DEVIL'S CHIMNEY

An absolutely gripping crime mystery with a massive twist

ADAM LYNDON

Detective Rutherford Barnes Mysteries Book 1

Revised edition 2022
Joffe Books, London
www.joffebooks.com

First published in Great Britain in 2012

This paperback edition was first published
in Great Britain in 2022

Cover art by The Brewster Project

ISBN: 978-1-80405-329-4

A NOTE TO THE READER

This book is set in 2001, when mobile phones were just that — with smartphones a distant dream — while computers were very far from being the lightweight, ubiquitous devices they are today. Additionally, while the collapse of Devil's Chimney and the relocation of the Belle Tout lighthouse are actual historical events, one or two minor liberties have been taken with the exact chronology — and the author begs the reader's kind indulgence.

PROLOGUE

They were filming something on Eastbourne Pier. Even here, four miles away and five hundred feet above sea level, Howard Van Leer could see the dawn patrol of white television trucks converging on the coastal appendage. Some World War II Hollywood blockbuster or other, he recalled, with the dogfights being filmed over the Channel.

As he scooped piles of sealed cigarette packets from the smashed-in vending machine into his rucksack, he frowned to himself. How would he have known that? Then he remembered — newspaper in the rec room. Prison had its good points — no way he'd have kept abreast of current affairs on the outside.

He moved to the till and started to prise it open. He might not have been a bad pilot, if his life had turned out differently. Or a bad soldier, come to that. He could have got involved in something worthwhile, travelled a bit, maybe even seen some action. But it was too late for that to happen. He'd have to ask for his life over again.

He felt air on his leg, and looked down at the white band above his ankle. Six weeks out and he'd prised off the tag — another tick in the box for the big house. Three squares of slop a day and he'd become a proper porky bastard, but six weeks back on the gear and he'd lost enough weight to slide the bloody thing off. Well, almost. His foot was a bit of an obstacle, but it only took some gentle persuasion with a screwdriver and it was off — intact. The tossers at Group 4 still thought he was tucked up in bed, on an early release home detention curfew. Thank you, Home Secretary.

He checked his watch. Two minutes down. Gavvers would be here soon. He laughed and made for the door. No prints, no fibres, no CCTV, no problem. He slung the bag over his shoulder and marched straight out of the front door of the Last Stop public house.

And stopped dead.

A cold spattering of rain and wind whipped across his face. It was only a couple of minutes since he'd crawled in through the toilet window, but the predawn sky seemed to be getting darker.

But it wasn't the sudden change in the weather that made him stop. It was something else. A low groaning sound that seemed to be coming from the edge of Beachy Head.

He looked east. The lights of the town had earlier been sharp, an audience for the rising sun, but now they were smudged against the wall of drizzle.

Unable to stop himself, Van Leer crossed the road and picked his way up the grass incline onto the clifftop.

The groaning grew louder, and the wind was now roaring so hard across the clifftop that he had to fight to keep his balance.

He inched forward, stumbling over ruts and dips concealed by the crazy dancing tongues of grass.

He dropped to his elbows and hauled himself forward, right to the edge. Any minute now he expected to see the black hulk of the landscape lit up by incandescent blue strobe lights, but he was compelled by something he could not name.

He chanced a look back, and saw nothing but the Seven Sisters stretching away behind him, like sentinels in the darkness, and twisted scrub-like trees blown horizontal after years of abuse from the raging gales.

As he reached the cliff edge, the groaning grew louder. The sea had been like a millpond — now it was churning and lashing on the rocks some five hundred feet below. Half a dozen rabbits out on the cliff approach stood up — twitching, sensing something in the air — then turned and scampered for cover.

The cloud broke, and Van Leer's vista was suddenly lit up by the moon. It shone from the sky like a powerful torch, illuminating the chalk cliffs; white slivers criss-crossed in a pathway over the waves, from the horizon to the water's edge. In the moonlight, Van Leer could just about see the Beachy Head lighthouse at the foot of the cliff, at this distance looking like little more than a candy-striped chess piece.

And then he saw it, tracing a line inland with his eyes from the lighthouse to the foot of the cliffs. A huge outcrop of rock, jutting out from the cliff; a giant chalk tower visible against the black sea. The groaning was accompanied by a new sound — *clack-clack-clack* — that made Van Leer think of a Newton's cradle.

The sound multiplied. Huge gashes appeared like black veins and raced up the tower with horrific speed. He saw particles of the chalk tower breaking off and rolling seawards like broken teeth, gathering pace and collecting larger fragments as they raced towards the water.

Van Leer could only watch, mesmerised, as the tower began to shake. Particles became rocks, which in turn became huge crags of chalk that began to fragment and tumble as the main outcrop was wrenched free of the cliff. The summit itself, a shard of chalk as sharp as a needle, keeled over and spun end over end towards the void. There was a low rumbling that he initially mistook for thunder, until it became so deafening that it filled the sky and even drowned out the sound of the sea. He clapped his hands over his ears and opened his mouth in a silent scream.

The whole bloody cliff's coming down.

And Devil's Chimney collapsed. Two hundred feet of chalk and stone, softened and battered by relentless winter rain, finally gave up and crashed into the sea. There was only a paralysing blackness at the bottom of the cliff, but Van Leer could imagine, all too clearly, the waves leaping up to claim the rubble. A blinding white cloud of chalk dust rose up from the shore, covering the cliff edge, and drifted away into the black sky.

Van Leer looked left and right along the undulating coastline, and it suddenly appeared to him that the edge of the land had been roughly incised, scythed away by the sea, the dazzling white cliffs like the very bones of the land.

He backed away from the edge, afraid to turn his back on the spectacle, panic seizing his movements. He tripped on a rock, and then turned and sprinted towards the road.

He grabbed his bicycle and belted off, away from Beachy Head, down into Upper Dukes Drive — the steep, winding coast road that led down towards the town. The spread of lights disappeared behind the treeline as he descended like an aircraft about to land.

A police patrol car, with the full blue light show going, raced up the hill in the opposite direction.

Despite his alarm, uncharitable thoughts flashed through his brain. *Stupid pigs*. Bicycles were by far the best means of getting around undetected — they hadn't even seen him.

Fear was still driving him, however, and he skidded off Upper Dukes Drive and crashed into a hedge.

He left the cycle and started to run down the snaking cliff road as it opened out onto the seafront. He ran past Helen Gardens, where the sheer drop from the Holywell cliffs was swathed in mist, and onto the wide boulevard of King Edward's Parade.

When he reached the pier, his legs buckled and he gave up. He leaned on his knees, trying not to vomit, taking huge, hoarse gasps of breath.

This wouldn't do.

As the sun rose, shafts of amber fell between the Victorian hotels jutting out from the land like so many crooked teeth. The roof of the amusement arcade, with the neon-red

"OPEN" sign still flashing silently on and off despite the burgeoning dawn, was like the back of a giant turtle held down and lashed in place with strings of light bulbs wielded by hordes of rancorous Lilliputians.

This wouldn't do at all.

Eventually his breathing eased, and he rummaged around in his rucksack for a smoke. Instead, he found the Stanley knife that he only ever carried for protection, for peace of mind.

Until now.

The voice in his head was loud, almost as loud as the fierce wind blowing in off the Channel.

Get a grip, little brother.

His fingers closed around the knife.

Get a grip.

After all, he still had a job to do.

CHAPTER ONE

Tonight was the night. They were going to get him. They could *feel* it. Barnes and Holden swung their patrol car around at the lights and parked in a crooked street off Victoria Drive. They emerged silently, and Barnes mouthed an instruction to Holden, his crew partner of thirteen months. She nodded back, and they moved off in opposite directions — Barnes six foot plus and lean, Holden small and slight; their quiet, controlled movements betraying a mutual keenness for distance running.

Foot patrol on night duty was a method which Barnes and Holden didn't really share with the rest of their team. At four in the morning, most of their colleagues either scoffed at the two uniformed constables and returned to a stack of DVDs or tried to catch up on paperwork. But the Old Town had been stung by night-time burglaries during March and April, and Barnes and Holden, with barely six years' service between them, were determined to nail the offender. They had, after all, been crewed together to get results.

Each burglary had the same MO: entry between 3 a.m. and 5 a.m. via rear fanlight windows or patio doors; handbags, jewellery and cash stolen from the kitchen, lounge and bedrooms. In most cases the householders had slept through it, but those disturbed had discovered, to their dismay, the offender's propensity for pulling a knife and making arcing lunges at anyone daring to challenge him. In nearly two months, six had been wounded, two seriously.

The Divisional Intelligence Unit was trying desperately to shorten the odds, but good information was in short supply. A surveillance team was on standby, but until they had a suspect to play with there was nothing for them. Scenes-of-Crime had yet to turn up anything of forensic interest either.

Acutely aware that an increasingly vitriolic press were screaming that people were not safe in their beds, the message from the Command Team had been clear:

Catch him at it.

The air over the Old Town was moist on Barnes's skin, an indication of an uncharacteristically warm April day ahead. The silence of the tree-lined street was broken only by his soft footfalls as he moved through the strange half-light of the breaking dawn.

The alleyways and twittens that threaded their way around the houses were like a web — routes so complex and confusing that they were practically designed to be of maximum benefit to the criminal.

He touched the transmit button on his radio.

"Harriet. What are you doing?" he whispered to Holden.

"Stalking the south side. What's up?"

"Just checking you're not back in the car, working on your CV."

"Yeah. Say that again when it's me that makes the arrest."

Barnes smiled to himself, already missing the competition for arrests that existed between them. Holden had passed the sergeants' exam and was waiting for various pieces of the administrative jigsaw to fall into place before taking promotion.

Barnes checked his watch — 4.38 a.m. He turned into an alleyway that led between two houses, taking slow, careful steps. He paused, and listened hard, trying to pick out any alien sounds. Hearing nothing but occasional lone birdsong and the silence roaring in his ears, he moved forward again, hungry eyes scanning front and rear, picking his way carefully so as to make as little noise as possible.

He crept down a side alley that serviced the rear gardens of a row of houses, and stopped at the gate of a house halfway along the row.

The garden was long and narrow, but he could clearly see that the rear patio doors had buckled and yielded to the force of an instrument. A spade lay nearby. He touched his transmit button again.

"Got something," Barnes whispered. "South of the car. Two hundred yards. Rear alley." He ended the transmission before Holden could reply.

He quietly unclipped a fastener on his belt and produced his standard-issue extendable metal baton. In a swift silent movement, he brought the baton down from his shoulder towards the ground, extending it to its full length. He held the baton aloft, behind his shoulder, and inched along the perimeter of the garden towards the house, careful not to disturb any forensic evidence left by the offender's likely trail.

He arrived at the patio doors. The net curtain billowed gently in the breeze.

All too aware of his own breathing, he tentatively stepped over the threshold into a small dining room. He could feel his heart drumming with apprehension — the intruder might still be here.

The dining room had been ransacked. The contents of a pine dresser lay strewn across the floor.

Barnes moved slowly towards the doorway and into the front hallway. He stopped, his ears straining for the sounds of movement. None came.

He moved into the front room, where evidence of the same chaos was apparent. It looked like the occupier had only just moved in — there were stacks of boxes in one corner. Both the boxes and what little furniture there was had been rifled through — drawers had been pulled out and upended, leaving the assorted fragments of a life evolving into domesticity scattered across the floor. Barnes shook his head. How was it possible to leave this much mess and not wake anyone?

He stepped further into the room and turned to look behind the door. He was jolted from his thoughts by the crude signage scrawled across the wall, dripping red onto a sofa.

DEAD COPS SLEEP LONG

He stared, trying to make sense of it, then photographed the writing with a small camera he kept on his belt. He removed a cotton bud from his pocket, and swabbed a tiny corner of the "G" before placing the bud into a polythene exhibit bag.

On the sofa lay a letter, the logo of a well-known television company catching Barnes's eye. He peered over at it curiously. It was partly folded over, so not all of it was visible, but evidently the recipient had a none-too-shabby singing voice. Opening with *Dear Contestant*, Barnes could make out an invitation to a further round of auditions for a reality television show looking for future pop stars.

He moved closer, intending to pick it up, but a gasp from behind him made him whirl around. Holden stood in the doorway. Her face was grey.

"I know. What a mess," Barnes said, moving towards the stairs. "I'll go alert the householder."

"I wouldn't bother," Holden said.

He turned back to her, confused.

"This is my house." She stared at him, wide-eyed and scared.

"Harriet . . ." he began, and then both of them jerked their heads around towards a faint sound from outside.

He held his breath, mouthed "*Just happened*" to Holden and pointed outside. She blinked rapidly, shock dulling her understanding, and Barnes retraced his steps down the garden, his baton ready for use.

He shut his eyes, trying to picture his quarry going about his business. He was still out here. Barnes *knew* it.

He came to a T-junction where the alley split and led to the rear gardens of another row of houses. He stopped and looked right. Nothing. He was becoming increasingly anxious that with every second that passed his target's chance of escape increased, and urgency began to govern his movements.

He ducked left and came face to face with a thin man clutching a rucksack.

He was standing by an open garden gate. A surge of make-or-break adrenaline pulsed through Barnes's body, and he recognised the man instantly — Howard Van Leer was a prolific burglar, only out of prison six weeks.

Their eyes locked, and Van Leer froze. The two men were barely six feet apart. Astonishment spread across Van Leer's gaunt face, but it quickly tightened into a look of grim determination as his body contracted and he took to his heels.

Barnes made a flailing grab but missed. He shoved his baton into his belt and took off after Van Leer, yelling into his radio.

"Control, this is Echo-Romeo two-one-seven. I have a runner in Old Town, heading south towards Victoria Drive. Backup, please."

The controller crackled a reply into Barnes's earpiece that he did not catch.

Van Leer came to a tall fence lined with barbed wire, and Barnes's heart sank as his prey scrambled easily over it. Barnes gritted his teeth and hauled himself up. He made it to the top and flung himself over — albeit much less gracefully than Van Leer — and felt a shard of fire as a barb tore into the soft underside of his forearm.

Barnes landed heavily, shockwaves racing up his legs, and continued his pursuit. He knew he could run, but he was hampered by his boots, body armour and belt, and the hunted man was running for his life. Barnes tried to keep a commentary on the radio for the units backing up, but he was using as much energy yelling as he was running.

Ignoring his throbbing forearm, Barnes yelled for Van Leer to stop, but the thin man paid no heed and sidestepped into a narrow street. Barnes cursed and followed, his lungs pounding in his chest. He was matching Van Leer, but he wasn't gaining.

In desperation, Barnes flung his baton at the sinewy burglar. It whipped through the air in a spin, and caught Van Leer a glancing blow on the left ear. He yelped and stumbled off balance but did not stop.

Van Leer turned again, up an alleyway that led between another two rows of terraced houses. Barnes followed him, some overhanging foliage sweeping his face as he rounded the corner. He wondered absently why he could hear drops pattering onto the pavement — there was no rain forecast for today.

Barnes's lungs were starting to burn, his boots heavy, his thumping footsteps like helicopter rotors in the still morning air. He knew he didn't have much left to give, but he was damned if he was going to let Van Leer get away.

Van Leer came to a fence at the end of the alleyway. He tried to scramble over it but lost his footing, and Barnes was almost upon him as he hauled himself over.

Barnes saw his chance. He made a final effort, planted his boot on the fence and vaulted over in one. He landed heavily on Van Leer, pulling him down, and the air was thumped out of the burglar as he found himself face down on the concrete, pinned prone by Barnes's knee on his shoulder joint.

"Don't move! Don't you fucking move!" Barnes roared at Van Leer as he pulled the burglar's arms behind his back and handcuffed him. There were splashes of red on Van Leer's tracksuit — being added to, Barnes realised as he pinned his captive, by the blood from the wound in his arm. It hadn't been raining at all.

For a moment there was no sound except the huge, wheezing gasps of the two men as they tried to catch their breath.

"What? What? Ain't done nothing, ya fuckin' pig!" Van Leer whined into the pavement, with a note of wounded outrage that Barnes had heard often in career criminals.

"Is that right?" Barnes panted, reaching down to Van Leer's left sock. He rolled it down and felt around. There was a small blue tattoo on the ankle. It simply said "Liam".

Barnes pulled Van Leer up into a sitting position and held a roll of cash up to his face. "Then how do you explain this?"

"Fuck off. I found it."

An unwashed stink rose off Van Leer. His grey skin was stretched tight over the bones in his skull, like cling film. His eyes were clear, however, and Barnes estimated that the burglar was at his most sober at this moment, somewhere between his last fix and the withdrawal that would consume his wretched body in the not-too-distant future.

With Van Leer safely cuffed and going nowhere fast, Barnes fished around in the first aid kit on his belt for a bandage. He wrapped it around his now-stinging forearm and continued his search. From Van Leer's rucksack he removed a Stanley knife and a can of red spray paint. There was also a credit card, embossed with the name HR HOLDEN.

He clicked his tongue against his teeth and slipped the items into polythene exhibit bags just as a patrol car pulled up alongside him and the section sergeant, John Callaghan, emerged.

Barnes's stomach fluttered as adrenaline pumped around his body. He *wanted* his skipper to see this. Callaghan — a career patrol sergeant — loved nothing more than booting in doors and chasing down fleeing suspects, and it rubbed off on the whole team. He had deliberately left Holden and Barnes alone to hunt down villains, and now they had something to show for it.

Callaghan was five-ten and as sturdy as a submarine. He kept his head completely bald — the hair, when it grew, was a vibrant red — and there was a long scar on his left temple that he never spoke of, but that everyone knew had come from his valiant attempt, off duty, to intercept two armed men robbing a bank up in Lewisham.

Barnes held up his bloodied arm as Callaghan walked over.

"That looks nasty. Tell me it was worth it," Callaghan said, the faintest hint of Limerick in his accent.

"Of course," Barnes said, pointing at the handcuffed Van Leer with his boot.

"Good *effort*."

Callaghan radioed for an ambulance, and then wrapped a bandage from his own first aid kit around Barnes's wound. Despite being only thirty-eight, Callaghan had a paternal tendency towards his younger charges. This irritated some, but it gave Barnes a comfort that he didn't always like to acknowledge.

Callaghan helped Barnes get Van Leer to his feet, and they manhandled him into the back of Callaghan's car.

"So, what?" Callaghan said, closing the side door and nodding towards Van Leer.

"Found him outside with a roll of cash in his sock and a credit card in his rucksack," Barnes said, watching Van Leer through the glass. He passed Callaghan an exhibit bag and winced as a fresh helping of pain scored through his arm. "Christ, that's hurting now."

"Keep it elevated."

An ambulance arrived and a sole paramedic began to clean up Barnes's arm while he spoke to Callaghan.

Callaghan turned the exhibit bag over in his hand.

"What a result," he whistled, and then frowned. "This card says HR Holden."

"I know. It's Harriet's house."

"You serious?"

"Yeah. And look at this." He held up his camera and showed Callaghan the pictures of the lounge wall. "He had spray paint and a Stanley knife in his bag. This isn't just a burglary. He's targeted her specifically."

"Jesus. Why HRH?" Callaghan asked, using the nickname Holden had unwittingly earmarked for herself as a result of her coincidental initials and occasionally sanctimonious personality.

"I don't know, but I left her at the house. Shit," Barnes said, fumbling with his radio.

"I'm here." Callaghan and Barnes turned to see Holden walking towards them. She was visibly shaking. Barnes noticed for the first time in thirteen months how small she seemed. He knew she was a fitness fanatic, and he had seen her take down enough male prisoners twice her size to know her slim body held surprising strength. He had learned the hard way to resist her frequent challenges to arm-wrestle. But she wasn't more than five-two, and now, all bravado gone, she seemed tiny. Her pale skin had always been prone to blushing, and her cheeks were pinched red now, hot from the embarrassment, fear and anger she had been made to feel in the last fifteen minutes. Her regulation bun had been dislodged and sat on her head like an octopus.

"Are you okay?" Barnes asked her.

"I've been better. Are *you* okay?" she said, pointing at Barnes's arm as the paramedic finished cleaning him up. "What happened?"

"I got him, Harriet."

"You got him? Then where . . ." Her voice tailed off as she realised the person responsible for wrecking her house was sitting in the back of Callaghan's patrol car. Anger flashed in her eyes. Barnes had met enough victims of crime to know that, in the immediate aftermath, they would give anything for five minutes alone with the offender.

Holden was no different. She stared at Van Leer, her nostrils flaring with the strength of her breathing.

Callaghan stepped in front of her, blocking her view of Van Leer, and pulled her to him in a tight hug. In the car, Van Leer pressed his papery face against the window and scowled. Saliva ran from his mouth and drooled down the glass. He started to bang his head on something below the sill, and Barnes realised he was headbutting the button that opened the window.

"Fuck you, copper," he snarled, craning his head up so his mouth was wedged in the tiny gap at the top of the window. "Nice fuckin' underwear drawer. Dirty slag."

"I'll get rid of him," Barnes said, walking over to the driver's door.

"You need stitches," the paramedic called. "And a tetanus jab."

"Later," Barnes said.

"He's right, Barnes," Callaghan said. "I'll get someone else to bring him in."

"No way." Barnes grinned as he opened the car door.

He got in the car and retrieved his spectacles, having carefully pocketed them before going out on foot. He glanced at himself in the rear-view mirror while he polished the lenses with his tie.

"You look great, darling," cooed a raspy voice from the back seat, breaking his concentration.

Barnes turned around in his seat to look at Van Leer and slipped his spectacles back on.

"Howard, I'm arresting you on suspicion of burglary. You do not have to say anything, but it may harm your defence if you do not mention, when questioned, something that you later rely on in court. Anything you do say may be given in evidence."

Howard Van Leer hung his head.

"Piss off," he muttered.

* * *

Like most fair-weather weekends in Eastbourne, it had been busy, the already stretched patrol teams fighting to curb the pockets of violence that had erupted around the seaside town. Around two that morning the custody block had been alive with drunk, fighting prisoners. By the time Barnes arrived the riot had quietened down and the early shift was starting to file in.

As he arrived at the station, he wondered how he was going to get Van Leer out of the car and into the booking area with only one good arm.

He needn't have worried. As he pulled into the cell block's cavernous holding bay, he saw five or six of his team colleagues lined up by the door. They were solemn-faced, but as he pulled in they began to clap and stamp their heavy boots on the riveted steel floor.

Word of the arrest had apparently spread fast. Barnes had barely brought the car to a stop before the officers flung open the car doors and dragged Van Leer out. He screamed a volley of frightened protest as he was lifted bodily and hauled through the pale-green, blood-spattered iron door into the main cell block.

Once the administrative formalities were complete — which consisted mainly of the custody officer grudgingly giving Van Leer his rights while Van Leer cursed the police with his every breath before being slung in a cell — Barnes went to the tiny medical room and began rifling through one of the cupboards with one hand, the wounded arm immobile and unconsciously tucked into his chest for protection.

"Coffee?"

He turned to see Holden in the doorway, bearing two Styrofoam cups. She frowned when she saw what he was doing.

"Let me help you."

Barnes sat on the edge of the small bunk while Holden retrieved the necessary supplies from a drawer. One of the station's more adroit first-aiders, she handed Barnes a cup and began to patch him up.

There was silence for a few minutes while she removed the bloody bandage and swabbed the wound. Barnes watched her work.

"Don't think I wouldn't have caught him." She looked up, caught his eye and forced a smile. "I'm faster over distance."

He didn't laugh, but gave her a sympathetic look. Her smile faltered.

"You okay?" he asked.

She nodded, her mouth tightly closed, and then her face contorted as the brave face slipped completely and she fought another bout of tears.

"Fucker," she said, shaking her head. He touched her shoulder with his good arm.

"Anything else missing besides the cash and card?"

"Can't get in to look. SOCO won't let me near it."

"Callaghan's got troops all over it. He had nothing else on him. If he stashed anything, Callaghan will find it."

She shrugged and resumed her work.

"I'm more concerned about your arm."

"I'll live."

"That you will." She applied some adhesive sutures to the wound. "It's a cracking arrest, whichever way you look at it," she said. "Could be your ticket to CID."

Barnes flushed. In this case his crew partner was the victim, not the competition, but he was still feeling the buzz from catching Van Leer.

"I think you can be forgiven for not getting there first."

"What does that take our league table to this year?"

"Don't worry, you still have the edge. Have you got somewhere you can stay? I could make up the spare bed . . ."

She leaned forward and kissed him on the cheek. "I'm sure your wife would love that. No, I'll go to my mum's. Thanks."

She finished wrapping the bandage around the dressing.

"There. Good as new."

She sat beside him on the bunk. Her feet didn't reach the floor, and she swung her legs back and forth while they talked. Barnes copied her, and she managed a laugh.

"At least let me drive you home."

"Honestly, Barnes, don't worry. I'm going for a run, anyway."

"Christ, Harriet, I like to run, but after nights? And ten *miles*?"

"Triathlon next month. Can't miss training. Maybe you'll join me one of these days."

There was a pause. Barnes stopped swinging his legs. Holden's eyes brimmed with tears again. Barnes thought of the letter from the TV company on her hall table, and thought maybe a gentle dig might lighten the mood. In the end he decided that it wouldn't.

He put down his drink.

"Why you, Harriet?"

"You tell me. I never met the little shit before."

"Didn't get him put away, pissed him off for some reason?"

"I've never met him," she repeated. "I only moved in a couple of weeks ago. Most of my stuff is still in boxes."

Holden had been hunting for a decent house for a while — in fact, as Barnes recalled, since the pair of them had worked together. She had lodged, rented and led a generally transient lifestyle around the town until settling.

"Barnes?" she said. "Do you think someone leaked my address?"

"I don't know."

He didn't elaborate, knowing that Holden had her fair share of detractors.

"I know what everyone says about me, Barnes. Sometimes they don't even try to wait till my back's turned."

"That doesn't necessarily mean your address was leaked," he said, without conviction.

"I know what they call me, Barnes," she said. "Her Royal fucking Highness."

Barnes felt the heat rise from his throat into his face. He couldn't recall ever using her nickname himself, but he felt guilty nonetheless.

"If I get married the initials won't fit. Maybe then they'll drop it."

"I don't . . ." he began.

"Don't worry. I'm used to it now." She hopped off the bunk, and he did the same. She turned to face him.

"The price of fame?" Barnes wondered aloud.

"Barnes, you have all this to come," she said.

She looked up at him with a sad half-smile, then squeezed her tiny frame past him and into the main cell block. He followed her out, and they walked together down the corridor.

She stopped abruptly and turned to him.

"Barnes . . . thank you," she said.

"I know you're there!" a voice shrieked.

They both turned, startled. It was Van Leer, screaming through the hatch in the heavy metal cell door. He had been placed in the cell furthest away from the main bridge, and his voice echoed around the cell block.

"I know you're there! You're dead, copper. You're fuckin' *dead*. Hear me? I know you're there. I can *smell* you, bitch! I know where you live, and I know who you're fucking! No one's gonna miss you. *You can jump into the fire, but you'll never be free . . .*"

His hoarse yells descended into hacking laughter.

Holden went scarlet and froze to the spot. Barnes took her arm and gently led her away out of the cell block and into the sanctuary of the main station.

* * *

With Howard Van Leer safely ensconced in a cell, and Holden giving her statement to the CID, Barnes began to write the report. He knew that he wasn't the best thief-taker in the district, not by a long shot, but he knew that where he would make this job count was in the write-up. He rubbed his face, slipped on his spectacles and continued typing, imagining every word being read aloud to a jury by some hotshot QC.

His typing slowed as he found his thoughts disturbed by Van Leer's outburst.

I know who you're fucking.
No one's gonna miss you.
You can jump into the fire, but you'll never be free.

Threats, abuse and an unholy rendition of Nilsson.

As far as Barnes knew, Holden wasn't seeing anyone, although she was fairly cagey about her love life. This was not unusual — cops that dated other cops often had to steel themselves against any developing relationship becoming public property, with gossipy colleagues recycling the details with the relish of a tabloid newspaper. Not for the first time, Barnes was grateful that he was married before he joined the police.

Barnes did not believe Holden to be promiscuous, and not just for virtuous reasons. She wasn't just unpopular — people went out of their way to avoid her. This was another reason Callaghan had crewed the two of them together — no one else, for one reason or another, could work with her for any length of time.

On paper, it didn't make sense. She was intelligent, young and pretty — that was usually enough for the dinosaurs, at least, to queue up to show her the ways of the world. She just somehow managed to rub people up the wrong way.

Barnes recalled a recent occasion where the whole of Callaghan's team had gathered to celebrate the capture of an elusive rape suspect. Holden had sauntered over to the self-congratulatory huddle and had suggested they get back to work. The suggestion was more or less ignored, but instead of letting it drop, she'd tried to pull rank by pointing out that, despite being the youngest one on section, she was the most senior.

Barnes still had no idea why she'd felt the need to voice this observation. It was technically accurate — the promotion board results having only been published a couple of days before — but it had served no other purpose than to irritate everyone, himself included, and things had never been the same afterwards. The nickname "HRH" had derived from there.

Barnes sat forward and began to type again. He couldn't understand how she managed to keep saying the wrong thing, but he felt she trusted him. They'd worked together long enough — certainly enough for him to be sure that she meant nothing by it — it was just that her attempts to lead were clumsy and ultimately misunderstood. Maybe he would take her to one side and talk to her properly about it. She might not like it, but she would thank him in the end. He shook his head. She just didn't seem to . . . do people.

At 7.10 a.m. he carried the file up to the CID office on the first floor, trying to ignore the dead taste in his mouth.

The fatigue had caught up with him now; as such, Barnes was unaware of the sense of victory radiating around the station now that the perpetrator was finally in custody and future victims were out of danger.

Many a probationary officer — Barnes included — had taken this long march to the CID office, clutching a carefully tended case file under one arm in the hope that they could persuade a detective it was something deserving of their attention. Many had walked it, and many had been laughed out of the office. But there would be no laughing today.

Pushing open the door to the office, he saw Callaghan talking to a female detective sitting with her feet up on a desk. Barnes marched over.

"This is a massive breakthrough," Callaghan said as he approached. "The Command Team will be singing your praises at morning prayers, Barnes. This is DC Cathy Nightingale. She'll be looking at your file."

Barnes wondered why his sergeant had felt the need to make his pitch for him. Perhaps he wanted to make sure his young apprentice would not be rebuffed. He hoped Callaghan wasn't there because he didn't think Barnes was up to it.

Barnes stuck out a hand. Nightingale was pushing forty-five, with burgeoning grey hair and smoker's teeth, but even sitting down her body was obviously as lean as a swimmer's. Her tightly parted marcel wave framed a razor-sharp jawline, and under a dark, arching brow her green eyes, smoky with make-up, reminded Barnes of a Twenties she-wolf.

She returned the handshake — and Barnes thought he saw her roll her eyes.

"So, I hear Mr Van Leer screwed the royal residence?" she said to Barnes.

"He certainly did," Barnes replied.

"Not a bad collar. Definitely worth a few beers."

"Well, actually, I don't really drink," Barnes said.

Nightingale's expression went from one of incredulity to wry amusement.

"That's very interesting," she said. "But I meant me."

There was a moment's uncomfortable silence.

"Search turn anything up?" Barnes asked Callaghan eventually.

"Not yet. They're still on it. You want coffee?" Callaghan asked.

"Can't drink it on nights, sarge. You know that — I'll be on the ceiling. Thanks anyway."

"You sure? Cathy will make that can of Coke last all day, so it's a cheap round otherwise." Callaghan looked at Nightingale, who put down the can she was drinking from.

"So, premature ejaculations aside, what's the evidence actually like?" Nightingale asked.

"He had cash and a credit card belonging to Holden on him. He also had a Stanley knife and a can of spray paint," Barnes said. "I found him outside the rear gate."

"SOCO?" Nightingale asked.

"At scene. They're working on it. Look at this." Barnes handed Nightingale some glossy A4 photographs, uploaded from his camera.

Nightingale surveyed them for a moment, then placed them on the desk.

"Howard Van Leer is a nobody. Too much smack and horror films," she said.

"'Dead cops sleep long'? Shouldn't we be treating this as a death threat?" Barnes said.

"Don't let it worry you. He can't get at HRH — or anybody — where he is. You saw to that," Nightingale said.

"How would he have got the address?"

"You tell me. He probably googled it. We don't protect our own as much as we think we do." She picked up the can again. "Any prints?"

"Nothing yet."

"Got witness statements?"

"All here."

"House-to-house?"

"No point at that time of the morning," Callaghan said. "I've arranged for the early turn to do it."

"And they'll check the linked logs for any other burglaries reported overnight. They booked on an hour ago. Look, it's all in the report." Barnes pointed to the file lying on Nightingale's desk, unable to keep the irritation from his voice.

"What about premises search?"

Barnes flinched. *I forgot to search Van Leer's home address.* He thought quickly, and managed to put forward a half-reasoned argument. "Not done yet. I found him virtually outside her house. Five minutes later and I might have missed him. There won't be anything in his address. He didn't have time to get there."

"What about his PACE rights?"

"PACE rights?"

"You held him incommunicado?"

There was a stilted silence. Nightingale sat forward and tapped on the computer keyboard, bringing up the custody log on screen.

"Says here he asked for his brother to be informed of his arrest. Call made at ten past five, according to this."

"So?"

"So, we have a good idea Howard is a serial burglar. His family now know he's in custody. How do we know the spoils of all his *other* burglaries aren't being flushed down the proverbial toilet as we speak?"

"That sounds pretty speculative," Barnes said, swallowing.

"How much service have you got, PC Barnes?" This time it was Nightingale's turn to sound irritated.

Barnes sighed; he'd known this was coming. "Two years," he replied, exaggerating only slightly.

"Well, I've got twenty-five, and I'll tell you what I tell every other uniform that comes up here. If you want the CID to take on a job then you've got to get the basics done before we can start on the secondary investigation. You nick someone for acquisitive crime, then you search their place. The basics."

"What secondary investigation?" Barnes pulled off his spectacles, as if to get a better look at the detective. "The evidence is all there. It doesn't need more investigation, it needs someone to interview and then charge him. All it's missing is the bow."

Callaghan and Nightingale glanced at each other. Barnes reached over and grabbed the file. He could feel himself becoming petulant, but he was too tired to resist it.

"You know what? Forget it. I'll process the prisoner. I'll be out of here by ten."

He blinked gritty eyes and walked out of the office, leaving Nightingale and Callaghan sitting in silence.

He stopped in the corridor, slapped the file down on a windowsill, and dragged his hand down his face.

Nice going, you idiot.

Here had been an opportunity to impress a seasoned detective with his efforts, and perhaps drop a few hints regarding future career openings.

Could be your ticket to the CID.

Holden's voice.

And he'd blown it with a sulk.

He went to the tiny kitchen that abutted the reports room to get some water. Callaghan appeared in the doorway.

"Barnes. Give me the file. DC Nightingale will deal with Van Leer."

"I told you — I can deal with it."

Callaghan snorted. "You know the CID spend most of their time trying to bat off crap jobs? People are always in their office trying to flower up an ABH as a wounding or a purse dipping as a street robbery, just so they can get rid of it. You come along and they can't get the file off you. You know how often that happens?"

"Surprise me."

"Well, it's not a lot. Barnes, look around. You know what's going on. The press are saying we haven't got a grip, that people aren't safe, that the criminals are taking over the streets."

"They're not far wrong," Barnes said.

"Exactly. This is a fantastic arrest. We can claw back a little dignity."

"How often do we get the chance to put away scumbags screwing houses like this? Especially cops' houses — a cop who's a friend of mine. Why would I *want* to hand this over?"

"Come on, Barnes. You're tired. You were due off an hour ago, and you really think the Command Team will authorise any more overtime when there's a detective sitting upstairs twiddling her thumbs? Plus, they want Van Leer remanded in custody by the magistrates. You've made a cracking arrest, but remand applications are their area of expertise. They'll take it."

"I missed the premises search."

"Don't beat yourself up over it. If anything, it's my fault. And Van Leer's going nowhere. If it bothers you that much, you can do the search tomorrow."

"Sarge . . . the message he left. It's a death threat. DC Nightingale didn't seem too concerned."

"Don't worry about it." Callaghan began to unbutton his epaulettes. "That's a CID problem. And as Cathy says, he can't do anything to her now. You've done excellent work, Barnes. Let CID take it from here."

Barnes looked at him. He trusted Callaghan, and so he picked up the file and thrust it into Callaghan's enormous hand.

"Let me know what he says in interview."

He found Holden sitting alone in an office. He touched her on the shoulder, and asked if she was okay. She smiled and touched his hand, and he told her to call him if she needed anything.

It was not yet eight, but the sun was already warm when he walked to his car. The streets were still quiet at this early hour, and at that moment they belonged to neither cops nor criminals, but seagulls. They swooped down to grab discarded kebabs, burgers and other rubbish littered across the road. The concentration of gulls was always greater after a weekend.

The sun reflected off the surface of the sea like mottled blue snakeskin as Barnes drove home. He replayed the conversation with DC Cathy Nightingale in his head, cringing inwardly as he did so. She didn't strike him as the voice of restraint, and no doubt the whole of the station would soon hear about his strop.

Great.

One thing he'd already learned during his short career was that deals were done, jobs were agreed and promotions approved on reputation. Not only that, but once you'd acquired one — for good or ill — it was hard to shift.

Barnes's desire to become a detective was such that he had absorbed all the study texts for the CID exam in his spare time — even though there was no suggestion at all that he would get to sit it. He'd put in his application some months back, and, to his surprise, Callaghan had rubber-stamped it. It had, however, been rejected at the personnel office.

No probationers allowed.

The exam was now only a couple of weeks away, and he would have to watch it come and go, and hope he could maintain enough interest in the studying to have a go the following year.

* * *

When Barnes got home, the curtains were still drawn throughout the house. His black Labrador Forbes — his wife had chosen the name — bounded over to greet him. Barnes rubbed the dog's neck and then gave him fresh water and breakfast.

He put the kettle on, and smiled when he saw Eve's textbooks and notes still covering the kitchen table from the night before, evidence of her own ongoing crusade to graduate from nursery worker to primary teacher. Her spectacles had been left on the open pages of one of the books.

Near the table was an easel. The canvas resting on it displayed the vivid acrylic colours of an unfinished poppy. Barnes was impressed, although this had as much to do with the fact that his wife of five years could create something so striking from a mere leisure pursuit as it did with the painting itself. Eve's hobbies generally resulted in a product of some description — boredom and wasted time seldom featured in her life.

He turned and noticed her nursery tabard hanging on the kitchen door. He frowned. She had usually left for work by this time.

He checked his phone. No messages. A wave of unease washed over him, and he crept towards the stairs, the kettle getting louder behind him.

He stopped to part the curtain covering the front door and looked through the glass. Eve's car was still out there. He spun around, half-expecting to see some slogan or another daubed across his living room wall.

Nervous now, he quietly ascended the stairs, keying "999" into his phone. His thumb hovered above the call button. Downstairs, the kettle boiled and clicked off. The ensuing silence was deafening.

He inched across the landing and gently pushed open the bedroom door, unable to quell his thudding heartbeat.

Eve's long, slim form was visible under the duvet. He crept towards the bed and paused, searching for any visible demonstration of her breathing. He waited — one, two, three, four seconds. Nothing.

Gripped with anxiety, he placed one hand on the bed, steeling himself for whatever violation awaited him under the duvet.

He touched her bare shoulder, the light suntan like cappuccino against the china white of the duvet. She stirred, and rolled over to face him. In the moment before she woke, he was struck by how peaceful she looked in sleep. Even when her eyes were closed her eyebrows were a perfect arch, as if permanently asking a question, one slender arm tucked under her head, her impossibly shiny Bournville-coloured curls strewn about the pillow.

"Hello, Chief," she whispered with a sleepy smile, touching his hand. Her dark, almond eyes filled with concern as she saw his bandaged arm. "Honey, what happened? Are you okay?"

Barnes shut his eyes as relief flooded over him. "I'm fine. It's nothing. Just a scratch."

"What happened?" she repeated.

"I didn't think you'd be here," he said, avoiding the question.

"I took the morning off from the little darlings, remember?"

Of course he remembered. At least, now he did. He went back to the kitchen to make the tea, shaking his head as he stirred. What was the matter with him?

He took a cup up to Eve and crept into bed beside her. She rolled over and draped her arm across his chest, more asleep than awake.

"I got him, Eve. Our burglar. The one terrorising all those people with a knife. Caught him at it, virtually. He'll go away. They're all safe."

"My hero," she yawned, and slowly brushed her palm down his chest and across his stomach, slipping two long fingers underneath the waistband of his underwear, at the small hollow between his stomach wall and hip.

He pulled her close, her body soft and warm with sleep. He slid his hand down over her hip, marvelling as he always did at the soft, vase-like shape that had awakened him on some primal level when they first met.

"Are you very tired?" she whispered.

His eyes fluttered closed before he could answer. Before sleep took him completely, one thought flew through his mind.

She's safe . . . isn't she?

* * *

About the same time, Police Constable Harriet Holden stripped off her uniform in the ladies' locker room of Eastbourne Police Station and changed into her running kit.

She walked out exactly on the hour. This early on a Sunday, the streets were virtually empty. Hands in pockets, she strolled along the wide flagstones of Grove Road and past the imposing town hall, where damp films of grimy confetti from a recent wedding were still smudged against the concrete steps. Several floors up, the bells chimed eight, punctuating her light steps.

An elderly gentleman walking in the opposite direction smiled as their paths crossed — in her sports gear she looked unassuming, bright, a little like a student.

She broke into a run, unsure of a route, unsure of a destination, knowing she now had nowhere to call home.

Thoughts see-sawed through her mind as she found her stride. Who was she trying to kid? Job aside, what adult in their right mind auditions for TV talent shows? *Just a bit of fun* was her standard brush-off, but who else fights the fatigue at the end of every night duty to run ten miles? Who fills their time off with ever more extreme adventure sports? Who, if not someone trying to fill a considerable void — someone running away?

The bells ceased as she rounded the corner into Saffrons Road, and silence enveloped the streets once more.

CHAPTER TWO

Barnes woke early Monday morning when the throbbing in his arm finally bored through his sleep.

He was in the shower, trying to wash off the jetlag that tended to follow a run of night shifts, when Eve knocked and opened the bathroom door a notch.

"Barnes," she said through the gap, her voice a conspiratorial whisper. "There's a phone call for you. It's work. Paul Hadian."

She was sucking the arm of her spectacles, her face anxious. Barnes turned the water off.

"The DCI?"

"I don't know. Is he? He said Paul Hadian from the CID."

"Oh, great. What does he want?"

"What's happened, Barnes?"

"Probably the DC I bad-mouthed has gone whinging to him about the probationer with the attitude."

"Oh Barnes, you didn't?" She ran a hand through her hair and left it there. "And he's calling you at *home*?"

"Yep. I had an opportunity to schmooze a detective, and I blew it."

"Well, come on. He's waiting."

Barnes pulled on jeans and trotted down the stairs bare-chested.

Dubbed with the oxymoron "Crime Manager", Detective Chief Inspector Paul Hadian had been a detective for twenty-seven years and was the head of Divisional CID, responsible for the management of all crime investigation across the whole of the East Downs Division. He was top of the detectives' food chain, and clearly he wouldn't be too impressed with some uniformed upstart troubling one of his most senior detective constables.

"Hello sir. Sorry to keep you waiting. I was in the shower."

"Don't worry about it. I'm sorry to bother you at home." The voice was deep, laconic and laced with a thick Welsh accent.

Barnes's brow furrowed. *Unusual way to begin a reprimand.*

"I had to get your home number from Personnel. Your first name — Rutherford, right? Or is it the other way around?"

"No, that's right. But everyone calls me Barnes," he mumbled.

"Well, Barnes, I've been reading some of your reports. Burglaries, mainly. Couple of robberies that we've picked up the secondary for."

"Yes?"

"And then you got Howard Van Leer last night."

"What happened?"

"Went 'no comment' in interview, and collected a burglary charge. Kept him in for court this morning, and Cathy got him potted."

"Potted?"

"Remanded in custody."

Barnes's stomach did a little somersault. *He* had done that.

"That was a superb arrest, Barnes. How's your arm?"

"It suddenly feels better."

Hadian laughed.

"A lot of people are sleeping easy in their beds, thanks to you. Not only that, but I've had word from Van Leer's probation officer that he might want to clear his slate."

"Oh, really?" Barnes said airily, the terminology escaping him a little now.

"*Tell him you want to be a detective*," Eve mouthed from the kitchen. Barnes didn't understand. Eve mouthed "*detective*" again and mimed, in an exaggerated fashion, the examination of a speck with a magnifying glass. Barnes made a shushing gesture and turned his back.

"Yeah, and Van Leer has been screwing houses and terrorising the occupants since he finished his last stretch. If he decides to cough them all now, the division's clear-up rate will go through the roof. It needs to be done carefully. Cathy Nightingale is going to visit Van Leer in prison in a few days. I want you to go with her."

"Come again?"

"Barnes, I've got something of a dearth of good detectives on division, or even potentially good detectives, for that matter. Uniformed coppers, they make the arrest, they put the file in and they forget about it until they're called to court."

"Yes, sir."

Was this going where he thought it was going? Barnes turned back to Eve, who unconsciously mirrored the disbelieving look of excitement on her husband's face.

"But detectives own the job from start to finish," Hadian continued. "You've got to hold the lawyers' hands half the time, until they get their head around a case. It's the DC that runs things, right up until conviction. Cathy Nightingale will make damn sure a jury convicts Van Leer, but, like I said, it was the arrest that made it."

"Right place, right time, sir," Barnes said, as modestly as he could manage.

"I don't believe that. I read your statement. Foot patrol on a night duty? What's your thinking behind that?"

"Well, any burglar out at that time of the morning is going to hear a car from at least half a mile away, and the odds of it being a patrol car are going to be pretty good."

"Not the most popular of pastimes, I must say. That time of the morning, most of the cops in this nick would have been dozing in a lay-by somewhere. You can call it luck if you want to, Barnes, but you made your own luck with Van Leer, and that's what I need in this office."

"Thank you, sir."

"But it's not just about flash arrests. Your reports are thorough and precise, and you don't shy away from the donkey work. You've got an investigator's head, Barnes."

Barnes, slightly uncomfortable with the praise, didn't immediately answer, and then he realised that Hadian was waiting for him to speak.

"So?"

"Sir?"

"I'm offering you a job in the CID. I noticed you put your hat in the ring some months ago."

Barnes shut his eyes and punched the air like a lottery winner. Eve, who had been like a rabbit in headlights up until this point, began to silently dance around the kitchen.

"Yeah. Personnel bounced it."

"I can sort out the bureaucrats. Can you help me out? I've squared it with Callaghan."

"Sir, myself and Cathy Nightingale, we . . ."

"Yeah, she told me about the tiff. Forget about it. You were tired, and Cathy can be a royal pain in the neck, particularly when she's grilling probationers."

"She did seem to blow hot and cold. Sir, I . . ."

He paused, and took just a moment to drink in the look on his wife's face.

"I'm not proposing marriage, Barnes," Hadian said in his ear.

"I'm in," Barnes said, as casually as possible.

"Well, I'm glad to hear it," Hadian said, with more than a hint of irony. "Your posting document will show you as a trainee detective constable. I'll get the paperwork arranged. There's one sticking point, however."

"Yes?"

"You'll need to take the detectives' exam, but it's only a fortnight or so away. The red tape says you'll have to at least have a crack at it . . ."

"Don't worry about it, sir. I've been . . . well, don't worry."

"Good answer." Barnes could hear him smiling. "I'll arrange some extra books. Crammer stuff. I'll also sort out your detectives' course, interview training, HOLMES, all that sort of stuff. In the meantime, hang up that uniform, get yourself to the office, then you can start locking up the nasty bastards."

* * *

Eve, perhaps even more excited than her husband, took Barnes shopping. She made a fuss of him — shortlisting, fitting and measuring. Combinations of ties and shirts were carefully matched, and the sales assistants were run ragged.

Barnes smiled as she ordered them about. His career was important to her — to the extent that she'd sidelined her own to support him. She had a resolute faith in Barnes's ascent, and did not anticipate setbacks. Despite their event-like status, days like these were, in her eyes, entirely predictable and featured prominently in the architecture of his career plan.

The odd bit of record-breaking didn't hurt either — she beamed with pride when he quietly told her that no officer in the force had ever been invited to become a detective while still in probation, and apparently it had caused no end of headaches for the personnel office.

There was relief there too. Eve had never liked Barnes working uniform: "cannon fodder" was the euphemism she had used throughout his career to date.

They eventually settled on four suits, two in navy and one in dark grey, and a more expensive pinstripe for court. New shoes — two pairs, eight shirts and an assortment of ties. Barnes winced when the sales assistant rang it all up, leaving Eve to pluck the card from his hand and thrust it in the direction of the till.

"Will the job pay for this?" Eve asked.

"I doubt it," Barnes answered. "Plain-clothes allowance went out of fashion about the same time as sheepskin overcoats and hip flasks."

"It's worth it," said Eve with admiration, fingering his lapel. "You look so good. Like a lawyer. You looked like Action Man in that uniform."

"I need to study," he said. The lawyer reference was no accident, either — Eve had never believed the ceiling of Barnes's career would be confined to the police service.

"Don't worry, I'll try to keep my hands off you. Just make sure you keep *your* hands to yourself when all those giggling WPCs start paying you lots of attention."

Barnes laughed and kissed her face.

"Don't be daft," he said.

They stopped home long enough to swap the shopping bags for Forbes, and parked near Chalk Farm. They let the dog off the lead and walked through a network of wooded paths traversing the South Downs up towards Butts Brow.

Barnes threw a ball for the Labrador, deliberately making him run down a set of wooden steps that led from the road down into the wood. Forbes disregarded the last three or four steps, instead launching himself into the air to clear them as he went after the ball.

The wood was shrouded in green, trapping moisture like a rainforest.

"You know CID work long hours?" he said as they walked, adjusting the camera strap over his shoulder.

Eve just squeezed his arm.

"I don't want you to . . ."

"Don't want me to what? Barnes, have you any idea how excited I am? It's all *happening*, right now. You can get the CID exam out of the way, and then once you're out of probation you can take the sergeant's exam, which is — when? Next year?"

He nodded.

"March. It does make sense. Half the syllabus features in the CID exam."

"Exactly. Economies of scale."

"Home comes first though, okay? If there's any danger of work taking over — I'll quit."

She stopped and turned to him, taking his face in her hands.

"Listen, Barnes, you don't need to reassure me. This is what it feels like when the future becomes the present. When your potential becomes realised. You can't *miss* this opportunity."

"There's rather an alarming divorce rate in the police," he said, thinking of the host of ring-finger tan lines that featured throughout the station.

"Barnes, you could be an inspector in three years."

He looked over her head at Forbes, who was inspecting a small clump of love-in-the-mist. A warm feeling flooded through him. When she put it like that, it did make sense. Inspector Barnes. It felt good. DI Barnes felt better. It made him *want* it.

"The extra money would be handy," he murmured.

They both fell quiet at the understatement, and continued walking, the two of them ruminating quietly on the possibilities of the future.

Neither of them was reckless with money, but nor were they particularly interested in managing it, either. In those long early days, hours and hours spent wrapped up in each other, sprawled on the sofa with movies and ice cream and sex, who could be bothered? She would touch his ear with her toes, and whisper, *"Chief, let's go out to eat. Who wants to cook?"*

Or he would get an idea for a romantic weekend in a remote B&B up in the Lake District or somewhere. The idea would snowball, he would plan and organise it meticulously and come home with a detailed itinerary, just to see that look on her face when he told her she had better pack quickly because they needed to get on the motorway.

It couldn't last forever. All too easy just to stick it on a credit card. Just lately, however, the piper wanted paying — they had tipped the balance between just about managing to meet the repayments and just falling short. With interest and charges, "just falling short" had meant that, over time, the debt had steadily grown into a seething mass.

Eventually Forbes returned from his exploration and trotted obediently beside them, usually a sign that he'd had enough. They returned to the car.

Eve flicked through Barnes's camera, chuckling at the pictures of Forbes. Barnes squatted down to lift the dog into the back of the car, and Eve laughed again when she saw the Labrador's solemn expression while his master struggled to carry him.

Once Barnes had liberated himself of the dog, Eve held up the camera and took a photograph of her husband. She smiled to herself.

"Tall, dark and handsome," she said. "I can see you doing interviews and stuff."

"Good face for radio, you mean?" he grinned.

She slid both her hands up his chest, over his shoulders and joined them around his neck. He wrapped his arms around her and squeezed.

"You're such a good dad to that dog," she said. "You'd be great with something smaller."

"Like a chihuahua?"

"I was thinking of something with only two legs, and less hair," she said.

This again, he thought. His phone vibrated loudly, several times. He tried to conceal his relief at the interruption.

"Looks like some missed calls," he said. "No number. It could be work."

"And so it begins," she smiled.

* * *

In the spring of 2001, Eastbourne's police resources were spread across the town. The sector patrol centre sat on the outskirts, near the arterial routes — a supposedly optimum location for rapidly accessing all areas of the town.

It comprised the uniformed response teams, community officers and the tutor unit — the first stop for all probationary officers after training school.

The CID lived in the police station in Grove Road, a square red-brick building with Georgian overtones right in the town centre. Unlike its sister site, which had a large sign over the door — "NOT OPEN TO THE PUBLIC" — the Grove Road station was the public-facing side of the business, where people came to report lost property, sign on for bail and produce driving documents to the counter clerks. The rear of the building housed a nine-cell custody block that was so ancient the stink of booze and various bodily secretions had seeped into the very bricks that held it together.

The remainder of the sprawling building provided accommodation for other so-called back-office functions such as file management and typing, the Divisional Command Team — and the CID.

In the locker room, deep in the bowels of the station, Barnes carefully knotted his tie with shaking hands. Van Leer's arrest on the Saturday, job offer from the DCI on the Monday, and here he was, day one as a detective — and it was only Wednesday.

He unknotted the tie and tried again, following the instructions he had printed from the internet and stuck onto the mirror with Blu Tack.

An image of his father rose in him. The memory was so powerful that it demanded his full attention; his fumbling hands slowed and then stopped. It took him a moment to work out that it was the act of knotting the tie that had triggered it.

Barnes's employment history prior to becoming a cop did not feature the kind of work that generally necessitated a tie. As such he had not, apart from two weddings, two interviews — one for university, one for the police — and his father's funeral, worn a proper tie since his school days. From the ages of five to twelve his father had carefully and expertly knotted Barnes's tie every morning before they departed for their respective institutions.

He finished his clumsy effort and stared at his reflection. His father was, what, twelve years dead? He hadn't been a chronic, before-breakfast alcoholic, but there had been too much of it at the weekend, along with too much rich food, too many cigars and no exercise. The sums weren't difficult to compute — with his genetic intolerance for such an imbalance, he'd been taken too early. Barnes's mind started to drift to that day, sixteen years old, but all he could really remember was his mother howling.

Another image surfaced — one of him knotting his own son's tie on his first school day.

He shook his head clear. He had to concentrate. Instead, he looked at the name badge on his lapel, but even that — POLICE CONSTABLE R. BARNES — was a reminder of his well-meaning immigrant father's attempt to give him an anglicised forename from a shortlist of notable historical figures. At least, that had been his mother's explanation. For all he knew, the old man had stuck a pin in a map of Scotland and picked the nearest village in the specious belief that every Tom, Dick and Harry was called Rutherford.

The net result was a double-barrelled legacy. One, he had left Barnes an archaic forename he wouldn't particularly want to use, especially not on a name badge; and two, as a consequence, he would forever use his surname in its place, to keep his father's memory alive. His mother had remarried — now he was the only Barnes in the family. Even his wife called him by his surname — was that normal?

Police Constable. He would have to get the badge changed. He stared at his reflection and tried to steady his nerves. *You're a detective now*, he told himself. *Start acting like it.*

Barnes stood in the doorway of the CID main office with a cardboard box of his belongings under his arm, hastily emptied from his locker at the patrol centre, feeling every bit the new boy in his suit and shoes.

DCI Hadian emerged from the Perspex box that passed for a corner office to greet his newest recruit. With a wriggling, autonomous black monobrow, rubbery lips and kind eyes, he looked a little like a university professor. His receding, jet-black hair was combed back on his head, which yawed from side to side as he walked, giving him the appearance of a jolly puppet.

"Welcome, Barnes," he said in his lilting Welsh accent while pumping Barnes's hand. "It's good to have you on board. Let's get you settled in."

He swept a welcoming arm around the office as if unveiling a statue, as he walked Barnes over to where Cathy Nightingale was sitting at her desk, still with her feet up.

Barnes steeled himself, expecting, at best, a curt greeting after their last encounter only days before, but Nightingale stood up to shake Barnes's hand and remarked on the improvement in his fashion sense.

Hadian thrust a twenty-pound note into Nightingale's hand, and the detective went out for fresh coffee and pastries while the other four or five DCs in the office queued up to meet Barnes, who was by now feeling mildly intoxicated by the attention of strangers.

Hadian pointed out an empty desk — one of several. Hadian hadn't been kidding when he'd said he had a dearth of detectives. Barnes strode over to the desk — and tripped over an unseen obstacle in the centre of the floor. The angle and timing of impact were such that his box of belongings went hurtling towards a window, while Barnes himself crashed headlong into the side of the desk.

He lay for a moment, stunned, wondering how to best deal with this hideous situation. He tried not to think of Eve's proud face. Hadian and some others made a dutiful show of concern, helping him to his feet and gathering his things, nevertheless unable to conceal their laughter.

Barnes looked for the accursed saboteur, and saw a cluster of brass telephone sockets in the middle of the floor, in a repeat pattern every two metres or so throughout the office.

He frowned at the incongruity.

"I suppose I should have mentioned those." Hadian saw where he was looking. "This used to be the area control room for Eastbourne. Before HQ centralised everything. Everything in this station used to be something else. Except the bar."

When Nightingale returned, Barnes took a coffee while the others gathered around, and decided to tell the slapstick story himself, pretending it had been deliberate, hoping to salvage some credibility as a team player. Nightingale was thoroughly vexed that she had missed it, but Barnes's self-deprecating account seemed to win them over. Someone asked him how he had nailed Van Leer, and he switched subjects with relief. A couple of them clapped him on the back while he spoke, while Nightingale toasted HRH and cracked a joke, and all the detectives roared with laughter.

"What's your first name?" someone called.

"Everyone just calls him Barnes," Hadian said, putting a heavy arm around Barnes's shoulders. "We've still got work to do. This is just till we get the champagne open in the pub."

"He doesn't drink, sir," Nightingale called helpfully.

"We'll soon sort that." Hadian winked at Barnes. "Welcome to the CID."

CHAPTER THREE

Flecks of drizzle had begun to patter against the windscreen of the unmarked Mondeo as they turned up the steep driveway of Her Majesty's Prison, Lewes. The uninviting stone and flint walls, crowned with rolls of razor wire, loomed against the darkening sky like a medieval fortress.

At the top of the driveway Nightingale stopped the car at the archway of the gatehouse. She barked into an intercom, and after a moment the enormous wooden doors slid open and they drove slowly forwards.

In the gatehouse, both Barnes and Nightingale surrendered their pepper spray, batons and mobile phones in exchange for remote panic alarms.

Barnes, unlike Nightingale, was a new face, and a young prison officer went over to him and began to pat him down.

"It's all right," Nightingale called over the roof of the car, not taking her eyes from Barnes. "I can vouch for him."

Another officer led them through the gatehouse and down a long driveway to the cavernous interview hall. The hall was empty, save for a single trusty mopping the floor between rows and rows of steel tables. Grey daylight cut in shafts across the top of the hall, through tiny barred windows near the ceiling.

The perimeter of the hall was lined with wooden, sound-insulated interview booths. All were empty. The prison officer led Nightingale and Barnes to one of the booths, and they were locked in while the officer disappeared into the wing.

They sat together on a steel bench fixed to the wall. Barnes was staring at the dirty corduroy soundproofing on the walls when the prison officer reappeared with Howard Van Leer in tow, wearing a grey tracksuit. The officer locked the door behind the three of them and disappeared.

It had only been few days since Van Leer's arrest, but swapping heroin for stodgy prison meals had already made his unshaven jowls noticeably more fleshy.

He slouched opposite the detectives with folded arms, his body language screaming defiance, but his eyebrows rose when he saw Barnes in a suit.

"Fuck's this? Promotion?"

"Something like that."

"Proper high-flyer, ain't cha?"

"How you doing, Howard?" Barnes asked.

Van Leer sucked his teeth and threw a hand in the air.

"It's prison, innit?"

"You get to see your son?"

Van Leer's animation ceased, and he stared at Barnes, nostrils flaring.

"What's his name?"

"Liam," Van Leer said, eventually.

Barnes had used an even tone in an attempt to identify with Van Leer so he would open up, but without sounding like a social worker. It wasn't working too well, and Nightingale cleared her throat loudly. Barnes recognised the "shut up" signal, as did Van Leer — he turned his head from Barnes to Nightingale, but his eyes took several seconds to follow.

"Know why we're here?" Nightingale asked.

Van Leer didn't answer. Nightingale fished a new pack of cigarettes from her jacket and tossed them onto the table.

"Ain't exactly a text letter," Van Leer sneered.

"Call it a taster," Nightingale said.

Van Leer flicked his eyes around quickly, then grabbed the pack and stuffed it into his sock.

"What's a text letter?" Barnes asked Nightingale.

Nightingale looked at Barnes, failing to conceal her irritation at being interrupted. "If a defendant facing prison decides to help us by confessing all their sins then we reserve the right to reward them by presenting the court with a text letter. We tell the judge how lovely the defendant's been, and the judge might knock a bit off their sentence."

Barnes sat back and mulled it over. He didn't want the world to know he was brand new, but as Van Leer knew anyway and it didn't look like Nightingale wanted to volunteer much, it seemed to be the only way to learn.

"Know why we're here?" Nightingale asked again.

"'Course I do. Ain't the first time I've had TICs. Make you look good, won't it, me admitting to all your burglaries?" Van Leer said. Barnes pulled at his tie, sensing a stand-off. Van Leer was a smart-arse most of the time, but today there was something extra-spicy in his arrogance.

"So I don't need to explain the benefits. Where do you want to start?" Nightingale asked, pushing a glossy leaflet across the tabletop to Van Leer.

"No, go on. Explain the benefits," Van Leer said, and slid the leaflet back over to Barnes without looking at it. Barnes looked down at the leaflet — *Asking for Offences You Have Committed to Be Taken into Consideration (TICs)*.

Nightingale smiled like a snake about to strike. "I will. You're on three strikes — your third house burglary in eighteen months, so you're going away — three years, minimum. If you ask for the other burglaries we suspect you to have committed to be taken into consideration by the judge, then you won't get any more on your sentence. If you don't admit them, then while inside you risk us getting together enough evidence to charge you with these other burglaries. We wait till you serve your time, then we arrest you at the gate on the new evidence, you go back to square one and you're back inside. How's that sound?"

"You make it sound very appealing, Officer. Hard sell and all that. But I think I'll pass."

Van Leer's tone was faintly mocking. Nightingale's predatory smile evaporated, and Barnes sensed her tense up. Her fists balled on the table.

"Between you and me, I ain't that mad for going back to the streets. Prison ain't so bad."

"You've only been in here five minutes," Nightingale said. "Let's see if you're still full of piss and vinegar when the judge gives you four years."

"Right now, my solicitor is on the blower to the pretty little airhead of a prosecutor that stitched me up at court yesterday, getting the charge downshifted from burglary to handling. If she doesn't want to do that then she risks getting the job chucked out altogether." He was in full flight now, drinking in Nightingale's incredulous expression.

"Are you pulling my pud, Van Leer?" Nightingale said.

"You can't prove I was in the house."

"What the fuck are you on? Barnes collared you outside the back door with the cash and paint still in your pocket." Nightingale's displeasure had caused her voice to go up an octave, and her cheeks were flushed with colour.

"You can't prove I was inside," Van Leer repeated.

"It's recent possession."

"It's handling at best. It might not even get sent up the road. I'm looking at six months, tops. I'll do most of that on remand." Van Leer sat back in his chair and laced his hands behind his head, a victorious smile on his smug face.

"You gave a 'no comment' interview. A jury will hang you out to dry."

"It'll get binned way before I need any sort of defence."

Nightingale sat back in her seat. Barnes saw her knuckles whiten as she glared at Van Leer.

"Besides, haven't you got more important things to be doing?"

"Don't tell me — this is the bit where you tell me I should be out catching rapists and serial killers."

Van Leer's eyes opened wide, and he grinned horribly.

"You don't know the half of it."

"Van Leer, what the fuck are you talking about?"

"Turned up for work, has she?"

The grin spread wider as Van Leer drank in the identical stunned expressions of the two officers.

"Big, dangerous world out there for a young lady living alone. Who knows what might happen to her?"

Barnes, now anxious, got up and left the booth. He had no mobile phone, so he called over one of the prison officers, who took him to a nearby office.

Barnes got the numbers from the area control room and made the calls. There was no answer on Holden's home number. She had two mobile phones — one personal, one issued by the job. Both were switched off.

As unease spread across his brow, he remembered she had voiced her intention to go to her mother's.

He didn't have the number, so he called the control room and asked for a patrol car to be sent to her mother's address. He told them it was urgent.

He paced around the desk for several agonising minutes while the prison officer made small talk. He was young and clearly a cop groupie. Barnes tried not to roll his eyes while the officer offered his canteen-psychology theories on everything from police paperwork to the causes of repeat offending.

Barnes tuned him out and fixed his gaze on the wall clock. The prison officer eventually got the hint and disappeared in search of coffee.

After twelve minutes the phone rang. Barnes grabbed it as the officer re-entered the room. The controller was only on the line for a few seconds before Barnes gently replaced the receiver.

He took slow steps back to the booth, escorted by the prison officer.

"She's not at home. She's not answering any of her phones," he whispered in Nightingale's ear. "And she never turned up at her mother's."

The two detectives turned to look at Van Leer. Seeing their faces, his grin faltered for just a second.

Nightingale leaned across the table. Her voice was low.

"What . . . do you . . . know?"

Van Leer just shrugged.

"You burgled her house."

"Allegedly."

"You daubed that ridiculous B-movie graffiti on the wall. You screamed those vile threats at her through your cell door. What's she ever done to you?" Barnes said, the frustration obvious in his voice.

"What can I tell you? I ain't seen daylight since you nicked me."

"What do you *know*?!" Nightingale yelled, grabbing Van Leer's jumpsuit. "Where is she?"

"Easy now, love, don't bust your groove."

"Cathy . . ." Barnes said, touching her arm.

Nightingale looked down at the hand on her arm, then up at Barnes, who held her gaze.

"This is crap," she said, and released Van Leer with an angry shove. She went to the door and banged on the glass for the prison officer.

"I bet now she's sorry," Van Leer said, mainly to himself. "Stupid bitch."

That did it. Van Leer's ill-chosen words caused what little remained of Nightingale's self-control to evaporate. She turned around and sprang across the table in a single movement, her sudden athleticism surprising both of the men in the room. She grabbed the panic alarm from her belt and crammed it into Van Leer's mouth. A high-pitched shriek filled the hall as the alarm activated.

"What's she ever done to you, you pond scum?"

Two enormous prison officers thundered into the hall, poised for action. They stopped in astonishment when they saw their prisoner eating a panic alarm. One of them unlocked the door and walked in, a confused look on his face.

"I ain't sayin' a thing," Van Leer yelled, pulling the machine out of his mouth. "You lot are well out of order. Get me my solicitor. *Now!*"

"What's going on here?" the prison officer asked, bewildered.

"You're obviously not feeding him enough," Nightingale said, through clenched teeth.

* * *

Nightingale made the call as soon as they were back in the car.

"You think the charges have been dropped?" Barnes asked.

"'Downshifted' is what he said. Either way we need to confirm it. Natasha Warwick is the prosecuting lawyer responsible for securing his remand in custody yesterday." Nightingale switched the loudspeaker on as the call was connected.

"CPS." The disembodied female voice swam into the car.

"Natasha, it's Cathy Nightingale. What the hell's this about Howard Van Leer's charge getting dropped?"

"Pull in your line, DC Nightingale, or I'll hang up the phone. It's not being dropped. It's being varied slightly." Her tone was terse, as if she were well used to admonishing stroppy detectives.

"You know as well as I do that 'varied slightly' means the difference between three months and three years."

"That remains to be seen."

"Oh, come off it. Why wasn't I consulted?"

"Your opinion won't sway anything. There are no forensics. We cannot prove Van Leer was in the house — ergo, we cannot prove burglary."

"He was found yards from the front door with her credit card and the can of paint on him. He was asked for his explanation and chose not to say anything. What other possible explanation is there?" Barnes could hear the frustration in her voice, frustration that what was patently obvious to the police seemed to be eluding everyone else.

"Coincidence is not enough to convict. I've spoken to McDermott. Van Leer will claim to have found the rucksack while out walking, with the paint and the credit card inside it."

"What about the cash in his sock?"

"He says it's his, and he keeps it in his sock for safekeeping. Before you start snorting with derision, and ludicrous as we all know it is, we cannot disprove this."

"Well then, why didn't he take the opportunity to inform us when he had the chance?"

"Apparently he had every intention of providing an explanation, but was intimidated and bullied by his custodians. Particularly the one who questioned him."

There was a stilted silence. To Barnes the defence suddenly sounded a little less implausible. He wondered if Nightingale was thinking the same thing.

"This is bollocks," Nightingale said, but without vitriol. "He's on his third strike, which makes this case indictable only. He should be looking at three years minimum."

"Cathy, I know exactly what you're saying," Warwick said, her tone softening a little. "But there is a real risk that we will lose this at trial. This way we keep him on remand for as long as we can, and if we take a plea to handling then at least we get some sort of conviction on his sheet."

"You know Constable Holden is a misper?" Nightingale said pointedly, as if this was a natural consequence of the CPS failing to deliver justice for the victim.

"She's a what?"

"A missing person. She's missing."

"She could just be . . ."

"In our line of work, 'missing' means she's in a situation where she can't help herself or she's dead. And chummy knows something about it. He's far too confident for my liking."

"I'll speak to you soon, Cathy."

There was a click.

"'*Yes, but, yes, but* . . .' Are we on the same side, or what? Total bollocks," Nightingale said.

"There's nothing to tie him to any of those other burglaries? They're all his MO," Barnes said, incredulous.

"No evidence. TICs or bust."

"Who's McDermott?" Barnes asked after a few moments.

"Van Leer's solicitor. Phil McDermott. Used to be a street boxer in the East End. Was pretty good too. Lost a couple of teeth, used his prize money to put himself through law school."

She became thoughtful. For a moment the only sound was that of the tyres on the road, then she punctured the silence with a loud belch.

"Little fucker didn't say a word through his interview. Was as cocky as you've just seen. Bullied, my arse. I should have videoed it."

"He's got a point. He's been in a cell since he was arrested, so he can't have done anything to Holden."

"Exactly. He's all talk. Let's not get ahead of ourselves."

The logic was sound, but Barnes could not ignore the anxiety in the pit of his stomach. Looking at Cathy's face, he could see she felt the same.

He also sensed her frustration at having to feed Van Leer's cryptic response back to Hadian. Nightingale found the number and slowly made the call.

"How are you getting on? Into triple figures yet?" The DCI's voice reverberated around the car.

"Paul, I don't wish to burst your bubble," Nightingale said. "But today's headline is that the CPS don't think there's enough to run against Van Leer with the burglary at HRH's place. Ergo, no TICs."

There was silence on the line.

"That isn't the best part, however," Nightingale continued. "He dropped some hints that HRH could be in danger."

"But Van Leer's in custody. He can't get at her," Hadian said, irritation in his voice from the first bit of bad news. "What are you worried about?"

"Sir, she . . . Harriet's missing. She was supposed to be at her mother's, but she never arrived," Barnes said.

More silence. All three were thinking the same thing, and the implications were descending on them like a fog.

"Phones?" Hadian asked eventually.

"Both mobile phones switched off. Long ring on the home landline," Barnes said.

"Sir, I don't have a terrific feeling about this," Nightingale said.

"Look, let's not jump to conclusions," Hadian said after a pause. "She's an adult. She's off duty, and according to your team's roster, Barnes — your *former* team's roster — she will be for a few days. She's entitled to do what the hell she likes. The only known threat to her safety is ensconced at Her Majesty's pleasure and has previous convictions for bullshit."

"He's got a point," Nightingale whispered to Barnes.

"We'll give it another hour, then you two revisit her mother's house. Keep trying the phones in the meantime. If she hasn't turned up by nightfall, I'll call a missing person enquiry."

The call was disconnected as Hadian hung up.

Barnes stared at a train matching them for speed on the Firle straight, his thoughts racing. Nightingale drummed her fingers on the wheel as she drove.

A car overtook them, just as the road began to bend to the right. It cut back in sharply. Nightingale went to yell out of the window, her hand simultaneously going to the horn. She checked herself when she saw the flash of blonde in the driver's seat.

"I don't know what it is, but there's something about aggressive female drivers that just does it for me," she said.

Barnes turned in his seat, pointing back towards the prison with his thumb.

"What's with the frisking on the gate? We put the prisoners *in* there — do they think we're going to break them out again?"

"Arse-covering, like most public sector jobs."

"Thanks for vouching for me, anyway."

"Forget it. Rules are rules, but their gaffer needs to tame their enthusiasm."

"The taming of the screw?" Barnes turned to look at Nightingale. There was a pause, and then they began to laugh.

"Hey," Nightingale said as the laughter subsided. "You know I needled you about not searching Van Leer's room?"

Barnes turned to Nightingale, wondering if this was a prelude to contrition.

"Well, now's your chance to redeem yourself."

Barnes faced ahead again. Clearly not.

"He's spoiled my day," Nightingale continued. "Let's go turn his room over."

Barnes frowned.

"It hasn't been done yet?"

"Oh yeah, it's been done. Couple of lids did it after you booked off. But a second look won't hurt. Boot up the MDT, will you?"

The car's mobile data terminal was a small screen fixed over the stereo. Barnes switched it on and drummed his fingers while it fired up.

"Look through the serials for April eighth," she said.

Barnes sat back in his seat.

"That's the day I arrested Van Leer."

"Correct-a-mundo. There should be one for the Atlantic Hotel."

Barnes brought up the operational incident system on the screen. He scrolled through every single incident reported to the police on 8 April, which meant untaxed cars, football in the street, noisy neighbours, abusive text messages, missing pets and a host of other banalities that people saw fit to report every single day — people who would quickly lose interest once they had been given a fifteen-minute platform to spout off at a copper.

There it was: serial 725. Reported at 10.21 a.m. 8 April. Location — Atlantic Hotel. Incident title — CONCERN.

The incident text was scant: *ANONYMOUS CALL REPORTING CAUSE FOR CONCERN. OCCUPANT OF ROOM 4C NOT SEEN FOR SEVERAL DAYS. OUT OF CHARACTER. UNIT TO ATTEND PLEASE TO CHECK.*

The call handler had then done some digging and had obviously unearthed the fact that the occupant of the room — Howard Van Leer — was safe and well and languishing in police custody. As a result, the incident had been marked as not requiring police attendance, and it was never brought to anybody's attention.

"No name given, but the number's a local landline," Barnes said.

"Yeah. I checked it against some linked calls. Number belongs to a payphone in the lobby of the Atlantic Hotel."

"So it could have been any one of the residents."

"It could have been anyone at all. But it's a way in."

Nightingale made a left and they headed along Royal Parade, the road that lined the seafront from the pier east to Princes Park. On this part of the seafront the procession of hotels and holiday flats was markedly less appealing than further west, with stalactites of rust and salt corrosion trailing down the exteriors of the faded paintwork. They continued past the Redoubt Fortress, the moated circular stronghold built during the Napoleonic Wars, and west onto Grand Parade, where the frontage started to bear picture-postcard familiarity. Past the Grand Hotel, Nightingale turned right into Jevington Gardens. She mounted the kerb and parked the car.

Barnes surveyed the washed-out pastel fronts of the hotels in an area that had once been the nucleus of the town's wealth. Jevington Gardens bordered the town centre and the ward of Meads, and featured three or four enormous hotels that had slid from being weekend retreats for the Victorian rich to bail hostels and social housing in less than a century.

Van Leer's own room was in the basement of a huge, jaundiced halfway house known as the Atlantic Hotel, an establishment both Barnes and Nightingale knew well. Five floors up, a massive gull shrieked its disapproval as they approached the building.

Nightingale pushed open the double doors and walked into the pea-green hotel lounge, which was crawling with sallow-skinned misfits — drinking, smoking and arguing. The cloying odour of cannabis was heavy in the air. Several pairs of dark, suspicious eyes turned to the detectives as they walked in. Two or three stood up and stared, motionless and slack-jawed.

"Jesus, it's like *Village of the Damned*," Nightingale muttered to Barnes.

A skinny creature in a string vest pulled himself off a moth-eaten sofa by the window. Nightingale strode over.

"Police. Where's room 4C?" she asked, flashing her warrant card.

"It's down the hall, in the basement," said the man in a thick Liverpool accent, sipping from a can of White Lightning. "But he ain't here. He's doing some bird."

"We know that," Barnes said. "We need to get into his room."

"Can't do that."

"Give us the key." Nightingale yanked the can of cider from the man's hand. She held it up, a smirk on her face, and slowly emptied the contents at his feet.

The man's eyes narrowed and his nostrils flared while the sickly-smelling liquid sprayed his sandals. His breathing grew deeper while he glared at Nightingale, who just fluttered her eyelashes. Barnes moved forward, thinking the guy was about to lamp her, but then he disappeared to a tiny office behind the kitchen, returning a few seconds later with a key on a paper fob. He held it out to Nightingale, and as she went to take it, he dropped it into the cider puddle. She smirked again and looked at Barnes, who fished it out.

The narrow corridor was dark, lit only by weak, naked light bulbs on fraying cords. The bare floorboards were sticky and rotten underfoot. The walls had once been white, but were now a dark brown from years of neglect and a gradual build-up of nicotine. The air was thick with acrid smell of body odour, cigarettes and damp.

Despite this, the intricate Victorian cornices, coving and ceiling roses were still obvious from when the hotel had first been built. Barnes wondered if the original architects could have foreseen its eventual use.

As well as being truly squalid, the hotel was a labyrinthine network of corridors, as narrow as diseased arteries, leading to all corners of the building. Rooms were hidden all over, in recesses and stairwells, and those rooms that actually had numbers on the doors appeared to be numbered in no discernible order.

Barnes and Nightingale doubled back on themselves twice, and eventually found 4C.

Barnes went to try the door handle. It was locked.

He turned to Nightingale.

"Van Leer was in custody when the call was made, so we can hardly pretend to be worried about him. We don't have the power to enter this room, much less search it. We need a warrant."

"Well, you know your stuff," Nightingale said, and pulled a crumpled piece of carbonated paper bearing the royal crest from her pocket. She waved it at Barnes.

"*Dieu et mon droit,*" she said, although her expression said, *Satisfied now?*

Barnes stared at her. It looked real enough, although Barnes's experience was limited to passing glances at the stacks of blank search warrants in the stationery cupboard.

"Probationers," Nightingale muttered to herself. She stuffed the warrant back in her pocket and inserted the key in the door.

Barnes said nothing, but a comforting thought came to mind. *Less than a year*, he thought, *and you'll be calling me sarge.*

Nightingale turned the key. Barnes placed a palm on the door.

"Do you think Harriet's alright?" Barnes said.

Nightingale looked at him. The door opened fractionally — and a putrid smell drifted through the narrow gap.

The detectives locked gazes, each mirroring the other's expression of realisation and fear. Far above them, the gulls continued to shriek.

No . . .

Harriet . . . ?

Together they shouldered the door open, and the stench hit them in a warm wave. It was a tiny single room — the bedroom and a small kitchenette occupied the same space. Light struggled to enter through what looked like a thick rug hanging up on the window.

The woman's body lay amid a pile of unwashed clothing and rotting rubbish. Fat bluebottles circled the corpse, their heavy buzzing sounding like distorted string instruments.

She was naked, lying awkwardly on her back, her left leg bent upwards behind her, her right sticking out almost perpendicular to her body. Her arms were outstretched to the side; the left was broken. Her hair was a dirty matted tangle of blonde, the face a badly mutilated succession of bruising, swelling and slash marks. At the crown of the head the blood was thick and dark, the skull crumpled and misshapen. It appeared, from the flat stomach and slender arms, that it was a woman in her twenties, but the damage to her face and body prevented much more in the way of immediate recognition.

Barnes's eyes roved over her body, his brain desperately trying to process the image of a violent death. His gaze paused at a tiny heart-shaped tattoo on the right hip bone, and only then did he realise the only sound in the room other than the bluebottles was his own shallow, rapid breathing.

Nightingale, with no outward show of emotion, pulled on some latex gloves and crouched by the body. She carefully examined the scene with a gloved finger, muttering observations to herself as she did so.

"Oh no. *Oh no*," Barnes said, his head spinning. He edged slowly towards the body as a child might — tempered by reticence but finding the horror irresistible.

"Poor cow," Nightingale said, not addressing Barnes directly. "That's what's done her. Look at the blow to the back of the head. This is murder, no question. Shit, what a way to go."

Barnes knelt beside the body. The face was frozen in horror — milky eyes wide open, fixed on a point somewhere in the corner of the ceiling, the mouth half open.

Barnes touched her shoulder lightly. Her cold skin was clammy and remained pitted where Barnes had touched it, yielding easily like a layer of icing, lividity like a halo around her ghostly, blue-white body. Blood from her wounds had pooled where she lay — the rancid smell of iron was overpowering. He could not channel his disbelief, and just kept shaking his head, vipers in the pit of his stomach.

"Is it her? Is it . . . Harriet?" he asked.

"You tell me. You worked with her," Nightingale said.

"I don't know. I . . . I can't tell. Her poor face . . ." She was beyond recognition, and yet he knew it was her.

"She have a tattoo on her hip?" Nightingale's green eyes bored into Barnes.

"I don't know," Barnes said, barely registering the insinuation through the shock.

"It must be her. Either way, I don't think we'll be waiting long to visit Mr Van Leer again."

Barnes's eyes flicked back and forth to the breasts and neat line of hair at her pubis. Feeling both guilt for his stolen glances and a desire to cover her last dignity, he reached for a nearby blanket and tried to cover the body.

Nightingale stopped him with a gentle touch of the hand.

"Can't do that. Got to preserve everything."

Barnes stood, and the room spun again. His vision darkened, and silence suddenly filled his ears. He grabbed for the wall.

"You okay?" Nightingale asked. Her voice sounded like it was miles away. She stood up and went to steady him — one hand on his shoulder, the other under his chin to steer his wandering eyes towards her.

"It's all right," she said. "Take it easy."

The faint passed, and Nightingale swam back into focus.

"It'll be okay," she said, releasing him.

Barnes looked around the room, shaking his head again at the squalid surroundings, trying to imagine her last moments, wondering what her dying eyes had seen last.

"She shouldn't have died like this," he said.

"No one should." With a heavy sigh, Nightingale slumped in a chair next to the body. "Call it in."

Slowly, achingly slowly, as if his limbs were no longer connected to his brain, Barnes fumbled for the radio on his belt.

"Sierra-Oscar . . . Echo-Papa nine-six . . ."

The controller responded with tinny urgency to the CID call sign.

"*Echo-Papa nine-six. Go ahead, over.*"

Barnes drew breath, yet to compose his next transmission.

"*Echo-Papa nine-six? Come in please, over,*" the controller repeated.

"Nine-six, I need . . . I need a patrol car to room 4C, Atlantic Hotel, Jevington Gardens. Also SOCO grade A, and you'd better get DCI Hadian down here as well. I have a crime scene."

"Nine-six, you're not assigned to any of my active logs. Do I need to input a new one?"

"Yes," whispered Barnes. "You most certainly do."

CHAPTER FOUR

The patrol centre briefing room was packed. Plans to launch a specialist Force-level unit dedicated to the investigation of major crime were still some months away from being realised, so Divisional CID ran the gauntlet — from burglary and car theft up to kidnap, rape and homicide.

Barnes had not met Denniker before, but knew him by reputation — like a Victorian headmaster, Denniker used fear and zero-tolerance discipline to keep hearts and minds in check. Barnes knew of two young constables who had been severely reprimanded for failing to wear their hats on a ten-foot journey from their patrol car to the front doors of the station. One of them had left in tears.

Chief Superintendent Denniker was not a tall man, but, at fifty-two, he was muscular, fit and totally untroubled by irritations like excess fat, although a closer look caused Barnes to wonder if the shirt was deliberately a size too small. Denniker's square lantern jaw was as sharp as that of a man half his age, and his thick thatch of white hair was cut with military precision.

Denniker moved to the lectern and spoke, killing the murmur in the room.

"Right, let's get this started. Everyone! Your attention, please." The voice was deep and clear. "For those of you that don't know me, I am Chief Superintendent Clive Denniker, the East Downs divisional commander. Alongside me is Detective Chief Inspector Paul Hadian, the senior investigating officer of this case."

He clicked a wireless mouse in his hand. An image blipped onto the screen. Blonde, smiling, the just-visible epaulettes of the dress uniform indicating to Barnes that this was Harriet Holden's passing-out photograph. He steadied himself and forced some deep breaths. Denniker continued.

"This murder investigation is codenamed Operation Christchurch. The victim is a female, twenty-six years old. Those of you that didn't know her will have inferred from the photograph that she was a police officer, and this is the reason that I am personally retaining strategic command of this investigation."

Subject matter aside, Barnes noted that Denniker had the full attention of his audience — his movements were confident, and during the course of his speech he had made eye contact with every single person in the room.

"Constable Harriet Holden had four years' service with this force, and worked on one of our local patrol teams. For those of you that knew her personally, the welfare department is organising ongoing counselling and debriefing sessions — dates and venues to be published. This will be an ongoing service during the course of the investigation. If at any time you feel your participation in this investigation is not one-hundred-per-cent impartial, then see me and we'll sort it. Any issues with that?"

The room was silent. Denniker stepped aside and Hadian took the floor.

"Okay then, onto the facts. Constable Holden was found deceased yesterday in a room at the Atlantic Hotel by two district detectives. She had been slashed with a sharp instrument over her body, possibly a Stanley knife."

Hadian clicked the mouse. Holden's smiling image jumped to a photograph of her corpse in room 4C, exactly as Barnes and Nightingale had discovered her. Barnes flinched.

An officer near the front of the room began to cry, and got up to leave when her sobs got worse rather than better.

Barnes stared at the picture of the corpse, although he didn't need to — the image was etched on his memory. He still couldn't reconcile the disfigured body with the pretty picture he had just seen, even with a confirmed ID.

"The slash wounds were concentrated on the upper torso and facial area. Cause of death was a heavy blow with a blunt weapon to the back of the head, causing massive haemorrhaging. The body was found naked, but there is no indication at this time that Constable Holden was sexually assaulted. Preliminary reports from the Home Office pathologist suggest that she was not killed in the room, but was put there post-mortem — she could have been in the room for anything up to about twelve hours. We know she left work about eight a.m. Sunday morning. Her body was found around four p.m. yesterday, which gives us an eighty-hour window for time of death."

In sharp contrast to the words he was saying, Hadian's voice was calm and gentle as he delivered the information like a university lecturer. The only indication that anything was amiss were his knuckles, which were chalk-white as he gripped the edges of the lectern.

"The room's sole resident is one Howard Van Leer, known to most district officers as a level-one drug dealer and petty thief. Van Leer was recently remanded in custody for the burglary of Constable Holden's home address, and is currently being treated as our number-one suspect based on the nature of the MO and subsequent threats made to the deceased. However, he was in custody at the likely time of death. So, although we are likely to be looking at a conspiracy, there are no other named suspects at present. Significant lines of enquiry will thus be determined by what Van Leer chooses to tell us.

"The hotel itself is well known to most of you, and is a pretty foul place — most of our regular customers can be found in one of the rooms at one time or another. The only blood found so far is that of the victim. However, given the amount of drug dealing and petty crime in and around that area, it seems highly likely that a number of transient persons will have been present in the room on a casual basis at one time or another. A number of exhibits have been recovered that will, likely as not, throw up full DNA profiles. Identifications are expected within seventy-two hours, and each one will be brought in." Hadian paused while papers were distributed.

"The press scrutiny will be intense," he said. "The media strategy is being handed out, and I want you all to familiarise yourselves with its contents." Hadian waited for the distribution to finish before continuing.

"You will see there is a blanket embargo on disclosing anything that does not appear on the sheet. Constable Holden was not killed in the line of duty; by the same token, facts about her death are currently in short supply. As such, giving the media the bare minimum will be extremely important in identifying her killer, and we need to keep our operational activities as quiet as possible. If you get approached by the press, refer it up. Any questions?"

The room was silent, and heavy with tension. Barnes could feel it in the air, like static electricity just waiting for an outlet so it could burst forth. Hadian sat down, and Denniker took over again.

"Ladies and gentlemen, Harriet Holden was one of our own. She was due to take promotion, and had a promising career ahead of her. Shortly before her death her house was burgled with an obscure threat left at the scene. Her personal life will be scrutinised, and if there is a leak in this station, I want to know about it. I want you on full alert, both for your own safety and in the event of the unthinkable possibility that we are being sold out by one of our own."

There was a murmur of disquiet around the room. Denniker allowed it to swell and then subside naturally — deliberately, Barnes realised, as a means of galvanising them into action. Nothing disturbs cops more than the thought of a carefully cultivated team bond being infiltrated.

Denniker continued his rabble-rousing.

"I know there are suggestions from other quarters that we should not be investigating this murder. But, at present, we are, and until such time as I am relieved of my command I expect all officers assigned to this case to display the high standard of professionalism I know you would in any serious crime investigation. We will find her killer. Uniformed officers, dismissed. Detectives, report to DCI Hadian after briefing and he will task you with your actions."

The uniformed constables began to leave, with a visible energy not apparent when they had arrived. The detectives queued up, Nightingale among them, to be further briefed by Hadian. Those waiting for colleagues stood around in huddles, talking earnestly in low voices.

Hadian picked up a slim white policy book, with *Op Christchurch* emblazoned on the front. As with any homicide case, such books formed the lifeblood of the investigation, and Operation Christchurch would necessitate the use of many more such books as it wound its course.

The strategic direction of the investigation would be catalogued here, providing an audit trail for every rationale, tactic and line of enquiry the SIO came up with, in the event of some reptilian barrister attempting to undermine the whole business at a jury trial.

Hadian produced an actions file and began tearing out carbonated pink chits and passing them to the detectives, who began to file out once they'd received their individual tasks.

After the briefing room had emptied, Hadian, Barnes and Nightingale returned to Grove Road and regrouped in Hadian's office.

"This isn't going to be a brass-tacks investigation. It won't be straightforward by any means," Hadian said as he distributed coffee from an impressive-looking machine on his desk. "Our answers are going to come from legwork, and I want you both on the outside enquiry team. Start on the outside and work in — that's where we'll find our answers."

As he spoke, the door opened and Denniker walked in. Barnes and Nightingale stood as if to leave, but the divisional commander shook his head and gestured for them to sit.

Denniker put down his briefcase and stood facing them, his hands by his sides. Barnes observed that, while this was a posture few men could carry off without looking awkward, Denniker managed it effortlessly.

The rank-and-file often spoke of command officers in the abstract. Commanders were "the job". Grizzled thirty-year cops would place a heavy arm around the shoulders of their younger colleagues and warn them about the job. *Log your hours. Record your own arrests. Don't crash police cars. Don't accept gifts. Don't date witnesses. Learn to look after yourself, young 'un, or the job'll fuck you.*

And now the job was right here in the room and abstract no longer. In his immaculately pressed uniform and dress shoes polished like mirrors, Denniker was thoroughly intimidating. Barnes wondered if he was always this well turned-out, or whether it was because the developments of the last twenty-four hours increased the likelihood of getting on television.

Having the DCI call him at home had been a closer encounter with a command officer than Barnes was used to, and yet here was another man two full ranks above Hadian, and the difference in status was palpable. Barnes noticed the change in Hadian's body language around the divisional commander; even without the epaulettes, there would have been little doubt as to who held the senior rank.

"Sir, Barnes is the CID's brightest new recruit," Hadian said when Denniker had said nothing after a minute. "I'm pleased to have him on the team."

"Ah, PC Barnes," Denniker said, extending a hand for a regulation bone-crusher. Barnes looked down and saw wrists almost as thick as his hands. "The man who nailed Van Leer. Excellent arrest, young man."

"Thank you, sir."

Barnes returned the shake, catching a trace of menthol and cigars. His eyes flicked to the crown and pip adorning the epaulettes on Denniker's shoulder. The commander caught this and smirked, lingering on the handshake before he finally sat down. He crossed his legs and laced his fingers on his shin.

"But perhaps you could explain to me how, with Van Leer in custody, another promising young officer has been deprived of the opportunity to celebrate her next birthday?"

Nobody spoke. Barnes noticed that Denniker had tiny feet — his toes barely extended beyond the sharp pleats of his uniform.

"He . . . he can't have been working alone," Barnes offered, when it became apparent no one else intended to speak.

"Exactly," said Denniker. "So what the fuck do you propose to do about it?"

His tone was as sharp as a Stanley knife. Barnes felt the colour rise in his throat.

"I don't need to remind any of you that this is a major embarrassment," Denniker continued, addressing all of them. "PC Barnes here went to the trouble of depriving Van Leer of his liberty, but the CID's subsequent complacency cost PC Holden her life. We — that is, the CID — missed a trick. And that pisses me off plenty."

"Sir, I'm not sure we could have done anything even if we thought Van Leer had an accomplice." Hadian's tone was brittle. "There was nothing to suggest that the burglary was a prelude to anything else, and certainly no evidence that he wasn't working alone."

"You won't mind if I quote you to the public enquiry, then?" Denniker snapped.

Hadian said nothing, but breathed heavily. His gaze was fixed on the divisional commander, and for a moment Barnes wondered if he was going to tell Denniker to go fuck himself. The moment passed, however, and the only indication of Hadian's discomfort at being rebuked in front of his juniors was the split second in which his gaze flicked to Barnes and back again.

"Sir, we will get this guy. I promise you." Not quite through gritted teeth, but almost.

Denniker opened his briefcase and produced a newspaper.

"If we don't get a quick result on this, people are actually going to start leaving town. The press have been muttering for weeks that the scum are taking over and the police are powerless. And now we've lost one of our own. I don't need to spell out the implications of this for you."

"Indeed not, sir," Hadian said.

Barnes picked up the newspaper. Even for tabloid hysteria, it made grim reading. He flicked through the pages. There was a local-interest piece about Devil's Chimney, a two-hundred-foot outcrop of chalk on Beachy Head that had collapsed the week before. The journalist's name was Emily Varela, and she had apparently reawakened local lore that a curse would descend on the town should the chalk stack ever collapse. Barnes wondered if there was any truth in it.

Hadian turned to Nightingale. "What did you get from the hotel?"

"Callaghan's team are doing the house-to-house as we speak. They've all got plenty to say, but none of it helps much." Nightingale produced a small tube from her pocket and applied it liberally to her lips. The smell of strawberry wafted across the room.

"The pathologist says she wasn't murdered in the room, but taken there post-mortem. You're not telling me you can smuggle a dead body into a pit like that undetected?"

"Paul, most of the residents of that street are comatose from filling their veins with shite. Even if they were compos mentis, most of them hate the police and wouldn't lift a finger to call us unless they could get something out of it. Not only that, a day doesn't go by without someone getting stabbed, beaten or robbed in that place. A roll of carpet being carried in at three in the morning probably wouldn't raise an eyebrow," Nightingale said.

"Cathy, I want you and Barnes back at the scene. Get your ears to the ground. Callaghan will do a good job, but he's uniform, and this will need some thinking outside the box. Lean on them if you have to."

"Not good enough," Denniker interrupted. "What I want, Paul, is a show of strength in that street. Speak to the intel unit. Get together every two-bit warrant we've got saved for a rainy day, every spare body, every shred of intel we've got, and kick in as many doors as you can. Make it loud, make it obvious and get the press down there. I want people to know we mean business. You can't just murder a cop and expect us to keep worrying about speeding tickets and shop-lifters. The community needs to feel *reassured*."

"Consider it done, sir," Hadian said, his expression neutral.

"Good. It's now down to you to find Van Leer's fellow conspirators or get enough together to charge him. Because at the moment, we've got two-thirds of fuck all."

Denniker stood up.

"You really need a computer in here, Paul," he said.

"Over my dead body." The DCI smiled politely.

Denniker eyed him for a moment, then picked up his briefcase.

"I have to go. I want twice-daily updates, Paul." He turned in the doorway and faced them.

"You find this bastard."

Denniker stalked out of the office. Nightingale and Barnes got up to go.

"Harriet's face was too much of a mess for her mother to make an ID," Hadian said. "We had to cross-check her fingerprints against the personnel database. If Van Leer had help, we need to raise our game, and you two are going to be the ones to do it."

The detectives nodded and turned to go.

"And Cathy?"

Nightingale turned in the doorway.

"You call me *sir* in front of the chief fucking superintendent."

* * *

Denniker's vision of the community reassurance phase of the investigation was called Operation Warlord.

Around 7 a.m. the following day, the early morning silence was shattered by six busloads of cops clad in NATO riot gear as they screamed into Jevington Gardens. Barnes and Nightingale stood outside the Atlantic Hotel as the door of nearly every bail hostel, B&B and halfway house within a hundred yards was simultaneously smashed in, and the ground shook with the ensuing yells, screams and ill-advised escape attempts.

The two detectives were meant to be following up on Callaghan's initial house-to-house sweep, but the colourful histrionics of Operation Warlord meant that the detectives were having difficulty keeping their witnesses' attention.

Amid the activity, Barnes saw a young woman with a microphone weaving carefully in between police officers, followed dutifully by a heavy man with a large camera.

He shook his head. Press.

Blue tape and high-visibility jackets swamped the hotel while the SOCOs continued their painstaking examination of room 4C. Barnes and Nightingale stood in the doorway. A couple of uniformed constables — one, a fifty-something woman; the other male, skinny and barely in his twenties — had been assigned to guard it. Barnes flashed his warrant card at them, and he and Nightingale stepped inside.

The SOCOs barely acknowledged them. Barnes watched them as they dutifully ensured that every last shred of evidence in the room could be packaged and accurately reproduced in court. Nightingale leaned up against the doorframe, blue tape brushing her shoulder: POLICE LINE — DO NOT CROSS.

The interior of the room had been torn apart. Everything had been removed, including carpets, wall cupboards and most of the floorboards. An image of Holden's dead body flashed through Barnes's mind, and he had to steady himself on the doorframe.

A SOCO in a white overall and blue facemask passed him in the doorway.

"You okay?" she asked, pulling down the facemask. She couldn't have been much older than Holden.

"Fine," Barnes said. "What do you think?"

"What can I tell you? We'll get fingerprints and DNA on any number of the jokers in this place, but I'm not sure any of it will prove who killed her. Good eyewitness is what you need."

"I wish. Thanks."

The SOCO left. Barnes stood in the centre of the room and surveyed it, trying to picture Harriet Holden's body being hauled through the door and dumped, then it became too much. He turned and followed the SOCO outside.

On the street, the woman with the microphone had joined the gaggle of other news crews on the scene. Her request for information was abruptly cut off when Nightingale stuck a hand over the camera lens and gave it a gentle but uncharitable shove.

"No press," she growled. "This is police work."

She turned to Barnes.

"Come on. I'll buy you an ice cream." She gestured to the car. "Won't get anything done while the storm troopers are getting their fix."

Barnes conceded the point and got in.

"Targeting cops," Nightingale said in the car, mainly to herself. "The nerve of these people."

"Let's hope the boss wasn't expecting Van Leer to admit the whole thing," Barnes said as they headed east along the seafront.

"Denniker's as sharp as an ice pick," Nightingale said, not looking at Barnes. "We joined in the same intake — went to training school together. He's been around the block. That said, he wants promotion to assistant chief constable. This year or next, and he makes no secret of the fact. An untidy result in a cop murder investigation won't look good."

"Is he married?"

Nightingale laughed. "Who, Clive the Cad? He certainly is, and has been for many years. But that hasn't stopped him from dipping his wick in anything young, uniformed and female that takes his fancy. There's a good few WPCs scattered around the division who have lived to tell the tale — just about. Wait here. I'm going to speak to that lot."

Nightingale pulled over suddenly and got out of the car. She walked over to the promenade to canvass some of the homeless street drinkers that occupied the dark spaces under the pier and furiously consumed Special Brew like their lives depended on it — which, in some cases, it did.

Barnes remained in the car and pulled a revision book out of his case. He had borrowed the books from Holden after she had passed the sergeant's exam, and her warrant number was still indelibly marked on the spine. He touched it lightly.

Apart from idly noting that house burglary and handling carried the same maximum sentence — and that Van Leer's choice of the word "downshifted" was erroneous as a result — he couldn't concentrate.

At this early stage of his detective's career, he was hardly an expert on murder investigations, but something was telling him this one was off to a slow start.

He pulled the folded pink actions chit from his pocket and opened it.

TIE CALLER ON SERIAL 725:8:4:01.

TIE: trace, interview, eliminate.

Someone had called the cops from the Atlantic Hotel's payphone. Someone professing concern for Howard Van Leer.

Or someone who *wanted* them to find Holden.

A resident? A visitor?

Or a killer?

A shout arose from nearby. Barnes looked up to see Nightingale tussling with one of the street drinkers, who turned out to be a grizzled individual named Garrett. Nightingale had evidently attempted to enforce the public-drinking ban by tipping away a bottle of Garrett's scotch and come dangerously close to getting thumped for her troubles.

By the time Barnes had jogged over, Nightingale had Garrett in cuffs for obstruction, but Barnes showed her the chit and reminded her they had better things to do. Nightingale reluctantly released Garrett into the custody of his peers, who obviously knew a fortuitous break when they saw one. They were at pains to reassure the detectives that they would make sure Garrett behaved himself and that there would be no more drinking today, thank you, Officers.

They drove back to the Atlantic Hotel, weaving their way around hordes of riot cops milling about in the street. Barnes and Nightingale climbed a wide staircase to the first floor, taking care to avoid holes and loose boards. The ornately carved banister was dull and greasy under Barnes's hand, and with faint disbelief he imagined an era of Victorian couples gliding down these same stairs in Sunday bests and summer parasols.

The flurry of police activity had sent most residents scurrying from the building. By the time Barnes and Nightingale got to the second floor, only two of the eleven doors they had knocked on had been answered.

Nightingale knocked on the door of room 12. A sinewy man answered. The smell of cannabis drifted into the hallway.

"Yeah?" The man squinted at Barnes's proffered warrant card.

"CID," Nightingale said. "Following up on all the excitement downstairs. Can we come in?"

The man stood aside with an exaggerated gesture. He was awkwardly dressed — the baseball cap, trainers and tracksuit bottoms were, from a distance, suggestive of a street corner adolescent, resplendent with gold hoop earrings and an ASBO. However, closer inspection showed him to be well into his thirties, and the gaunt, lined face, grey complexion and slight stoop made him look even older.

"I'm DC Barnes, this is DC Nightingale," Barnes said as they entered the bedsit. "What's your name?"

"Robbie Fortune," the man answered, lighting a cigarette.

The room was barely big enough for the three of them to stand a safe distance apart. The single bed and white chest of drawers looked like Salvation Army cast-offs and took up half the room. There was a Thin Lizzy poster on the mildew-caked wallpaper, and half a joint rested on the edge of an ashtray apparently stolen from a pub. Besides that and two bin liners full of damp-smelling clothes, it was more or less untroubled by clutter.

"You know the occupant of room 4C?" Nightingale asked.

The man called Fortune shrugged.

"Only been here a few weeks," he said.

"Where were you living before that?"

Fortune rolled his eyes. "Come on, Officer, where do most people living in this fleapit spend their spare time?"

Nightingale scanned the room. Her green eyes finally came back to rest on Fortune.

"Long stretch?" she asked.

"Long enough."

"Got some ID?"

"Nope."

Nightingale rolled her tongue over her teeth, a mannerism Barnes had noticed she used when irritated by something. She knew she had no power to compel Fortune to prove who he was, and he certainly wasn't going to help any more than was necessary.

"Well, anyway, someone used the payphone downstairs to call us and report their very grave concern for the occupant of room 4C. When we went to check it out, we found a dead body, and all the time said occupant was in a police cell. It's a matter of some importance to us that we identify the person that made the call. Any ideas?"

"None at all. Sorry." Fortune smiled sweetly.

Nightingale moved closer to Fortune and eyeballed him. It was a calculated move to get well inside his personal space.

"You sure about that? The occupant of room 4C is called Howard Van Leer. Know him?" she said.

Fortune stubbed out the cigarette and sighed heavily.

"Look, Officer, I didn't really know him from Adam, but he gave me a sub for some weed when I was brassic, which makes him all right in my book. If a smackhead ain't going to rob your supply, then he's gotta be sound."

While Nightingale wrote this down, Barnes took in Fortune's physical appearance. At first glance he appeared of slight build, but closer inspection suggested the man had a wiry frame, each muscle clearly visible under almost translucent skin. Barnes suspected the man was a good deal stronger than he looked.

A black cat leapt up onto the sill of the open window from outside. It sidled over to Fortune and began to arch its body against his legs. Fortune picked it up and stroked it.

"Nice cat. Yours?" Nightingale asked.

"Not mine. She visits every so often. Got a nose for 'nabis. Might have to name her after a copper. Not that I smoke it, 'course." He grinned.

While Fortune was talking to Nightingale, Barnes noticed something else. Fortune's teeth were brilliant white, and when he grinned they appeared positively luminescent against the sallow complexion.

"Have we met before?" Barnes interrupted.

"Don't believe so, Officer, don't believe so." The cat wriggled free and jumped onto the sill.

"Are you sure? Didn't you report a robbery last year? Right here, in fact, in this street. Two men, one with a baseball bat. I remember thinking it seemed like a DSS fiddle."

Fortune cackled. "I'm hurt, Officer. You might find a junkie making up stories to get some compo, but not me."

The cat watched Barnes for a moment and then disappeared out of the window. Barnes moved to the window and peered out, but the cat could not be seen. He noted that room 12 was more or less directly above room 4C, separated by two floors.

"The only thing I reported last year was recurring insomnia," Fortune continued. "And that was to the screws.

Being robbed in the street would almost be worth it, just for being outside in the fresh air. No fresh air in prison, Officer Barnes. It's damp, and it smells like fear."

Barnes turned back from the window and looked at Fortune.

"How do you know my name?"

Fortune's black, needle-prick eyes bored deep into his.

"Your colleague here informed me. Just now, while we were speaking. Didn't you hear?"

Barnes, uncomfortable, held Fortune's gaze, but read nothing in those black eyes.

"Come on. There's nothing more we can do today. Let's get a drink," Nightingale said, tugging at Barnes's sleeve.

"What about this guy? We need a statement," Barnes said.

"Don't worry, I've noted his remarks, and I'll file them along with the wisdoms of every other crackhead in the place."

Fortune scowled. Nightingale smirked and disappeared down the corridor. Barnes turned back to Fortune.

"You sticking around, Robbie?"

"Not likely. I'm supposed to be rehabilitating, but somehow my licence don't quite stretch to a desk job and a company car."

"You ought to have a word with Probation about that."

Fortune didn't laugh.

"It ain't an exact science, Officer. You get your money from the social, you get your bedsit in junkie land, then you're expected to keep your head down and stay clean. I've been tempted, DC Barnes, I've been tempted. And I'll slip off this perch before too long, I'm sure."

"Someone was murdered, Robbie. A young woman. She didn't die happy. Someone chose room 4C to dump her. Why would they do that?"

Fortune looked solemn but didn't answer.

"I want to find who did this, Robbie."

"That much is obvious. Look good on the CV, won't it, you solving this all by yourself? They might promote you."

Barnes felt himself go cold. Fortune opened the door to the corridor and didn't meet the young detective's eyes.

He caught up with Nightingale further down the corridor.

"What do you think?" Nightingale asked.

"I'm not sure. Something . . ."

"It's bullshit, is what," Nightingale said, interrupting. "These vultures don't look out for each other. The minute they hear one of their cronies is inside, they're kicking his door in looking for his stash."

"Anyone in his room would have got a nasty shock."

"No one's been in there since the body was dumped. It was secure. They might not call us to discharge their civic duty, but they would tell us about a body, if only to save their own skin. Someone made that call because they *wanted* us to find Harriet's body."

You read my mind, Barnes thought.

"Are you coming for a drink or what?" she asked.

"I don't drink."

"Yeah, you said. I thought you were taking the piss."

"Well, I wasn't. Besides which, it's not even lunchtime."

Nightingale stared at him a moment, then walked ahead, muttering, "*What is the world coming to*" and similar objections.

By the time they left the hotel the sun had disappeared behind cloud. On the way out Barnes was stopped by the matronly constable guarding room 4C.

"Excuse me, sir," she said, calling up from the basement steps. "Do you know when we will be stood down?"

Barnes almost corrected her misuse of the word "sir," but something stopped him. He checked his watch.

"Soon, I imagine. Give me your number. I'll check with the SIO and someone will get back to you before the end of your tour."

"Did you know her, sir?"

"Not as well as I should have."

Nightingale already had the engine running and told Barnes she was off to the pub. She made one final, brave attempt to overcome Barnes's teetotal tendencies by pointing out that a hot debrief over a cold beer at the New Inn was an important rite of passage for a young detective. Barnes mutely observed that most young detectives became old, divorced detectives, and declined. Nightingale shrugged and left.

As Barnes made his way towards the seafront and his own car, he did not look up at the crumbling facade of the Atlantic Hotel. Had he done so, he would have seen the man called Robbie Fortune staring at him from an upstairs window, hate filling his black eyes.

While Fortune stared, the black cat reappeared on the window ledge. Fortune stood at the open window and stroked the cat absently, not taking his eyes from the detective. Then, in a single movement, he lifted the cat, snapped its neck, and dropped it into a skip below.

CHAPTER FIVE

The Major Incident Suite was on the same site as the patrol centre, but it was situated about fifty yards behind it, on the spread of wasteland adjacent to the Willingdon Levels. The centre was two storeys of concrete, glass and steel, and it was — if you believed the press releases — a tribute to modern architecture, boasting an air-conditioned briefing and conference room, spacious offices for the SIO and their team, a CCTV room, dining and kitchen facilities, exhibit stores like bank vaults, state-of-the-art video interview facilities and a brand-new Scenes-of-Crime base. Most of the detectives agreed that it was great to have so much space, but where was the bar?

Until the Major Crime Branch was out of the gate, Divisional CID had the run of the place, and as a consequence it had been used precious little — investigations into two rapes and a couple of robberies had barely touched the surface of its capacity and hadn't used up much more than an office or two. Privately, the senior officers, police authority and other investors believed that as yet they hadn't really got their money's worth, that what they really needed was a high-profile murder case investigated under intense media scrutiny. It was something of a pyrrhic victory, however, that the case they had hoped for had turned out to be the murder of a police officer.

Constable Harriet Holden's death had caused the MIS to come alive. Most of the Divisional CID strength had relocated from Grove Road to the incident room; the offices buzzed with telephonists, intelligence analysts, HOLMES indexers and typists. SOCOs breezed in and out, laden with huge sacks of scene exhibits, muttering their thanks for the transit elevator that carried the procession of exhibits from their ground-floor base to the top-floor exhibit stores. Detectives darted about from office to office — ploughing through CCTV, scribbling in notebooks and earnestly discussing the favoured hypotheses in the corridors. A dozen telephone conversations were going on at once, interspersed with clipped segments from the area control room's airwaves.

The bulk of this activity was taking place on the top floor of the MIS, where the offices were arranged in a square circuit around a glass-walled canteen kitchen at its hub. Outside the SIO's office was a massive board, embossed with the words *OP CHRISTCHURCH*. Underneath this was a poster-size copy of Harriet Holden's passing-out photograph. The few various and suspected scenes that had so far been discovered — Howard Van Leer's bedsit and Holden's home address, car and body — were itemised in boxes on the board, with key bullet points listed underneath. Adjacent to this was a computer-generated timeline showing Holden's last known movements and the people that had interacted with her on that day.

Usually, timelines created for investigations of this nature were a sprawling complex of intertwining arterial links, often too complicated to immediately decipher. In this case, however, the timeline was worryingly bare.

Detective Chief Inspector Paul Hadian surveyed the board and the same thought occurred to him. The investigation was now just shy of a fortnight old — more intelligence would be submitted, more witnesses would come forward, more results would wend their way to him from the Forensic

Science Service laboratory, and the suspect would be found. But he couldn't shake the feeling that this was not a straightforward case, and that they would be found wanting.

Chief Superintendent Denniker had wasted no time in politely reminding Hadian that the force boasted a one-hundred-per-cent detection rate of its recorded murders — in ten years there had not been a single case where a suspect had not been charged. He had made it clear that, with the prospect of his promotion to assistant chief constable looming, he did not intend for that record to be damaged on his watch. He had also hinted with little masquerade that, if it were so damaged, then DCI Hadian would be looking for work elsewhere.

Granted, there had been one or two really difficult cases where tireless hard work and excellent investigative skills had resulted in the killer's detection, but Hadian had refrained from reminding Denniker that many of the cases had been relatively uncomplicated domestic murders — the husband had gone one step too far, or the wife had finally snapped and taken her retribution for decades of torment. In those cases, it was often the murderer who made the 999 call. The cases were simple — the suspects were found at the scene, they often made admissions, they often pleaded guilty.

In this case, however, there hadn't even been a 999 call. What did they have? Two detectives shouldering in the front door of a drug-addicted burglar — a burglar with a grudge against a particular police officer, the provenance of which remained elusive. But they'd caught and potted him almost immediately, and there had been no suggestion of any other suspects being involved, despite the threats. Recidivist cop-hating offenders often yelled obscenities from their cells — it was nothing new.

But Denniker had framed his warning with the suggestion that the CID's premature celebrations of Van Leer's arrest had contributed to Holden's death. Hadian thought this to be something of a non sequitur, but that was irrelevant — a bad result always needed a scapegoat, although *accountability* was the word Denniker had used.

The filthy room in which the officer's body had been found had been occupied by Howard Van Leer. The body had been taken there post-mortem, which meant there was another scene out there somewhere, as yet undiscovered.

House-to-house enquiries had not yet turned up anything from the street where she was found. Forensic evidence in the room had, as predicted, identified a number of the town's unsavoury customers — kith and kin to the burglar Van Leer. Teams were being tasked to do early-morning knocks — turn them over, bring them in, one by one.

The media coverage was, as expected, intense and had gone national. Eastbourne was used to TV crews filming documentaries and period dramas on its beaches, but national news networks swamping the town were a different matter. National news. *Crimewatch*. TV. Radio. Calls for an enquiry. Calls for the police to be armed. *Have you turned up any leads? Do you have a suspect? Do you have anything?* The only thing keeping a ceiling on the enquiry monopolising the media was the fact that the victim did not appear to have been killed in the line of duty.

The crank calls and insane claims of guilt were being received in volume by the telephonists, and each was being bottomed out by a detective on the outside enquiry team, just in case. CCTV was being checked thoroughly by two trainee detectives and two uniformed constables. Hadian eyed them as they diligently ploughed through the jerky frames of coarse, barely viewable video footage for just a snapshot of Harriet Holden — and, if they were really lucky, of her killer.

They'd torn up Holden's Old Town house. She lived alone in Monceux Road, had been there only a couple of weeks. The state of the house offered no further clues beyond the burglary.

There was no private or police CCTV covering the street. There were no suspicious cars in the street that anyone noticed, but then people parked up and down this and surrounding streets to walk into town. All of the residents in the street were interviewed — a mix of students, young families and retirees. They had seen and heard nothing out of the ordinary. One or two greatly resented the intrusion, but of those that had noticed the new resident, none of them had a bad word to say about her.

The house was being dusted, swabbed and scrutinised by a swarm of SOCOs. Most of the results were unsurprising — Holden's fingerprints had been found, as had her hair and fibres from her uniform. DNA profiles were taken from unwashed cups and glasses in the kitchen — all hers.

Itemised billing records had been retrieved for the landline telephone — both the most recent outgoing and incoming calls had been to and from her mother's number.

The local informants were being plugged and pumped for information. They got the message — this was personal. Cash was on the table for decent intelligence, but it had been offered too early and was proving counter-productive as a result. The informants only managed to creatively gild what they already knew, which was limited to rumour and snippets from the newspapers. Reliable intelligence did not appear to be circulating in the town's underbelly — that, or, as Nightingale had suggested, the murder of a police officer had not engendered much sympathy in the hearts of some of the town's lowlifes.

Interviews were conducted and full reports taken from Callaghan and the remainder of Holden's team, including those who were not on duty during her last shift.

Had she been behaving strangely? *No.* Did she seem depressed at all? *No.* Did she receive any unusual calls or visitors? *No.* Did she have a boyfriend? *Don't think so.* Was she involved with anyone? *Don't think so. Might have been seeing someone.* Who was she seeing? *Don't know.* Was it a police officer? *No.* Did she live alone? *Yes.* Did she spend any protracted, unexplained periods of time away from her duties? *No.* Was her performance substandard in any way? *Certainly not.* How did she get to work? *Walked, ran or cycled.* Had she been threatened or intimidated by any of the prisoners she was responsible for? *Don't think so.*

Barnes himself submitted a full report on his involvement, which Hadian had interviewed him about — as her crew partner and the last person to see her alive, Barnes was a key witness. The pair had worked together for about a year, and since the beginning of the spring they had resolved to hunt down the man responsible for the series of knife attack burglaries — Howard Van Leer.

She had finished her night shift and had, like the rest of her section, begun a period of four rostered rest days. Her body had been discovered eighty hours later. She had been killed while off duty — this too may or may not have been coincidence.

Motive appeared to be eluding them too. Holden hadn't been sexually assaulted, so a frenzied sex attack by a stranger was ruled out. And she had been taken to Van Leer's room *after* her death — this had to be an indication of something, but Hadian didn't know what. At this stage his strongest theory was that Van Leer had schemed with someone to murder Holden and then carved out a convenient alibi for himself by getting himself arrested — either intentionally or otherwise. He had been found in possession of a can of red spray paint and had red splashes of paint on his clothing. The splashes matched the paint in the can, but neither matched the crude, red graffiti on Holden's living room wall. This had been photographed, sampled and analysed — a precipitin test had confirmed it was animal blood. Not only did this explain why they had been unable to forensically link Van Leer to the inside of the house — and why the charge had been altered from burglary to handling — but also that it was looking increasingly like he was a decoy.

This hypothesis was bolstered by Van Leer's refusal to implicate the principal killer, but it still didn't explain why Van Leer would want to murder Holden. He didn't like the police — most criminals don't, including the long list of Van Leer's associates — but why choose her? According to the sprawling network of intelligence, Van Leer was linked to most other street criminals in the town, not to mention an entire family with form, including a miserly mother, an older brother and the long-separated, disgruntled mother of his child.

Could she have been killed by a jealous colleague? She was a high-flyer, a fast riser, and it was common knowledge that her abrupt manner had not endeared her to some — well, most — of her colleagues. Many of them blanked her on principle, but did someone hate her enough to kill her? Had she rebuked one of the old sweats a little too sharply, and caused bitter resentment? It seemed unlikely. Harriet Holden was not the first bright young woman the service had ever seen, and she wouldn't be the last. And, in Hadian's experience, most ambitious female officers had had to develop balls of steel to stay afloat and contend with their male counterparts. None of *them* had been murdered.

Could she have been bent? All of the signs pointed to the contrary, but you could never tell about the quiet ones. Yet she was an exemplary officer with an impeccable track record — she'd never even had a complaint made against her.

Hadian wanted to know about the boyfriend, but it seemed Harriet was intensely private, and no one seemed to know for sure if she was seeing anyone.

Hadian had ordered a search of all the bins — for condoms, tissues, paper cups, anything that might identify a partner. This turned up nothing — by the time they got to the house the collections had been made and the bins in the house had only recently been emptied. What little they found was seized, itemised and sent to the lab.

Of her two mobile phones, her own could not be found; the job phone held nothing useful. Address books and diaries had also been uplifted from her house — those, along with her emails, were being trawled for names to be traced and either implicated or eliminated. So far it had only been the latter — mainly old friends from university, who had alibis or were without motive or both.

She had told Barnes that she was going to her mother's, but her mother confirmed that she had never arrived. She hadn't gone back home — that scene was still locked down. She was fond of walking and running along remote routes — it wouldn't have been difficult to kidnap her undetected, possibly into a van.

Hadian stood by the desk, sadness in his stomach. To neutralise any later suggestions of his impartiality being compromised, he had stayed away from the funeral. He now found himself desperately wishing he had attended. The overriding picture coming into focus for Hadian was that Harriet Holden was something of a loner, with few friends or confidantes within the service. Poor bloody girl. Ostracised for having ambition, and for doing her job properly. *Did you upset someone enough to kill you?* The MO was brutal and deliberate, but there was also an element of calculation present — she had been slashed to ribbons with the knife before being bashed over the head, and now the rest of the district's workforce were uneasy, on edge, looking over their shoulders and checking all the locks twice before going to bed.

Hadian stared at the huge photograph of Holden on the wall.

"We'll find him, love," he muttered.

His thoughts were interrupted by the tinny theme tune from *The Sweeney*. He pulled the phone from his pocket and answered it.

"DCI Hadian."

He sat down on his desk for the remainder of the brief conversation, and all he had to say was, "You fucking what?"

* * *

On the day of the detectives' exam, Barnes awoke early from a dream about Holden smiling and walking in a wood while bagpipes played.

He kissed his sleeping wife softly on the forehead, resisting the urge to climb back under the duvet and share the warmth of her body. He pulled on shorts and running shoes and padded downstairs. He kicked aside the post as he went out the door, the gesture revealing one or two envelopes with angry red frames.

Holden's funeral had been two days ago, but the tears and music were like a hangover that refused to budge. She'd been dead two weeks, and the aftermath was proving to be a raw, draining business, with the funeral a particular low point. Barnes hoped the run would clear his head before the exam.

The day was already warm, but the seafront was cool and pleasant; morning dew clung in beads to plants and trees and he held his hand out as he ran along King Edward's Parade, feeling the cold prickles on his palm.

The wind chilled his scalp through his newly cut hair, and he rubbed the nape of his neck as he ran. Since finding out how much he paid a high-street professional for what was essentially the jarhead look, Eve had purchased some cheap clippers and insisted on doing it herself — one of hundreds of little everyday savings that she was convinced made an exponential difference overall.

It took her a little longer than the barber, but the pay-off was that when she cut his hair, she did it completely naked. This was on the proviso that he kept absolutely still and did not touch her until she had finished cutting — by which time he was virtually drowning in his own anticipation.

He smiled as he thought of it. Eve had turned what should have been a rather mundane monthly necessity into something he couldn't wait for. That was one of the things he loved about her — she could turn anything into a good time. These days he found himself looking at his reflection, willing his hair to grow faster.

He showered and changed into his suit at the station, taking deep breaths to steady his nerves. When they married, Eve had tried to tell him children would not be easy. Barnes, twenty-three at the time, was not thinking about kids. Eve, the more strategic of the two, had tried to talk about the long-term, that he might not want kids *now*, but he might do *later*. Barnes, intoxicated by his young love, had wondered how he could possibly want for anything else. Now, with thirty on the horizon, he was changing. In those early days, during Eve's cautionary forecasts that he might resent her ten years down the line, he had idly wondered how it would manifest itself. How going from not wanting to wanting would *feel*.

Now he knew.

Just lately, he was finding wonder in toddlers messing around and laughing as they passed him on the street, and he had started having B-movie dreams about trying to save babies from various disasters. Now he knew how *want* felt. There was an ache there, and he knew it was like being in love.

He wondered if Eve could sense his changing heart. Or perhaps it was the prospect of her thirty-eighth birthday looming on the horizon. In either case, she had been dropping hints with increasing regularity of late.

Disappointment had been alien to him then, but it would crush him now. He knew she kept her pain just below the surface, and he didn't know if he could expose himself in the same way. It was all so *complicated*, and as with anything that did not seem remotely feasible in life, his instinct was to bury it and move on to something else. And how the hell were they supposed to afford it, anyway?

He finished dressing. Perhaps, with his burgeoning detective's career, Eve felt there would be an opportunity before the window closed completely.

Assuming he could pass the bloody exam, of course.

The three-hour exam was held in the town hall in Grove Road, next door to the police station. A gaggle of hopeful men and women had congregated on the steps and were excitedly discussing the revision notes and subject matter. Barnes stood a little way from them and tried not to listen to their conversations.

Eventually they formed an orderly line and filed inside, filling the lines of empty desks in formation. Barnes had always been comfortable with exams. The reverberating tones of the invigilator, the strict rules, the silence, the tension, the rows of individuals straining for clarity — all the things that made most people nervous had the opposite effect on Barnes. He took some deep breaths and waited for the exam to start.

The exam was three hours long, with ninety multiple-choice questions. Barnes quickly calculated two minutes per question. He saw someone a few rows away from him checking their watch and working out the same thing.

When they were given the signal, all 102 candidates turned over their exam papers and began work. Barnes settled down into a trance-like state of concentration and began to race through the questions.

After an hour and a half he put down his pen. He looked around. All the other candidates were still immersed in their papers. He couldn't leave yet, surely. He checked his paper thoroughly, and then checked it again. Still no one else had finished.

Eventually he decided that there was nothing more he could physically do, and he raised his hand to let the invigilator know he had finished. She walked briskly over and permitted him to leave.

He stretched in the sunshine. It wasn't even midday. He couldn't remember any of the questions, but there was a confident feeling in his veins, and he knew he'd nailed it.

It was written somewhere in the web of police regulations that a three-hour promotion exam counted as a full tour of duty, so Barnes bought coffee and cake and drove straight home, already thinking about the sergeant's exam the following March. He could do it. He knew he could. Eve was right — economies of scale.

She was immersed in her own books when he arrived home.

"You're early. I hope you checked your answers." She kissed him while hanging off his neck.

"Of course I did."

"Just let me finish this paragraph. I can't concentrate today. Nothing's going in."

"Old age, darling. You're losing your marbles."

She stared at him, not even remotely amused.

"You keep that up and I'll start calling you by your *first* name."

"Don't you dare."

"Well then."

"Eve, come on," he laughed, kissing her on the forehead, surprised by the look on her face. "It was a joke. Look, I have cakes."

Eve pulled off her nursery worker's tabard and they went to the living room. Her laptop was on. She went over to it and shut the lid, a little too quickly. Barnes noticed.

"Something you don't want me to see?" he asked.

"It's nothing," she said, blushing.

They stood together by the window. A swirl of fog lay in the basin of the Downs, and Eve sipped from her cup while staring out at their lovingly tended garden.

"You haven't planted those dahlias yet," she murmured.

"I will. The digitalis has finished for this season. Should I deadhead it?" Barnes put down his cup on the coffee table and moved closer to her.

"No, leave it. I want it to seed."

Barnes moved behind her. He pushed her hair to one side and touched her skin with his lips. She set down her cup and turned to him, taking his face in both her hands.

They didn't make it to the bedroom. They made love on the staircase, Eve holding her husband tight with her arms, both for support and to ensure he understood the urgency of the embrace, the importance of the closeness to her. Five years of marriage had not dampened their passion for each other, for the fervour that was like an addiction for both of them.

If there had been a correlation between the strength of their union and the statistical likelihood of conception, Barnes thought, they wouldn't have had a problem.

Afterwards Barnes knelt a few stairs down from Eve, his head resting on his wife's stomach. He could hear her heartbeat, the sounds of her insides, and wondered if he could hear the rogue inside her.

"I was looking at a fertility clinic when you came in. They have a website," she said.

He shut his eyes. He'd known this was coming, one way or another. It didn't make sense, even to him — now he wanted kids himself, he was afraid to take the risk.

"Is that what you didn't want me to see?" he said.

She shrugged.

"I guess I'm worried I already know what you're going to say."

"So why mention it at all?"

"I thought you might have changed your mind. You're not twenty-three any more. I'm not going to pretend that I don't want children. That's not the issue here. The issue is talking you into it."

"Eve . . . I just don't see that it's possible."

"Don't worry about the logistics. There are options, Barnes. This is the twenty-first century. They can do all sorts."

He didn't say anything. She stroked his hair.

"What is it?" she asked, her voice soft.

"Can . . . can we talk about this later?"

"It's okay, Barnes. I'm not going to force the issue. I'll always want children, but if you don't . . . I would love to at least talk about it."

Barnes touched her hand, and looked up at her from where he lay — from this angle he could make out the inch-long scar in the flesh under her chin. She saw him looking and fingered the scar absently.

He knew she hated it, but it didn't bother him at all and he didn't think about it much, usually because he was taller than her and didn't often see her from this angle. The first time he had noticed it they had only been on a handful of dates, and Barnes, stomping over their budding relationship with typical tactlessness, had asked her how she had got it. Embarrassed, Eve had refused to answer. Barnes had apologised several times — Eve was magnanimous about his lack of sensitivity — but that didn't stop him feeling bad incessantly afterwards, longing to replay that evening and make amends.

That evening came seven months later. They had been eating ice cream on the seafront, when, unbidden, she told him about her long-dead father — a bear of a man who would drink until his insides were filled with rage like a petrol tank. Eve had been thirteen when he'd gone after her with a razor blade. But for her gymnastic abilities, the damage might have been much worse.

Barnes, acutely aware of the opportunity to make up for his previous insensitivity, listened patiently. When she had finished her story, he pulled her to him, held her close and kissed her forehead. They were engaged the following week.

"What are you thinking about, Chief?" Eve asked him.

He grinned at her. "When I proposed to you."

"Liar."

"No, honestly I am."

She reached down and grabbed his crotch playfully.

"Make love to me again."

Barnes's mobile phone rang. His hastily removed jeans were hanging half-off his ankles, and he fumbled around in the pockets until he found the phone.

"It's the boss," he said, checking the display. He gently pushed Eve's hand away; she took the hint and went upstairs.

"Barnes, it's Paul." Hadian's voice was strained.

"What's up, sir?" Barnes tried to pull his jeans on, the phone wedged between his ear and shoulder.

"Listen, I know I gave you the afternoon off, but I need you in."

"Is everything okay?"

"Van Leer — the little pissant — has been given bail."

"Oh, shit." Barnes sat down heavily on the stairs. Two weeks in custody, and Van Leer was already out? "How did *that* happen?"

"Never mind, I'll tell you later. Just get yourself down to the court. We've missed the application, but if we're lucky you can get surveillance on him before he's physically released."

"I'll be there in half an hour. Where's Cathy?"

"My second problem today. She hasn't shown up for work, and I can't get hold of her."

Barnes was silent, the implications circling his head like stars. Surely Cathy couldn't be missing?

"Sir, you don't think . . ."

"No, don't fret," Hadian interrupted. Barnes wondered if he didn't want the possibilities spoken aloud. "It isn't the first time she's been here in spirit only. But it's because of that we've missed the bail app. Just get yourself down to the court."

Not the first time? Hadian didn't sound even remotely convincing, and Barnes was not reassured.

Barnes clapped the phone shut and poked his head around the bedroom door.

"Sorry, darling, I've got to go," he said.

"Already? You haven't been home five minutes. I thought you had the afternoon off." Her hair and clothing were dishevelled, her underwear visible, and Barnes felt another surge within him, but fought it back down.

"I know. I'm sorry." He was too. The last thing he wanted was to go back to work. He walked over and pecked her on the cheek. "I'm hoping it isn't always like this. 'Baptism of fire' doesn't even come close."

"Barnes, it's okay. But I do need to talk to you about this. About our baby." She stared up at him with a smile and squeezed his hand.

"We'll talk about it later, I promise."

Barnes dressed quickly. Eve kissed him on the mouth, and he ran out to the car.

* * *

Barnes raced into Lewes Crown Court. He flashed his warrant card at the security staff and ran across the rich red carpeting to look at the day's listings. *Shit*. Hadian was right. Van Leer's bail application had been heard before lunch.

He ran back outside and stood on the court steps, scanning the crowds on the high street for Van Leer's familiar scraggy face. Nothing. He ran back inside, unsure of himself, of what his next move should be. Where the hell was Cathy?

There was a cluster of people lining up outside a huge pair of oak doors. A large court usher had arrived to open them while trying to breathlessly organise various unruly members of the bar.

Barnes made his way over and showed his warrant card to the woman.

"It's all right, Officer. You don't need that," she said, in a kindly Yorkshire brogue.

"Can you please tell me if Howard Van Leer has been released?"

"Who, dear?"

"Howard Van Leer," Barnes repeated, trying not to show his exasperation.

"I believe I might be able to help you, Officer."

Barnes turned, and found himself facing a squat, solid man, whose square jowl was framed by a goatee and a short flat-top the colour of custard.

"You mentioned the name Van Leer?"

"That's right," Barnes said.

"You're the officer in the case?"

"By default. Who are you?"

"Well, it just so happens, Detective, that I am prosecuting this case. Perhaps, now that Mr Van Leer is at large, you might be good enough to tell me your plans regarding enforcement of his bail conditions. Covert surveillance, perhaps? Late-night visits by uniform patrols?"

Barnes did not immediately answer, distracted as he was by the mode of address — as yet, no one had referred to him as "Detective". He opened his mouth to answer, but the conversation was interrupted by a female voice and a blast of perfume.

"Not very subtle, Phil." The voice came from behind him, and it had been from public school to Oxford and thence to Gray's Inn without many detours along the way.

They were joined by the voice's owner — a tall, positively statuesque woman of about forty. She was wearing a pinstripe jacket and her hourglass figure had been shoehorned into a tight pencil skirt. Her short, dark hair was cut into a sharp pageboy parted on one side, and she was clutching a bundle of thick files.

"Passing yourself off as a prosecutor is a new one, however. Officer, have you met Phil McDermott? Mr Van Leer's defence solicitor?"

The man named McDermott scowled, flashing a gold incisor.

"The police are not averse to using underhanded tactics, Ms Warwick. I am simply ensuring equality of arms." He turned back to Barnes. "I am reliably informed that you visited my client earlier this week, Detective."

Barnes didn't answer, feeling rather out of his depth.

"Not very appropriate from your point of view, I must say. My client has already told me all about it, and a coercive prison visit with a conspicuous absence of access to legal advice makes your questioning rather tenuous. Speculation among the judiciary as to just what might have been discussed will be rife, I'm sure."

McDermott's theatrical dialogue was a deliberate ruse, intended to both unnerve young police officers and also to remind himself that he was a blue-collar boy who had made good.

Barnes found his tongue.

"Your client should worry. He's got to answer questions in a murder investigation yet."

McDermott showed no reaction to Barnes's calculated impudence — even though it had surprised Barnes himself.

"We wait with bated breath for your latest trick, Officer."

"I'm sure you'll let me have it in the witness box."

"If it ever gets that far, Detective, which I sincerely doubt, then yes, there will be plenty to discuss. But frankly, *res ipsa loquitur*, and I don't see that this prosecution has the legs."

Barnes looked blank. McDermott sighed.

"Another policeman punching above his weight. Let's just say that, now my client has rightfully regained his liberty — albeit conditionally — I expect minimal interference from the police. If he is further harassed, I will take further action. *Alea iacta est.*"

McDermott turned on his heel and strode off, the bald rolls at the back of his head glowing red. Barnes exhaled and dragged a hand down his face, not quite believing what had just happened.

"*Nil carborundum illegitimi,*" said the woman in the pinstripe suit.

Barnes turned to his rescuer, still looking blank.

"*Don't let the bastards grind you down,*" she explained with a gentle smile. "I'm afraid Phil likes to use Latin to disarm his opponents, particularly when he's been caught misbehaving."

"Thanks. I'd have told him half our plans if you hadn't showed up," Barnes said.

"What plans?"

"You'll forgive me if I ask for some ID."

The woman laughed and stuck out a perfectly manicured hand. "Natasha Warwick. I really am prosecuting this case."

"DC Barnes." He took her hand, noticing a tiny tattoo on the inside of her wrist. "Pleased to meet you. So that was the Phil McDermott I've heard so much about. He just passed himself off as a prosecutor — isn't that an offence or something?"

"Yes, the Law Society has quite a file on Mr McDermott. He's represented most of the Van Leer family at one stage or another."

Barnes looked past the prosecutor, his eyes scanning the corridors for Van Leer.

"I'm sorry to be abrupt," he said, his eyes coming back to Natasha Warwick, "but has Van Leer been released yet?"

"No, but he isn't here."

"He isn't?"

"No. Bail applications are generally made *ex parte*; that is, without the defendant being present. He's still in prison. He'll be released shortly." She seemed faintly amused.

Barnes exhaled with relief, and his hand went to his mobile phone.

"Do you know about this case?" she asked as he held the phone to his ear.

"Sort of. I arrested him."

"Oh, I didn't realise that was you. I read your statement. Exciting stuff. Though I'm sure it said something about being in full uniform."

"The DCI was nice enough to recruit me into the CID on the strength of it."

"Really? Good for you. So you'll be aware that I shifted the charge from burglary to handling?"

Barnes removed the phone from his ear and put it back in his pocket. Apparently the conversation wasn't over yet.

"Cathy and I had a fairly forthright conversation about it the other day," she continued.

"Yes, I heard it. You were on loudspeaker."

Natasha Warwick grinned. "I should have known. Where is she, anyway? I was expecting her here to oppose the bail app."

"She's . . . sick. Swine flu."

"That's a shame," she said, clearly not believing a word.

She took a second look at Barnes, from the feet up, and took her time about it. "You look awfully young to be a detective," she said, smiling.

Barnes felt colour rise in his face. He was fairly used to being patronised — it was a daily occupational hazard for probationers — but the woman had caught him off guard.

"They can't give the job away these days," he said, trying to hold his own by matching her banter. "I'm shadowing Cathy while I learn the ropes."

"Oh . . . sweet," was all she said, clicking her tongue hard on her teeth to emphasise the "t".

There was a pause. She held his gaze, and only broke it when she saw a younger woman hurry past, whom she hailed like a taxi in order to offload her armful of files. The woman scurried off in silent acquiescence. To Barnes the contrast between trainee detective and senior lawyer suddenly seemed all too obvious. Maybe he was lucky to get away with only being patronised.

"Sorry about that." She turned back to him.

"You know this is now a homicide investigation?" he asked.

"Only from what I've heard on the news, which isn't much. I'm due to meet DCI Hadian tomorrow for a full briefing. I understand this is just the tip of the iceberg, though."

"And then some. Van Leer getting bail is not very good news at all," Barnes said.

"Well, the alternative charge is only half the story. I think he will still be imprisoned for handling, but it's been undercut somewhat by this bail application. Normally, with his previous convictions and the likelihood of his re-offending, I would say any bail app would have been refused. But he's put forward a new bail address that doesn't sound like a room in some grotty B&B."

"Where is it?"

Natasha Warwick fished around in her case for the address and moved to stand next to Barnes so he could read over her shoulder. "Here we are. Santa Ana Court, Barbuda Quay. Do you know it?"

"It's in the harbour. Somehow I don't think it's within Van Leer's budget."

"My thoughts exactly. I emailed Cathy with the details, asking her to check it out. Who lives there, *et cetera*. Do you know if she did?"

Barnes flushed, and pulled at his tie. "No, I'm afraid I don't. He'd already been granted bail by the time I got the call."

Natasha rolled her eyes. "Did she even get the email?"

Barnes, distinctly uncomfortable by now, flushed for the third time in as many minutes. "I don't know."

"Don't worry. It gets worse."

"Go on."

"Well, this really clinches it for him. Some company has agreed to stand surety to the tune of one hundred thousand pounds for him. Do you know what that means?"

Patronising was beginning to rub shoulders with intimidating. Barnes looked her in the eye. Senior lawyer or not, he was going to show this woman that he knew his stuff. "It's a security. If he fails to answer bail then they forfeit their money."

She smiled. For a moment Barnes thought she was going to say, *Well done.*

He frowned, focusing on the picture that was being painted for him. "But it doesn't make sense. He's a smack-addicted career burglar. No one in their right mind would think he's a good bet. Who's the company?"

"Sovereign Holdings."

"Never heard of them."

"Me neither. I thought it was a put-up, until a very smug Phil McDermott rang me to say that said company had sent them a cheque for fifty thousand pounds as proof of their goodwill. Phil cashed it and sent me a photocopy of the bank statement with kisses on."

"This McDermott isn't really going up in my estimation." Barnes took out his phone again. Hadian really needed to hear all this.

"Join the club. Van Leer's got conditions — a curfew at the address between seven p.m. and seven a.m., not to contact any prosecution witnesses, and to comply with the probation service in relation to drug testing. If you catch him in breach he'll be straight back inside *and* this mysterious company will forfeit their money," she said.

"That's very useful. Thank you," he said, holding the phone to his ear.

"Thanks for coming, Officer," Natasha Warwick replied, sticking out her hand again, slender fingers brushing the inside of Barnes's wrist, lingering there for just a split second longer than was absolutely necessary.

* * *

Barnes left Lewes Crown Court and jogged down the concrete steps to the pavement. He ran back to his car, and made the ten-minute journey to HMP Lewes in the unmarked Mondeo. He parked in a residential cul-de-sac nearby with a view of the main entrance, and wondered what would happen to Van Leer once his bail had been granted. Would McDermott telephone the prison, or drive there and give him the news in person?

And once the release formalities were completed, how would he get back to his bail address? Would McDermott give him a lift? Walk? Train? Perhaps Van Leer would walk right past the car. Perhaps he would run. Or perhaps he would turn to Barnes and give a little wave before disappearing.

One thirty-second call from his mobile to the prison and Barnes established that Van Leer had yet to be released. He called Hadian and relayed details of the bail address.

"That's a new development. Lots of empty houses. We might be able to get an urgent OP."

"I'm outside the prison. He hasn't been released yet."

"Thank Christ for that. Stay on him. Chief Superintendent Denniker has approved an urgent RIPA for the follow."

Over time, acts of Parliament — like most police vernacular — tended to become acronyms, which in turn became phonetic nouns in their own right. It took Barnes a moment, but he worked out that Hadian was talking about an authority under the Regulation of Investigatory Powers Act 2000, the legislation under which all covert surveillance had to be authorised.

"Sir, you know I'm not surveillance trained?"

"Who is? Just use your loaf and don't get made."

Barnes was silent.

"Okay, look. You're new to the department, and I understand that without Cathy Nightingale I'm tasking you with far more than is right for your level of experience. I'm also aware that you took your exam this morning and deserve the afternoon at home. I owe you a beer and a day off. But later. How did it go, by the way?"

"Okay, I think. It wasn't easy."

"I'm sure it wasn't. You need to think about things on a different level than when you were in uniform."

"I'm reasonably confident, sir."

"Good. Because, like it or not, you are smack bang in the middle of this investigation, and at this early stage you have more of a handle on it than anyone else. If *you* miss something, we're all fucked."

Barnes's stomach did a little flip. No pressure, then. He was already aware that the need to find Holden's killer was under his skin and in his bones, but no one had yet put it in such bald terms.

"Sir, I don't want to be treated with kid gloves. I can do this properly." He meant it too, even though his answer was largely intended to maintain the confidence of his new boss. It didn't seem the right time to mention that his first few days as a detective had felt a little unorthodox — besides, for all Barnes knew, this was normal.

"That's what I want to hear."

"Did you get hold of Cathy?" Barnes asked.

"Not yet, fortunately for her."

"Sir?"

"That warrant, the one you used to get into Van Leer's room. It was duff."

Barnes was stunned.

"Are you serious?"

"She wrote it, signed it and rubber-stamped it all herself. We'll be lucky if only half the scene evidence is chucked out. As you can imagine, I'm having a real sense of humour failure today."

Barnes suddenly sat up straight in his seat as he saw the familiar stooped gait of Van Leer shuffling down the ramp leading from the prison to the road. He had a duffle bag over one shoulder and was accompanied by an animated Phil McDermott. From the body language, he might have been admonishing his client.

"Boss, I've got to go. He's on the move, with McDermott. Prison crossroads. If they're going to the bail address, they'll be on the A27 eastbound in about five minutes."

"Okay. Good luck. I'll call you about the OP."

Barnes flipped the phone shut without bothering to ask what an OP was, and kept his eye on Van Leer and McDermott. The pair disappeared out of sight into another residential close, and Barnes started the engine, his heart suddenly in his mouth. He edged the car forward and saw a sporty yellow Honda pull out of the close and head onto the main road, with Van Leer and McDermott in the front.

Barnes counted to ten, and followed the car at what he thought was a safe distance.

During the initial part of the follow McDermott stuck to the speed limit, and the main road allowed Barnes to keep a visual on the car without being too obvious.

Then, at the bottleneck outside Lewes, McDermott suddenly opened up the Honda, cutting in front of seven idling cars at the roundabout, leaving Barnes way behind.

Barnes cursed and strained to see the Honda. At Beddingham the road dipped, and he caught a glimpse of yellow firing off into the distance.

He took a deep breath, dropped a gear and hammered the Mondeo into the offside lane on the approach to the roundabout, triggering a riot of angry horns, but managed to overtake four cars as he did so.

It was tight, especially at speed. The rear wheel clipped the roundabout, and launched the rear of the car into the air. Not high enough to flip it, but high enough to feel like it. Barnes's yell matched the shriek of the accelerating wheels suddenly touching nothing.

The rear of the car thumped onto the road. The impact forced Barnes's tongue between his teeth. The car swerved, the rear fishtailing wildly, and with tremendous effort he wrestled it under control.

And then it was over. He returned to a steady fifty miles an hour, his heart pounding in his chest, and saw that McDermott was only two cars ahead.

He checked his mirror. The driver behind was on his phone, doubtless calling 999 to report another maniac on the A27. Hadian can sort it, Barnes thought, and returned his attention to McDermott.

To his surprise, McDermott continued the rest of the journey at a normal pace. It wasn't until they neared Eastbourne that Barnes realised the tactic had purely been to flush him out, and in doing so McDermott had got the answer to his earlier question about surveillance. *QED*, as McDermott might have said.

He cursed inwardly. This reptilian solicitor had got the better of him twice in as many hours. Hadian had told him not to get made, and he'd blown it.

"I don't know . . . what I'm fucking *doing!*" he yelled, tasting blood.

His mobile rang again. He glanced at the display. Hadian, of course.

"Boss?"

"You still with him?"

"Yeah."

"If I'm right, SV should be taking over any minute."

"SV?"

"Surveillance."

Barnes craned his head to look in the rear-view. A black, powerful-looking Chrysler was just sliding into view behind him, cutting in front of the line of increasingly disgruntled motorists. There was a man and a woman inside, both wearing sunglasses.

"I think they've found me."

"Okay. Back off, let them take it, and get your arse back to town. I still can't get hold of Cathy. She isn't home. I don't like it. I need you to find her. Do it quietly, but if you can't find her by morning, I'll make it official."

Barnes clapped the phone shut.

"With fucking pleasure."

The investigation was only a fortnight old, and now another cop was missing.

CHAPTER SIX

As Hadian had not defined "quietly," Barnes decided to reduce the margin of error by spreading the load a bit. He confided in one or two of his more trustworthy uniformed colleagues to keep an eye out. One offered to check the local hospitals, and another volunteered to discreetly check Nightingale's vehicle movements using the automatic number plate recognition software plumbed into traffic cameras all over the county.

Barnes made attempts to call the DC's mobile phone periodically, the call going straight to voicemail each time, suggesting the phone was either off, without a signal or damaged beyond repair. Barnes shuddered as he thought of the times he had called a missing person's phone with the same result, only to find later that the phone, like the misper, was destroyed and lying at the bottom of Beachy Head.

Barnes had obtained Nightingale's photograph and her home address from the personnel office. Her address was not, Barnes realised, a million miles from his own house. He drove straight there.

Willingdon Triangle was on the main road leading north out of Eastbourne, a small patch of green traversed by a cluster of shops and a sprawl of quiet residential roads.

The local pub was a long Tudor building called the British Queen, which sat invitingly just off the main road, the South Downs looming constantly on the horizon like a watchful parent behind it.

Nightingale's flat was in a straight, tree-lined suburban road that branched off from the triangle itself. It was a purpose-built place tucked behind a newsagent's, and it took Barnes a while to actually find it.

He walked around the side of the shop to the flat itself. It seemed to defy most design conventions. There was no front door, just a set of PVC double doors that opened out onto a tiny patio.

After knocking for a minute or so without an answer, Barnes tried the doors. They were unlocked. With unease starting to flicker in his stomach, he stepped into a sitting room barely big enough for two, with a small sofa, coffee table and television taking up most of the meagre space. The fixtures, fittings and carpets had the hallmarks of a new build, but the place was a wreck. Clothing and rubbish were strewn everywhere, and the whole place smelled of damp, cigarettes, old food and sweat.

Unable to suppress a grimace, Barnes took tentative steps through the mess. He was aware of anxiety tightening his chest, and he spun three-sixty as he walked through the sitting room, expecting at every turn to see dripping red letters smeared across the walls. The last time he had been inside a colleague's house, that same colleague had been viciously butchered only days later.

A short counter separated the sitting room from a kitchen area that was little more than a store cupboard with sticky chessboard lino. Beyond the sitting room was a hallway, roughly the same size as a telephone box, which led to the only bedroom and a bathroom. Besides the unmade mattress on the floor and the cheap canvas wardrobe, the bedroom had no furniture. Also on the floor was an old portable television and a lot of mess, but not much else except a full ashtray and several empty beer bottles on the floor.

A cursory check of all the rooms did not take long, and a relieved Barnes exhaled deeply when he realised that Nightingale's blood-spattered body was not lying prone in any of the rooms, and that the walls were untouched.

He returned to the kitchen, amazed by the sheer number of wine, whisky and beer bottles that occupied nearly every available surface. One wrong move and the whole lot would go over like pins at a bowling alley.

Feeling rather awkward about invading the privacy of a colleague he didn't know particularly well, he picked his way through the bottles to examine a calendar on the wall, but it was largely untouched. An address book in a kitchen drawer was empty.

There was a letter on the fridge door, held in place by a leprechaun magnet, confirming a consultant's appointment. The logo of the local hospital trust was familiar to Barnes, but it was the subheading that caught his eye — *Dept. of Psychiatry*. Barnes checked the calendar. The appointment had been and gone.

Barnes realised in an instant that all the banter, back-biting and banality that goes on between cops in the station was just a front, only ever what others were permitted to see. In some cases what lay below the surface was stable and innocuous — in others, it was troubled and considerably darker. What demons were plaguing Cathy Nightingale?

He went back to the sitting room and looked around for a landline phone, and when he found the empty telephone socket he realised Nightingale didn't possess one.

On the floor by the sofa, next to yet more beer bottles, was a three-day-old newspaper. Barnes squatted down and flicked through it, looking for scribbles and notes.

Barnes stood up and saw a framed photograph of a small child hanging above the sofa. He frowned. He didn't think Nightingale had children, but the portrait — of an angelic blonde five-year-old — was professionally done.

He turned. Behind him, hanging above the television, was another framed photograph — exactly the same as the first one. On the coffee table was a third photograph — again, exactly the same.

The revulsion Barnes had felt at the state of the flat turned to a horrible sadness as he realised that the frames were all empty — the picture he could see repeated through the flat was just a stock insert. Barnes picked up the photograph and leaned his head against a doorframe, eyes gazing up at the ceiling. Nightingale had presumably acquired the frames with intentions of homeliness, but hadn't got around to putting anything in them — that or she had nothing *to* put in them.

As Barnes put the photo frame back on the coffee table, a small rectangle of white caught his eye. He picked it up — Phil McDermott's business card. He flipped it over. It looked new and was free of any scribbles. Barnes stood for a moment, trying not to leap to any conclusions. He put the card in his pocket, stacked Nightingale's mail in a neat pile and left the flat.

On the way back to the car, Barnes showed Nightingale's photograph at the newsagent's and got a vacant response. A small gaggle of raspy urchins were exchanging cigarettes outside the shop — Barnes showed them the photograph and got a similar response, along with a few fucks and jeers. Barnes walked to his car and paused with his hand on the driver's door. The image of the bottles appeared in his mind, and he walked a little further down the road to show the photograph in the British Queen.

The landlord was a sixty-year-old Scot with skin like cowhide, and, yes, he knew Cathy Nightingale very well. She hadn't been in the pub for nearly a week, which was unusual for her. What was she like, Barnes wanted to know. The Scot said she was quite a character, quite a teller of tales, but although she was popular with the other drinkers, she always came in alone. That is, apart from the last time she was in. She'd been having a drink with a short, solid man with a bright yellow flat-top and an expensive suit.

Barnes thanked the landlord and walked slowly to his car, fingering Phil McDermott's business card in his pocket as he went. Cathy had dealt with McDermott many times, and could have inadvertently brought a card home, forgotten it and found it in a pocket when doing the laundry. Equally, a seasoned cop drinking with a defence solicitor was not necessarily indicative of anything other than a long-standing professional association.

A perfectly plausible explanation, but something told Barnes, as he unlocked the car, that it wasn't the reason at all.

* * *

Eve was not home.

The sun was dipping behind the South Downs when Barnes finally pulled onto the driveway, and cast enough golden light across the front garden for him to tend to his roses while he waited for her. She had left the stereo playing loudly. Barnes switched off "Dancing in the Dark" — the silence was heavy and sudden.

He didn't know where she had gone, but he pruned, watered and fed the flowers until the sun sank behind the Downs and all that was left was a pink glow, like the dying cinders of a furnace burning somewhere in the west.

He called Eve's mobile, and then the nursery, and got voicemail on both. He made a light dinner for the two of them, and, as the kitchen table had been lost to study books and revision notes, sat on the sofa to eat.

He knew she was struggling with the work, and guilt crept up on him. Just lately, it seemed she was a little more sensitive to his teasing. He told himself it was bound to happen — to some, a nine-year age gap was just a quirky feature; to others, it was getting on towards the realms of tabloid journalism and gaudy TV chat shows.

He ascribed it partly to the studying. A fifteen-year advertising career in the media and marketing department of a reasonably prominent airline had been abandoned — partly to escape the relentless gossip, partly to consolidate the fresh start she had made with Barnes. And now she'd made the decision to return to her first love of teaching, using the part-time nursery job as a way of learning the ropes and getting sponsored for courses. But starting completely afresh — financially, at least — was not easy, and with her dissertation deadline looming the idea was seeming less attractive.

Everyone at the airline company had known of her previous marriage, had thought they were the perfect couple. The fact that the guy had been a complete arsehole remained well and truly below the surface — something Eve regretted, for a variety of reasons.

On paper, the story was a torrid one, the stuff of soap operas. A passionless marriage between senior finance manager and marketing executive dissolves after three years when she, aged thirty-two, leaves him for a twenty-three-year-old temping as a post room worker.

A significant amount of effort had been invested in justifying their union to friends and colleagues, something they both found exhausting. Reactions ranged from the bemused to the overtly hostile, and eventually they gave up their attempts to convince others of the integrity of their marriage.

Barnes recalled one such exchange, overheard when he arrived to collect Eve one evening from the airline's Crawley offices. A God-fearing colleague of Eve's who rather fancied herself as both a confidante and relationship counsellor had taken Eve to one side and hissed, "For heavens' *sake*, Eve, what are you going to do when everything starts to sag?"

Eve had mulled over the question with mock-thoughtfulness before settling on an answer.

"Gosh, I don't know. Chuck him, I guess."

Barnes, unable to suppress a laugh, had put his coat around her shoulders and led her to the car.

Barnes imagined the tongues, relentless with envy:

She'll want children.

He doesn't earn a tenth of what her ex did.

They must only stay together for the sex.

These remote observations made him think of royal legacies dissected by pragmatic historians who talked of heirs and bloodlines — nowhere was there mention of how they *felt* about each other.

It was the self-righteousness that got him. The way people felt empowered to offer their opinions from both barrels when the scent of the unconventional was in the air, as if they were helping save the pair of them from a dreadful mistake.

So he enjoyed the kudos of having an older wife, of the ever-stronger bond between them, of the unabashed smugness and *told-you-so's* he felt legitimised to level at the naysayers with each new anniversary, and of the validation Eve could celebrate as he ascended from post room worker to police officer and thence through the ranks.

But the barren space between them where there should have been a child still remained empty, being filled instead by gradually accumulating material crap. Barnes knew those pious fuckers would raise disapproving eyebrows at this quite demonstrable punishment.

And this made him angry. *Losing* made him angry. His marriage being endlessly remarked upon like public property made him angry, which was one of the reasons he kept his — admittedly rather limited — social life well outside the police. He'd had enough of feeling like a kid with a toy marriage — he was a detective now, and he didn't have to justify himself to anyone.

He finished eating and tried to put his feet up on Forbes — the Labrador nosed at his ankles and ran off.

He dozed off in front of the television. Once he had stopped fidgeting, his dog came over and lay next to his feet.

He awoke some hours later to find Eve kissing his neck, her hand stroking his stomach. Her breathing was heavy, and he could smell chardonnay on her breath. Her lips found his, and he met them gratefully, glad for her warmth and tenderness. He tried to ask where she'd been, but she shushed him with her mouth, pulled him off the sofa and took him to bed, holding him close. She murmured in his ear — "I want your baby."

* * *

Barnes awoke early and called at Nightingale's again on his way to the MIS. He yelled through the letterbox four or five times, only to be rewarded with a heavy silence.

He stood for a moment.

At the MIS he rang through to the call-handling centre and requested a copy of the call made on serial 725 on 8 April. The supervisor told him the recording would take a day or two to reach him, but she played the call back over the phone for him.

It was a short call, and the serial text was more or less a verbatim transcription.

Police contact centre, what's the nature of your call?

Yeah, I . . . er . . . haven't seen my neighbour for a few days. I'm a bit worried. It's not like him at all . . .

Barnes closed his eyes and concentrated on the voice. Could it have been one of the residents they spoke to at the Atlantic Hotel? Could the voice belong to the man out on licence, Robbie Fortune?

It was certainly feasible, but not conclusive. The line was bad, and the caller had been breathing heavily into the receiver.

Barnes thanked the supervisor and hung up.

DCI Hadian had made himself at home in the SIO's office — a red dragon adorned a corkboard behind his desk, alongside a poster bearing a sideburned rugby team and the words "WALES — FIVE NATIONS GRAND SLAM 1978". His desk was clear apart from his policy files, the impressive coffee machine that had found its way from his Grove Road office and a small DAB radio with another dragon, this one tiny and brass, sitting on top of it. There was still no computer to be seen, something virtually unheard of in the world of modern policing.

Barnes arrived and peered through the glass in the office door. Hadian was at his desk, facing down a shapely woman with short dark hair and a smart suit. Her back was to the door, and it took Barnes a moment to realise it was Natasha Warwick, the prosecutor he had met the previous day.

She had mentioned meeting Hadian for an Op Christchurch briefing, but when she turned slightly Barnes could see her cheeks were flushed, and it looked like a very animated conversation. Barnes made to go, but Hadian beckoned him in. Barnes caught the tail end of the conversation as he closed the door behind him.

"... Van Leer has to be charged with Constable Holden's murder. I *want* him charged."

"DCI Hadian, it isn't going to happen." Natasha Warwick's jaw was set with weary stoicism.

"Have you any idea what the media are saying about us?" Hadian was staring at her intently, his leg jiggling up and down like he was frantically inflating a tyre with a foot pump.

"Paul, at best he is an accessory. A conspirator."

"We can still charge him without the principal." The irritation in Hadian's voice was obvious.

"I'm well aware of that, but it would not hold up, and I will not sanction it. I cannot alter the burden of proof just because you're feeling the pressure of the media."

"The body of a copper was in his room, found three days after he burgled her house and made serious threats. He's a conspirator and an accessory."

"An accessory with a pretty good alibi," Natasha Warwick said, gathering her things. "Perhaps you should worry less about charging Van Leer and more about finding whoever it is he's protecting."

"He's involved, dammit!" Hadian raised his hand suddenly, as if to hit the desk, but then appeared to think better of it. He lowered it slowly. "And I *will* find out how."

"I really hope you do. Talk to you later. Officer," she said, nodding at Barnes as she left the office. The mischievous tone of the day before was absent. In Hadian's presence she was all business.

The DCI watched her leave. "I may as well be speaking Russian. Great arse, though," he said, switching on the radio to some easy-listening station. "This thing's fantastic. The wife got it for my birthday."

"She has a point, sir. Van Leer's alibi is indisputable."

Hadian looked at him. Barnes thought he saw a faint shake of the head.

"It's tactical. Only two ways you get someone like Van Leer to talk. Hand him an envelope full of money or hand him a charge sheet with the promise of serious jail time. I'm flat broke, so option one is out."

"I see."

"Greed and fear aren't so different," Hadian said, getting up to fiddle with the coffee machine. "It won't go anywhere, of course, but it'll make him think twice about keeping quiet. Unfortunately the CPS don't share that view. In their world people tell the truth, clean up after their dogs and don't get charged unless the job is a stone bonker. So I could do with some good news."

The coffee machine burbled into life.

"Well, there is one resident at the Atlantic Hotel that is of some interest," Barnes said.

"Go on." Hadian sat on the edge of the desk, his attention now fully on Barnes, who sat down in one of two small wooden chairs opposite the DCI's desk.

"Goes by the name of Robbie Fortune. Cathy and I spoke with him on the house-to-house, trying to identify the caller of serial 725, the cause-for-concern report at the Atlantic Hotel. I just listened to the recording of the call."

"You think the caller is this guy Fortune?"

"Not one hundred per cent, but very similar. If we could get him on tape, maybe some voiceprint analysis . . ."

Hadian screwed up his face as he handed Barnes a coffee — his expression read, *That ain't going to happen.*

"What else do we know about him?" he said.

"Well, nothing," Barnes answered, suddenly wondering if he should have bottomed out the enquiry before briefing his boss. "He told us he was just out of prison, but I can't find anything on the system on the details he gave us. Cathy asked him for ID, but he didn't exactly bend over backwards to help."

He put the mug back on Hadian's desk.

"Alias, no doubt," the Welshman said. "Not unusual if he's just out of custard. Need to confirm his ID, pronto. Leave that with me. I'll task the intel cell to do some digging on him and speak with Probation. Anything else?" Hadian stood up and drained his coffee.

"Sir, I'm worried about Cathy. She's disappeared completely. It's been almost two days."

Hadian pursed his lips, holding Barnes's gaze, his face rigid with tension at the mention of her name.

"I got her circulated this morning. It's now a missing person enquiry, and I'm keeping the reins on it. We'll go wide on it — bank accounts, itemised phone billing, vehicle movements, the whole shebang. I just hope she hasn't gone the same way as Harriet."

"Do you really think that's possible?" Barnes's voice was almost a whisper. He'd been worrying constantly about this very eventuality, but the fact that someone else had articulated it seemed to make it a reality.

"I really, really bloody hope not. Losing two cops in a fortnight is just bad manners, and Denniker will put my head on a spike outside the nick."

"Her flat looks like a landfill site. No one's home," Barnes said, deciding for now to omit the empty bottles, the psychiatrist's letter and the probable rendezvous with McDermott.

"If we don't find her by the end of tomorrow, then we'll start issuing warnings to the staff. I don't want people to panic, but we need to consider their safety. I'll speak to Denniker, see if he will lift the embargo on officers taking their protective gear home."

"Yes sir."

"But this enquiry stays within the walls of the station. No uniform will be assigned, only detectives. And I do *not* want any publicity at all. If the press think someone's picking off cops then it'll be open season. Christ, I hope I can find my pepper spray."

"Sir . . ." Barnes hesitated.

"Yes? What's on your mind, lad?"

"I . . . I'm sure Cathy is fine, but . . . do you think I should be assigned another mentor? This is all still new to me, and I . . ."

Hadian interrupted him with a wave of his hand.

"I hear you, Barnes, but you saw the office. The empty desks outnumber people to sit at them by about three to one. I would love to partner you with someone else, but I just can't spare anyone. As soon as we get some more people through the door, I will sort it."

"I understand, sir."

"Besides, if it wasn't this, it would be something else. There's no such thing as normal in this office. What's the saying? Sink or swim?"

"Something like that," Barnes said.

Hadian stood up and stretched, belly straining against his shirt.

"I want you assigned to the surveillance watch tonight," he said. "You know Van Leer, and I want us in place if he breaches. If he's going to screw a house, let him do it, but make damn sure you catch him coming out."

"Yes sir."

"Oh, and one more thing," Hadian said, throwing on his jacket. "The boss wants you at Grove Road."

Barnes swallowed. "He does?"

"Don't look so worried. You haven't been here long enough for a bollocking."

Barnes thought of his amateurish attempts to pursue McDermott and said nothing.

Hadian stopped in the doorway and turned.

"And Barnes?"

"Yes?"

"Lock your doors."

"You too, sir."

The DCI hurried out. Barnes looked at Hadian's battered leather swivel chair and suddenly felt the needle of his own ambition, the hunger to ascend. He considered sitting in the empty chair, just to get a feel for it, but Natasha Warwick beat him to it.

She appeared in the doorway and walked over to the desk just as Barnes was standing up. She looked even taller than the day before, then Barnes noticed the four-inch heels.

She made herself comfortable in Hadian's chair. Barnes sat down again.

"Fifteen minutes he was spouting off at me. He didn't even invite me to sit down." She spun the chair from side to side on its castors, removed her shoes and tucked her legs under her.

Barnes was instantly cautious at the playful tone.

"Think yourself lucky he didn't make you stand to attention."

Natasha laughed. "Didn't you tell me you've only just been made a detective?"

"Not quite. I only took the exam yesterday. Just waiting for the result. I was hoping for the afternoon off when I was ordered down to the court."

"Well, I hope the day wasn't a total disappointment."

He raised his eyebrows.

"I hope you get the result you want. Just don't let them change you too much. I don't know how much you heard of the conversation he and I were having, but he's feeling the strain."

"He's under pressure."

"Oh, come on. Paul Hadian is one of the most experienced detectives in this force. Which might be part of the problem."

"How do you mean?" Barnes frowned. He felt a natural instinct to defend his boss, but found insights into the weaknesses of anyone more senior than him to be fascinating.

"Don't get me wrong, I have tremendous respect for the police, but when things like this come along it's all too easy for them to fit the suspect to the evidence, not the other way around."

Barnes noticed that she said "them" not "you". He sat back and crossed his legs, trying to keep on an equal footing with the prosecutor. She was still swinging the swivel chair from side to side.

"Do you think it might have something to do with the fact that he's right in the firing line? The police will be hung out to dry if this goes bent. Publicly. Named and shamed. The CPS probably won't even get a mention. I think DCI Hadian feels you might be putting forward your ideas from behind the sandbags."

"DC Barnes, are you being provocative?" Playful.

"Maybe." Deadpan.

"Don't lose sight of your objectives. You seem to be a fair and objective officer, and, provided you hang onto it, it will be your biggest strength."

"That's very insightful, considering I only met you yesterday." He folded his arms.

"I can read people extremely quickly. Hidden talent, you might say."

"Now I'm nervous."

She smiled.

"You needn't be. But if you charge too early on this case, it will be fatal. Do right by Constable Holden. And don't make the mistake of thinking I am not interested in prosecuting her killer."

Barnes returned the smile and made his excuses.

* * *

Through the mid-morning traffic, the three-mile drive from the MIS to Grove Road and Chief Superintendent Denniker's office seemed to take an age.

He knocked three times on the royal-blue door and paced outside while he waited. The hospital-green wall outside the commander's office bore the monthly performance graphs, next to a glossy oak panel listing the names of officers killed in the line of duty. Barnes knew on which he would rather feature.

"Come!" Denniker shouted, after an inordinately long pause.

Barnes entered and stood to attention. Denniker was seated behind his desk. He was writing something on a pad — forehead resting in his left hand as if shielding his eyes from the sun, elbow on the desk. He appeared not to notice Barnes, and continued writing for another half-minute or so.

The office was free of any clutter and immaculately presented. The high, white walls were bare aside from a smattering of awards and a poster that read, "LAZINESS WILL NOT BE TOLERATED." Barnes tried hard to decide whether or not this was intended as a joke, then decided it was most definitely sincere.

Eventually Denniker stopped writing. He put down his pen, sat back and peered at Barnes over half-moon, gold-plated spectacles. Barnes suspected these were intended to enhance his Victorian-headmaster image, but they just made him look old.

"Stand easy, son." Denniker discarded the spectacles and came around from behind the desk to shake Barnes's hand.

"You wanted to see me, sir?" Barnes did no more and no less than Denniker's instruction, and stood with his hands clasped at the small of his back, feet shoulder-width apart.

"Yes, I have an action for you." Denniker perched on the edge of the desk. "DCI Hadian originally assigned Cathy Nightingale to the task, but it appears she has better things to do than turn up for work."

"Sir, about Cathy . . ."

Denniker raised a hand, and Barnes was silenced.

"I want recordings of the telephone calls Van Leer made from prison. Inmates' calls are routinely recorded."

"Yes, sir."

"Do you know how to go about doing that?" The commander's voice was patient, but his eyes were fixed on Barnes, who sensed that he was being tested.

"I'll need to apply to a Crown Court judge for a production order under section 14 of the Police and Criminal

Evidence Act 1984, which will need to be served on the prison."

"Good. I want you to draft the application for my approval immediately, taking account of collateral intrusion risks and proportionality."

"Has he . . . do we know if he's called anyone?"

Denniker's eyes narrowed.

"His network of malcontent associates is extensive, I'm sure. And no doubt what's left of his bottom-feeding family will have been in touch. Not to mention his lawyer."

"Sir, any conversations with his solicitor will be subject to legal privilege and will therefore constitute confidential material."

Denniker gave a thin smile and returned to the seat behind his desk. The spectacles went back on.

Message received.

"Yes, sir." Barnes cleared his throat. "Sir, Van Leer has an alibi."

"I know — he was in custody when Constable Holden was last seen alive and did not get bail until after her death. What about it?"

"Sir, other than the risk of other officers — specifically Cathy, after today — meeting a similar fate, nothing." He paused. "But I am concerned about the placement of the body. It was put in Van Leer's room post-mortem."

"And?" Denniker steepled his fingers and rested his elbows on the desk.

"Well, moving a body anywhere is risky, not least a hotel, even if the residents aren't terribly helpful. I'm thinking the placement might be significant. It might be a sign. Or a warning."

"To whom?" Denniker's eyes had wandered to the window, where a queue of stationary traffic in Grove Road below was in danger of becoming disorderly.

"I don't know. Maybe Van Leer himself. Maybe it was Van Leer's co-conspirator stabbing him in the back. Or maybe it was a warning to us — she was a police officer, after all. The day I arrested Van Leer, someone used the Atlantic Hotel's phone to report the fact that he hadn't been seen for a few days, and it just doesn't scan. Someone *wanted* us to find her body."

Denniker cleared his throat. Barnes suddenly felt stupid, and Denniker's disinterested body language only made it worse. He had two years' service. Did he really think that he could come up with theories that career detectives hadn't thought of?

"Barnes, you are clearly a very bright and enthusiastic young officer," Denniker said softly. "And I am not oblivious to the fact that you fancy yourself in my chair. With all due credit, I expect you will get this far one day. I have to leave early today. Draft the application and bring the papers to my house."

Barnes looked at his feet. "Sir, I'm assigned to Van Leer's surveillance detail tonight."

"You'll have plenty of time to come to mine before you are deployed."

Barnes thought of Eve and didn't answer.

"Moreover, I expect you would probably like to know your exam result?"

Barnes looked up sharply.

"The results are in, Barnes."

"Already?"

Denniker smiled. "Come to my house, and you will have yours."

Denniker resumed writing. Barnes dug his hands into his pockets as he left, so the divisional commander wouldn't see them shaking.

* * *

With the evening appointment at Denniker's and the night surveillance duty both looming, Barnes made a point of being home by five. May was only a few days away, and the afternoons were growing warmer. Eve poured some sweet-tasting fruit cocktail of her own invention and sat with Barnes on an old wooden bench in their front garden, watching the sun inch slowly towards the massive green baize of the South Downs in front of them. Forbes frolicked on the lawn and tried to chase a bee. The smell of a barbecue drifted past them from a house a few doors away.

The garden was in the full explosion of late spring. A sprawl of clematis entwined itself around the trellis next to the bench on which they sat, and an array of bluebells, celandine and lily of the valley, all carefully planted and tended by Barnes and his wife, flourished in the tiny patch of garden of which they were justly proud.

The house itself was at the foot of the Downs, one of a row of small terraced houses built in the 1920s on a bank steeped in foliage. An unmade path led up some stone steps away from the main road into an area that was quiet and full of greenery.

"You know, I could settle for this," Eve said, as the dog lay down at the foot of the garden next to a patch of sage and panted. "It's not quite paradise, but with that view, it's not far from it."

Since they had met, Barnes and Eve, like many couples scraping a living, had yearned to live in the undisturbed tranquillity of the countryside. Planning their future in meticulous detail — a fair amount of which included renovating and decorating the house — around Barnes's career ascent was something Eve particularly enjoyed. Barnes was inclined to agree with his wife about it being somewhere close to paradise, but didn't feel he could echo the sentiment until a bit less than ninety-five per cent of the house belonged to the mortgage company.

"Wait there. I want to show you something." Eve darted into the house, taking their empty glasses. Her legs brushed against the sage as she went, and the aroma filled the air around him.

While she was gone Barnes turned his attention to the day's post — junk, bills and a steadily increasing wave of final demands. As a child he had loved getting letters; now, as an adult, he dreaded their arrival.

On the top of the pile next to him was an envelope he recognised as his payslip. He tore it open, curious to know how much the round-the-clock lifestyle of a detective was actually worth, and nearly choked.

The overtime payments themselves were more than he had ever earned before, but there was another figure as well — one he had not seen before, but one that doubled his take-home pay that month. His eyes roamed the small slip of printed paper for an explanation. "SPECIAL BONUS" was all it said.

From inside, some Latin music began to play out through the open windows. Barnes didn't recognise it, but enjoyed the lilting sound of an acoustic guitar, soft horn and whispery vocals.

Eve returned with more of that unnamed fruit punch for her husband, having herself switched to gin and tonic. The sun cast long shadows across the lawn and turned Eve's skin and the edges of her hair golden. She had also changed from her nursery garb into an ankle-length skirt with plum-coloured high-heeled boots.

"What do you think?" she asked, with a graceful twirl, moving in time to the music. "Pretty, isn't it?"

"Where did you get it?" he asked, feeling the fabric of the skirt. It was like velvet.

"I didn't *buy* it. I *made* it," she said.

"You did? When?" He was genuinely impressed. His house seemed to become a hive of creative industry when he wasn't in it.

"This week. While you've been working all this overtime."

"On which note," he said, thrusting the payslip at her, "we might have cleared one hurdle, at least."

She stopped twirling and took the piece of paper from him. He smiled as her eyes widened.

"Bloody hell! Nine hundred quid in overtime? And this two thousand pounds? What's a 'special bonus'?" she asked.

"I haven't the faintest idea. Maybe I should ask someone."

"No, don't do that. Gift horses and mouths, and all that."

"It might help towards a nice holiday."

"It might help towards our baby."

There was a pause — both of them thinking the same thing. She knew he had a chip on his shoulder about the lifestyle she had left behind when she married him. She was always at pains to say that she'd rather be poor and happy than rich and miserable, but he didn't always believe her. Besides, he knew he was trying to prove something to himself just as much as Eve, and with this single bloody payslip it seemed like the tide was finally turning.

She sat close beside him. "So, you like the outfit?" She was a little tipsy.

He touched her thigh.

"I was just going to say — you look stunning. For a gin-soaked lush, that is." He grinned.

She leaned towards him and smiled. Her dark brown eyes sparkled. They looked black in the fading light. "Looks aren't everything, you know."

She placed a hand on his knee and squeezed. Then she took the glass out of his hand and moved her hand up his leg. He tensed.

After scanning the area for inquisitive passers-by and neighbours, she surreptitiously undid his belt. Adrenaline surged through his body, and butterflies began to roam around his stomach.

She was still grinning. She hitched her skirt up a little way and deftly sat astride him.

"It's what I'm *not* wearing that probably interests you most," she murmured into his ear as she carefully lowered herself onto him.

She dropped the long skirt down around them. She stayed absolutely still for what seemed like an eternity, and then began to move slowly with him, so slowly that anybody walking past would think she was innocently sitting on her husband's lap, enjoying the sunset.

Forbes rolled over to face the other way. The traffic rumbled in the distance, and the heavy sun continued to inch slowly west.

* * *

If Barnes was not enamoured of the prospect of going from a day shift to a night shift via his boss's house, then Eve's unexpected garden seduction made him feel even less inclined. He felt that perhaps a quick run would refresh him, and went upstairs to change into his running shorts and trainers.

When he got downstairs there was a small fire burning in the grate, despite the warmth of the early evening sun. Eve was on the sofa with her slim legs tucked under her, a glass of Oyster Bay on the coffee table. The bottle beside it was newly opened, and there was a second, empty glass with it.

She was tearing pages out of a folder, which she crumpled and tossed onto the flames.

"Where are you off to, Chief?" Eve asked, her eyes on her folder. "You've not been home long."

"Just a quick run."

She looked up sharply.

"Now? It'll be getting dark soon." There was an edge to her voice.

Barnes frowned. Running late in the day was not unusual for him — in fact, he preferred it. Then he saw the anxiety in her face and realised she was — perhaps not unreasonably — worried. A colleague of his had been murdered a fortnight ago, after all.

"Don't worry, I'll be fine." He bent down and kissed her on the cheek, then leaned on the mantelpiece to stretch his calves. He had chosen not to mention Cathy Nightingale's absence to his wife, which was just as well, or she'd have probably chained him to the cooker.

"Why don't you sit down and spend a bit of time with me instead? I haven't seen much of you lately," she said, sliding the empty wine glass towards him. "Plenty for two."

He frowned. Eighty per cent of the time Eve respected her husband's teetotalism, but she didn't particularly like drinking alone, and every so often she would try to persuade him to join her — and the frequency seemed to increase as her assignment deadlines drew nearer.

"What's that?" he asked as he stretched, nodding at the folder in Eve's hands.

"Draft one," she said, tearing out another page.

He stopped stretching and stared at her. Evidently the fire was purely functional.

"Don't worry, I've saved it on disk. This is purely a ritual. You don't think I'd just chuck ten thousand words, do you?"

"It's going well, then?"

"Why do you think I've got the bottle open?"

He smiled at her.

"Exercise is good for stress. Why don't you come out with me?" he said, already knowing the answer.

"What? Running?" she scoffed.

"Yes. Why is that such a silly idea?"

"I don't think so." She picked up the wine glass and took a sip.

He sat down next to her, suddenly serious.

"Yes, why don't you come with me? It would be nice to have the company. I won't go too fast, I promise."

"Oh, you think I won't be able to keep up?" She punched him on the shoulder.

"Sounds like a challenge."

"Actually, I probably *wouldn't* be able to keep up." She hung her head in mock shame.

"Of course you will. Come on, it will make a change."

"I've got a dissertation to burn. Besides, I haven't a thing to wear."

He rolled his eyes, stood and made for the door. "Suit yourself. I won't be long."

His hand was on the door handle when she called him back.

"Barnes?"

He stuck his head round the living room door.

"Be careful."

He blew her a kiss, left by the back door and took off down the road. The sun was beginning to melt behind the Downs, the evening still warm and pleasant as it enveloped him. But Christ, his quads felt heavy and sluggish after the little tryst with his wife. Maybe a run wasn't such a hot idea after all. What was that line from *Rocky*? Something about women giving fighters weak legs?

After five minutes or so, however, he found his rhythm, and his feet began to pound out the miles. His breathing started to come with metronomic control, like a train moving steadily across the land.

When he turned into his circuit home, he sensed something in the periphery of his vision. Distracted by the music in his earphones, and one of his senses impaired as a result, a shiver ran across his back and he snapped his head round. He could see nothing.

As he headed back off the main road towards his house, the traffic thinned considerably. Then he sensed it again. He jerked his head round and again saw nothing. He yanked out his earphones. Now the only sound was his own breathing and the light padding of his footsteps. With all his senses returned to him, he relaxed a little.

Then he heard the footsteps. He turned, still running, and could make out a figure, also running, about a hundred yards behind him. The person was too far away to identify in the half-light of the approaching dusk — all he could tell was that it was a male, slim, about five foot eleven, nothing on age.

The adrenaline was flowing now. Barnes thought about slowing down or stopping, maybe even challenging his opponent. But his instinct told him to do the opposite, so he opened out his stride and began to increase the speed, keeping it steady as the pavement began to incline. This should lose him, he thought.

He increased the pace until he was not quite sprinting, then he slowed down and risked a glance over his shoulder. No sign. He had lost him. He brought it back down to a jog and began to ease off for the home stretch.

To his dismay, he heard the footsteps again. He spun around wildly and scanned the street for the figure. No sign. Off balance, he collided with the wing mirror of a parked car and grabbed at his hip in pain.

Panic crept up his spine, and he turned back onto the home stretch and ran full pelt for home. As he drew parallel with his front door he kept on going and cut back to the main road so as not to lead his pursuer home.

He slowed to a walk and paced around for five minutes outside a twenty-four-hour petrol station not far from his house. After he'd got his breath back he ducked into the brightly lit shop and bought a box of Milk Tray for Eve, earning a distasteful look from the cashier as sweat dripped off his brow onto the cellophane wrapper.

Eventually he decided it was safe to go home. This was ridiculous. Police officers running from unknown pursuers? How could the police keep the streets safe if they turned and bolted for cover every time there was trouble? Why hadn't he turned around and challenged the guy?

Because, he said to himself, *you're off duty, you had no kit with you, and then there might be three dead cops instead of two.*

He shook his head. Nightingale wasn't dead, just missing. One officer was dead. Only one.

As he arrived back at the house, he took a moment to stretch and get himself together. The back of the house was completely cut off from the setting sun, and the cooling air chilled the sweat on his neck. After Holden's murder, he didn't want Eve worrying any more than she already was, which meant he had to present himself as calm and composed.

Even if he didn't feel it.

He walked in the back door and put the chocolates on the dining table. The house was quiet. He locked the back door behind him and went into the living room, taking a bottle of water from the fridge as he passed.

She was still on the sofa, the folder beside her now devoid of pages. Draft one had been consigned to history. Draft two was full steam ahead. She had her glasses on and was writing on one of a small tsunami of notepads and textbooks that surrounded her.

He sat beside her. The fire was still burning, and something that sounded like Miles Davis was playing quietly from the stereo.

"Good run?" she said, not looking up. The pen continued to move across the pad.

"Fine." Now he was back in the warm, brightly lit house, he felt even more ridiculous about how scared he'd been. "See? I was quick, as promised." He began to nuzzle her neck. She shrieked with laughter and dropped the pen.

"Remember you said we could talk about babies?"

"You mean the practical?" he said, moving to her ear lobe.

She pushed him away gently. "I went to the doctor today. He referred us to the fertility unit. They'll see us tomorrow."

"Tomorrow? Jesus, I thought we were going to talk about it first." He sat back on the sofa, his sweat-drenched T-shirt cold on his back, and swigged from the bottle of water.

She looked a little defensive.

"He just picked up the phone while I was in the surgery. They gave us the date there and then. It all happened before I realised what was going on. Are you angry?"

He was staring at his feet, the sudden news of progress like a thunderclap. He didn't feel ready. She moved into his line of sight as she spoke, trying to catch his eye.

He looked at her. She was plainly worried about his reaction. How could he be angry?

"I thought referrals took weeks?" was all he could manage.

She smiled. "That's what happens when you go private. You pays your money and takes your chances." She laughed, while he wondered how she'd managed to pay for a private referral. "Tomorrow. The letter's on the kitchen table. Have a look at it."

"I'm working tomorrow . . ." he began, weakly, hating himself for draining the hope from her face.

"Can you . . . take the day off?"

"It's not a good time. With Holden's murder, it's a busy time. I need to be around."

"I know, but you're not the only detective working on this. They can surely cope without you for an hour."

"Where's the clinic? London?" he asked.

"No. Town centre." She smiled. "It'll take ten minutes to get there."

"How are we going to afford it?"

"It's only an initial consultation. Hundred quid. At least we get the ball rolling."

Barnes didn't argue further. She leaned into him.

"Or is that not really the reason? I can't keep second-guessing your thoughts, Barnes. All you do is pout when I mention children."

"Why are you doing this, Eve?" he said eventually.

Her patience evaporated, and she stood up, hands on hips.

"Why am I doing what? You make it sound like I'm dragging you off to have a molar extracted. I just thought if we met the doctor, he could explain what treatments are available, tests, costs, and you could make an informed decision from there."

"It won't *change* anything . . ."

"This house is so damn quiet when you're not here. I listen to kids all day in the nursery, then when I get home, it's like a morgue. I'm *lonely*, Barnes. I want us to have a family. Don't you?"

He sat forward and looked at the floor.

"You have no idea how much," he whispered, then shut his eyes, the feeling of vulnerability that flowed through him hot and uncomfortable.

She stopped, stunned, and then sat back down next to him.

"You do? When did this happen? Why the hell haven't you told me?" Tears were forming in her eyes — tears, he knew, of relief.

"Because I'm scared, Eve," he whispered.

"Scared? Of what?"

"Of everything. I'm scared it won't work. I'm scared of having twenty strangers poke and prod us in an operating theatre when we should be upstairs doing it alone in bed. I'm scared because there is no way on this earth that we can afford it. And I'm scared of disappointment."

"We just need to be positive," she said. "If it works, there'll be no need to *be* disappointed."

He covered his face with his hands.

"Okay," he said finally. "We'll go. I'll make some calls. Don't worry about it."

She laughed through her tears and pressed her forehead against his, her hand on the back of his neck.

"I just wish you'd told me how you really felt," she said softly.

He kissed her on the mouth, and with slow, heavy movements, went to shower and change.

After he'd kissed Eve goodbye, he went out through the kitchen. As he passed he noticed the box of chocolates he'd forgotten to give her, and he scribbled a quick note — *Love from your passing ship*.

Next to the chocolates was the pile of post, his payslip lying on top. He picked it up and looked at it again, trying to process the numbers. It was difficult to ignore the excitement in his stomach — especially when he remembered Eve's stunned expression — but there was another feeling there too.

An uneasy feeling.

A special bonus was all very nice, but was he really that special?

Something this good, someone will want something in return.

CHAPTER SEVEN

Denniker lived in the Belle Tout lighthouse atop Beachy Head, the massive chalk cliff that overlooked the town like a sentinel. Barnes drove through Old Town to get there, rather than heading for the coast road. As Paradise Drive swept upwards through Meads under a cool green canopy of oaks, Barnes glanced backwards over his shoulder to take in the sprawling view of the velvet-green Royal Eastbourne golf course, bathed in the last glow of the sunset. Beyond that lay the town and seafront, with the blue stripe of the Channel visible on the horizon. Eve had spoken before about moving to this part of town — one day, when they could afford it. *When you get promoted to chief*, she would often say.

He took Carlisle Road up through Meads straight through onto Upper Dukes Drive, where it joined the Beachy Head road. Barnes braked sharply, causing a sheaf of papers he'd printed from the daily briefing pages to spill out in the passenger footwell.

The ascent continued until he reached Beachy Head. He followed the snaking road along the cliff edge and then turned into Denniker's long driveway — a sharp, straight incline that led up to the lighthouse itself.

The driveway opened out onto a gravel standing that was bordered by an impressive fish pond recessed in a concrete patio and a framework of halogen lamps buried in the ground. Barnes parked the car, and as he collected up the briefing pages from the footwell, the top item jumped out at him. It had a simple banner headline:

MISSING — DC CATHY NIGHTINGALE

He locked the car and walked up to Belle Tout, forcing himself not to look over his shoulder.

Barnes climbed a set of stone half-moon steps to the front door, which was actually at the rear of the main building. The lighthouse itself acted as a barrier from the powerful wind swirling across the clifftop.

As he rang the doorbell, thinking of Cathy, the thought that this visit may yet have an exponential bearing on his own career was suddenly sharp in his mind — his stomach surged with nerves and he gripped his hands together behind his back to stop them shaking.

A tall, handsome woman in her fifties answered the door, dressed in evening wear as if preparing to go out. She extended a bejewelled hand. Barnes took it. The hand was soft and warm, and he felt a moment's fleeting comfort.

"How very nice to meet you. You must be Barnes."

"Pleased to meet you, ma'am."

"Oh, please! My name is Ellen, and you must call me so. I've no doubt Clive insists on being reminded of his rank at every turn, but I expect no such formality. In any event, he was once of the same rank as you. Not so long ago, either. We are all just people, aren't we?" She laughed loudly.

"Indeed we are," Barnes answered, not quite believing it.

"Listen to me — I haven't even invited you in yet. Please." She swung the door wide, and Barnes stepped into a narrow hallway with a stone floor. There was a small oak table with a collection of tribal ornaments under the main staircase; besides this, the hallway was empty.

"Clive is in his study. Please follow me."

Ellen Denniker led Barnes along the hallway, pointing out two guest bedrooms as they passed.

"We've just had these done for visitors. We're very pleased with them. When we moved in there was a foot of standing water under the floorboards."

Barnes peered in as they walked. The bedrooms certainly looked very new, with parquet floors, spotlights and all manner of nautically themed ornaments.

The "study" was in the lantern room, in the very top of the lighthouse tower itself. Barnes followed Ellen Denniker through the main living area and up an extremely narrow spiral staircase, steadying himself more than a few times on the cold brick walls. The staircase wound around the keeper's loft, a tiny room with a ladder leading to a recessed bunk, and came up through the floor of the circular lantern room, which was surrounded completely by floor-to-ceiling glass. Through these windows Barnes could see the last of the daylight, like mauve-and-yellow tiger stripes over the Channel.

Denniker was standing with his back to the pair, apparently drinking in this sweeping view of the horizon. Ellen stayed at the door and ushered Barnes in.

"Your guest, Clive. Can I get you a drink, Barnes?" she asked.

"Just some tea, thank you. I'm on duty later."

"And for me, darling," Denniker echoed.

Ellen glided away without another word.

"Please sit down, Barnes. Welcome to my home," Denniker said, with what appeared to Barnes to be something of a flourish. Barnes sat down on a vinyl seat that stretched around the circumference of the lantern room. Denniker had arranged the west half of the room into an office space, with a small desk, armchair and bookcase. He sat down in the armchair.

"Thank you for coming."

"My pleasure, sir." Barnes stood up to place a sheaf of papers on Denniker's desk. "The application for the prison tapes," he explained.

"Good. I'll look at them later." Denniker nodded towards the space his wife had just vacated. "Thirty-five years we've been married. Not all plain sailing, but if the good hadn't outweighed the bad we wouldn't be here today. You must excuse her eccentricity. She had a couple of small strokes last year."

"I'm sorry to hear that, sir."

"Nothing too serious. She has always been a trifle . . . unconventional, which is one of the reasons we ended up in this place." He waved a hand, indicating the lighthouse.

"I certainly didn't have any trouble finding it. I didn't know Belle Tout was occupied." Barnes shifted in his seat. This insight into the commander's personal life made him slightly uncomfortable, although to term their relationship "friendly" might have been stretching it a bit, especially as an element of formality — and rank — remained between them.

"George V used it as a residence in 1935, after a new lighthouse was built on the rocks in 1902. Alas, perpetual chalk collapses have brought our home perilously close to the edge of the cliff, and I am undertaking something of an ambitious project to move it away from the edge."

"You're going to move your house?"

"Exactly. New foundations will be built, and the entire structure lifted up and slid backwards to the new site. I will show you the plans later. It's all rather exciting. As I said, it's ambitious, but neither Ellen nor I could face the prospect of our home falling into the sea. This will at least prolong its life a little while longer."

"Good luck, sir."

"Thank you. I must confess to an irresistible urge to defend the history of the town. William Cavendish conceived the borough of Meads as Eastbourne's own Belgravia; also the Winter Garden, our wonderful tri-level promenade, our parades and our enduring tradition that the seafront should be free of shops. There is a saying, Barnes, often attributed to Cavendish, that the town was planned by gentlemen for gentlemen. I would love to preserve that."

"Yes, sir."

Denniker's eyes narrowed, and he smiled. "I apologise for my meandering, Barnes. I am something of an amateur historian at heart."

The sound of rattling china drifted up from the staircase, and Barnes got up to intercept the tea tray from Ellen Denniker and save her any further struggling on the steep staircase. She smiled at him gratefully.

"Are you married, Barnes?" Denniker asked as Barnes returned. He set the tray down and Denniker waved a hand — *proceed*.

"Yes sir. Five years," Barnes said, pouring the tea.

"A good police officer needs a solid marriage. Helps keep him afloat. Gives him a sense of perspective, a sense of what's important in life. And —" he paused to open a cigar box on the desk — "it ensures one keeps one's feet on the ground. Particularly when on the ascent. Ellen helped me with that during my formative years, and I suspect your good lady wife may find herself discharging the same duty."

"Thank you, sir," Barnes said, declining a cigar.

"No need to thank me, Barnes," Denniker said, taking one for himself and making a show of unwrapping, cutting and lighting it. "It's a statement of fact. An officer's potential to succeed is identified very early on. Paul Hadian clearly sees it in you, and I can see why. You are a very bright young man, Barnes. Tell me, what is the secret of your soon-to-be-realised success?"

Barnes thought before continuing. He sensed something wholly theatrical about the entire encounter, which, he supposed, was Denniker's skill.

"I suppose . . . well, sir, my heart's in the right place."

Denniker liked this. He laughed, and blew smoke rings at the ceiling.

"Good answer. With a degree of affected modesty, I suspect. Don't worry about that. When you peak in this job, Barnes — and it will happen around about twelve years' service — people will stop pushing you forward and you will have to start pushing yourself. *Selling* yourself. To get ahead. I make no secret of my desire to ascend to assistant chief constable and beyond. To act humble is to clip one's wings. So remember, one day you will have to jettison the humility entirely, although at present it's rather endearing."

Barnes looked at the commander, disturbed briefly by this analysis of his personality. He thought of Eve, alone in the house, and for just a moment wondered if she was okay.

"Well, I won't keep you in suspense any longer." Denniker set his cigar down and retrieved a slim brown envelope from the top drawer of his desk. He slid it across to Barnes. Barnes hesitated for a moment and then grabbed at the document.

"You needn't be too nervous," Denniker said reassuringly. "I wouldn't have invited you here if you'd failed it."

Barnes ripped a single sheet from the envelope and his eyes roamed the paper, processing the news.

"Well? How did you get on?" Denniker laced his fingers in front of him and rested his elbows on the desk.

Barnes shrugged. "I didn't do too badly."

"That modesty again!" Denniker laughed. "You scored highest in the force. Third highest nationally."

Barnes looked at him.

"I thought the results took weeks to come in."

"Nonsense. The answer sheets are scanned by computer, and the results are provided instantly. You just have to know who to call," Denniker said with affected embarrassment. "I know all promotion exam results before the candidate. It isn't public knowledge, and I certainly never disclose it to the staff. There's no need."

"Why the exception now, sir?"

"Purely because there should be a degree of ceremony involved, which demands a little insider information, don't you think?"

"I suppose so."

"You're not offended, are you? If you look hard enough you will find it on our policy database, so strictly speaking, it's not a secret. In any event it would only be an issue in the event of failure. In this case it's a cause for celebration. The third highest score in the country, and still a probationer? That's nothing short of exceptional, Barnes."

Barnes's natural sense of modesty did battle with the hot feeling of elation flooding through his veins. He wanted to yell, and jump in the air. Instead, he looked at his shoes while his hands trembled.

"I trust the bonus payment was satisfactory?"

Barnes stared at the commander.

"You arranged that? I meant to ask you . . ."

Denniker showed Barnes his palm.

"Consider it a reward for your excellent exam result, but also a generous golden handshake for your inauguration as a detective."

"Generous is an understatement."

"Barnes, there are reasons why I invited you to my house, and not Hadian, or Callaghan, or that moron Nightingale, wherever the hell she is."

Barnes grimaced. Was he the only one worried about Cathy? Okay, so the DCI had made a feeble mention of this not being her first unexplained absence, but hadn't Denniker already made the point about complacency costing Holden her life? Was this so different?

Denniker continued, in a low voice.

"This investigation is already running cold. There is insufficient evidence against the principal suspect to bring a charge, which means poor Harriet will not see justice done."

"Sir, there are still enquiries that could lead us to the killer."

Denniker hit the desktop with the palm of his hand.

"There are no other suspects! Howard Van Leer — for whatever damn reason — knew we would find her body in his dingy little room. Maybe he thought that by leading you to her he could somehow assuage his own grubby conscience and pass the guilt onto us. Well, it won't work."

"Sir, it just doesn't gel. I don't see what possible reason Van Leer would have for wanting to murder Harriet Holden. He's a thief and a drug addict. That's all."

"Drug addicts are capable of wanton violence whenever their physiological deficiencies demand it."

"But I still don't see that he has a motive. Not only that, he has a concrete alibi. We should be looking at other suspects — suspects who might make attempts on the lives of other officers, and who may have already got to Cathy Nightingale."

"Barnes, Van Leer's unwillingness to cooperate with us and help us seek the principal suspect indicates to me that he is guilty of conspiracy at the very least. We have been made to look stupid by this imbecile, by resting on our laurels and popping the cork the moment he was in custody. We took our eye off the ball, Barnes, and that mistake led to Harriet's death. There is a leak in our workforce, and it has cost an officer their life. I *will* salvage what is left of our collective pride." He hit the desk again.

Both Denniker's passion and seniority curbed Barnes's confidence in further arguing, although he still could not understand the reluctance for looking beyond Van Leer.

"Sir, I am only a DC in this investigation. I will pursue whatever lines of enquiry you or DCI Hadian give me."

Denniker ran a hand through his hair, the exasperation obvious.

"Barnes, two minutes ago I advised you to jettison your humility. In anticipation of your future ascent, practise now. Paul Hadian and myself, we digest the theory of what has been collected and concoct strategic hypotheses. We write our thoughts in lists and hand them out for the rank-and-file to action. You are the investigator, you are the officer on the ground that sees these awful people in person, sees them for what they are. A slight mannerism, an averted gaze, a delay before answering, those are the things you will see and report back. Those are the things that will direct the investigation. This is in your hands, not mine."

"That may be the case, sir, but I don't see anything in Van Leer that makes me think he's guilty. Nor do the CPS."

"Van Leer may not be absolutely guilty of murder in legal terms, but he is certainly not innocent. He is in this up to his smack-addled neck, however much he protests, and he needs to be punished. Barnes, do you understand what I am saying to you?"

Barnes tensed, and sat up a little straighter in his chair.

"Van Leer is guilty. And we will see justice done for Harriet. We will undo our mistake, one way or another." Denniker slid an A4 envelope across the desk to Barnes. Barnes opened it. A single sheet of paper bearing neatly typed print was inside.

"You are an integral part of the investigation, Barnes. But now you could make the investigation."

Barnes read the paper. A simple instruction, no more, no less. He stood up, cold prickles sweeping across his back.

"Sir, I'm not sure we should be having this conversation at all."

Denniker moved around to the front of the desk and stood in front of him.

"Please don't think of it as something as banal as planting evidence on an innocent man. The real world is not nearly so simple. Our victims, witnesses and offenders are interchangeable on a weekly basis, depending purely on who happens to dial 999 first. Harriet Holden — bless her heart — was a true, unfortunate victim."

Denniker placed his hands on Barnes's shoulders. Ten minutes ago, Barnes would have felt decidedly uncomfortable at what amounted to an excessively paternal gesture, but by now Denniker — the consummate performer — had him completely mesmerised.

"Van Leer is a conspirator and a procurer. The mechanics of our justice system rely on convenient, neatly packaged morsels of evidence, but the truth, the truth of what actually happened to poor Harriet may never be known. Even if it was, it would be an abridged and sanitised version that would eventually be spouted in court. But we, the police, can make our own justice. We can make our own *rules*. Barnes, the effort required on your part is minimal. No overt tactics, no obvious fabrications, no names. Just a gentle shaping of what we already have. Your conscience will be clear by Christmas."

Denniker laughed loudly. Barnes could smell the stale cigar on his breath. Barnes knew, could *feel* that he was being seduced with the promise of success, and that Denniker's faintly sinister intentions were the price he would have to pay, but he felt powerless to do anything about it.

"Van Leer was in prison when Harriet died, but this will provide the motive and the association for a charge of conspiracy to commit murder. And he will be convicted. What are your immediate plans for promotion, Barnes?"

"I . . . I'm planning to take the sergeant's exam next year."

"Do it. Pass it. I will guarantee your promotion. New sergeants are assigned to a mandatory twelve months on uniformed duties, minimum. Not for you. I'll post you straight back into the CID. Major Crime Branch if you want it, when they finally get it going. Can you deal with that, Detective *Sergeant* Barnes?"

Barnes felt his loins twitch as adrenaline surged through his body. He'd felt it before — on being headhunted by Hadian, on completing the detectives' exam, on getting his result, and now here. Denniker must have sensed this, for he smiled.

"Success feels good, doesn't it? But I warn you, it becomes an addiction."

"Does it?" Barnes croaked.

"I rose rapidly, Barnes. You will too. But such ascension has a price. I paid mine. This is yours. Earn your place. You will be an inspector in eighteen months."

Flash frames of Robbie Fortune and Howard Van Leer slammed into Barnes's mind, and were gone just as quickly. Denniker gently removed the sheet of paper from Barnes's hand and slid it carefully through a compact paper shredder on the edge of the desk, overhanging the wastepaper basket. Barnes watched the strands of paper fall and thought of long, white tears.

"I trust you have committed the details to memory?"

Barnes nodded.

"Then go. Find the right time to do this."

Barnes turned and left Belle Tout in a daze, the darkness outside sudden and complete. His body felt numb. He walked down to his car, so wrapped up in his thoughts that he didn't see the metallic-green Mercedes speed away from where it had been parked at the end of Denniker's drive.

* * *

Barnes decided the right time was immediately.

Harriet Holden's mother lived in a terraced house in Channel View Road, which would indeed have had a view of the Channel if not for the sharp deviation in the road and some obstructive foliage. Barnes parked up shortly before nine that evening, calculating that he had time to visit before he was due to deploy to the surveillance detail.

Barnes had briefly met Sally Holden at the funeral. At the time she had been sporting a large purple welt under her left eye, which Barnes later learned she had sustained after collapsing in the doorway when told of her daughter's death, catching the doorknob full in the face.

She let Barnes in without complaint, a slim woman with a face grey and tired out by grief. Barnes allowed himself to be led through the narrow hallway into a sparsely decorated front room that smelled strongly of lavender.

The walls were adorned with family photographs — Harriet as a baby, Harriet as a child, Harriet with her parents on a sunny pebbled beach somewhere, Mr and Mrs Holden's wedding photograph and subsequent anniversaries.

The house was simple, but tidy and well-kept. Sally Holden had the look of a career housewife — she was only in her fifties, but the white lace, neat corners and dust-free surfaces spoke of an era of scrubbed doorsteps and Dunkirk spirit. Barnes noticed there was no television.

She brought tea on a tray and gestured for Barnes to sit down. She had not yet questioned the purpose of his visit, and her actions as hostess were mechanical. There was a pack of cigarettes on the tray. She picked it up and then put it down again. The welt under her eye had started to fade.

Barnes took some tea. "Mrs Holden . . ."

"Sally, please," she interrupted. Her voice was weak and hoarse — from crying or smoking, Barnes didn't know. "At least if you call me by my first name you don't seem like quite so much of a stranger. And there have been so many strangers this week."

"Sally it is," Barnes replied.

She set down her cup, as if noticing him for the first time.

"I've had a couple of your Family Liaison people round this week. They're lovely, the pair of them, but Lord knows why I need two. I feel like asking if they shouldn't be out catching burglars or something."

Barnes smiled.

"There's only so much reassurance a person can take. Sometimes I wish someone would slap me round the face, tell me to get a grip . . . Nothing prepares you, you know."

Barnes was silent. Sally Holden looked over at the photographs on the wall. She was breathing through her mouth — Barnes could hear tears, thick at the back of her throat.

"You don't know what to do with yourself. People phone, they come round, they ask if there's anything they can do. But it's the quiet hours, that's when it gets you. All those minutes and seconds, they tick by, and it feels like I'm getting further away from her. Then there was the funeral, the investigation, the inquest to come . . . it's like she doesn't *belong* to me anymore."

She took a couple of deep breaths, slowing herself down before the rollercoaster came off the rails. Barnes thought he caught a faint aroma of gin on her breath. Even the Dunkirk spirit needed to refuel, he supposed.

"It's nice to see you again, Mr Barnes," she said, resuming the role of the hostess admirably. "Why did you say you were here? You've already paid your condolences."

"I just thought I'd see how you're doing."

She didn't answer. Barnes continued.

"Harriet and I, we were friends. We're the same age, give or take."

Sally Holden's eyes dropped to Barnes's wedding ring.

"We weren't, you know, close, but we did get on. I was her crew partner for over a year. She had her eye on the top, and some might say there was a comparison."

"You have your eye on the top?" She sounded cautious, as if this might have been the thing that did for her daughter.

Barnes dropped his gaze. "Not exactly. But I have ambition."

"She wasn't finding it easy — the higher she went, the more resistance she seemed to encounter, particularly from her *colleagues*." She spoke the word with sudden rancour, and Barnes wondered if she knew more about the obstacles Holden had faced in her professional life than she let on.

"I know. I also know you'd probably think someone of equal ambition would more likely be a detractor. A professional rival."

"And that wasn't the case?"

"No. You might even say we had something in common. She needed support wherever she could get it. But she was ahead of me on the ladder, which is why I'm only realising this after . . . afterwards."

"Because now you need support wherever you can get it?"

"Something like that. We're investigating the murder of one of our own officers. The fact that she wasn't killed on duty is the only reason the investigation hasn't been taken out of our hands at all. Even now I'm not sure it won't be, it's just a question of when."

"And that worries you?"

"I thought earlier that for an officer of her service, there didn't seem to be many people that knew her well. I certainly didn't, and now I'm wondering if I should have tried harder to resolve that."

"To clear your conscience?" Barnes couldn't decide whether her paraphrasing was a gentle interrogation, or whether she was genuinely trying to understand.

"Perhaps. Even though it might be too late, I can still get to know her. But if the investigation gets taken away from us, then it may be too late for anyone to know her."

Sally Holden stood up suddenly and walked out of the room. Barnes waited a moment, unsure of himself, then followed her up the stairs to a small bedroom at the rear of the house.

It was a room awaiting its owner's return, an owner who had stayed and left and returned many times. There were ring binders and promotion study texts on the floor, faded teen idol posters on the pink walls and soft toys on top of the wardrobe. Barnes took in the room and its contents, feeling like an intruder. Sally spoke, guessing his thoughts.

"She never really moved out. She left it as it was when she left school for university. Got a two-one in performing arts. She visited every weekend until she graduated, then went straight into the police. After that, she had the money for her own place, but she never got round to moving all her belongings out. I'd been on at her to do it. Told her I needed the space." Her voice hitched as her speech gave way to a huge sob. As she tried to catch her breath it sounded for a moment like she was drowning.

She moved towards a large cardboard box. In it were some of the belongings from Holden's house. Right on the top was a demo CD, Holden's name and the date scrawled on the surface in marker pen. Sally Holden went to play it on a very old stereo that sat on a bookcase, but her hand began to tremble. Barnes gently took the CD from her.

"Take it with you," she said, gesturing to the CD. "Listen to it. She had such a beautiful voice. She . . ." Her voice cracked again.

"Do you mind if I have a quick look?" Barnes asked, deliberately avoiding attempts to comfort Sally. She gestured acquiescence with her hand, her face still contorted with trying to control her expression of grief.

Barnes moved to the wall opposite the door, next to the bed, where a row of photographs hung in small plastic frames. Holden's graduation picture was there, as was her passing-out picture. Both parents were present in the former, only her mother in the second. Below these was a montage of her life — pictures of her in dark nightclubs with friends clutching cigarettes and cocktails, pictures of her skiing with two other friends, pictures of her horse riding at a local contest. And her brother featured — pictures of him at football matches, on the beach, as a sleeping baby being fussed over by his nine-year-old big sister.

There was another photograph, but it wasn't in a frame and it did not form part of any montage. It was loose and sitting on its own on a shelf, wedged between two small framed pictures. There was a thin film of dust on the glossy surface.

It showed Holden on a sunny day in Paris, seated at the foot of the Arc de Triomphe. She was wearing mirrored aviators, a rucksack and a plain white T-shirt. Her arms were stretched out either side of her, resting on the concrete, and her head was cocked to one side, aiming a lopsided grin at the camera.

Barnes could still hear Sally Holden sobbing quietly. He braved a look over his shoulder. Her eyes were screwed shut as she fought back tears. She was not looking. He reached forward for the photograph and took it in one hand, holding it carefully.

He heard her breathing gradually slow down and return to normal. The sobbing stopped. He tried to distract her with more talk.

"Do you mind my asking what happened to Harriet's father?"

"Benjamin died shortly after Harriet graduated. He was a good man, but vice got him in the end. Cancer of the lung.

Thirty-two years we were married. He only wanted the best for her. I'm just . . . I'm just glad he didn't have to see Harriet in the ground. No one should . . ."

The tears came again. He rose, still with his back to her, then slipped the photograph quickly inside his jacket pocket. He shut his eyes momentarily, then went to her, although he wasn't sure he could say anything more to comfort this poor woman. He didn't know what else to do, and so he touched her hand, then pulled her to him in a hug. She clutched at him and the tension seemed to ease from her body as she cried freely into his shoulder — big hiccupping sobs as though she'd been holding her breath since answering the door.

Eventually he released her, then turned silently to go. Sally Holden followed him to the door. He thanked her for the tea, and she touched him gently on the arm as he left.

"You know, seeing you look at her pictures . . ." Her voice tailed off. "You two would have looked good together. Not like some of the idiots she dated."

"Cops?"

"Mainly. The latest one was married."

Barnes raised an eyebrow. Was this news?

"Do you know who?"

"No idea. Never met him. She wouldn't tell me about him. Not even his name. She really knew how to pick them."

"Have you told anyone else this?" Barnes asked.

She shook her head.

"They didn't ask."

"Neither did I."

She shrugged.

"Those other policemen, they came round here, did tea-and-sympathy for quarter of an hour, then looked at their watches and started on the questions. They just wanted to talk about her death. You're the only one that seems genuinely interested in her life."

Barnes closed his eyes briefly, thinking of the picture in his pocket.

"Do you have children, Mr Barnes?"

Barnes felt goosebumps swarm all over his body as he managed a slight shake of the head. Sally Holden gave him a little nod, and for a moment he thought she understood.

"Don't let what happened to Harriet stop you," she said. "There's nothing better on this earth."

He thanked her again and walked back to his car.

He sat for a while in the driver's seat, thinking about going back and asking her to call in with the information about Harriet's relationship. After all, he had not been sent to her house — the FLOs had already done that — and he'd had no real reason to go other than to indulge the subterfuge with which Denniker had enveloped him.

He retrieved the photograph from his jacket pocket and stared at it, lingering on Holden's happy face. Her tiny frame, tousled blonde hair and look of lazy contentment stirred a horrible, aching feeling of loss within him. It was only a fraction of what her mother must have been feeling, but it was the insidious realisation that no one would ever see her again, a feeling that had been steadily growing since he found her violated body. Barnes hoped that Sally Holden would never have the misfortune of seeing the last ever pictures taken of her daughter.

He had carried out part of Denniker's scheme. There was a second part to go. He stared at the photograph one final time — tried to summon some justification for what he was doing, some bypass of his integrity, to give him the will to continue. *I'm doing this for you, Harriet.* He forced himself to believe it was the right thing to do. *I'm doing this for you. I'm going to find who killed you, and I don't care how.*

He put the photograph away and held his fist to his forehead, almost overcome by the sudden urge to drive straight home and pull his wife close to him.

He didn't notice the green Mercedes drive slowly past his window.

* * *

Van Leer's bail address was in Santa Ana Court, a yellow-and-blue block of brand-new apartments on eight floors. It was one of six blocks that, together, were decked out with some modern-art fixtures that Barnes supposed were meant to convey an abstract ocean liner. The underground car park was covered by a long, dark wooden deck dotted with tall arc lights that resembled masts, which were just beginning to come on as Barnes arrived at the nearby site. The halogens projected pale, ghostly beams onto the buildings, which were themselves shrouded in huge white metal canopies intended to resemble sails. These cast long shadows across the face of the deck and the churned, boggy mud and machinery of an adjacent site still under construction. Very few of the apartments were yet occupied, and the entire area was still and eerily silent.

Barnes followed Hadian's instruction and backed the Mondeo into the garage of a nearby townhouse, which formed part of another block opposite Santa Ana Court that, Barnes presumed, gave a decent view of Van Leer's bail address. He rummaged in the boot and found a reflective jacket, hard hat and clipboard, which he took for a crude site foreman disguise for officers on surveillance.

Further searching yielded a pair of binoculars, and he took the entire ensemble with him. He opened a door connecting the garage to the house proper and entered a hallway with a tiled floor.

He stood for a moment in the silent hall, unsure if he should announce himself, or make himself at home, or what. He surmised he ought not to ring the doorbell.

Eventually he followed the sound of low voices and walked up to the second floor. The day watch officers were in what Barnes supposed was a living room, but apart from two camping chairs, a cool box and a table with a load of equipment on it, it was empty.

The day watch turned at the sound of Barnes approaching, and Barnes saw that one of them was his former patrol sergeant, John Callaghan. Barnes's surprise must have been obvious, because Callaghan laughed as he shook the hand of his former charge.

"Hello, Barnes."

"How you doing, sarge? Since when do you work surveillance?"

"The boss thought a change of scene would do me good, so he stuck me on an LST."

Barnes nodded. Local Support Teams were specialist units comprising a sergeant and six constables, permanently on standby for whenever their skills were called for, be it searches, surveillance or riot control.

"I don't mind, actually. I worked SV some years ago, and I can't say I'm sorry to be out of the limelight. No probationers to wet-nurse on the LST, either."

Barnes grinned.

"How are you doing, anyway?" Callaghan asked.

"Pretty good, I suppose."

"CID already. I always knew you'd go far. Just don't forget the little folk when we all have to call you sir. Or your wife, for that matter."

"You know something I don't?"

"Only that detectives tend to view divorce as a fashion accessory. Make time for her."

"Good advice. How . . . how's the team?"

"They're pretty resilient. They lost Holden, they lost you and now I've been replaced. Being busy helps. Hey, did you hear about Cathy Nightingale?"

"What about her?" The hairs on Barnes's neck stood up in anticipation of whatever news was coming.

"She's missing."

Barnes breathed a sigh of relief as he realised he wasn't behind with the updates after all.

"Yeah, I know *that*. Christ, I thought you were going to say they'd found her body or something. Hadian's running the enquiry, got a bunch of us running around trying to find her. He's been trying to identify a relative, or any family she might go to."

"Who, Cathy? She hasn't a soul in the world."

Barnes was quiet for a moment as he thought of the empty photo frames in Nightingale's flat.

"Sarge — what's OP?" he asked.

Callaghan raised an eyebrow and indicated the apartment with his hand. "You're standing in it. Observation post. The point from which you will observe Monsieur Van Leer. Who's your oppo?"

"DCI Hadian's supposed to be sending a crew partner. Apparently they're not here yet."

Callaghan frowned and gave Barnes a briefing. They walked to the window. It had an unobstructed view across an open courtyard into Van Leer's bail address, which was about a hundred yards away in a fifth-floor apartment in a corner block directly opposite the OP. The main lobby door was the only way in or out, so there was no coverage of the rear.

From the ground floor lobby there were two exits — the main door and a fire door — with another door leading to the car park on the lower ground-floor level under the decked walkway. The surveillance detail would lose visual on anyone taking the lower exit to the car park, but would pick them up again when they came out, and any vehicle would be held up at the gates before it could get onto the main road.

There were no external fire escapes, so anyone evacuating would have to come down the main stairwell. Barnes peered out. The stairwell was illuminated all the way down, and if Van Leer left the apartment there was a clear line of sight right into the lift.

"What's he been up to?" Barnes asked.

"Well, he's keeping to his conditions, so far," Callaghan said. "He didn't score, he didn't contact any witnesses and he was back here by six-thirty tonight."

"He must be bored out of his mind. He's going to breach, I'm sure of it. Has he had any visitors?"

"Only McDermott. Been round a couple of times."

"Okay, thanks. You want to get home?"

"I do, thanks. Call me if you get stuck."

"Thanks, sarge. Take it easy."

Callaghan and his partner left the room and disappeared down the stairs. Barnes moved to the window and settled down with the audio-visual equipment. He looked at his watch and hoped his partner would be turning up soon, because he certainly didn't know how to work any of this stuff.

Night was like a thick blanket threatening to smother the amber arc lights of Santa Ana Court. As it began to envelop the largely empty site, Barnes felt his phone vibrate gently in his pocket. He pulled it out, the green backlight casting a pale glow around the room.

He rubbed his eyes, the inertia of his body causing him to realise just how tired he was. He'd been at work all day, and apart from the brief hiatus in the front garden with Eve — which had just made him want to crawl into bed with her even more — he had now gone straight into a night duty surveillance detail from his boss's house, via Sally Holden's, of course. If Van Leer stayed in bed all night, Barnes wasn't sure coffee alone was going to help him last the night.

What was that, eighteen hours on in a twenty-four-hour period? The box of Milk Tray had been a good idea.

To his surprise, the text message was not from Eve.

Hope u not bored 2nite. If he runs, get him! C u soon x

Barnes thought for a moment, and then keyed in a reply.

Who's this?

He only had to wait a few seconds before the phone lit up again.

Natasha W ;-)

Barnes slowly tucked the phone back into his jacket, his mind and stomach racing. He wondered, albeit idly, how a CPS lawyer would know the finer details of a covert police operation — or, for that matter, how she'd got his number. After some deliberation, he decided not to reply — and then, as if to cement the decision, he sent a message to Eve's mobile, telling her he missed her and he hoped she slept well.

His meandering thoughts were interrupted by the sound of a creaking floorboard in the stairwell behind him. His head jerked upwards and he moved away from the window.

He turned and picked out the clear sound of somebody ascending the stairs. He *was* expecting someone to crew up with him, but he'd had no name and no contact, and with Phil McDermott's anti-surveillance tactics he wasn't leaving anything to chance.

Wide awake now, he crouched down behind the door and tensed his body like a sprinter in the blocks. The person in the stairwell was moving slowly, carefully, their feet making tiny tapping noises on the uncarpeted stairs.

The walls of this new build were like paper — as Barnes pushed his ear to the wall he could clearly hear the rustle of clothing governed by the quiet ascent.

Somewhere near the top of the stairs the person stopped and audibly exhaled. Adrenaline began to pump through Barnes's body, and for a second he thought cramp in his right foot was going to betray him.

The figure appeared in the living room. Barnes sprang forward from behind the door, planting his hands onto their shoulders like a lion pouncing on its prey, and forced the unfortunate individual onto the floor.

"Police! Who the hell are you?" Barnes yelled.

"Will you get off me? It's me! It's . . . Cathy."

Barnes jumped to his feet.

"Cathy? What the hell are you doing here?"

There was a moment's pause, and then, too dumbfounded to do anything else, Barnes extended a hand. Nightingale took it and got to her feet.

"I'm assigned to tonight's watch," she said, smoothing down her clothes.

Barnes stared at her. Surprise and relief pushed a hundred different questions to the surface.

"Where the hell have you been? You know the DCI's called a misper enquiry? After what happened to Harriet, half the division is waiting for your body to turn up. Who knows you're here?"

Barnes pulled out his mobile phone and scrolled through the contacts until he found Hadian's number.

"Who are you calling?" Nightingale sounded as irritable as ever.

"The boss needs to know," Barnes replied, not looking at her.

"I went to Hadian today. *He* assigned me to the OP, okay? I was never missing, okay? I just have some . . . problems."

Barnes looked at her for a moment and then put the phone away. Relief gave way to anger.

"Problems? Like using a fake warrant to get into Van Leer's room?"

Nightingale opened her mouth to speak, but Barnes wasn't done.

"What the hell were you thinking? Hardly anything from the scene is going to be admissible. I mean, is this what it means to be a detective? Warrants for any occasion? What else do you . . ."

The sound of an engine revving caught Barnes's attention. He moved to the window and saw a car driving away from the house. The driver was a thin female with a solemn face, no more than twenty-two. She had lank, yellow hair with dark roots, and she wore a white vest. Her thin arms were covered with tattoos and bangles.

He turned to Nightingale and jerked his thumb back towards the window.

"Who was that? It seems like the world and his wife know about what's meant to be a covert operation. Should we add unauthorised disclosures to your list of indiscretions?"

"Don't worry, she's job," Nightingale said, ignoring the sarcasm. "Works out of HQ. Hadian cleared it. She only gave me a lift."

She didn't elaborate. Barnes eventually relented, and they settled in to watch. The lights of the stairwell opposite were a cool blue, and only one apartment window was illuminated. The block was quiet.

"What kind of first name is Rutherford?" Nightingale asked eventually. "Your parents have a thing for American presidents or something?"

In the darkness, Barnes rolled his eyes.

"Not exactly. Scientists, maybe. Besides, everyone calls me Barnes," he said, on autopilot.

"I'm not bent, you know," she said, suddenly ending the small talk and meeting Barnes's unspoken accusation.

Barnes didn't say anything.

"How long have you got in?" Nightingale said. "You did tell me, I know."

"Two years."

In the gloom, Barnes saw Nightingale shake her head.

"What's your problem?" he said.

"There's no point me explaining. You're just a pup, but you'll find out yourself, soon enough. If you want to be a detective, if you want to get the results, you have to cut a few corners. You know, bend a few rules."

As recently as last week, Barnes might have met this remark with "*Bullshit.*" But since then, he had entered into a clandestine agreement with Chief Superintendent Clive Denniker, and even as Nightingale spoke he wondered if he was already on the road she was talking about.

"I thought we were just going to have a sniff around Van Leer's room," she continued. "Obviously if I'd known we were going to find a cop's body and a homicide scene I might have been a bit less cavalier about the whole business."

"Well, that's good to know," Barnes said, anger gradually dissolving into sarcasm.

"Naive you may be, but you've done well. I wouldn't have made detective in my probation. I'm a woman, of course, which has its own challenges, but I imagine my male counterparts would say the same. So, are you a graduate? Accelerated promotion?"

Barnes thought of Denniker gripping his shoulders and didn't answer.

"I'm just curious," Nightingale said. "You're at the core of a homicide investigation — barely out of nappies and you're assigned to a surveillance watch."

"What's your point?"

"Doesn't it strike you as . . . unusual?"

"Which bit?"

"Come on, Barnes. Harriet was marginalised by her colleagues. You probably knew her better than anyone else, and not only that, you were the last known person to see her alive."

"And?"

"And now you're getting deployed to jobs that normally require specialist training. You don't think that's odd?"

"I haven't really had time to think about it."

"Hadian's no fool, Barnes. Some of the actions he's been slinging your way are double-edged — he gives you a leg up the greasy pole, but he also gets to keep you nice and close. Keep an eye on you."

Barnes inhaled as the penny dropped. "Wait. Are you trying to say . . . I'm a *suspect*?"

"It's a possibility, that's all. Think of it as a heads-up."

"You've got a fucking nerve. If anyone's down as a suspect, it's you. Someone leaked Harriet's address — someone with a lot to lose."

Nightingale didn't answer. Barnes turned back to the window.

"How did Van Leer get himself a place in Sovereign Harbour?" he said, mainly to himself. "This place is meant to be exclusive."

"Don't kid yourself," Nightingale said. "This is Toytown. Give it ten years, it'll just be another council estate. And besides . . ."

"Sash. *Look!*" Barnes hissed.

There was movement in the building opposite, in the fifth-floor hallway. Barnes checked his watch — 2.37 a.m.

He scribbled on the log, moved to the window and squinted. He picked up the binoculars and looked out across the lock.

"Here! Move back from the window," Nightingale whispered hoarsely.

"Ssh! I'm trying to see . . . Van Leer! It's Van Leer! He's left the apartment. He's taking the stairs, all the way down. He's running!"

Nightingale made a grab for her radio. The static and feedback whined as she switched it on.

"Control, this is Hotel-Sierra nine-one-eight . . ."

Nightingale's words were cut short as Barnes whipped round and clapped the radio out of her grasp. The handset clattered across the parquet floor.

"What the fuck are you doing?" Nightingale yelled.

"Don't call it! Let him run. He's in breach."

"Yeah, which means we keep the OP static and call up for local units," Nightingale said.

"Are you serious? They won't get here in time. Do they even know we're here? I'm going after him."

"You're bloody well not. We do not blow the OP, we call for local backup."

"Look at him. He's running flat out!" Barnes cried.

Howard Van Leer was indeed running. His face, in the pale-blue interior lobby lights of the apartment block, was drawn and pinched with fear. He charged down the stairs, stumbling several times, before he collapsed in the lobby. He hauled himself up and ran through the door connecting the lobby with the underground car park.

"He's in the car park. He's in the fucking car park!" Barnes yelled.

"I've got to call this," Nightingale said. "If he's got a car then we're fucked, and it'll be my arse all over for letting a pursuit happen."

Barnes watched through the window. No car came, but after about fifteen seconds a dark figure emerged from the underground car park. Howard Van Leer was huddled over a pedal cycle, freewheeling across the courtyard.

"He's on a bloody bike," Nightingale said.

"I'm going after him," Barnes said.

"Fuck you, PC Barnes. You stay put. This is my OP, and I'm ranking officer here!" Nightingale barked in a cracked voice.

Barnes stared at her for less than a second.

"Like hell you are."

He turned and raced out of the house.

CHAPTER EIGHT

Barnes gunned the car onto Atlantic Drive. His heart was in his mouth now — he had taken the risk of preventing patrol cars from flooding the area, but if he hadn't been quick enough to keep sight of Van Leer, then it was an ill-conceived gamble.

The road ended by a boatyard. A path led past the yard to the massive lock gates joining the north and south harbour, and Barnes ditched the car. He continued on foot and broke into a run — Van Leer had been out of sight for three or four minutes, and the need to find him overrode his need for caution.

His feet landed heavily on the metal plates that formed the crude walkway across the lock gates. The metal buckled slightly under his weight, and the dull clanging sound thundered around the lock. He grimaced and froze, his eyes scanning frantically for any movement beyond the lock that might indicate that he'd betrayed his position.

Beyond the lock, out on the sea, the dredger *Sospan Dau* was performing her annual task of regurgitating the shingle around Sovereign Harbour. A sludge of water and recycled shingle spurted from a pipe on her bow like a geyser, the noise a distant, steady rumble.

An empty lifeboat and a fishing trawler were the only two vessels in the lock. Barnes sensed movement, and his eyes came to rest on the trawler, its faded paint and grimy hull in stark contrast to the fleet of sleek yachts and cruisers that floated in the marina.

Barnes edged along the walkway, and saw two fishermen — one young and skinny, the other middle-aged and heavyset — arranging nets on deck, their faces intermittently illuminated by the pulsing red light at Langney Point.

They saw him, alerted by the noise he made on the walkway. He locked eyes with them, and they met his stare with expressionless gazes. Neither side broke the stare for several seconds, each trying to gauge the intentions of the other. Barnes eventually dug in his hand for his warrant card. He held it aloft, a silent talisman to ward off suspicion.

The older fisherman nodded slightly, raising a finger towards the residential area in the north harbour beyond the lock gates. Barnes nodded back and crept across the walkway. The dark green surf in the lock churned and seethed as the water levels rose to allow the lock gates to yawn open. Barnes turned to look and saw nothing beyond but black.

He followed the path underneath the huge, elevated hulls in the boatyard and into Pacific Drive — a sweeping road circumventing the residential building sites. A cool wind was rolling in off the Channel, masking any sound that might have alerted Van Leer to Barnes's presence.

Pacific Drive rounded ninety degrees and curved into a handful of new developments — detached family houses, apartment blocks and pastel four-storey townhouses. The residential areas were flanked on all sides by skeletal breeze block carcasses reinforced by steel rods and scaffold. These unfinished buildings sat on muddy, remote sites littered with machinery and had a frozen, unfriendly feel; bereft of any lighting, they loomed black against the maroon night sky.

Pacific Drive swept round to the left and Barnes broke into a trot — he couldn't be far behind Van Leer, but he was in danger of losing him in the jungle of machinery and scaffolding.

Just as his hand went to his radio to call off the embargo, Barnes spotted Van Leer's cycle lying on a grass verge. He slipped the radio back into his pocket and followed the path into one of the few completed residential estates. The spread of townhouses was sporadic, and the amber wash created by the street lights shrank away from the darkness of the huge unfinished construction sites.

Barnes stood at the corner of a cul-de-sac and scanned the houses frantically, trying to banish the feeling that he had lost Van Leer.

Then his eyes became fixed on a white sugar-cube corner townhouse. He stared at the house, trying to fix on why it seemed out of place, and on a second sweep he saw the wide-open downstairs window, the curtain fluttering in the breeze.

Barnes edged forward and crouched behind a car parked on the street, concentrating fiercely for signs or sounds of movement. Van Leer was in the house — he *had* to be.

He held the radio up to his mouth, then hesitated. Should he call this? Or should he wait for Van Leer to come out, wait until his pockets were stuffed full of whatever the unfortunate householder owned, so there could be no doubt, no loopholes at all for him to wriggle out of? He considered it briefly — waiting would mean apprehending Van Leer on his own, which he had done before without any misgivings, but he had seen the look on Van Leer's face when he ran out of his bail address, and he *knew* he would fight.

The silence was suddenly broken by the elastic howl of a fox from a nearby garden, and Barnes jumped in shock.

"Jesus *Christ!*" he exclaimed, flattening himself against the car and taking huge breaths as the adrenaline continued to surge around his system.

Barnes wondered what Nightingale was doing. Would she have called it in after he'd left? She had no reason not to, but he couldn't rely on that — she didn't seem to be quite functioning on a linear plane of logic at present.

He fished around in his pocket for an earpiece and attached it to the radio to minimise the risk of being overheard. He jabbed the transmit button and whispered into the microphone.

"Sierra-Oscar, Hotel-Sierra nine-one-eight."

A beat.

"Nine-one-eight, go ahead, over." The controller's voice sounded loud in his ear. Barnes turned the volume right down.

"Nine-one-eight, surveillance unit on suspect Howard Van Leer, date of birth twenty-seven, twelve, nineteen seventy-four. Burglary in progress — he'll be coming out in a minute. Requesting marked units to assist with detention and transport. And a dog handler if there is one. Silent approach, please."

"What's the location, nine-one-eight?"

"St Lawrence Way, Sovereign Harbour North."

"Roger for that." The controller rattled off the information over open air — four cars called up at once. After a one- or two-minute interlude, Barnes saw the familiar blue strobe of police cars radiating from over on the coast road about a mile away. *No lights, no lights*, he muttered to himself.

As if answering Barnes's silent plea, all the lights were shut off as the cars got closer. As they approached, the controller began to direct them to the front and rear of the townhouse, placing another on a static point on Pacific Drive. A dog handler was directed to the point of entry.

Come on. Barnes clenched his fists. *Come on.*

* * *

"Please . . . don't hurt me."

The woman shrank against the cupboards, a prisoner in her own kitchen. She tried to pull the flimsy silk robe around her naked body, and in doing so the glass of water she had come downstairs for fell from her grasp and spilled across the linoleum.

The intruder stood in the doorway, a large Puma hold-all on one shoulder. The woman recognised it as her husband's, and the intruder had presumably filled it with their belongings.

The woman managed to regain some semblance of control.

"Please . . . just take what you want. I won't stop you."

Hoping desperately that the children would not come downstairs, she moved her hand an inch towards the phone on the worktop. The LCD display on the handset read 2.51 a.m.

"I couldn't sleep. I just came down for a glass of water. Please . . ."

"Get out . . . my fuckin' way," he snarled, advancing.

She inhaled and allowed her robe to fall open. The intruder stopped. She watched his eyes drop to her breasts, following her gym-fit stomach down to the tiny triangle of black.

As a hungry scowl crossed his face, she wondered if she'd made a terrible mistake, but she had to assume her distraction attempt had been successful, and she made a grab for the phone.

She froze when the Stanley knife appeared.

Howard Van Leer chopped the blade down onto the Formica worktop, and whipped it across the surface towards the woman's hand, knocking the phone onto the floor.

"You bitch," he said. "*Bitch!*"

He took three quick steps towards her. She backed away down the kitchen into the dark dining room, the blade at his waist glinting even in the gloom.

"Please . . ."

She got no further. Van Leer lunged forward and brought the blade up diagonally in a slashing arc from his waist up to head height, slicing the woman across her robe as he did so. She stumbled backwards, tripped on a coffee table and fell in a heap. Van Leer paused again, to watch the thin ribbon of red erupt across her chest, the edges of the wound curling back like waves breaking away from the shore, and then he stepped out into the night.

She tried to pull herself to the phone, a trail of blood slicking out across the carpet, her mouth opening and closing as she silently begged for her husband.

* * *

The front door to the house opened. Howard Van Leer stood in the doorway, carrying the Puma holdall over one shoulder and a black bin liner full of somebody's belongings in the other hand. *How is he going to carry all that on a cycle?* Barnes wondered absently.

He immediately regretted asking himself this, because Van Leer walked over to a brand-new silver Audi TT parked in the driveway, put down the two bags and pointed something at the car which made the hazard lights blink a couple of times in unison, making a *blip-blip* sound as they did so.

Barnes hissed into his radio.

"Oscar, nine-one-eight. Suspect Van Leer is out of the house. Repeat, suspect has left premises."

"Roger that, nine-one-eight. You still have visual?"

"Yeah, but not for much longer. He's stealing the car."

"Index please, nine-one-eight?"

"It's, er . . . Papa . . . Charlie . . . Mike . . . One. Cherished plate. Silver Audi TT."

"Keep the commentary coming, nine-one-eight. Units almost with you."

"He's in the car! Suspect making off in the car . . . oh fuck it . . ."

As Barnes heard the car start, he dropped the radio on the ground and sprinted over to where Van Leer was fumbling with the Audi's transmission. Barnes saw the reverse lights illuminate and the car began to edge out of the driveway.

He covered the fifty yards in only seven seconds or so, but it was enough time for Van Leer to have pulled out onto the road. By the time Barnes was within grabbing distance of the driver's door, Van Leer had seen him. Panic lit up the burglar's face when he saw the policeman at the window.

In the split second before Van Leer stamped the throttle, Barnes made a brushing, flailing grab for the door handle. The car headed out of St Lawrence Way just as a patrol car swung in. Barnes ran forward, waving his arms at the Audi, but the police driver was already turning around in the road. Blue lights ignited the street and the patrol car flew after the Audi.

Barnes, some considerable distance from his own car, ran after the two vehicles, collecting his radio from the pavement without stopping, picking up segregated clips of radio traffic as he ran.

"... suspect headed east on Pacific Drive in silver Audi TT, speed fifty miles per hour ... failing to stop ... right-right-right off Pacific Drive into Wimpey unmade building site ... believe will decamp ... dog please ..."

Barnes ran flat out along Pacific Drive, following the direction of the blue lights.

"Suspect has decamped . . . repeat, suspect has decamped . . . need containment on now . . . more units please, and where is the dog . . . ?"

Van Leer had abandoned the car outside a building site about two hundred yards up the road. Barnes got to the mouth of the site — and pulled up short.

Provided the patrols had Van Leer contained, the burglar was bang to rights. There would be no downshifting of charges this time. Would Barnes's presence jeopardise that? Would him being here taint his later identification evidence, creating some kind of Code D get-out clause? Did he even *need* to be here?

Then he recalled the times he'd been on patrol and turned out en masse with his team to a barely coherent radio shout from some covert operation that had got unexpectedly messy — nine times out of ten they had cursed the fact that a detective wasn't present to make some sense out of all the chaos.

Something else occurred to him. If Van Leer *was* bang to rights, a better opportunity to indulge Denniker's whims would be unlikely to present itself. Once Van Leer was back inside, it would get a whole lot more complicated.

Barnes ran past the car onto the murky site, leaving the bright glow of the residential street lighting behind him. The moonlight reflecting off the puddles meant he managed to pick his way through most of them, but the unmade ground was still difficult to negotiate.

Ahead of him was a black, unfinished apartment block. Two patrol cars had already pulled up — four officers in high-visibility jackets were standing at various corners of the building. Another two marked cars and a dog handler roared past Barnes to meet up with the others.

There was a bolt of movement in the darkness as the dog handler pulled up. Two uniformed officers sprinted after the blur, followed by the dog handler, who released her charge from the cage of the van.

Barnes heard "Runner! Runner! Into the building . . ." on the radio, and there was silence. Thirty seconds passed, and then a strangled burst of activity filled the airwaves.

". . . dog's got him . . . bitten . . . resisting with a golf club . . . some help please . . . one officer injured, but not badly . . . still fighting . . ."

The remaining officers ran into the building after their colleagues and, a minute or so later, Van Leer was carried out in cuffs and full restraints. He was struggling furiously.

Barnes walked over to the Audi and peered inside. DVDs, two laptops, a few mobile phones and a handbag were among the spoils of Van Leer's venture, spilling across the rear seat in the pursuit. Barnes wondered if he'd been stocking up for the winter.

Barnes moved slowly around the car, careful not to touch anything, when a glint caught his eye. He leaned in through the still-open driver's door, and shone his torch on the front passenger footwell.

His eyes widened with alarm as he registered the blood-spattered blade of the Stanley knife.

"Hey," he called to one of the uniformed constables. "Stay with the car."

Barnes ran back to the house, barking into his radio as he did so.

"Sierra-Oscar, Hotel-Sierra nine-one-eight."

"Nine-one-eight, go ahead."

"I need an ambulance to the burglary scene, please."

"Age and condition of casualty, nine-one-eight?"

"I'll let you know. Just get them rolling."

He ended the transmission and arrived at the house. A trail of blood spots began on the driveway — where Van Leer had flung the knife into the car — and led back towards the house.

Barnes snapped on some latex gloves and followed the blood into the house, urgency taking over his movements as the blood trail went from spots to splashes to a substantial pool by the dining table. Barnes swallowed and shone his torch frantically around, wondering what he was going to find.

From the blood pool in the dining room the trail changed to a long, continuous drag mark that led to the living room. Barnes ran into the room and switched on the light.

"Oh, shit . . ."

She had managed to pull herself onto a sofa and was barely conscious — either from shock or blood loss, Barnes was unsure. He shoved his torch into his pocket and yelled into his radio to get the ambulance there, quick.

The silk robe was sodden with blood, and had fallen open like a flap of soggy skin where she lay. Barnes grabbed a throw from the back of the sofa and clamped it over the wound, trying to preserve her dignity at the same time.

She was murmuring something unintelligible. Barnes brushed hair from her pale, clammy forehead, and told her in a soft voice not to worry, that everything would be fine. He asked her if there was anyone to call, but she was too weak to make sense.

Blue lights strobed into the living room from outside, and two fit-looking paramedics thundered into the house, utility belts bumping against their green uniforms. The male paramedic scrabbled around in an orange go-bag, while his female counterpart, clutching a defibrillator, rushed forward to check the woman's vitals. They went about their business with urgency and confidence, and Barnes's breathing and pulse slowly returned to normal.

He backed quietly out of the door, returning to the scene of the arrest with his warrant card out. A single uniformed cop was standing by the rear of the patrol car, writing in his notebook. As Barnes approached, he recognised the cop and slowed his pace. His old team were on night duty tonight. He should have realised.

"How you doing, mate?" Barnes said, brightly. The lad had been one of Holden's pallbearers.

The cop squinted in the gloom. "Barnes? That you?"

"I'm afraid so."

"You're the one called it in? You're not happy unless you're ruining Howard Van Leer's day, are you? Good little job, this."

"The car's full of the stuff from the house. Plus the knife he stabbed the occupant with."

The cop's eyes widened. "Bad?"

"She'll live." Barnes looked past the cop's shoulder at the site. "The others stand down already?"

"No, they're doing a sweep with the dog. Think he might have ditched some stuff before we got him."

Barnes nodded. "Good. Thorough."

"We do function in your absence." The cop wasn't smiling. "Nice for a detective to turn up, though."

"I didn't mean—"

"Listen, seeing as you're here, you mind watching him for a moment?" The cop nodded towards the interior of the patrol car. "The others could probably do with some help."

The cop disappeared off into the darkness without waiting for an answer. Barnes looked down at his hands. The blue latex gloves had been turned purple by the woman's blood. He pulled them off and dumped them in a biohazard receptacle in the boot of the patrol car, then pulled on a clean pair.

He shut his eyes, feeling for the presence of the thin envelope in his pocket. He put one hand on the door handle — and hesitated.

Was this even necessary? Third-strike burglary — three years' minimum, aggravated by possession of the knife. Stabbing the householder — that added a wounding charge. The evidence was overwhelming — assume a guilty plea. Even so, that had to make it at least seven years' imprisonment.

That was still well short of a sentence for a murder conviction. And he thought of Phil McDermott, and the slippery defence case he would no doubt mount — had *already* mounted. Barnes had thought the burglary of Holden's house was watertight, but he'd quickly been proved wrong.

He opened the door.

He got in next to Van Leer. The air in the back of the car was thick with pepper spray residue, which wormed its way into Barnes's throat and eyes.

Van Leer's hands were cuffed behind him, forcing him forward. He was still suffering the effects of the pepper spray — his head was slumped downwards, his eyes clamped shut, and strings of saliva and mucus hung thickly from his nose and chin. He didn't — couldn't — acknowledge Barnes, or even register his presence. In the quiet Barnes listened to his laboured, staccato breathing.

"Howard?" Barnes said. "What are you running from, Howard?"

"Fuck . . . you . . ." Van Leer managed between breaths. His voice was shrill.

After another five minutes or so Van Leer's breathing began to ease.

"Howard, who killed Harriet Holden?" Barnes's voice seemed to have dropped an octave, and he barely recognised it. He stifled a cough.

"Don't know no fuckin' Holden. Fuck, that stuff hurts."

Barnes produced a packet of fresh cigarettes and unwrapped it. He did not smoke, but during his brief partnership with Cathy Nightingale he had discovered that two essential accessories for a detective — fake warrants notwithstanding — were new cigarettes and cash. He pulled out a cigarette and placed it between Van Leer's lips.

Without his eyesight, Van Leer flinched at the thing in his mouth, then he realised what it was and his brow furrowed at this unexpected act of charity. He twisted his head dumbly towards Barnes. The spray had worn off a bit, and he was able to open his eyes enough to squint, like a newborn starling coming into the light. When he realised it was Barnes, some of the aggression seemed to seep from his body.

"You again? Fuck, you get around. Loosen these off a bit, would you?" Van Leer asked, shaking the cuffs behind him. "They're killing my wrists."

Van Leer shifted in his seat so he was facing the window, and Barnes removed the handcuffs and arm restraints.

"So, this where the detective saves me from the storm troopers and tells me how much trouble I'm in, right?"

Barnes shrugged. "You don't need me to tell you that. But don't say anything. All in good time."

"What are you doing here, then?"

Banes shrugged again. "Someone's got to sit with you till it's time to go. The others are still busy."

"I'm not complaining. Something about that uniform. The only way they know how to talk to people is like they're a piece of shit."

"Do you get to see your son?" Barnes asked, lighting the cigarette. Van Leer sucked at it desperately, like it was the last one he'd ever get.

"Now and then. Depends how bad into the gear I am. You know what it's like, copper. A junkie on a bad one can't think of no one but himself."

Barnes said nothing. The vapour in the car was stinging his eyes and caking on the back of his throat.

"She won't let me see him when I'm using. I don't blame her. She's clean now, so she don't want me near her or the baby. I respect that."

"That's a good incentive for getting clean, then, isn't it?"

Van Leer didn't reply, but continued to smoke in the darkness.

"I mean, what are we looking at here?" Barnes continued. "Aggravated burglary, maybe robbery, wounding with intent, aggravated TWOC, resist arrest, assault police, failing to stop." He made an exaggerated show of doing sums on his fingers. "If you kick while you're in prison, then you might get to see him by the time he's old enough to vote."

Van Leer didn't say anything, but his eyes gleamed in the darkness, and it was a second or two before Barnes heard him start breathing again.

"Why did you run, Howard? What are you scared of?"

"Fuck off."

"I don't get it. Why don't you start being a bit more helpful? We know you're not the only one involved. Why take the rap for someone else?"

"I've been in prison a couple of weeks, Officer. Pretty good alibi."

Barnes moved closer to him and touched him on the shoulder. Van Leer hung his head again and wouldn't meet Barnes's eye.

"Yeah, you have. But we know you know something about it. Telling us might just make you another witness. Not telling makes it conspiracy."

Barnes turned as the ambulance raced past them towards the hospital, blue lights flashing. He needed to get a move on.

"You made a right mess of that lady." He turned back to Van Leer. "And at the moment you're the only one under the spotlight. Whoever you're protecting, you think they'd do the same for you? They're probably all off somewhere, laughing at how easy it was to leave all this shit at your door."

"Yeah, I'm under the spotlight. And so are you." Van Leer looked up and parted his dry lips in a gummy grin. The dirty light from the construction sites made it look like a grimace.

"What do you mean?"

"You're going places, Officer. It's obvious even to a smackhead like me. You're on the up-and-up. People like you have a lot to gain, but you've got even more to lose."

"What are you talking about?" Barnes had been unsettled once before by Van Leer's sing-song arrogance, and it made him uncomfortable.

Van Leer dropped the butt and ground it into the floor of the patrol car with his foot.

"You think I'd be this stupid? To get caught for all this lot? Breaching my bail and all the rest of it? I could have just slept in and ordered pizza."

"Looks to me like that's exactly what you've done. I'm just trying to work out why. Why make life so much worse for yourself?"

Van Leer didn't answer, but hung his head and hissed laughter through his teeth. Barnes got annoyed. The hard bit wasn't going to require quite as much Dutch courage as he'd thought.

"You really fucked this up, didn't you? Whatever idea you had about helping us, helping yourself, helping your kid, you cocked it up from day one. Too much of your solicitor making you believe you're the victim in all this, too much feeling sorry for yourself and too much bloody gear."

"Fuck you, copper." The grin evaporated. Barnes shoved him up against the window and reapplied the handcuffs and seatbelt.

"Ouch! Christ . . ." Van Leer said to the glass.

"You had one go at your life, Howard, and you flushed it down the toilet. You made your own bed, but what really gets me is that you and some other junkie scumbag managed to bring a child into this world. You made your own choices, Howard, but you've already made them all for your son as well. You've managed to fuck up Liam's life already . . ."

Van Leer's head snapped round from the window, and he spat violently in Barnes's face, strings of saliva and snot spattering over Barnes in a sticky web. Before Barnes could react, Van Leer was launching himself at the detective — screaming, kicking and butting like a billy goat, despite being somewhat restrained by the cuffs and seatbelt.

Three uniformed constables heading back from searching the apartment block carcass saw what was happening. They ran over, flung the doors open and attempted to subdue Van Leer on the back seat, while Barnes removed himself from the rear of the car.

He moved quietly away while they wrestled, and touched a forefinger to his face. The mess was already starting to dry off, making his skin itch. The feeling of sticky wetness was revolting; some was hanging off his top lip. Resisting the urge to wipe it off, he carefully removed the envelope from his jacket.

He extracted a single piece of paper from the envelope. He touched his face again, and transferred some of the viscous muck to his gloved finger. There was a strong south-westerly blowing off the Channel, and the paper flapped in the wind, making a sound like a rapid drumbeat.

He moved over to the partial shelter of a huge yellow JCB and crouched below the scoop. When there was a lull in the gusts, he collected more of the fluid on his thumb and finger, and smeared it onto the paper as carefully as possible. When this was done, he inserted it back into the envelope.

Van Leer was still struggling in the back of the patrol car, which was rocking on its suspension as though containing passionate lovers. One of the constables emerged and went round to the driver's door while his colleagues continued to fight with Van Leer in the back. The wheels spun and the engine howled as they took off in the car, strobes lighting up the street in a blue corridor through the darkness.

Barnes stood up and stared after them. He pulled off the gloves, flung them into the darkness, and slid the envelope back into his jacket pocket. Alone now in the empty construction site, he watched the blue lights become a blip on the coast road and fade to nothing in the distance.

"Gotcha," he whispered.

CHAPTER NINE

When Barnes arrived at the station, his three uniformed colleagues were dragging their captive up the concrete steps in the police station garage through to the main cell block. Van Leer had stopped fighting, but he was still violently cursing the officers and anything else he apparently thought of.

Van Leer was marched to the charge desk and the custody officer began scribbling details on a clipboard — the creeping vines of information technology had yet to penetrate the custody records system — while Van Leer was searched and had his property removed from him. Barnes had not seen the custody officer before — she was young and pretty. He shook his head. He seemed to be seeing Harriet everywhere.

The iron door clanged behind him, and he turned to see Phil McDermott standing behind him. *Christ, that was quick,* Barnes thought.

"Mr McDermott? We're quiet tonight." The custody officer stopped writing and scratched her temple. "I didn't know you'd been called. Are you here for another client?"

McDermott didn't answer.

The custody officer continued, "Your client's been arrested for burglary and wounding. I'm just giving him his

171

rights. He's asked for his brother to be informed of his arrest, but I'm holding him incommunicado, I'm afraid."

McDermott remained silent. He looked tired, as if he hadn't been awake long. He was dressed in jeans, trainers and a Millwall football shirt. He wore no socks, and he was unshaven. His eyes were bloodshot under his heavy brow, his head tilted to one side like a curious primate.

The custody officer, a little hesitantly, continued writing. One of the constables removed Van Leer's handcuffs and then turned to Barnes expectantly. The other two patrol cops followed his gaze.

Barnes hesitated for a moment. Strictly speaking, he was part of the surveillance operation and therefore wouldn't normally be quite this close to a suspect, but then he figured that Van Leer had seen him so often recently he practically had him on speed dial. Besides, Barnes had caused this mess, and it wouldn't do much for uniform relations if he were not around to help mop up afterwards.

Barnes began to address the custody officer directly, explaining the grounds for the arrest. When he mentioned that Van Leer had been seen entering and then leaving the house laden with stolen property, and that the householder had suffered slash wounds, Barnes turned away from the custody officer to look at Van Leer.

He would have done better, however, to remain fixed on McDermott. Barnes was suddenly aware of a flash of movement in the periphery of his vision, as McDermott sprang at Van Leer.

McDermott, snarling, fired two quick jabs at Van Leer's face and two more at his torso. Van Leer was on the floor before any of the officers present had time to move.

Barnes was the first to react. He grabbed McDermott from behind and pinned his arms back, but McDermott, an ex-street fighter, was strong and broke his grasp quickly.

He leaned over Van Leer and continued to fire punches at him. Van Leer howled on the floor.

"You fucking prick!" McDermott yelled as he swung shots into Van Leer's skinny frame. "You break into my house? You stab my wife? You cut her up! I'll fucking murder you. I'll fucking . . ."

By now all the police in the room had taken hold of McDermott and pulled him away from his victim. In his rage, McDermott had entirely forgotten his affected diction — his furious volley of expletives had been delivered with a thick East End accent.

The officers now had McDermott pinned prone, and Barnes felt the tension suddenly abandon the solicitor's body. The custody officer hauled Van Leer off the floor and into the medical room while the others dragged McDermott to a cell. McDermott lay on the cold floor in an incoherent ball, wailing sobs convulsing his body.

One of the cops slammed the cell door shut and the group dispersed to their respective duties — which, in all cases, involved a lot of writing.

The cell block corridor was suddenly quiet. Barnes felt a sudden urge to get out of there, pronto, but as he walked past the medical room, the custody officer beckoned him in. It stood to reason — a violent assault had happened right in front of her, and *she* wasn't going to be the one writing it up.

The custody officer was treating Van Leer. He had two impressive black eyes, and his nose was a misshapen mess. Barnes tried not to dwell on the fact that the last time he'd been in here, Holden had been alive and treating *his* wounds.

"I ain't being interviewed," Van Leer said, while the custody officer dabbed at his face with cotton wool. "I got nothing to say."

"Then you risk being charged without having the opportunity to put forward your side of the story," she said, holding a compress to Van Leer's face with a gloved hand.

Van Leer snorted hollow laughter into the compress.

"Me own defence brief done ABH on me. It don't get much worse than that, does it? Charge me, missus, and let's call it a day."

"This officer will take your statement," the custody officer said.

"We'll prosecute him," Barnes added from the doorway.

"Be a waste of your time and paper. I got nothing to say about it."

"Okay, have it your way. See you in court."

Barnes turned to go.

"Listen, copper." Van Leer's voice was cracked and hoarse.

Barnes stopped, and turned back. There was resignation in Van Leer's eyes.

"I'm sorry I spat in your face. You said some pretty rancid things, though. Didn't think that was your style. I almost thought you was winding me up on purpose."

Barnes stared at him for a second, then turned and left the cell block.

* * *

In the car, Barnes carefully removed the envelope from his jacket, and sealed it inside a polythene evidence bag. He took a deep breath and filled in the details.

The exhibits store was closed. All out-of-hours seizures were logged into the property store, a huge warehouse that sat between the patrol centre and the MIS.

A security light flicked on as he approached the transit store, a tiny cupboard adjacent to the warehouse where stuff was dumped out of hours for sorting in the morning. The transit store was all-purpose — whereas major crime exhibits would be taken direct to the MIS during the day, after 4 p.m. they shared the same space as volume crime exhibits, lost property and anything else that couldn't be housed.

Barnes exhaled heavily and logged the photograph into the property system and generated a receipt, which he marked up OP CHRISTCHURCH — EXHIBITS OFFICER.

No going back now. A shudder passed through him — was this what Denniker had meant when he had spoken of cops making their own justice? Barnes didn't suppose it was meant to feel quite this horrendous.

On a shelf in the transit store was a massive polythene bag stuffed with items from Holden's house. A SOCO — or whoever — would carry the whole lot up to the exhibits officer in the morning for it to be logged onto HOLMES. Barnes tucked the slim evidence bag in among framed photographs, books, CDs, videos, the contents of a bin, some stuffed toys — the stuff had yo-yoed from packing boxes to shelves and dressers and then back into storage, only now their owner was dead, and the purpose of packing it all up quite different.

Barnes stood back and surveyed the bag of stuff. It looked like it had been slung in without a care, as if in anticipation of taking it to a boot fair or the rubbish tip. He'd had misgivings about Denniker's plan remaining undetected, but now, looking at the jumble of stuff, the likelihood of the photograph being lost in the pack and given only cursory attention seemed considerably better.

He shut the door of the transit store and walked towards the MIS. The massive building was still and silent in an unreal orange glow, and seemed twice its normal size in the darkness. Barnes posted the envelope with the property receipt and walked to his car, looking at shopping trolleys and other nameless detritus floating in the Horsey Sewer as it trickled alongside him on the other side of the perimeter fence.

The entire site was entrenched in the midst of an industrial estate. Even at this deathly hour, it was alive with the hum of factory units and the pulsing buzz of a huge electricity pylon immediately overhead. Opposite the patrol centre sat a cement mixing plant and industrial laundering depot, frozen in the glow of powerful security arc lights.

Barnes drove to the hospital, taking the long, straight avenue of Lottbridge Drove, where the bright neon trademarks of the motor and fast-food industries lined either side of the road. At that time of the morning, A&E was mercifully quiet, and he had his face properly flushed and a blood test for hepatitis within minutes.

He wondered how soon it would be before Van Leer's profile was flagged up on the system. Forensic submissions for a murder investigation were fast-tracked — it could be less than twenty-four hours. When a fingerprint match or a full DNA profile identified a suspect on an otherwise cold investigation, the system went bananas. Alerts went off, the report had "FORENSIC HIT" stamped all over it, the briefing system put out automatic disseminations, and half the district got an email about it, even if it had nothing to do with them.

And this was just for routine volume crime. For murder enquiries the forensic process was a painstaking affair, and nothing happened without the SIO knowing about it. With the current situation, the most complicated part of the process would be adding the photograph to HOLMES, the operation's indexed investigation database, and making it look like it had been seized along with everything else in Harriet Holden's house.

But that was Denniker's problem.

Daylight was a couple of hours away when Barnes finally crept into bed. Eve was sleeping on her side. He curled up behind her, reaching over with his arm to pull her to him.

"I love you, Eve," he whispered into her shoulder, hearing the guilt in his own voice. "More than you can know."

He wrapped his arms around her and held her close. He tried to speak, tried to apologise for not being there, his mind still plagued by what he had done and what he might yet do.

"Ssh," she whispered, reaching back to touch his hair. "Ssssh."

She turned over and nestled in the crook of his arm, her head on his chest. He stroked her hair till she fell asleep. He gently kissed the top of her head and inhaled her smell.

The curtains in the bedroom were open. A bright slit of crescent moon rose across the sky into his view, casting a chalky glow across the walls. The refracted headlights of cars rumbling past rolled across the ceiling. He remembered being a child, remembered the movement of cars outside and their lights entering his room, and how it comforted him in the darkness, how it kept the bad dreams away. He clamped his eyes shut, a feeling of helpless, desperate need suddenly powerful inside him. Where was the child he could protect? Why could he not be a father? Why was it so difficult?

Barnes squeezed Eve close to him, suddenly overcome by a need to protect her. After tonight, he already felt like she had lost a little bit of him to his work, along with a little piece of his integrity. He did not want his career to be the only thing about him; by the same token, he did not want his wife to be forever defined by the thing they could not have.

She made a tiny sigh in her sleep. Barnes lay back and stared at the ceiling, feeling his eyes begin to prickle. He tried to push the feeling away, but a tear as cold as steel ran down his cheek and fell onto the pillow, while the moon continued to slowly rise.

CHAPTER TEN

Constable Harriet Holden had either been killed for no reason by an untraceable someone, or she had been killed by
her mysterious boyfriend — whom no one could identify,
despite the painstaking investigation.

Paul Hadian found the former hypothesis highly
improbable, but could not discount it. He found the second
theory much easier to digest, because he was convinced that
if they identified the boyfriend, the motive would present
itself. Yes, this theory was far more palatable, all except the
part where they could not actually identify him. This didn't
sit well with the DCI. It stuck in his throat and made him
choke. Hadian didn't drink to excess; instead, he internalised
his stresses. He was a coronary waiting to happen. He knew
this, and it worried him, which in turn only increased the
risk.

The forensic strategy for Op Christchurch had become
increasingly broad. When the primary lines of enquiry —
eyewitnesses, murder weapon, CCTV of her last movements,
an inescapable motive — had dried up, identifying Holden's
boyfriend had become the priority objective by default, and
so, working on the assumption that whoever it was had been
to her house, they had started with the obvious — glasses,

cups, knives and forks. When that drew a blank, they moved onto CDs, gloss-covered books, tissues recovered from the bin, the works. Holden's entire life was being shipped up to Lambeth by the truckload.

Hadian knew that he had reached a bottleneck in his career, that he would ascend no further before retirement or a premature death claimed him. Attaining rank had not come easily to him. His detective's brain had got him this far, but above and beyond here the requirement to be able to regurgitate politically friendly psychobabble was mandatory — all clever labels for common police sense, in Hadian's view, dreamt up by some overpaid graduate at Bramshill or somewhere. He would never get around to being able to spout drivel for the cameras like Denniker. Hadian would never make assistant chief constable. Crime and criminals were all he knew.

Even this, however, had caused him some disillusionment in recent years. He had begun to convince himself that there was no secret skill he possessed that allowed him to catch the nasty bastards before others did, no magic formula that allowed him to follow up on gut instincts and make daring extrapolations to link hitherto independent theories.

No, in Paul Hadian's view, a successful investigation came down to luck. Your witness makes a positive identification at a parade, it's luck. Your armed robber happens to be caught on CCTV leaving the scene, it's luck. Your car thief cuts himself escaping after a chase, leaving his DNA at the scene, it's luck. That, and the stupidity of the criminal who's so off his tits on heroin that he passes out in the house he's trying to burgle. Diligent, meticulous investigation might shorten the odds a fraction, but it really all came down to luck and stupidity. That was what Paul Hadian believed he had based his whole career on, and it was why the police clear-up rates hadn't changed much since the Bow Street Runners.

And so far, in this investigation, he'd chanced upon no luck at all, nor stupidity on the part of the murderer. He was beginning to get the distinct impression that the investigation was slipping away, and that Harriet Holden's vicious — and apparently motiveless — murder would go unpunished. The same tried and tested lines of enquiry that would be followed in any investigation had turned up nothing. No CCTV, precious little forensic evidence, hardly any intel, no eyewitnesses, no motive, no weapon — just an impossible theory about Howard Van Leer.

Natasha Warwick had refused to sanction a charge of Van Leer as a conspirator, and she had warned him about putting all his eggs in one basket. He knew she was right, but in the absence of any other workable leads there was little else he could do, and he was tired of hitting the usual CPS brick wall.

He tapped his pen on the keyboard of the computer that had been forced upon him the previous day. The police were losing their autonomy, and he was losing his grip. Before long the lawyers would be coming in and running the investigations, like they did in the bloody States. Seemed like he couldn't even wipe his nose without referring it to the CPS first. What had happened to the days where the police formulated the charges and decided who they were taking to court? What had happened to the days of presenting a case properly to the jury and letting them decide on the facts? If the police believed a person to be guilty, why not present the jury with the same things the police had seen and let the jury make up their minds? He liked Natasha Warwick, but the CPS's insistence on deciding the outcome themselves before it got anywhere near a court was draining him.

It was all numbers, of course. Performance and statistics. The police didn't want to be filing jobs when they knew who was responsible — they wanted them in court and another solved crime on the books. The CPS didn't want to run a job that wouldn't succeed at court, because they had targets to meet as well — too many acquittals and withdrawals did not make a pretty graph. What sort of eulogy was that to give to a poor dead copper?

Van Leer screwed a copper's house and left a death threat on her wall. When they checked out his room, they found the same police officer's dead body. He'd obviously known about it, even if he didn't actually do it. *What more do you want, Ms Warwick?*

He was distracted by a pop-up message on his computer — YOU HAVE NEW MAIL.

He leaned forward and clicked on the box, and his email program appeared on the screen. It really was quite easy to use. The subject field read: OP CHRISTCHURCH DNA IDENT — SUSPECT TO SCENE.

Hadian sat forward, a little more interested, but also annoyed. The SIO of a homicide enquiry ought to get a phone call from the lab, at least, not a stock-generated email.

He opened the email. His jaw dropped.

OP CHRISTCHURCH
CRIME NUMBER: E41/2831/01
HO CLASS. 1/1 (MURDER — VICTIM AGED
ONE YEAR OR OVER)
DNA IDENT[1] SGM+
SUSPECT-TO-SCENE[1]
EXHIBIT PRH/37 — SEIZED FROM SCENE(1)
— 4 MONCEUX ROAD, EASTBOURNE
(HOME   ADDRESS   OF   VICTIM).
PHOTOGRAPH   BEARING   SUBSTANCE
BELIEVED SALIVA. FULL PROFILE MATCH
— VAN LEER, HOWARD. D.O.B. 27/12/1974.
PNCID 485838/86B.
THIS EMAIL HAS BEEN FORWARDED TO
THE SIO. PLEASE ADVISE THE CRIME
DESK OF INTENDED ACTIONS.

"I'll tell you my bloody intended actions," Hadian muttered as he picked up the phone and began to jab the buttons.

* * *

Eve clutched her husband's hand as they rode the lift to the top floor of the hospital and stepped out into the reception area. Barnes read the plaque on the wall — *Assisted Conception Unit.*

The hospital was in Hartington Place, nestling between the seafront and the town centre. It was an imposing white stucco building set in tranquil green grounds. The inside was like a country hotel, with the kind of trappings that Barnes assumed were *de rigueur* for private healthcare, but the long corridors and high ceilings spoke faintly of wartime casualties and anguished convalescence.

Barnes had only managed to sleep for a couple of hours. It didn't feel like his feet had touched the ground. He'd had no time at home, no time with his wife, no time to stop and think about anything. He was getting paid for it, but six-teen-hour days were not healthy for anyone. He'd had more energy working nights in uniform, for God's sake. Life was easier then.

And the thought of the photograph, safely ensconced in the HOLMES system and somewhere between here and Lambeth, was like a cloud at the back of his mind, know-ing that Hadian would soon get notification of the forensic result, and then it would be all systems go. This feeling on his conscience was clawing at him, dragging him downwards, and the sickness in his stomach refused to be shifted.

As such, despite his promise to Eve, he had made no calls to arrange for the morning off, other than to the court to establish that Van Leer's court hearing was not until after lunch. This was no small relief to him, and it did not take much inward persuasion to simply switch his phone off and accompany his wife without a further word to anyone.

The bottle had claimed his father prematurely, and so Barnes's own teetotalism was self-imposed for health reasons — the feelings of being virtuous and being able to run faster and faster sufficiently intoxicating.

At least, they had been, to date. The thought of one or two ice-cold beers to help him unwind and forget — about the case, Van Leer, the stack of unopened bills, everything — for a few hours was suddenly irresistible.

He blinked tired eyes as he announced their arrival to the receptionist, and waited for her to tell them to sit down. He was surprised when she handed him an envelope and a small plastic pot.

"What's that for?" he asked.

"You have to provide a sample before the consultation." She was young-looking, with an angular face and a tone like a butcher's knife.

He leaned forward across the desk.

"Er, I don't think it's me that needs assisting, if you see what I mean."

"It's mandatory, sir. Have you given a sample before?"

"Well, no. But . . ."

"The room is just down the hallway and on your left."

The conversation was over. Barnes turned around and looked at his wife, who was grinning more widely than he had ever seen her grin before. He padded down the corridor with her and found the door. It was the only one without a name plate on it, so by process of elimination Barnes assumed it was the correct room.

"Shall I wait out here?" Eve asked, still grinning.

"Are you joking? I need moral support."

"I'm not sure that's allowed."

Barnes went in. He paused for a moment in the doorway; Eve looked left and right, then, when the coast was clear, snuck in too.

It was like a tiny room in an old run-down hotel. The high walls, ceiling, pipes and ancient radiator were all pink, and a couch lay in the corner, underneath a frosted window. A coffee table was situated next to the couch, covered in several well-thumbed pornographic magazines.

"Oh, *yuck*!" Eve exclaimed, picking up a magazine and flicking through it. "This is so gross. I mean, is this stuff supposed to *excite* you?" She held up a centrefold and showed it to Barnes.

He didn't answer.

She bounded across the room and sprang onto the couch. She patted the space next to her.

"Come on, Chief, you don't need porn. I'll sort you out." She hadn't stopped grinning.

He began to protest, but then thought about it and sat obediently next to her.

"Where's your pot?" she asked. He gave it to her.

"You could put on a bit of a show or something," he said, laughing now.

"Don't be daft. This is *medical*."

"At least undo some buttons."

"Okay then. There. Now, you'll have to hold the pot, I think. Make sure you aim right, or we'll be here all day waiting for another go."

"That doesn't sound so bad."

"Are you joking? This place charges by the *hour*. Now, concentrate."

She got into her stride, and began to whisper and moan seductively in his ear, punctuated as it was by a giggle every few seconds.

Fifteen minutes later, Barnes emerged with the envelope and handed it to the receptionist, engaging her in conversation while Eve crept out of the room.

Eve was more cheerful than he had seen in a while, and Barnes realised he had underestimated just how much this meant to her. It meant a lot to him too, but the fear of failure and disappointment was enough for him to long to call the whole thing off.

The consultant was kind, and took them through the possibilities, the risks and the costs. It was really just an information session, but they booked the next appointment and arranged some tests. They didn't speak in the car, but Eve smiled as she looked out of the window, and held her husband's hand all the way home.

* * *

The magistrates' court was deserted, apart from two scraggy-looking creatures sitting in the foyer.

"Pig!" one hissed at Barnes as he walked past into Court 1.

"Pond scum," he muttered in riposte, albeit under his breath.

Barnes entered the empty courtroom, a huge, windowless wood-panelled chamber. The royal crest adorned the wall behind the bench. Other than a low whirring noise from somewhere deep in the building, the place was silent. From the back of the court Barnes recognised Natasha Warwick. Her jacket lay on the seat beside her, and the tight pencil skirt was making another appearance. She stood alone at the prosecutor's seat, sifting through the stack of files that formed her afternoon's remand cases.

"Listen to this," she said, not looking up. Her voice echoed around the empty courtroom. "Petty thief arrested for receiving, yes? According to the officer's report the stolen property was recovered after conducting enquiries at the local 'porn' shop." She spelled out the word. "P-o-r-n."

"I can top that."

"Pah!" Natasha Warwick threw down her pen and folded her long arms.

"A bunch of intel reports came our way last month about a guy who keeps sawn-off shotguns under his bed. He'd been bubbled up by his Auntie Virginia, who thought planning armed robberies wasn't a very Christian thing to do. Unfortunately, four syllables threw the submitting officer a bit — so he went for V-a-g-i-n-a."

"And people wonder why the CPS have this apparently ill-conceived notion that police officers don't have two brain cells to rub together," she said in exasperation.

She leaned against the green leather seat, as if only just noticing Barnes.

"I see you're here with Mr Van Leer again. Getting to be quite a couple, you two."

"We caught him doing another burglary," Barnes said, sitting down on the edge of the clerk's desk.

"Then that's three strikes for Mr Van Leer. Very straight-forward — section 51 transfer, straight to Crown Court. And there's no lay bench today, it's District Judge Melville."

"The stipendiary?"

"Yep. Defence solicitors tend to throw in the towel when there's a stipe sitting. Phil McDermott will be spitting when he finds out the surety's been forfeited."

"Er, you could be more right than you know."

Natasha Warwick stood with an open mouth and wide eyes while Barnes recounted the story of the previous night, and the injuries with which Howard Van Leer would be appearing in the dock. Her eyes moved around the courtroom as she processed the news, and questions began to surface.

"So . . . so who's representing him?" she asked when she had recovered from the shock.

"I've no idea."

"It wouldn't be ethical for anyone else at Wedderburn's to do it. It would have to be another firm entirely. What are you doing about the assault allegation?" The question sounded like a demand.

"There won't be one," Barnes said, stiffening slightly. "Van Leer won't put pen to paper."

"Balls. There must be CCTV or something." She seemed genuinely indignant. Barnes tried to fend her off as casually as possible.

"Mrs Warwick, anyone would think you *wanted* to see Mr McDermott prosecuted."

"Well, it would make a change from his standing next to me spouting Latin and being obnoxious. And it's 'Miss'."

She emphasised the correction by holding up her naked ring finger.

"My apologies."

"Charge him with violent behaviour in a police station. No bail. I'll sanction it. Will his wife be okay?"

"Traumatised to hell, but she'll live. She lost a fair amount of blood, but they patched her up well."

"Thank God you found her when you did. Poor woman. Phil isn't the most popular of defence solicitors — and that's saying something — but I wouldn't wish that on anyone."

She was quiet for a moment. Barnes looked up as people began to fill the courtroom — probation officers, a small flotilla of defence lawyers and a thin woman sitting in the public gallery. She was ebony-haired, with a hurriedly constructed ponytail, and looked no older than about twenty-five. She wore thick glasses and was scribbling furiously on a notebook. Barnes recognised her as one of the gaggle of reporters he had seen in Jevington Gardens during the execution of Operation Warlord.

He turned back to Natasha Warwick.

"How have your seniors decided to progress the murder charge in light of my advice?" She punctuated the word "seniors" with the raise of an eyebrow.

"They've let it go, for now. But they won't let it rest. Denniker's convinced Van Leer's a conspirator and should be prosecuted as such. We're looking to seize the records of Van Leer's telephone calls to and from the prison."

"Are you applying to the Crown Court for the recordings?"

"Yes. I could do with your help, actually. The application is drafted, but . . ."

"Don't worry. I can hold your hand."

She had switched back from dragon-lawyer to concerned mentor. Barnes was starting to feel a little bit like a plaything, but the conversation was cut short by his mobile phone. He retreated outside to take the call.

"Hello? DC Barnes."

"Hello, Mr Barnes. This is Helen from the Assisted Conception Unit. I'm sorry to trouble you, but . . ."

He sighed. "I'll call you back, okay?" He ended the call.

The phone rang again, almost immediately.

"Look, I said . . ."

"Barnes." It was Hadian. "Where the hell are you?"

"At court, sir. Van Leer," he said innocently, as if it were the most obvious thing in the world.

Hadian was quiet for a moment.

"Don't tell me he got bail."

"His case hasn't been heard yet, sir. In fact . . ."

"I've heard the McDermott story," Hadian interrupted. "As long as he's potted, I'm happy. Just get back here as soon as you're done. Christchurch briefing. New information."

Christ, that was quick. The excitement in the DCI's voice was palpable. Barnes closed his eyes. He'd known it was coming, just not quite this soon.

"Really?" he said, not sure if he should be sounding casual, pleased, surprised — or all three.

"I'll tell you when you get here. We'll be in the conference room."

Barnes ended the call. Information was only as good as the people being informed.

He sat on a low wall outside the court building, staring at his shoe. The wan look Van Leer had given him in the medical room wormed its way into his mind and refused to budge.

Denniker had tried to convince him that Van Leer was guilty, and that this was the only way to achieve justice and see Van Leer punished for his part in the crime and his refusal to implicate his associates. The Chief Superintendent had tried to blur the moral boundaries separating the legal from the factual, and had insisted that, although they were playing outside the rules, the result would be the correct one.

But, whatever the nature of Denniker's proselytising, Barnes had planted evidence on a suspect and taken money for it. Denniker had blinded him with promises, but now he realised that words like "inauguration" and "golden handshake" were purely euphemisms for simple bribery. That was the naked truth, and Barnes suddenly had a horrible suspicion that the issue of Van Leer's guilt was not so clear-cut.

Despite wearing his arrogance like a shield to keep the cops out, Barnes had seen the look on Van Leer's face when he ran from the apartment. Real fear. He'd never let on — at least not to the police — but something spooked him that night. He'd gone on to burgle a house of someone known to him, but why? For convenience? Because he needed gear promptly and knew what he would find?

He drummed his fingers on the wall and thought about Eve. She would be disgusted with him, perhaps more so than if he were actually unfaithful. And it was the extra money that was going to fund their fertility treatment — unlikely they could afford it otherwise.

He screwed his eyes shut and pinched the bridge of his nose. How would he tell her? How do you tell a child that they were conceived with dirty money?

Oh God, what have I done?

"That was a big sigh."

He looked up. Natasha Warwick. He stood.

"You're done already?"

"Uncontested hearings with unrepresented defendants seldom tend to be complicated."

"How did it go?"

"Remanded in custody. Prelim's next week — Lewes Crown. I need you there, really."

"Consider it done."

She touched him lightly on the forearm and grinned.

"Got time for a coffee?" she asked.

Barnes hesitated. He was not sure he could go another round of sparring with Mrs Robinson, but equally he was in no hurry to face Hadian, which greased his thoughts.

"I'm buying," she added.

"Something tells me you wouldn't take no for an answer."

They walked past the station, down Grove Road, and sat outside the coffee bistro opposite the Central Library. Natasha ordered two cappuccinos and Barnes carried them to the table. The bistro called the street-side seating a terrace, but it was really no more than part of the pavement covered by an awning. Natasha took off her jacket and hung it on the chair, then stretched in the sunlight.

"I hear you aced the detectives' exam." She added sugar to her cup, and then produced a cigarette. She held it up in between two scarlet fingernails — *Do you mind?*

"Yeah, I did okay," Barnes replied, shaking his head. He looked over at a short queue of traffic as it stopped at the pelican crossing.

"Modest as well," Natasha said. She lit the cigarette and sat back, crossing her legs. "So, Detective, presumably you have concocted a hypothesis about this murder investigation?"

Barnes shrugged. "Technically, I'm only looking after the burglary charges. Murder hypotheses belong to the DCI." He sipped his coffee, and the bell of the town hall further up the road chimed three.

"The cases are all part and parcel. The burglaries will keep him off the streets for the foreseeable future, but you're an integral part of the murder enquiry as well. Come on, what are your thoughts?" Her tone was eager, like a professor trying to extricate the maximum potential from an errant student.

"Well," Barnes began slowly. He didn't want to be openly disagreeing with a senior officer in front of the CPS. "I think Van Leer is the tip of the iceberg. Without wishing to undermine the SIO's policy, I think to put the focus solely on Van Leer may be at the expense of identifying others who may be involved."

"Yes, my thoughts exactly." Natasha leaned forward. "What I can't understand is *why* Chief Superintendent Denniker is so keen to focus purely on Van Leer when he is, as you say, the tip of the iceberg. Or, perhaps more anecdotally, he is just garnish."

"He has an alibi," Barnes said in a monotone.

"*He has an alibi*," Natasha repeated. "Like you, I don't doubt that he knows something about it, but that isn't enough to charge him — or anyone else for that matter." Her voice got louder as her thoughts gained momentum. "Personally, I think the police have got this wrong by hanging him out to dry. With his new charges it doesn't matter whether he's convicted of burgling Constable Holden's house or simply handling stolen goods. He's going away for a long time in either case."

Funny, I said something similar to him last night, Barnes thought.

"He's a broken man, DC Barnes. You should be exploiting that. He no longer has a lawyer. Cosy up to him, treat him as a witness. Buy him a McDonald's — anything to get him to open up. If you can just get him onside, I'm sure it will snowball."

Barnes blinked rapidly in the sunlight while Natasha used him as a sounding board. As well as making perfect sense, this woman's insights and interest in the case were disturbing him. Could it really be that easy to get Van Leer to talk? Had Denniker's plan been completely superfluous — and, in turn, the shame he now felt?

He shifted in his seat, suddenly uncomfortable. He felt like he was in an Edgar Allen Poe story — much more of her theorising and he might jump up and run down the road, screaming his guilt to the heavens.

"You know, for someone with such a low opinion of the police, I almost think you secretly want to be a copper," Barnes said as casually as he could, in an attempt to cauterise the conversation.

Natasha smiled at him and blew some of the froth from her cup.

"Delusions of grandeur." They locked gazes for a moment. Barnes looked away. "So, what does your wife think of your rapid career ascent?"

Barnes paused, trying to think of a neutral subject. He didn't want to talk about the case, but he wanted to talk about Eve even less.

Natasha's eyes bored into him while he fumbled for an answer, and then his phone rang. It was Hadian. He mouthed *"Excuse me . . ."* and took the call, the discomfort in his veins momentarily neutralised.

"Barnes, are you done at court yet?" The DCI sounded impatient.

"Yes sir. Just this second. Remanded in custody."

"Good. Get your arse back to the office."

"I'll be right there, sir."

He shut the phone, glad of the excuse to leave.

"Duty calls?" Natasha asked.

"I'm afraid so. Urgent meeting. Thanks for the coffee."

"I'll see you next week. At the prelim." She smiled and stubbed out the cigarette.

He nodded and began the short walk back to the police station, feeling her eyes on his back. He paused on the steps of the station to turn his face briefly up at the sunshine.

His phone vibrated in his pocket. He pulled it out and read the text message:

Keep meaning to ask — what's ur FIRST name? NW x

He didn't reply. As he made to go, his phone rang again. He took a deep breath before answering.

"Hello?"

"Mr Barnes?"

"Yes?"

"This is the ACU. We've tried to call you a couple of times."

"I'll have to call you back, okay? Now isn't good."

"But . . ."

He hung up.

* * *

Barnes slipped inside the conference room and apologised for being late. Hadian and Denniker were waiting for him.

"What have you got?" Hadian asked, eyeing Barnes as he sat down.

"Van Leer was remanded in custody about half an hour ago. He wouldn't have legal representation — refuses to have it — and I imagine he'll plead guilty at some point soon. Prelim's next week."

"Good work. I apologise for the impromptu conference — it's deliberately small-scale. We've had something of a new lead in the Christchurch investigation," Hadian began. "We've had a DNA hit on our friend Mr Howard Van Leer.

His saliva was discovered on a photograph — a photograph found in Constable Holden's house."

Barnes looked at his feet, unable to meet his boss's eyes. Hadian addressed Denniker.

"Sir, I plan to produce him from prison and interview him about this. I am then going to charge him with conspiracy to commit murder." Hadian was clearly excited.

Denniker folded his arms.

"Saliva?" was all he said.

"Obviously we'll need to interview him about it, but it's possible that he kissed the photograph," Hadian said.

"Demonstrable sexual obsession, perhaps?" suggested Denniker, looking at Barnes.

"Or aggression. He has previous for spitting at police officers," Barnes replied, looking at the floor. "It's just as likely that he was making a point."

"That would certainly correspond with the message he left at her house. In any event, we can now forensically place him inside the house — at the very least, the burglary charge will stand. We just need Barnes to sort out the prison's recordings of his phone calls, see if he dropped himself in it, and then we'll charge the bastard."

Barnes tried to gauge the commander's expression — what could a conviction do for his promotion prospects? Denniker's eyes seemed glazed, as if he were already rehearsing the speech, or mentally trying on the title *Assistant Chief Constable Clive Denniker* for size. Perhaps he was imagining how his new chief officer signature would read.

"He has an alibi for the murder, but he threatened her from his cell, made oblique references to her safety while in prison, and her body was then found in his flat by two police officers. With his refusal to explain, there is more than enough circumstantial evidence to charge him, and I don't give a damn what the CPS say." Hadian was standing ramrod-straight, his fists balled by his sides, the scent of success renewing his confidence in both himself and the investigation.

"Good work, Paul," Denniker said quietly.

Barnes tried not to grimace. He caught Denniker's eye and the unspoken contract passed between them. Guilt and shame had threatened to cripple him from the moment he slipped the photograph into the exhibits store, but this was now being superseded by fear — fear of being caught.

"Sir, you will need to arrange some form of press release when he's charged. There will be national interest, I've no doubt," Hadian continued.

"Doubtless, Paul." Denniker sounded like a parent trying to settle an overexcited schoolboy. Barnes wondered if he was feeling the same, or whether this was all water off a duck's back to him.

"Barnes?"

"Yes?" Barnes nearly leapt out of his seat at the mention of his name.

"I want you to get Van Leer out of Lewes Prison as soon as possible for interview. I will fast-track the production order with the governor. We're going to nail this bastard."

"Okay, sir," Barnes said, trying to share his boss's enthusiasm as a means of ignoring the nausea that was now churning his stomach. The production order Hadian was referring to was a formal request made of the prison by the police. If granted, it allowed the police to take a prisoner out of prison to a police station to be questioned about matters other than those for which the individual had already been imprisoned in the first place.

"I will assign you a new partner for the production. I don't want either of you to think that Nightingale's misper enquiry is being sidelined, but this takes precedence."

The image of Van Leer's wretched face had been swimming, ghost-like, around Barnes's mind, but at this latest disclosure from the DCI it vanished. He looked up sharply.

"Missing person enquiry? Nightingale isn't missing."

There was silence. Barnes could hear traffic outside. Hadian sat down, his voice dangerously quiet.

"What do you mean?"

Barnes took a breath, knowing something was wrong — more wrong than it already was. He placed his palms flat on the table and steadied his breathing.

"I worked the OP with her last night. She turned up twenty minutes after me. Said you'd deployed her."

"I haven't seen Nightingale for days," Hadian said through gritted teeth. His eyes flicked from Barnes to Denniker and back again. "What did she have to say for herself?"

"Not a lot," Barnes said. "Said she was there at your instruction. Said she was never missing. Then Van Leer tried to do one, and the conversation kind of ended. I pursued Van Leer. I left Nightingale in the flat."

"What else?" Hadian asked, barely controlling his anger.

Nightingale's remark about Barnes being a suspect crossed his mind, but he kept quiet, instead trying to recall what else Nightingale had said to him the night before.

"Well, there *was* one other thing. She was dropped off at the OP by some woman. Said she was job, that she works at HQ. Said you'd cleared it."

"Case closed?" Denniker enquired of Hadian, with more than a trace of irony. He produced a futuristic-looking mobile phone and began tapping a message.

"Something is very wrong here," Hadian murmured, more to himself than anyone else. "If she's been absent from work for nearly three days, how the hell would she know about the mechanics of a covert investigation?"

"I don't know, sir. But at least she's alive," Barnes said, trying to remain upbeat.

"Believe me, being dead is the least of her worries," Hadian snapped. He rubbed his forehead with the back of his hand. "Thank God I kept this meeting low-key. What the sodding *hell* is she up to?"

"Question for you, Paul," Denniker said brightly, putting the phone away. He seemed to be almost enjoying the DCI's discomfort.

Hadian shut his eyes. "Go ahead, sir."

"If Nightingale is in fact alive and well, where the hell is she now?"

CHAPTER ELEVEN

Cathy Nightingale sat at the gym bar, watching men enter from a packed car park. The gym was one of several leisure, retail and entertainment bolt-ons built to service the surge in the construction of new residences in the Sovereign Harbour development.

There was a standing joke around the station that, in keeping with the characteristics of the harbour's inhabitants, the only people that patronised Levine's were cops and criminals. Like all good jokes, it was based — at least partly — in fact.

The clusters of heavy men continued to swarm out of the April sun into the refrigerated building. None of them were over twenty-five, Nightingale mused. Back when *she* was twenty-five, this consumer's paradise hadn't been here. Back then, fat families in tracksuits did not descend for an afternoon of spending other people's money. When *she* was twenty-five, all those years back, she'd already been in the job five years, and her occasional weekends off had been set aside for football and overtime.

Her mind drifted further back. When she'd been a little girl, her dad had taken her shrimping when the Crumbles had been nothing but a spread of mudflats from Eastbourne to Pevensey. Then development had spread like a malignant tumour — a nightclub and holiday park for the baby boomers at King's Park had had the fun knocked out of it in the 1980s by a particularly rough patch of social housing. This had been followed by retail warehouses — multiplex, supermarket, discount furniture and sportswear — at the back end of the twentieth century, around the time they started digging up the harbour. Then the residential part of Sovereign Harbour itself had started to erupt — houses and apartments shooting up like mushrooms, to meet a hungry demand from Londoners and others who wanted some weekend sunshine by the sea. By the time they'd finished, Nightingale mused, the inhabitants would be like sardines in a concrete tin.

She signalled for another drink, recognising the heavy curtain of depression that had been sinking over her for some time. Being alone with her thoughts and memories was only accelerating its descent.

She looked up at the clock over the bar, and idly noted that she'd been here over three hours — one hour working out, two perched on a stool knocking back double G&Ts. *A lady's drink*, she thought, and guffawed inwardly. Her limbs had been aching from lifting weights, but the booze was warming her muscles through nicely.

She sensed someone next to her at the bar. He was wearing a pale-yellow gym singlet with a blue Nike logo, and his bare, heavily muscled arm brushed hers. He was right in her personal space, and she could smell his sweat and sickly-sweet deodorant. He was so close that conversation of one form or another was unavoidable. She fixed her gaze ahead, buggered if she was going to be the one to initiate it, unless it was to tell him to get fucked.

She had a good three inches on the man, who was a few years younger and solidly built. He had a scar at his left temple and a zero-crop all over that, had it been allowed to grow, would have been a vibrant red.

John Callaghan.

The barman brought Callaghan a tall glass of sparkling water, and he perched on the bar stool.

"What are you having?" Callaghan asked her, pulling the towel from around his neck to mop his brow.

She didn't look at him, but waved her empty glass at the barman, who brought another G&T without a word.

"Good workout?" Callaghan asked.

"Yep. A thorough afternoon session, to blow out all the cobwebs and keep my GP happy." Her sing-song sarcasm was bordering on bitter.

"Was it a heavy night?" he asked. His voice was soft, and she thought she detected a note of pity.

She finally turned to him, fire in her green eyes.

"Why don't you just say what's on your mind?"

He spread his hands in a conciliatory gesture.

"Okay. Are you planning on driving home?"

"What's it to you?"

"You stink of booze. I can smell it on you from a mile off."

"Do me a favour, okay? Leave me alone."

"You shouldn't drive. I'll run you home."

"You can keep the intervention for another day. I don't need saving." She sank her G&T in one and got up to leave.

He touched her lightly on the arm. "Don't do it. I'll drive you home."

She snatched her arm away, picked up her sports bag and left the gym.

Callaghan cursed his rotten luck. He waited ninety seconds, then pushed his own drink away, grabbed his bag and followed Nightingale.

He ran out of the double doors at the gym entrance and scanned left and right. The car park was heaving with Saturday afternoon shoppers and cinemagoers, and Callaghan thought he'd lost her. Then he saw a flash of pink from Nightingale's tracksuit bottoms. She was about a hundred yards away, dumping her sports bag into the boot of her Audi.

"Cathy!" Callaghan called. Nightingale appeared not to have heard him as she walked to the driver's door. Callaghan began to jog over. Nightingale opened the driver's door and stepped in, inserting the keys in the ignition before closing the door.

"Cathy!" Callaghan yelled again. People heard the shout and turned to look at him. He broke into a trot, then a full sprint as Nightingale started the engine.

Callaghan reached the car and banged on the window. Nightingale had not yet put the car in gear. She wound the window down, like she'd never seen him before.

"What do you *want*?" she said.

"Cathy, for Christ's sake, it's not worth it. I can drive you home and even bring you back for your car tomorrow, if you want."

"I *said* I'm all right." Her lips curled in an angry scowl.

"Cathy, suppose you hit someone?"

"Don't preach, John." Her tongue was thick with booze.

"Who's preaching? Why are you being so fat-headed?"

Nightingale put the car into gear and gently squeezed the accelerator. The revs climbed a little.

"Cathy, for Christ's sake. Don't put me in this position."

Nightingale released the handbrake slowly, as if she were taunting Callaghan. The car began to edge forward. Callaghan walked alongside the car as it rolled forward into one of the car park's exit lanes. She took her hands off the steering wheel and folded her arms.

"Cathy, what's the matter with you? Someone's going to call this in."

The car picked up a little speed. A four-by-four laden with children and shopping bags in equal measure bore down on Callaghan and Nightingale. It angrily belted the horn and swerved around them at the last minute. A small crowd had gathered to watch the unfolding spectacle.

As Nightingale's Audi reached the end of the lane leading out of the car park, Callaghan realised she had hit her self-destruct button. A hypothetical image of a nine-year-old lying crumpled on the side of the road appeared in his mind, and he made his call.

In one swift movement Callaghan grabbed the handle, flung the door open and snatched at the keys. He switched off the ignition, and the engine shuddered and died.

Nightingale made no effort to resist. The car continued to coast forward with what little momentum it had left.

"Cathy, dammit! This is dangerous. Hit the brakes, will you?"

Nightingale softly pressed the footbrake, and the car rolled to a stop. The crowd of spectators had now tripled in size. Some of them were speaking on their mobile phones.

Nightingale sat motionless. Callaghan pocketed the keys and squatted down beside her at the open door.

"Hey, Cathy." His voice was soft. "Cathy, are you okay?"

Nightingale said nothing. Her eyes were glazed and staring somewhere off in the distance, maybe looking at the gulls pirouetting over the harbour. She was breathing heavily, and she reeked of drink. Callaghan was amazed that she'd even managed to get the keys in the ignition.

"Are you all right, mate?" The voice was gruff, but not unkind. Callaghan sensed the man appear behind him. "I've called the cops. Lucky this silly cow didn't hit a kid."

Callaghan shut his eyes.

"Thanks," he said, without looking round.

Nightingale's green eyes began to mist with tears.

Callaghan stayed where he was, his hand on Nightingale's shoulder, while they waited the seven minutes for the traffic car to arrive. Not a further word was said between them.

The spectators had started to lose interest, but it was quickly rekindled when the powerful Volvo traffic patrol car roared into the car park with lights and siren blaring. Callaghan couldn't stifle a grimace.

The patrol car pulled alongside Nightingale's Audi; the tyres screeched and the car rocked forward on its suspension as it came to an abrupt halt. A traffic inspector got out of the passenger's side. The driver, a constable, produced a breath kit. Callaghan didn't recognise either of them. Like cobras moving in for the kill, they both donned their white hats and walked slowly over to where Callaghan stood with his de facto prisoner.

"Just step away please, sir," the constable said, placing a palm on Callaghan's chest. "We'll take it from here."

Callaghan bristled. The constable was little more than twenty-six. The temptation to swing for the guy — or worse, get his own warrant card out — was strong.

He mustered his self-control and moved several paces away from the car. He turned around and shut his eyes, and didn't turn back until he heard the unmistakable sound of ratcheting steel.

He turned and saw the constable with his handcuffs out.

"Is that really necessary?" Callaghan asked the inspector. Both traffic officers glanced at him just long enough to impart their thoughts, which Callaghan correctly interpreted as, *You've done your bit, now we've got it, so fuck off.*

"Just back off, sir," the constable said with a poorly concealed sneer. The *sir* was redundant — he may as well have been addressing Callaghan as *scumbag.* Callaghan, like many supervisors, did not relish dealing with complaints, but these two definitely deserved a couple. If they spoke to everyone this way, it was no wonder people hated the police.

The constable went to clap the cuffs on. Nightingale offered no resistance.

"Your warrant card, Officer." This was the inspector. Nightingale did not answer. Callaghan wondered idly how they had worked out Nightingale was a police officer. Had they already checked the car out before arriving and recognised the name? Or maybe Cathy had already told them, out of Callaghan's earshot.

The inspector fished in Nightingale's inside jacket pocket and pulled out a small black leather wallet. She began to cry softly as she was marched to the patrol car and put in the back. "And the car keys, please, sir."

This was to Callaghan. The inspector's attempt at *sir* was slightly more convincing, but not by much. Callaghan tossed the keys to him without a word. The inspector missed them, and scowled at Callaghan as he scooped them off the tarmac.

The inspector walked to the other rear passenger door and opened the flap of Nightingale's warrant card to look at the photograph and badge. As he did so a small piece of paper fell out of the leather wallet and fluttered to the ground. The inspector didn't notice, and climbed in next to Nightingale.

The Volvo was roaring away before the inspector had shut his door. From arrival to departure, the traffic boys had been on scene less than six minutes. They were nothing if not efficient.

The spectators gradually melted away into Asda and Sportsworld and the multiplex, leaving Callaghan alone with Nightingale's car. He walked over to the Volvo's tyre marks and picked up the tiny piece of paper from the dusty concrete.

It was a passport photograph of a man. It was an old photograph, but Callaghan recognised him as Nightingale's ex-husband. He turned it over. It read, "*To Cathy. With all my love always, Mike. Sep '87.*"

Callaghan wasn't sure, but he thought Nightingale had been divorced for over ten years.

She still kept her ex-husband's picture in her wallet.

Callaghan slipped the photograph into the breast pocket of his shirt and vowed to return it.

* * *

Barnes walked into the kitchen to find an excited Forbes, who nearly knocked his master over with his enthusiastic greeting. He fetched food and water for the beast, and walked into the living room. Eve was sitting on a chair by the window, busy with her sewing machine. Rays of evening sun flooded through the bay window, casting a soft, golden glow on his wife's face and highlighting the tiny, almost invisible hairs on her arm as she worked.

He sat down on the sofa next to her and pulled his tie loose.

"Hello. What are you doing?"

"Making some curtains." She didn't look up. Forbes nosed at her feet. "Go away, dog. Or lie down quietly."

She hung the first curtain. Forbes got the message and slunk over to Barnes, who fussed over him for a moment until he settled. The Labrador sat next to Barnes, stealing doleful glances at Eve.

"It looks fantastic. Brightens the place up. Maybe you should sell some. You're good enough."

"Thank you." She still didn't look up, but instead put the sewing down. She hung her head, and Barnes noticed her shoulders start to gently shake.

"Eve, honey, what's the matter?" She did not answer. "Eve?" His voice was quiet.

She looked up at him. Tears were starting to well in her brown eyes. Barnes felt a sinking in his stomach as he wondered if she was going to say, *I know what you did, and I can't believe it,* and he vowed there and then that this was the only secret he would ever allow himself to keep from her. He did not want to live a life where every night he came home worrying that his wife would have discovered his latest professional disgrace. It hurt him to realise how easily he could make her weep.

He went over to her, and cupped her face in his hands.

"Eve . . . what is it? What's going on?"

Her lips were tight, pinched white with self-control.

"The doctor called. He's put us on the waiting list for a donor."

"That's good, isn't it?"

She shook her head.

"It could be months. Maybe even years. No guarantees. And he gave me an estimate."

He shut his eyes. "Go on."

He held her hand when she gave him the astronomical figure. The little avenues of hope were slowly being severed by slamming doors. How the hell were they going to get that much together?

"I can't believe it. I just can't," she murmured. "All this, just because of a missing tube or whatever. All because of *me*!" She prodded at her stomach angrily.

"Hey," he said gently, taking her hand. "Don't do that."

He kissed her on the forehead. A sob escaped her. She stood and went upstairs. Forbes made to follow her, his tail wagging, but he became doubtful and lay down at the bottom of the stairs.

Barnes sat on the sofa for a long time. Eventually he crept upstairs and peeked around the bedroom door. Eve was lying on her side, with her back to the door. Barnes covered her with a blanket and went downstairs again.

His willingness to answer his phone had been waning of late, but it suddenly occurred to him that the hospital had been trying to call him too. He picked up the phone to check for messages, but it rang before he could listen to them. He jumped up to shut the door so it wouldn't disturb Eve. The DCI's number appeared in the display. His heart sank, and he ignored the call.

It rang again. Like the cantankerous detective he could see himself becoming, he cursed the device and yearned for the days before such things had been invented.

"Hello?"

"Barnes? I hope I'm not disturbing you."

"No, sir."

"Well, I've got good news, bad news and something in the middle. Which do you want first?"

CHAPTER TWELVE

"She was *what*?"

It was Monday morning. Barnes was sitting in Hadian's office. The Welshman was tapping a can of Coke on his desk with a pencil.

"Arrested. Saturday afternoon."

"What for?"

"Drink-driving. Thursday night she showed up at the OP under the radar. Friday afternoon we got the DNA hit and the revelation that she wasn't missing at all, thank you very much. Then, Saturday afternoon, the silly arse decided to go on a bender after a workout. She bumped into John Callaghan, who smelled the booze and decided to do the decent thing and nick her. Traffic came right along, and once *that* lot were involved, it was always going to be textbook. About as flexible as a cruise missile, the fucking wooden-tops. CID and uniform relations have been set back a hundred years."

"Jesus. Will she plead?" Barnes ran a hand through his hair, unable to believe what he was hearing.

"It would be difficult for her not to, but it depends on the advice."

"Who's representing her?"

"You'll like this. Want to guess?" Hadian's tone was sour. Barnes closed his eyes.

"Don't say Phil McDermott."

"In one."

"What's she thinking of? What about her job?"

"The disciplinary stuff will be put off till after the court case. First hearing's next week. She's on suspension, and unless she's acquitted, which is unlikely, she will almost definitely lose her job. God's *sake*. Couldn't Callaghan have just given her a lift?"

Hadian's eyes had been roaming around the room while he spoke, and Barnes wondered if he were talking more to himself.

"Mate of yours, isn't he?" Hadian's eyes had now settled back on Barnes.

Barnes frowned at the DCI's accusing tone. "He was my sergeant when I was on section. Just before I came to you."

Hadian said nothing, but held Barnes's gaze.

"Turns out this wasn't just a bender, though," the DCI said after a moment. "I knew Cathy liked a drink, but she's got a full-on problem."

Hadian finally stopped tapping and pushed the Coke can across the desk to Barnes. Barnes said nothing. He sniffed it. Tasted it.

"Vodka."

"She's been drinking on duty for years. I never realised."

Barnes thought of the cans of soft drink that lasted all day, and the powerfully scented tubes of lip balm Nightingale used on a regular basis. He thought of the acres of empty bottles in Nightingale's flat, and realised he wasn't surprised in the slightest.

Hadian was shaking his head, clearly intent on self-blame.

"I'm sorry, Barnes."

"What for?"

"For compromising a new detective. Not only that, but — word to the wise — some of the other detectives know you're friends with Callaghan. They may give you a hard time."

Barnes looked up.

"I had nothing to do with it. I'm hardly *responsible* for him."

"Loyalties run deep in this job. Fanatically so. Just be careful," Hadian sighed. "Now for the good news. I called the prison today, see if I could put some weight behind Van Leer's production order, speed things up a bit. Spoke to one of the screws. 'That's a coincidence,' he says. 'We were just going to call you.'"

Barnes frowned. Speeding up the production order was the last thing he wanted. "Oh, yes?"

"Yes. Mr Van Leer has found God — or something. In any case, he's had a touch of the seconds and wants to talk. He knows we've got DNA evidence, and he knows he's going to cop a charge sheet, so he's decided to save his own skin and turn Queen's."

Barnes said nothing.

"Did you hear what I said? The little skaghead is finally going to tell us who the real killer is. He doesn't even want immunity from prosecution — by cooperating he can wriggle out of a conspiracy charge anyway, and frankly, I don't think he minds being in prison. He hasn't even asked for a lawyer."

"That's . . . good news."

"You see? Tactics." The relief on the DCI's face was palpable. "Mr Denniker is over the moon. He might salvage his career yet, and I might get to enjoy my retirement in peace."

"Has anyone told Harriet's mother?"

Hadian frowned. "Well, let's not count our chickens, eh? Let's hear what his information is like, then get the horrible fuckers in the bin first."

"Okay."

"As soon as you get that production order, you let me know, okay? We can't sit on this."

"Yes, sir. Wasn't there something else? We've had the good news and the bad news."

"Oh yes. Thank you for reminding me. There's a community partnership conference next week. Denniker wants me to go, and I'm buggered if I'm going alone. So I suggested it might be a good opportunity for an ambitious, up-and-coming young officer. He thought that was an excellent idea."

I bet he did, thought Barnes, realising that the divisional commander had him over a barrel. "Okay. No problem. What's a community partnership conference?"

"Oh, you'll love it."

Barnes raised an eyebrow to further prompt his boss. Hadian just grinned.

"Wait and see. Just wait and see."

* * *

It was the same receptionist on the hospital desk. She smiled this time, and seemed generally more agreeable. This, in Barnes's book, meant bad news. The giving of a sperm sample was meant to be a formality, but something told Barnes that, in this case, that it was not.

He drummed his fingers in the waiting room, trying not to look at maternity catalogues, *Mothercare* magazines and other apparently innocuous reminders. He checked his watch. He'd shouted over his shoulder as he left the office that he was going to get some lunch, and he'd only been gone twenty minutes. He hadn't thought the consultation would be a long one, and he didn't want to trouble Hadian by asking for time off for personal problems.

Eventually he was called through. The consultant looked harried. Wisps of wiry blond hair stuck out from his head at various angles. He squinted at the piece of paper in front of him, frowned and rubbed his chin.

Barnes shut his eyes and gripped the arms of the chair while the consultant spoke. He started off cold, businesslike — then, as it appeared to dawn on him that the information could probably use a small dose of tact, he began to stutter sympathetic platitudes as he delivered the news that the sample Barnes had produced was useless. He was infertile.

Barnes only spoke once — in a shaky voice — to politely ask the consultant not to refer to it as a *diagnosis*, unless he believed Barnes to be ill. He tried to process what he was hearing, tried to decide on a sliding scale of emotions. It wasn't just Eve. It was both of them.

The consultant, in a voice that sounded like it was thousands of miles away, tried to outline what this unexpected turn of events meant in practical terms. Other procedures were available, he explained, that meant fertility treatment was still an option, but they were protracted, the chances of success were greatly reduced and it would all cost a great deal more money.

But Barnes, his fist pressed against his mouth, was not really listening. He was thinking of Devil's Chimney, collapsing in the night while the waves lurched around it. He wondered if anyone had been around to hear it. As he walked to the car, his hands hovering over the keypad of his mobile phone, a heavy, numb feeling in his heart, he wondered how he was going to tell Eve.

* * *

The next stages of Howard Van Leer's inexorable decline took the form of a preliminary hearing on the Friday, exactly four days later — four days during which Barnes had not told his wife that, like her, he was not able to conceive naturally.

He couldn't quite articulate the reasons for withholding the news. He and Eve had barely spoken for those four days. He'd tried to comfort her, to extricate her from despondency, but had been bruised by rejection and didn't want to compound that by lumbering her with his own problems. His helplessness had left him confused and frustrated, so to compensate, he had gone into overdrive trying to find out what solutions were available so he could at least attempt to rescue her by presenting some actual routes out of the mire that currently held her. So far, however, all the options were too costly, too far away or too remote in their chances of success. So he had settled into inertia, and now events were overtaking him.

Inter-agency communications meant that the preliminary hearing happened before Van Leer's production order had been granted — for this, Barnes was grateful, and had not exactly tried to rush it through.

Barnes stepped out of Lewes Crown Court and blinked in the sunshine. April had become May, and the weather had improved on cue. Both the preliminary hearing and the application for the telephone recordings had been quick and straightforward — Natasha Warwick had rattled off the circumstances and outlined a fairly damning case, and then made the application for the recordings of Van Leer's telephone calls while in prison. Natasha had also pointed out that, technically, this was Van Leer's second stint behind bars in as many weeks, and the wisdom therein of redrafting the application to cover both periods. The judge had approved it and made the order on the spot. Now Barnes had only to serve it on the prison and await the tapes.

Van Leer had again refused to have legal representation, and had entered no plea. He had been quickly indicted and remanded in custody until the plea and directions hearing.

Barnes smoothed down the pinstripe suit that he kept back for Crown Court, and turned to walk back towards the railway station.

"DC Barnes?"

The voice came from behind him. Barnes turned and saw the ebony-haired reporter he had seen in the magistrates' court the week before, only this week the ponytail had been discarded in favour of a thick plait. The thick, red-rimmed glasses were still in evidence, however, and she was dressed simply in a crisp white shirt and black slacks, with a black satchel slung across her body. She was thin and very short — up close, twenty-five might have been a generous estimate. She was probably closer to thirty, but her general demeanour gave the impression of an art student.

"DC Barnes. Could I ask you a few questions?" She seemed a little out of breath.

"Who are you?"

"My name's Emily Varela. I'm . . . *Sussex Times*." She thrust her press ID and a business card in Barnes's direction, pushing her glasses up her nose as she did so.

"I thought I recognised you. Saw you in Jevington Gardens a couple of days after the murder." Barnes recognised the name as well, though he wasn't sure from where.

"Op Warlord. It was . . . subtle."

"Saw you in court last week as well, come to that. What would you like to ask?" Barnes's experience of the press was limited to a handful of fishing trips while on scene guard, but he had seen officers from constable all the way up to brass fudge and fumble their way around reporters, and they only ever succeeded in looking evasive and cagey. Barnes thought being candid was a much better approach, especially if it meant one could avoid looking like a numpty. Certainly the media awareness course he'd been on suggested this was a good idea — particularly as the press, if handled well, could prove a useful ally.

"Do you mind if we sit?" she asked, gesturing towards a bench further up the street. Emily Varela found a clean sheet of paper in her pad. "I've just come from the court. I wanted to ask about Howard Van Leer. This is his second burglary charge in a fortnight, isn't it?"

"Not quite. About three weeks."

"Right, okay." She made a note. "Are you the officer in the case?"

"I'm OIC, yes."

"Is he a drug user?"

"I believe his criminal behaviour is fuelled by his drug habit, yes." Barnes crossed his legs and sat back on the bench, finding the experience curiously enjoyable.

"Can you explain why he chose not to have legal representation this morning?"

"No, unfortunately I can't. You'd have to ask him. It was his choice."

"Did he have representation while in police custody?"

"He was given his rights when he arrived at the station. Beyond that I can't comment further. Like I say, it would have been his choice."

"And can you explain the injuries he has?"

"Those injuries are the subject of an active investigation and unfortunately I can't disclose any of the details. Sorry," he added. Talking to the press wasn't as easy as he'd thought. Journalists want to extract as much information as they can, and the police only want to release certain details. The stuttering and the stammering came about when the two came into conflict while people like him tried to remain within the bounds of politeness.

"Did he have them before he was arrested?" Emily Varela was scribbling quickly.

Barnes stiffened a little as he realised what was being implied. He gently pushed her pad down and took her pen.

"Come on, Detective. I'm touting for the local rag here, and I'm barely making enough to eat. Any unusual case could be my next couple of meals if I get the scoop. Talk to me, and I won't misquote you."

"That sounds like blackmail." He wiggled her pen between his fingers.

Emily Varela's olive skin went red — a small victory for him. "What I meant was, it's a two-way street. The more detail you give me, the more you can guarantee decent, positive police exposure with no, er, inaccuracies."

Candid and frank it was, then.

"Okay then, how about this? Howard Van Leer burgled his own solicitor's house and stabbed his wife. When his solicitor found out about it, he decided to fill him in. And, unfortunately for Mr Van Leer, his solicitor just happens to be a former boxer. Unsurprisingly, not many people want to represent him now."

Emily Varela went quiet as she tried to decide whether or not Barnes was being serious. Finally she spoke.

"I think you're making fun of me," she said.

Barnes handed her pen back. "Well, it appears you'll never know." He stood. "I don't think I can help you."

She stood up as well. "Thanks for your time." She sounded glum.

Barnes watched the reporter walk away and then he slipped her business card into his pocket and stood up.

He paused a moment, alone on the wide pavement outside Lewes Crown Court, and stared down the street at the latticed Tudor shopfronts — tiny buildings crammed into crooked spaces, the ground-floor windows at knee height. Barnes watched some al fresco diners, and pictured himself and Eve doing the same, sharing a joke over coffee, enjoying each other. Many of the diners were feeding young children with gleeful faces, and he realised that such scenes would forever be tinged with longing, a constant ache in the pit of the stomach, and the peaceful tableau suddenly seemed a million miles away. He resolved to drive straight home and give Eve the news. They were both infertile. It was a problem shared.

And a bill quadrupled, he thought.

Without warning, he suddenly thought of Holden's smiling face, and the children she would never have.

A white security van rolled into Barnes's line of sight, obliterating the vista. It was Group 4, taking the remand prisoners back to HMP Lewes and elsewhere. He squinted, wondering if he would be able to make out Van Leer's profile through the blacked-out windows.

The van stopped at traffic lights. Barnes walked towards it, thinking about buying a lottery ticket.

The shriek of an engine suddenly came from behind him, so close it made him jump like he'd been stung. Even in his interrupted reverie, Barnes realised that the car would have to stamp on the anchors to stop in time at the lights.

He turned to see a black Land Rover with bull bars hurtling past his shoulder, the engine screaming. The car was brand new, with surfaces waxed like mirrors and opaque windows the same colour and finish as the bodywork.

It raced on towards the queue idling at the traffic lights, the howling engine incongruous within the otherwise normal street scene. With no sign of brake lights, and clearly no time to stop, Barnes braced himself for the impact.

The Land Rover broadsided the van at around forty miles per hour, with no slowing or braking whatsoever. It collided with a jolting, deafening bang, and the van was launched sideways by the force of the impact. Glass sprayed over a row of coffee tables on the terrace of a nearby café. The prison van teetered on two wheels briefly, before coming to rest again in the middle of the high street.

In the immediate aftermath of the impact, the street was silent, as if the collision had switched off all the ambient noise in the street. Barnes stood frozen, the only sound coming from the glass particles as they tinkled onto the tarmac.

The screaming began just as four men in balaclavas emerged from the Land Rover and ran over to the van. Each carried a sledgehammer, and they moved to tactical positions around the van, baying orders in deep, rasping voices at both the occupants and the few onlookers that had gathered at the roadside.

One young man watching from the kerb held up a camera to capture the scene. Balaclava 1 ran over to him and knocked it out of his hand with a single swing of the hammer. Barnes heard the young man's wrist snap, followed by the dislodged camera smashing on the ground, and the man collapsed, howling in pain as he cradled his shattered hand. The onlookers scattered amid cries of fear.

Balaclava 2 ran to the cab of the van and began screaming orders at the driver. The unfortunate man emerged onto the road and was frogmarched, cowering, to the rear of the van.

Prisoner transport vehicles were not like cash transit vehicles — there were no failsafe countermeasures, no areas of the van that were off-limits to the drivers, no public-address alert systems and no crime scene dye chemicals to render the proceeds useless in the open market.

Barnes did not have time to speculate on whether such differences represented the competing demands of protecting cash over prisoners, nor was he in any doubt about who they were after.

Of the thousand different thoughts vying for prominence in his mind, one thought galvanised his frozen body into movement.

They're breaking him out.

He sprinted towards the van, tie flapping, dialling 999 on his mobile as he did so. When the call was connected, he barked "Lewes High Street, prisoner escaping" at the call taker, and then shoved the phone back into his pocket, leaving the call connected and the loudspeaker on.

He could hear the call taker's tinny voice calling "Hello? Sir?" as he ran. He ignored it, focusing on the details of the scene that appeared as he got closer — a plume of white vapour hissing from the Land Rover's engine bay; the smoking black tyre smudges on the road surface; the angry, red, grime-caked gash on the van driver's forehead.

Barnes dug in the pocket of his pinstriped jacket for his warrant card, but as his fingers curled around the leather, he thought again, thinking he was probably going to need both his hands. Instead he dropped his shoulder, like a lock forward defending his try line, and charged full pelt into Balaclava 1.

The guy was knocked off balance, but didn't drop the sledgehammer.

"Police!" Barnes yelled. "Drop the hammer."

Balaclava 1 resumed his balance, quicker than Barnes was expecting, and swung the hammer around with a snarl. Barnes managed to duck out of the sledgehammer's arcing path, and — on the assumption that the gang was wearing body armour — used his hips to drive his fist upwards into Balaclava 1's testicles.

It was a reasonably solid strike, and took the wind out of Balaclava 1, who doubled over in pain. Barnes moved forward, intending to follow it up with an elbow to the back of the neck, but instead he looked up and froze.

Right in his line of sight, the driver of the Land Rover was sitting motionless behind the wheel. Shrouded by a balaclava, Barnes met the cold, green eyes for a split second through the windscreen. They widened in alarm as they met Barnes's own eyes. There was a flash of recognition.

Cathy?

While Barnes was staring, Balaclava 2 appeared from behind the van and, with an angry yell, crashed the handle of his hammer into the side of Barnes's head.

The world darkened, and Barnes felt his knees sag. He fell backwards against the side of the van and then sank onto the concrete. With considerable effort he managed to haul himself onto his hands and knees, his head feeling like it was underwater.

He tried to inch forwards, tried to shake his head clear, but his body wasn't having any of it, and he collapsed face first onto the road, nausea lurching in his stomach. He managed to turn his head, grit scraping his cheek, and could only watch as Howard Van Leer, screaming in protest, was hauled bodily into the back of the Land Rover.

CHAPTER THIRTEEN

Barnes drummed his fingers on the trolley in A&E. He was still in his now-crumpled and grubby pinstripe suit, the tie pulled loose, the shirt stained with blood droplets — whose, he wasn't quite sure.

He was bored. The CT scan was clear, but they wanted to keep him in overnight. A hammer to the skull is enough to spoil your weekend, they said. All the staff seemed to know about Van Leer's kidnap, and then he realised the whole thing had happened right in front of that skinny reporter, the one whose name he had momentarily forgotten.

One of the doctors winked and said he was a brave man. A nurse told him he was stupid and should have let the geezer rot. Let the police deal with it, she said. He'd started to politely say, "*Well, actually* . . ." but she'd been called away.

Eve's face had been pinched with worry when she'd come running into A&E, eyes red, flinging her arms around him, handbag tossed aside, whispering, "*Thank God, thank God*" and "*I don't know what I'd do . . .*"

He'd tried to reassure her. She'd kissed him. They held each other and made romantic plans of dinner and holidays to lessen the immediacy of the situation, while machines pipped and beeped around them, disinfectant scenting the air.

Eventually she went home to feed and walk Forbes and maintain the domestic routine that ploughed on regardless of Barnes's setback. He smiled to himself. Her concern was so real, so strong, so stripped of any surface pretensions, that he had found himself enjoying the attention. He was mature enough to admit that. For this reason — the minor fracas in Lewes High Street notwithstanding — he hadn't quite got around to mentioning the news he had promised himself he would give her. He would, though. When she came back to the hospital.

He quickly discarded this plan when his next visitor arrived, who had neither sweet-smelling hair nor soft, womanly curves. Instead, he had a houndstooth jacket, a wriggling monobrow and a thick Welsh accent.

"You went and found out what a community partnership conference is, didn't you? I would have done anything to avoid it as well, but this seems a bit extreme."

Barnes smiled.

"How's your head?" DCI Hadian asked.

"It hurts. Scan's clear, but they want to keep me in. Cautionary tales about concussion."

"How do you feel about that?"

"Not terribly keen, actually."

"Good." The DCI handed Barnes his shoes. "Buggered if I'm going to let you stand me up."

* * *

The glass-fronted, union-owned conference centre, incongruous to its Victorian surroundings, stood adjacent to Wilmington Square, opposite the Redoubt.

Hadian and Barnes stood on the mezzanine level, right at the back of the brightly lit conference hall, watching hundreds of heads bob and nod in rows while Chief Superintendent Denniker stood on the podium, delivering a speech about falling crime rates and the need for communities to be vigilant and look after one another in the fight against antisocial behaviour.

Hadian grabbed two glasses of champagne from a passing waiter, and drank them both when Barnes refused one.

". . . we know that many ordinary citizens would, given the opportunity, stand up and take action in saying no to the most egregious of crimes. The challenge is for us to *activate* and *protect* these citizens . . ." Denniker was moving around the stage, gesturing while he spoke.

"I'll give him his due, he puts his weight behind it," Hadian whispered. He nudged Barnes. "Give it a few years, that will be *you* up there, using words that nobody understands."

"Who are all these people?" Barnes whispered back.

"These are the people that make the wheels turn," Hadian said. "County councillors, regional government, community safety groups, think tanks, social care, neighbourhood panels, residents' associations, anyone you can name that has a brick in the infrastructure. They all make up the partnership — the annual conference is where they try for a bigger piece of the pie."

Barnes looked down at the agenda in his hand. Denniker's speech was third on the bill — something that Hadian said had rather displeased the divisional commander, who felt that the police input should form a natural conclusion to the event.

". . . our workforce comprises staff who show the utmost moral courage and professional integrity. We have put the right people on the streets to deal with the issues the public tell us matter to them . . ."

Barnes felt sick. How could the man look himself in the mirror?

"This is politics," Hadian said, as though reading Barnes's thoughts.

". . . and these changes have manifested themselves," Denniker droned on, "in real results. Overall crime down thirteen per cent, violent crime down eighteen per cent and property crimes down eleven per cent . . ."

There was a change in the atmosphere. A murmur fluttered around the room and then subsided. A small, elderly man with baby-pink skin had asked about the rubbish, vomit and unconscious revellers that littered his street on a Sunday morning. What kind of society, he wanted to know, encouraged people to drink all night in nightclubs and only leave when it was daylight?

Denniker made some remark about his double-strength weekend patrols, and then cleverly foisted the rest of the blame onto the government's licensing laws.

The genie was out of the bottle, however. People began to stand up and say that the figures were skewed, that the reality was different, that crime had become more prevalent and more overt in their streets. One woman mentioned an old lady she knew who had been robbed on the seafront. She'd clung bravely onto her handbag straps and had been dragged along the promenade. Eventually she gave up, and while she lay there, her assailant had kicked her in the ribs a few times, just for the heck of it. The black bruising, the woman said, had covered the entire left side of her body, making her look as though she'd been burned in a fire.

Then someone mentioned Harriet Holden's murder — the murder of a *police officer*, no less — as a clear example of the lawlessness.

"Fancy a drink?" Hadian whispered.

Barnes and Hadian slipped through the doors at the back of the conference room. Like the conference room, the mezzanine level was also brightly lit — through the windows, the English Channel was only a black void.

"I hope he gets out alive," he said.

"The boss, you mean? He's faced worse. Like at the Gold Group meeting for Christchurch earlier this week. He got creamed."

Barnes did not know what a Gold Group meeting was, but he surmised, more or less accurately, that it involved the senior echelons of the police service. It also involved some of its significant partners, and discussed matters of strategic interest pertaining to the operation: investigative ownership, finance, resources, reputation, the media, public interest — and self-preservation.

"The chief tore him up for arse paper. This thing isn't going away. HQ is all over it now. HMIC and the PCA are sniffing around it as well. Even the Home Office is asking how we managed to let the only suspect in a cop murder find his way out of a reasonably sturdy prison van."

Barnes noticed that there was a thin line of sweat on the DCI's brow.

"For Christ's sake, Barnes, will you have a drink?" Hadian said as Barnes poured some water into a glass from a jug on the bar.

The doors of the conference room opened and the delegates began to swarm out. The bar was suddenly engulfed by thirsty men, most of whom were aged over sixty and wore grey suits and spectacles.

A short man in a tweed suit, no less than seventy-five, carried an empty brandy tumbler over to the bar. He had the vacant smile and slightly wavering gait of the career conference delegate. In profile, the loose globule of flesh under his jaw looked like a teardrop.

He looked as if he were about to join the conversation, but he smiled, handed Barnes the empty glass and disappeared.

Barnes's head had been feeling better, but now it was hurting again. He dug in his pocket for some of the triple-strength painkillers the hospital had given him, and gobbled them down with the water.

"You okay?" Hadian said.

"I'm fine. It's . . . just my head," Barnes said. "Would you excuse me, sir? I need some air."

He backed away towards the stairs. As he went, he saw a red-faced Denniker emerge from the conference room. The divisional commander scanned the mezzanine, ostensibly looking for Hadian, while Barnes turned and disappeared down the stairs.

He stood outside the conference centre. The air felt good, but his head was pounding. He walked east towards the town and stopped outside the Cavendish Hotel. It was one of the seafront's larger hotels — a huge white Victorian building with a prosthetic east wing that had been rebuilt with a decidedly Brutalist look after it was bombed during World War II.

Barnes and Eve had spent a weekend in one of the corner suites when they were first dating. Barnes smiled to himself as he got caught up in the memory. On the rare moments they actually ventured out, they had walked along the seafront, holding hands, eating ice cream and buying bottles of wine that they had smuggled into the room to avoid being charged corkage. He looked up at the hotel. The suite was on the first floor, right on the west corner. He squinted. It was shrouded in darkness, the curtains on the tall picture windows wide open. The silhouette of a chandelier was visible in the gloom. No guests.

Further down Grand Parade, his eye was distracted by two small cars racing up and down Devonshire Place, skidding around the statue of William Cavendish, seventh Duke of Devonshire, that stood at the seafront mouth of the broad avenue. Barnes stared at the statue, and thought of what Denniker had said — built by gentlemen for gentlemen. He thought of Van Leer, Denniker and the two boy racers, and wondered where the gentlemen had gone.

Further east, opposite the pier, the white stucco entablature of the Claremont was swathed in an ultraviolet glow from its ground lights. He crossed the road and walked down the steps to the promenade. The sky had turned a dark crimson and thick cloud had begun to roll in. Barnes could feel the storm in the air. He sat on the edge of the bandstand and swung his legs, watching the flimsy fabric of the deckchairs writhe as the wind began to swell.

A pulse of lightning flashed on the horizon, electricity snaking and thrashing like veins into the clouds. He counted the seconds, like his father had taught him to, years ago. The growl of thunder followed seven seconds later.

His phone rang. He cursed aloud. No doubt the DCI wanted to share some of the abuse Denniker had surely just meted out.

He frowned. There was no number on the display.

"Hello?"

"This DC Barnes?"

"Yes. Who's this?"

"How about you tell me why you wanted to speak to Mr Van Leer?"

Barnes went cold. "Where is he?"

"How's your head?" The voice was deep and had a ratchety South London accent.

"If this is a ransom demand, I think you're being optimistic. Howard Van Leer isn't worth the shit on my shoe," Barnes said, the pain in his head concentrating his anger.

The ratchety voice laughed — a rasping, throaty cackle.

"You see, that's where you're wrong, DC Barnes. We know you want him. We know you're planning to fit him up for murder — and it *is* a fit-up, Officer."

"We? Who's we?"

"It's all a bit transparent, you know. I read the papers. You lot, you look fucking desperate."

"What do you *want*?"

"It's funny . . . how much he's suddenly in demand. It's just a shame we got to him first."

"Wait . . ."

"Go west, young man."

The call was ended.

Barnes looked up. Further along the upper promenade, to the west, he could see the figure of a man, partially concealed by the railings and a concrete portico that acted as an additional seating area for the bandstand. With the string of lights suspended from the gaslight lamp posts behind him, he was little more than a shadow.

Barnes scrambled to his feet, and raced for the steps leading to the upper promenade. The figure was on his toes and running before Barnes had even got to the bottom of the steps.

He would lose too much time ascending the steps. Instead, he began to jog west on the lower promenade, parallel to the street above him.

The first fat drops of rain began to fall. Barnes inclined his face to the street above to seek out whoever had been watching him and felt the water splash on his face. It helped wash away the pain in his head. The smell of the water battering the warm, dusty concrete rose up from the ground in a vapour.

As he reached the bandstand the prom meandered outwards to circumvent the makeshift auditorium. This section of the prom was under cover, blue neon strips of light illuminating the otherwise black underpass. His footsteps echoed and squeaked on the wet concrete as he ran past the bandstand's glass doors, where the publicity posters were beginning to pucker in the rain.

Barnes couldn't see him, so he took staccato steps up to the upper promenade. The figure was gone. Barnes dropped to one knee and clutched his head — the exertion of running up the steps had made the blood pound in his skull. It felt like razor blades see-sawing his brain.

He shook it clear and started to jog west, turning one-eighty on the spot as he did so. Back past the Cavendish Hotel, past the conference centre.

He started to pick up speed, feeling his heart thumping in his chest and his lungs pulling at air, the pain in his head starting to ease as the painkillers finally got to work.

He jog-walked for several hundred yards, then cursed. He had lost his shadowy accuser.

He kept going. Grand Parade became King Edward's Parade, and as he passed the Grand Hotel, the Western Lawns were suddenly illuminated by powerful lights coming from behind him.

Anxiety began to gnaw at his stomach. He looked over his shoulder as he ran. The car was cruising behind him, matching him for pace, the tyres rumbling quietly along the road, the chrome grille glinting like teeth in the gloom.

It clearly had no other intention than to follow him. Barnes increased his pace, and then stopped and spun on the spot. Caught in the headlights, he broke the stand-off and began to advance towards the car.

"What do you *want?*" he yelled at the unseen driver.

He broke into a run and charged for the driver's door. In riposte, the main beams came on, dazzling him, and then there was a shriek of rubber on tarmac as the car accelerated towards him.

Fear threatened to paralyse him, but at the last second Barnes dived across the middle of the road. As he rolled, the mobile phone in his pocket took the brunt of his body weight. He heard it crunch. He got to his feet, and saw a flash of metallic green.

The brake lights of the green car glowed like red eyes in the dark as it came to an abrupt halt. Then the reverse lights illuminated and the tyres squealed as the car moved backwards and started to turn around. As if the devil himself were now chasing him, Barnes headed back east, darted down Silverdale Road and pinned himself against the wall of the Grand Hotel, his breath coming in fearful gasps, his pulse enveloping him like a rhythmic thunderclap from the sky.

The car rolled past. Barnes squinted, and then froze as the Mercedes stopped at the mouth of Silverdale Road. Like a frustrated predator it sat for a moment, the engine idling, and then turned around and headed back towards Holywell.

The sound of the car dwindled and then disappeared altogether. Barnes dropped his head and exhaled with relief, the only audible sound now the low humming of the blue neon hanging over the entrance to the Mirabelle restaurant.

He walked further down Silverdale Road towards the rear of the hotel. Down here the white stucco cornices and Byzantine cherubs of the building's exterior were caked with grime, and the street lighting was poor. The hot smell of clean laundry from an industrial dryer engulfed him from a vent somewhere below ground level.

He heard laughing and cursing in what sounded like an Eastern European tongue. It was loud in his ear, and he turned with a start. Two waiters in black tie were smoking in a darkened doorway. They stopped laughing and their smiles vanished. They locked eyes with Barnes. The startled detective, feeling like a hunted fox, saw only hostility in their eyes, and he backed away across the road to the corner of the Grand Hotel's perimeter wall.

There. Across the road, by the lifeboat museum. A solitary dark figure, stock still, hands in pockets.

Staring right at him.

The pain had abated, but it was still fuelling his anger. They were *playing* with him. He ran across the road, but in the time it took to check for oncoming traffic, the rain had fallen in his eyes and the figure had disappeared.

West of this point, Grand Parade started to incline upwards, but the promenade remained level. Barnes moved west, flicking his eyes from the rain-slicked concrete of the promenade to the road above as it inclined further away.

Beyond the spiky fronds of yucca surrounding the Wish Tower, the intervals between cafés and ice cream kiosks became greater, giving way instead to a number of beach shelters that habitually housed the street drinkers and the homeless.

Then he saw him, up ahead. A dark figure, running west along the prom. He had about a fifty-yard head start. Barnes wanted to chase him, but the see-saws in his head were threatening to put him on his knees, and all he could manage was a stagger.

The figure disappeared.

Barnes's vision started to blur — from the rain or the concussion, he wasn't sure. He stopped, taking a moment to make sure he wasn't going to pass out, then moved gingerly along the prom.

He was passing one of the shelters when there was a flash of movement in the corner of his eye.

A lone figure sprang from the gloom. It was tall and thin, and it slowly advanced. Barnes adopted a defensive stance, with his palms out in front of him.

"Stay back," he warned in a shaky voice, not fancying his chances at all. He recognised his fight-or-flight instincts kicking in — as well as realising he was not really in a fit state to do either.

The figure shrugged off its outer garment and swung it onto the floor. Barnes set his feet and clenched his fists as best he could, recognising the invitation to fight.

"Keep back. I've told you once." Shit, *shit*. He had nothing on him. No spray, no phone, no cuffs — nothing. This was going to be over quickly.

The figure continued to advance, then crept forward into the orange wash of a street light — and Barnes recognised the street drinker, Garrett.

"Stefan. What are you doing?" Barnes dropped his hands.

Recognition sprawled slowly across Garrett's craggy, unshaven features. He had a thick head of salt-and-pepper hair in a long-expired crewcut and equally thick eyebrows. His narrow, pointed nose had been broken many times, and under it was a downturned mouth in a state of permanent disapproval that cut deep lines in his face. He gave Barnes an exaggerated bow, which, affected or otherwise, only heightened the impression of a Dickensian villain.

"Hiding from the rain, sir. You startled me." He shoved his fists into his pockets, as if he did not fully trust them to do as they were told. His jittery eyes flicked from Barnes to the sea and back again.

"Likewise." Barnes leaned forward and rested his hands on his knees, relief and nausea dancing a jig in his system.

"Show me a gooseneck?" Garrett asked with sudden enthusiasm.

Barnes managed to wheeze a laugh. On each of his encounters with Garrett he had requested a demonstration of one of the police repertoire of defensive techniques.

Garrett was no problem, really. He had been a violent offender in his youth, but now the sole cause of his police attention was limited to complaints from tourists about being harassed by a drunk while they walked along the seafront.

His mood depended a good deal on how much he had had to drink and who was attending the complaint — some of Barnes's colleagues found it easier to wind him up and take him in. He was easy to antagonise, but Barnes had never been given cause to arrest him.

"Stefan . . . were you watching me?"

"You looking for the man who killed that copper, ain't you?"

Barnes froze.

"Do you know something?" Barnes was aware of the desperate edge to his voice.

"Maybe I does, sir." Garrett began to gnaw at a grimy fingernail.

Barnes's hands began to tremble. It was easy to write off the street drinkers as hallucinating crazies who had turned their brains to porridge with triple-strength cider, but on more than one occasion Barnes had found their insights to be right on the money.

"Well, what?" Barnes demanded.

"There's new people in town. People you don't see. People with money. They's scaring all us folk."

"Who are they? And what have they got to do with the murder?" Barnes checked himself and clamped his mouth shut — one question at a time, don't confuse him.

"You don't see 'em. But you hear about 'em. That's worse." He lowered his voice and looked over his shoulder, in case someone was listening. "It's the Dutchman I'm scared about."

"Who's the Dutchman?"

"I don't know. But he slashed her. Laughed while he did it, I heard. Bashed her bonce with a bust of Beethoven."

Barnes could take no more. He grabbed Garrett by the upper arms and shook him.

"Who killed her, dammit? If you know, tell me!"

With surprising ease Garrett extricated himself from Barnes's grip and retched. He spat a gob of blood onto the beach, where it disappeared amid the pebbles.

"Ain't no need to be roughing me up, sir. You always talk nice to me. Ain't no need for that."

"Stefan, I'm sorry. I'm sorry." Barnes took several deep breaths. He had scared himself with his own desperation to make something of the tiniest lead.

"Been roughed up enough in my time by you fuckin' coppers." Garrett made a show of straightening his unwashed clothes. Barnes could smell the damp on his body and the cheap cider on his breath. Garrett spat blood again.

"Stefan, a police officer is dead."

"I don't piss in the street, sir. You know that."

"I know that. Who killed her? Who is the Dutchman?"

"Denizens! Damn the disfiguring Dutchman!" he shrieked.

"*Who killed her?*"

Garrett did not respond. His face had contorted with fear.

"Stefan?" Barnes said, alarmed by the change in Garrett's face. "What . . ."

Garrett was looking past Barnes, his fearful expression now illuminated by flickering orange. His mouth opened and closed, but no sound came.

Barnes spun round. The last shelter on the prom was fifty yards or so away, just under the Holywell Tea Rooms, where the incisor-like symmetry of the toothpaste-blue beach huts ended and the black sprawling rocks at the foot of Beachy Head began. Barnes tried not to think of the number of bodies that had been recovered from these rocks.

The fire had consumed most of the shelter already, and the rumbling of the flames drowned out the sound of the waves. As he approached, Barnes realised he could hear screaming from within the shelter, engulfed by the growl of the flames.

"Oh, Jesus," he whispered.

Barnes grabbed Garrett's heavy coat from where he had flung it on the ground and moved towards the shelter, the pain temporarily forgotten as a second dose of adrenaline was released into his system in as many minutes. The heat beat him back, and he paused for a moment, paralysed with fear and a panicked knowledge that the window of opportunity for rescue was so tiny that it rested on his shoulders alone. The screaming reached a crescendo — a strangled, gargling, inhuman sound. Barnes imagined the fragile physical construction of the victim's throat and voice box being decimated by the fire.

As his eyes grew accustomed to the light, he saw the black silhouette of two legs sticking out of the shelter, twitching and jerking in the flames.

Barnes felt the coat — wet, but not wet enough. He ran down over the haphazard, pebbled beach to the water's edge and soaked the coat. The tide was in; even so, the stumbling journey to the shore and back seemed to take forever. He wrapped the sodden coat around his hands and crawled forwards, his body pressed flat to the concrete, knowing deep inside that it was already too late.

Barnes clenched his jaw and grabbed at the feet through a shimmering curtain of black and orange. The screaming had stopped. The legs had stopped moving. The first grab had him clutching at nothing but rapidly disintegrating clothing. He would have cursed, but the heat dipped white-hot fingers down his throat and seemed to be yanking the very breath out of his lungs.

He stretched out for a second attempt. The heat punctured his hands through the garment, but he found enough purchase to pull the feet clear.

"Stefan!" Barnes roared. "Grab my feet."

Garrett did as he was told.

"Pull!"

Garrett did so. The pair rolled backwards and pulled the body clear of the flames. Barnes doused the flames with the coat, rolling the body over and over like he'd seen in fire safety videos.

Eventually the flames succumbed. Choking black smoke took its place, rising off the body in wisps, like its last breaths. The corpse was skinny, and appeared to be male. Barnes could see at least seven black, eye-shaped wounds in the side of the body. Someone really hadn't wanted him to survive; if the flames hadn't got him, the blood loss almost certainly would have done.

The fire had eaten most of the clothing. The head and most of the upper torso had suffered full-thickness burns, the flesh still crackling and popping like a roasted leg of lamb. Streaks of melted white tears trickled down from the now-hollow eye sockets. The lips had curled away like burnt paper, leaving only an insidious grin.

The cloying, burnt-pork smell suddenly made Barnes's stomach lurch. He covered his face with his tie, and frantically scanned the corpse for something to help with ID.

On one ankle there was a white band of undamaged flesh. Blue writing was visible. Barnes carefully pushed down the sock to read the tattoo.

It simply said "*Liam*".

Barnes closed his eyes. His breath was coming in thick, gulping coughs, and his head was swimming, intoxicated by the smoke and the concussion. The shock of the discovery was compounded by his sudden understanding of the earlier call. This had been organised. Someone wanted Van Leer dead, and they wanted the police — Barnes — to have a front-row seat.

This far west, the prom remained at sea level, while the road high above snaked sharply up towards Beachy Head. Had Barnes looked up, he would have seen the green Mercedes parked in the Holywell Retreat. He would have seen the driver flick a cigarette out towards the sea and then get in the car. But for the rumble of the fire, he would have heard the Mercedes engine starting up.

But he did not look up. He could not take his eyes from the charred body of Howard Van Leer.

CHAPTER FOURTEEN

The fire was out, but the smell of burning flesh still filled the air. The blackened shelter was cordoned off by blue tape. Patrol vehicles and dutiful uniformed officers kept the onlookers at bay. A scene tent protected the remains of Howard Van Leer, who remained in situ under the gaze of a Home Office pathologist.

Barnes watched from a distance. In the daylight, the flurry of activity did more than simply preserve a crime scene. It was intended to reinforce the semblance of order, to show that things were now under control. It was a far cry from the horror of the previous night.

Barnes shook his head. From one extreme to the other. He looked up. Last night he had only been able to imagine the cliffs in the darkness, but now the white heights of Beachy Head towered above him.

Hadian joined him from where he had been speaking with the pathologist. He was drinking coffee from a paper cup, and handed one to Barnes, who handled it clumsily. His hands had escaped serious damage, but a diligent paramedic had still applied a pretty decent burns dressing.

"The PM is this afternoon, but he's riddled with stab wounds." Hadian nodded at the scene tent.

"He was still alive when they set him on fire."

"Let's wait for a pathologist to tell us that, eh?"

Barnes folded his arms. "I heard him screaming. He couldn't get out."

Without warning, a short, dumpy SOCO in a scene suit walked over, and, using a white plastic object that resembled a credit card, scraped a sample of singed, crispy hairs from Barnes's forearm. They yielded without difficulty and tumbled into a plastic exhibit bag.

"Is that it then? Is it over?" Barnes asked, rubbing the now-bare patch on his arm.

Hadian snorted. "Depends what you mean by over. The principal in a cop murder was snatched from under our noses and dumped here for a seagull's barbecue."

"Sir, I tried . . ."

Hadian looked at him. "It isn't your fault, Barnes."

"Sir, when they took him. Outside the court. The driver . . ."

"What?"

"It looked like Cathy."

Hadian's eyes widened for a moment, and Barnes faltered.

"I . . . I couldn't be sure," he said. "They all had balaclavas, but the eyes and mouth . . . it could have been her."

Hadian turned back to the shelter. "We can add kidnap to the list of charges, then. She's still suspended, so I guess her time is her own." His tone was bitter, and Barnes didn't know whether his boss believed him. Maybe he just didn't *want* to believe him.

"They led me here."

"Come again?" Hadian dumped his cup in a nearby bin.

"They *led* me here. I got a cryptic phone call minutes before the shelter went up, and nearly got pasted across the bumper of a car on the way here. They *wanted* me to find him. Me specifically."

Hadian shrugged. Barnes looked over at a blue plastic crate by the scene tent, which contained a number of exhibits in sealed polythene and brown paper bags. Some of the items were innocuous — drinks cans and cigarette butts gathered from the floor of the shelter. Others contained incinerated scraps of clothing. Through the narrow window of one bag Barnes could see a butcher's knife mounted in a box, Van Leer's blood scorched black on the blade.

One of the bags contained the remains of Barnes's mobile phone.

He turned back to his boss.

"Sir, am I a suspect?"

Hadian didn't answer. His eyes were fixed on the scene.

"Nightingale mentioned it," Barnes continued, hearing the shake in his voice. "Said that a brand-new detective wouldn't get this much action so early on, that the only reason for keeping me so close was so you could keep an eye on me. I thought maybe it was just because I'm new, but every time Cathy gets sidelined I end up working solo again."

Hadian was not quick to reassure him.

"All my detectives work solo. On the planet where I've got enough detectives to work in pairs the rivers run with honey and my clear-up rate tops out at forty percent."

Hadian turned to face him.

"Barnes, if you were a suspect, do you think I would tell you? Not only that, but it would be a cold day in hell before you could make a Force surveillance team."

"Thanks for clearing that up," Barnes said, unable to keep the sarcasm from his voice.

"Barnes, you have the makings of a fine detective. But trouble seems to have a way of finding you."

Hadian's voice was quiet. Barnes felt himself go cold.

"Sir, you surely don't think I had something to do with Van Leer's death?" Barnes's voice was shaking.

"Look, Barnes, Christchurch has been a proper clusterfuck. It will probably cost Denniker his promotion."

"Sir, with respect, I'm more concerned with finding Harriet's killer than with the boss's career plans."

"Barnes, you're missing the point. Heads will roll." Hadian's shoulders seemed to slump a little. "You're being pulled off the enquiry."

"What?" Barnes actually laughed, although when his voice snapped it sounded more like a shriek — a pained, incredulous sound.

Hadian waved an arm towards the town.

"Plenty of other crimes to solve. Can't ignore them forever."

"Is that the real reason?"

Hadian shook his head. "It's what I'm telling you."

* * *

Barnes went back to the office and mechanically started sifting through his caseload, the shock of displacement like a heavy weight on his shoulders. He flicked through the two-foot stack of case files that had he had inherited on his arrival in the CID office, the day he had tripped on his way to his new desk. There they had remained, untouched since the discovery of Harriet Holden's battered body.

He wrote several contrite letters to victims of robbery, burglary and assault, apologising for the delay and explaining that there were no lines of enquiry, and took an armful to dump in the mail room. While it was more an administrative process than an investigative one, he couldn't help feel that it was more in keeping with what a normal day as a detective looked like — even if "normal" did seem to be largely relative.

On the way down the corridor he heard raised voices. As he passed Denniker's office, the voices reached a crescendo.

The divisional commander's office had an outer door with a glass pane, beyond which was a solid inner door, with a small workstation for his assistant in between the two.

The outer door was shut, the inner door open. Barnes edged towards the door and peered in at the edge of the glass. Denniker and Hadian were standing in the centre of the room, the distance between them just enough for a boxing referee.

". . . we're into damage limitation now, Paul — the success or failure of which will largely determine whether or not you keep your job."

"Are you serious? I've got no staff and those I do have are just the right side of amateur. You can't pot an organised crime group that way."

Denniker looked at his watch.

"Paul, calm down. Van Leer's death can quite easily be worked to our advantage. It is merely a question of delivery — in fact, I can dictate the press release now. Howard Van Leer, remanded in custody on charges of assault, burglary and wounding, and the principal suspect in the murder of Constable Harriet Holden, was found dead on Eastbourne seafront last night. Recent evidence in the form of DNA suggested Van Leer was directly involved in the murder of Constable Holden. We, the police, intended to charge Van Leer with conspiracy to murder in the immediate future. We are confident that he would have been convicted in the event of trial. Howard Van Leer's death presents an abrupt and unfortunate end to the investigation, and it is our great regret that we will now not achieve justice for Constable Holden. However, we can rest easy in our beds knowing that this dangerous killer is no longer at large to prey on other innocent victims."

"Very nice," Hadian said, folding his arms as if to keep buried some truths about Denniker's grandstanding that he would later regret.

"Let me know how you get on," Denniker said, and went to sit down behind his desk, the conversation apparently over by his reckoning.

Hadian looked up sharply.

"Sir?" His voice was like cold steel. Barnes had not heard him like this before.

"Well, I believe you to be eminently capable of running this press conference, Paul. You are the SIO, after all."

"And you are the divisional commander."

"I know that, I know that. But you are the one with your finger on the pulse. The nuts and bolts of the investigation and all that." Denniker waved a disinterested hand.

And all that? Barnes chewed his lip, unable to believe what he was hearing. Did Denniker care anything at all for finding Holden's killer?

"Sir, with the greatest respect, this is the murder of a police officer. There is national interest, with an unexpected twist to the story to disclose. I think the divisional commander owes it to the victim to take the bloody press conference!" Hadian shouted.

Denniker stood up.

"One more insubordination like that, Detective Chief Inspector, and you and I will fall out."

Barnes accidentally nudged the door with his knee. Denniker and Hadian turned to the source of the sound and saw his face at the glass. Barnes froze, the eavesdropper exposed.

Their stares remained locked in a stand-off. Then Denniker, without breaking Barnes's gaze, marched over to his inner office door and kicked it shut.

* * *

The trainee cashier at the building society on Bankers' Corner was barely twenty, not long with the firm. She was being tutored on the job by a more senior cashier — a middle-aged woman with a complexion like semolina.

The younger cashier was getting flustered. It was hot, there was no air conditioning and she had already caught herself miscounting a stack of notes with her sweaty fingers.

Only the two of them were working on this Saturday. They were both acutely aware that Saturday trading hours ceased at midday, but this was at odds with the queue of customers stretching out onto the pavement.

Desperate to serve the queue and get home, the cashier paid no attention to anyone but the customer immediately in front of her. She certainly did not notice the tall, thin man that stepped into the branch as the queue gradually shortened.

It was 11.28 a.m.

* * *

At 11.29 a.m. Barnes was back at his desk, still ploughing through his case files. There had been two serious assaults during the night — one with a suspect in custody, one without. Both needed secondary investigation, but he couldn't concentrate. He felt like he was waiting to be summoned — by whom, he wasn't sure. His mind was an agitated scramble of thoughts struggling for coherence. Even sitting at the desk, his pulse felt like that of a racing driver on the starting grid.

He flicked through one of the assault files that had been dumped on his desk by the night turn patrol officers. The detail was scant. There was plenty of work needed to bring it up to scratch — not least locating a suspect.

He pulled a videotape out of the file. The handover sheet promised that the assault had been captured on CCTV.

The telephone on his desk rang. He cursed and wiped sweat from his brow. He should have unplugged it. Unexpected telephone distractions were the curse of the diligent. He answered it, but deliberately didn't identify himself.

"CID."

"Good morning. Is this DC Barnes?" The diction was careful, but Barnes detected the strains of a South London accent.

"Yes, this is DC Barnes. Who is this?" Barnes held the phone between his ear and shoulder and continued to write on the report he'd been reading.

"I want DC Barnes. I'll only speak to him."

"I just told you — this is DC Barnes. What do you want?"

"I have some information for you, DC Barnes."

"What kind of information?" Barnes sighed, like this was the last thing he needed.

"Useful information."

"Yeah, what kind? I'm very busy."

"You ain't too busy. Or rather, you won't be when I tell you what it is I've got to tell you."

Barnes stopped writing, his curiosity piqued. He put the pen down and held the phone with his hand, glancing around the office for the fourth time that morning to verify that, in fact, there was only one other detective on duty, and they were down in the cell block wading through a queue of Saturday morning prisoners.

"So, I'm listening," he said, in a tone that was more controlled than he felt.

"Your office is in the town centre, yeah?"

"Yes."

"Not far from Bankers' Corner, yeah?" The accent was blatant now, all efforts to disguise it dispensed with. Maybe he had just been making fun of Barnes.

"Yes. Will you be getting to the point today?" Barnes wanted to scream at him.

"Indulge me, Officer, indulge me. I'm enjoying this."

Barnes shut his eyes and concentrated on the voice. The same one that had called him at the conference? He couldn't be sure. He didn't immediately recognise it.

"Go on."

"So, if I'm right, it wouldn't take you very long to get from your nick to Bankers' Corner? Five minutes?"

"I could . . . I could run it in two." His heart was thumping now.

"Nah, you'll want a car."

"Okay then, less. Traffic permitting."

"You'll want a car with all the flashing lights and sirens and whatnot."

"Who *is* this?" Desperate.

"There's that little building society on Bankers' Corner. Little one. Up the road from the big banks. Only a couple of staff. Tiny counter. If you leave now you'll get there before they close. It's Saturday, you know."

"Why would I want to go to the building society?"

"You might want to make a withdrawal. You might want to deposit a cheque. Or, you might want to arrest the geezer that's about to go in there with a shotgun and rob the place."

* * *

"Can I help you, sir?" The young cashier didn't look up.

The man standing at the counter didn't answer. After a second the cashier looked up, but not at the man. She checked the countertop for a deposit book, a pile of cash or something else indicating a desire to transact. The countertop was bare.

Now she did look at the man. He was tall, with a thin, deeply lined face and craggy features. He was dressed in black, dirty clothes with a tweed cap and an olive-green rucksack on one shoulder. He smiled without parting his dry lips.

Her eyes narrowed. Something was not right, but she could not immediately identify what it was. There was a sickly smell coming off the man, and he did not look like the kind of person that frequented building societies very often.

This particular building society was distanced from its larger cousins up the road by both geography and operating budgets. It was a small, independent enterprise, and it did not have the same design, technical facilities — or security features.

The security screens that sat on the counter and separated the staff from the customers were only about two feet high — above them there was nothing but six feet of air, right up to the ceiling. The screens ran the length of the counter, but were separated at intervals by three-inch vertical gaps through which cash and cheques could be passed through — not quite big enough for the human hand, but the perfect size for, say, the stock of a shotgun.

She stared at him.

"I said — can I help . . ."

She didn't finish her sentence. The man jerked the sawn-off from below the counter up into her line of vision, through the gap in the screens, and smashed the stock into the bridge of her nose.

The force of the blow sent her toppling heavily backwards off her chair. The cashiers' working area was small — her head struck the wall behind her, and she landed in a heap behind the counter, blood spurting from her face. She whimpered quietly, and her lips trembled. Unconscious.

The man vaulted the counter with little difficulty, only dimly aware of the shocked cries and gasps from the queue behind him. He grabbed handfuls of cash from the open drawer under the counter and shoved them carelessly into the rucksack, notes fluttering to the floor around him like parade ticker tape.

The older cashier had jumped to her feet, toppling her chair, and she was standing rigid with her hands clasped to her bosom as if in prayer. In a life given over to the banking industry — and despite innumerable training scenarios — she had never experienced anything like armed robbery.

Her eyes were wide and milky, robbed of everything but insane terror, and they flicked mindlessly from her unconscious junior to the assailant and back, her entire body rigid. Her breath sputtered out in little bullet-whispers as shock spread through her system and paralysed her.

She was standing by a second cash drawer, also open. The man saw it and advanced, making a low, throaty growl as he did so. His movements were swift, like a cat, and when he was within a foot his attention moved from the cash drawer to her, and she could take no more. Her eyes widened, rolled upwards and she fainted, collapsing in a crumpled pile like a marionette whose strings had been cut.

The man snorted like a satisfied predator and helped himself to the cash from the second drawer, stuffing it into the rucksack. He looked at a small button under the counter and sniggered. Security countermeasures were only as good as the person that activated them.

The episode thus far had unfolded in just a few seconds, and the customers in the packed branch were only just

beginning to realise what was happening. The man unloaded
a round from the shotgun into the ceiling, and that was
enough to shepherd the customers' collective decision-making. The huge, alien sound made the panicked crowd dive to
the floor as one, screaming and crying as they did so. Many
of them covered their ears.

The man vaulted back over the counter and darted for
the doors, while fragments of ceiling tile descended behind
him.

* * *

Barnes tore out of the garage under the station and spun
the Mondeo onto the road towards the town centre, trying
to keep calm. He hit the lights but did not want the sirens
scaring anybody off. He shouted into the radio as he drove.

"Armed robbery . . . Cornfield Road . . . building society . . . male suspect with shotgun . . . anonymous info . . .
backup, please."

The area around Grove Road and South Street was
known as Little Chelsea for its boutique clothes shops, funky
café bars and second-hand treasure troves, and it was uncom-
mon for the mid-morning traffic to be anything other than
heaving. Barnes crawled towards the intersection outside the
town hall, thumping the horn in lieu of the sirens, but this
only caused his disgruntled fellow road users to dig their heels
in and throw some abuse his way.

At the end of Grove Road he had intended to head left
down South Street — the most direct route to the building
society — but progress was impossible thanks to two unload-
ing delivery vans snarling up the whole traffic flow.

"Fuck this," he muttered to himself.

Beyond the intersection Grange Road was clear. He
dropped the car into first and wrenched the wheel to get out
of the queue. Then he stomped the throttle and took the car
up over a small traffic island to get over the junction into
Grange Road. The car made a deafening *clang* as the floorpan

scraped the kerb, and then he was over the junction and the road was clear.

He took the Mondeo to sixty in second gear, screaming up towards Eastbourne College. Students in striped blazers turned to look at the lunatic racing up Grange Road. Barnes pulled the car left into Blackwater Road doing nearly fifty, and felt the back start to slide as the tyres scrabbled for a grip on the road.

He screamed to the end of Blackwater Road and stood on the brakes when he was alongside Devonshire Park — the speedometer needle dropped in an instant from up near sixty to around twenty. He swung the car left and headed into Cornfield Terrace as casually as possible.

He stopped the car in a loading bay just south of Memorial Roundabout. Bankers' Corner was straight over the roundabout, at the end of Cornfield Road.

He shut the engine off and paused for just a second in the car, suddenly aware, in the instant silence, that he was gasping for breath. What the hell could he be walking into?

He was hedging his bets that anyone wanting to make an escape would head his way, as the other direction was heavily populated by shoppers, CCTV cameras and town centre foot patrols.

He got out and forced himself to walk, eyes straining for signs of anything out of the ordinary, any sign of being under observation — or, indeed, any sign that he might be attacked again. He was in plain clothes, and he'd been given a tip. He might get the advantage.

Having dealt with the immediate challenge — getting quickly to scene — his thoughts slowed a little. Should he really be doing this? On the one hand, and for all he knew, anonymous tip-offs direct to the CID office about juicy jobs happened with monotonous regularity. On the other, however, the last time he'd received a cryptic phone call like this he'd walked straight into a burning corpse. Who was to say he wasn't being led like a lamb to slaughter for a second time?

There hadn't been anyone in the office to tell, but, as a concession, he had at least tried to call Hadian before he'd turned out, and had only got the DCI's voicemail.

He decided he couldn't chance it. Couldn't just ignore the possibility of catching an armed robber. It would practically be a neglect of duty. He'd called it in, but if the information was good they wouldn't make it in time.

The controller was desperately trying to get him back on the air to clarify the information. Barnes quickly repeated it, then turned the volume on the radio handset down and stuck it in his pocket. He could hear sirens in the distance. He reckoned thirty seconds, maybe a minute's advantage, then the cavalry would be here and — likely as not — the perpetrator would be long gone.

He quickly crossed Trinity Trees and walked as calmly as he could towards Bankers' Corner. He scanned the street, his heart like a pneumatic drill in his chest. It was a normal street scene. No cars accelerating away from the kerb, no screaming members of the public, no one running, no gunshots. Was it a hoax?

He crossed again by the roundabout and headed towards the building society, the urge to run almost irresistible. There was electricity running through him — he knew only too well that the window of opportunity to catch criminals leaving the scene was slim at best, and that ninety-nine times out of a hundred the cops turn up too late. With every second that passed without a result, the window was rapidly closing. Barnes felt all dressed up with nowhere to go.

The building society was almost in view. The street was busy with shoppers, but not so busy that he would miss anyone matching the very specific description given to him by his anonymous informant.

Then he saw them, about fifty feet ahead. A tall, thin man, aged about fifty, wearing a black raincoat and tweed cap, holding the hand of a younger, skinny female who seemed vaguely familiar. They were walking straight towards Barnes, but they did not appear in any rush. In fact, the man was looking upwards and whistling. He had an olive-green rucksack on one shoulder.

Clever, thought Barnes. The man matched the description given to him to the letter, but because he was hand in hand with a woman like any other couple, Barnes had barely given him a second glance.

As the suspect got closer, Barnes recognised him as the street drinker, Stefan Garrett. Barnes frowned. From his youth Garrett had form for all manner of colourful offences, but for the last ten years his pre-cons consisted mainly of drunk offences and shoplifting Special Brew. Armed robbery was not something Barnes expected of him.

In any case, Barnes darted into a small alleyway that led down to the front door of an employment agency. The couple had not seen him. Barnes extended his baton, his heart racing, the adrenaline threatening to overtake his movements. After what seemed like forever, he suddenly worried that they might have crossed the road or changed direction while they were out of sight.

But the whistling got nearer. Barnes pictured their steps in his mind, trying to estimate when they would draw level with the alleyway. He leaned his head against the wall of the alleyway, the brick cool on his head, and forced himself to breathe quietly. There was a blue ribbon of sky visible in the gap between the buildings above him, and just for a moment there was nothing but the ambient sound of the street, the traffic, the caw of gulls passing overhead . . .

Then they were right there, passing the alleyway, within two feet of him. Barnes shut his eyes, counted to three, then sprang out. He wasn't quite behind Garrett; he caught Barnes in the corner of his eye and started to instinctively spin round, raising his arm as he did so. Barnes didn't let him get any further.

He swung the baton two-handed, like a baseball bat, as hard as he could. It connected full force with Garrett's shoulder. The woman screamed. The Garrett cried out and collapsed onto one knee. Barnes swung the baton again and connected with his triceps. Garrett shrieked and clutched his arm. The sirens got louder.

Barnes planted a boot between Garrett's shoulder blades and kicked him prone, then pinned his shoulders with his knees.

"Police! Don't fucking move!" Barnes yelled, and clamped the cuffs tightly around his wrists. Garrett lay still and moaned softly. There would be no fight.

Barnes ripped the rucksack from Garrett's shoulder and pulled it to him, feeling the bulk of the firearm inside. With Garrett under control, Barnes looked around wildly in case the female was going to try to attack him — or, indeed, if there was some other ambush in the offing — but she was long gone. Barnes knew he'd seen her before now, but couldn't think where.

Garrett moaned and tried to say something, but failed. His breathing sounded laboured. Barnes sat him up a little.

"Stefan, what the hell are you playing at? Armed *robbery*?"

Garrett moaned again. He was incoherent, and, unsurprisingly, he wasn't sober. Barnes shook him gently and started to speak again, but he was interrupted by the ringing of his mobile phone. He stayed firmly fixed to his prisoner, while he fished around in his pocket. The phone was a new one — his own was still in the exhibits store — and it took him a moment to answer it.

"DC Barnes."

"DC Barnes, this is Inspector Toynbee from the FCC."

Force Command and Control. The ones who make the plan if the shit hits the fan.

"Hello, sir. Can I help you?"

"You've called in an armed robbery with next to no information. I need some things clarifying before I broadcast the deployment method."

"It was a tip-off. Here and now. I didn't have time to get the ins and outs of a duck's arse."

There was a pause.

"DC Barnes," the inspector said slowly, with tightly controlled patience. "Needless to say, if there is a firearm involved then local, unarmed units are to keep clear and wait for the ARVs. Particularly if there is a suspect sighting. That includes you."

"Sorry, sir. It's a bit late for that."

* * *

The headline of the evening edition was bold, simple and consisted of only two words — *HERO COP*. Hadian spread the newspaper out on the desk, and turned it around to show Barnes. Underneath the headline was a full-colour picture of Barnes pinning the armed robber called Garrett to the pavement. There was nothing else on the front page. The story continued inside, augmented by CCTV images from the building society of the vicious assault on the cashier.

"Well, you'll get a lot of publicity out of this, Barnes." Hadian's voice was cautious. Like so many devotees of the Welsh forward pack, he believed in graft rather than glory.

"You don't sound very happy about it, sir." Barnes stood in front of Hadian at the desk, with his hands clasped behind his back. The pose was deliberately rigid, for fear that his body might betray his frustration at wondering if he could do anything to please his boss.

Hadian rose.

"You and I need to have a talk."

They walked over to the New Inn, Barnes now wondering if rugby analogies would soon be the least of his worries.

The pub was quiet. Hadian went to the bar while Barnes pored over the headline, unable to deny the exhilaration he felt from seeing his name in the paper.

"How's the girl?" Hadian said as he sat down. He passed a lemonade to Barnes and wrapped his thick hands around a pint of Speckled Hen.

"Fine. Broken nose. She'll make a full recovery. Have a headache for a while, but no permanent damage."

"I bet she was pleased to see you."

"Sir, I sense there's more to this." Barnes could stand the tap-dancing no longer.

Hadian put his drink down and folded his arms.

"Okay. First off, you nailed a horrible villain leaving the scene of a nasty armed robbery. He still had the cash and the nostrils on him and if he doesn't plead guilty at first appearance he'll want to seriously reconsider who he instructs for legal advice." He spoke with his eyes on his pint, only raising them to Barnes when he'd finished speaking.

"Go on." Barnes thought this sounded better than "*Get to the point.*"

"But whether you like it or not, high-profile success will always piss off some of your colleagues. Some do it on principle, some are just bitter, but some might have a half-genuine reason."

"Such as whom?" Barnes frowned, unable to mask his defensive tone.

"The source unit have got the knock because it's the first decent tip we've had since the unit was formed, and it didn't go to them. They're jumping up and down saying that if you've got an informant giving you A1 1 info then you should be turning him over to them — only a half-genuine reason, as I said."

"It was an anonymous call. He asked for me specifically. He took ages to get to the point. If I'd had more time I would have submitted the report and let them have it."

"I know you would. But people in this job will make the circumstances fit their agenda. You'll come to learn that."

"I tried to call you too. There was no one else in the office. I wasn't particularly keen to go at all, given my track record with anonymous phone calls."

"The other beef is with FCC." Hadian acted like he hadn't heard.

Barnes looked up at the ceiling. He barely knew of the source unit's existence, let alone that he'd pissed them off by arresting someone. But he'd sort of known this next bit was coming.

"You went unarmed to the scene of an armed robbery. Tactical parameter for a spontaneous firearms incident is that unarmed units keep well clear until the ARVs turn out."

Barnes spread his hands.

"We didn't have time. If I hadn't left as soon as I got the call, we'd have lost him. I didn't have time for anything. I took the car, went straight down there, asked for backup, and then I saw him."

"The phrase he said you used was 'the ins and outs of a duck's arse'."

Barnes shook his head, wondering how he'd managed to piss so many people off by doing his job.

"I was rolling around on the floor trying to arrest this bloke. I was on my own, trying to get the job done, and they're stuck in the fucking ivory tower trying to cover their own arses."

"Spoken like a Pontypridd prop forward," Hadian said with a smile. Now he'd done the uncomfortable bit, the DCI was more sympathetic. "But don't get exasperated. I'm not criticising you, but this has been fed back to me, and I've got to sound you out on it. As far as I'm concerned, you did everything right in the circumstances."

Barnes breathed deeply. At least someone was on his side.

"Thank you." His voice was quiet.

"But I'll tell you something else for free." Hadian sipped from his pint, leaving a line of white foam on his top lip, and leaned forward. "You've got nearly twenty-eight years left to serve, and there will be plenty more opportunities to piss people off by doing your job properly, and quite often it will make no sense to you."

Barnes suddenly felt old, like the strength had left him.

"Just don't get cocky, for heaven's sake," Hadian continued. "If you give the dissenters reason to dislike you, it will last your entire career."

He wiped his lip and picked up the newspaper.

"The byline belongs to someone called Emily Varela. Do you know her?"

Barnes looked his boss dead in the eye.

"No."

Hadian held his gaze. "She was on the scene awfully quickly to get that picture of you making the arrest."

Barnes said nothing.

"You say this informant asked for you specifically?" Hadian said.

"Yes. He wouldn't speak to anybody else, which was strange."

"How do you mean? It would only have taken a phone call to the contact centre to find out what shift you were working."

"Well, I wasn't working my rostered shift. I was down to work a three-to-midnight, but I came in at ten to catch up on some paperwork, and I only changed it a couple of days before. If I'd worked the regular shift I would have missed all this."

"So how would this guy have known when to get you? Are you suggesting this came from the *inside*?"

"It's possible, but I don't think so. I can hardly see any of the bobbies in this station donating a collar like this one. Although the arrest was bizarre in itself."

"In what way?"

"Our armed robber is a guy called Stefan Garrett. He sleeps rough on the seafront, spends most of his life pissed on White Lightning and is usually brought in for minor disorder and drunk offences. He's a street drinker, not an armed robber."

"He looked like one to me."

Barnes conceded the point with a shrug.

"The night Van Leer died, Garrett helped me pull him out of the shelter. He mentioned 'the Dutchman'. He said the Dutchman was responsible for Harriet's death."

"Van Leer is a Dutch name," Hadian murmured.

"That's what I thought."

"I *knew* the little fucker was involved, but since he's now little more than charcoal, it's a moot point."

"Did we ever find a murder weapon for Harriet?"

"I wish."

"Garrett talked about a bust of Beethoven. Admittedly he was only half coherent — which is about as good as he gets — so I don't know if it's kosher information or just the DTs."

"He's probably talking to Beethoven in his cell right now. Getting legal advice." Hadian gulped down the rest of his drink and checked his watch. "Won't hurt to question him about it, though. I'll send someone over to see him. I'll see you, Barnes."

Barnes watched him hurry out of the pub, a nagging feeling at the back of his mind. He knew he'd had nothing to do with contriving or calculating Garrett's arrest, even if his boss didn't entirely believe him. There was one way to find out who had, however.

He pulled Emily Varela's business card out of his jacket and dialled her number on his phone. He hadn't wanted to lie to his boss about knowing her, but he had been laid bare by Hadian's cross-examination and his natural response had been to guard himself. Still, the lie felt like another step down a road he hadn't wanted to travel.

It was well after hours, but she answered on the second ring.

"Emily Varela, news desk."

"Emily, this is DC Barnes. We met outside court—"

"I know who you are," she said, a note of excitement in her breathless voice. "I've been trying to get hold of you all afternoon for a quote. I had to go to press without it or I'd have been trampled in the rush for the evening edition . . . Did you like it?"

"It was quite a spread. My boss thinks I engineered the whole thing."

"That the same boss that wouldn't let me speak to you? Hadrian, is it?"

Why am I not surprised? Barnes thought.

"Hadian. DCI. He's old-school. He doesn't trust the media," he said.

"Him and every other cop under the sun." She clicked her teeth. "But it *was* rather fortuitous, I grant you. Did you get a tip-off?"

"That's why I'm calling. What's your story, if you don't mind my asking?"

She didn't answer immediately.

"We got a tip as well. Male voice. Came straight through to my desk, although he didn't ask for me specifically."

"What did he say?"

"Not a lot. Just that an armed robbery was going down there and then. He gave me the location, and also said that it was the sort of job a certain young detective could make his career on if he hurried. Looks like you succeeded."

"What did he sound like?"

"Rough. Gravelly voice, London accent. He was a bit theatrical as well, if you know what I mean."

"I think I do. Sounds like the same guy."

"Looks like someone wants us to be together."

He took the phone away from his ear and looked at it. She must have sensed that he was about to end the call, for her words all tumbled out in a rush.

"I wasn't joking, Barnes. I'm getting some good stories out of you. We could help each other."

He slowly put the phone back to his ear.

"What are you suggesting, exactly?"

She exhaled heavily.

"You throw me your jobs on an exclusive basis, and I'll make you look good. You could call the 'hero cop' piece a line of credit, if you like."

There was a slight edge of desperation in her voice, and Barnes sensed that she was trying to carve out a place for herself in a cut-throat world — not unlike him, he realised. Whether you wanted to call it corner-cutting, rule-bending or just showing initiative, Barnes understood the unspoken caveat that any scheme couldn't involve the bosses.

"Barnes?" She was still waiting for him to speak.

"You're pretty direct, aren't you?" was all he said.

"Is this linked to the murder of the police officer? Harriet Holden? You were on the enquiry team, weren't you?"

This threw him.

"What makes you think that?"

"Well, I ran the story for the *Sussex Times* — not that you'd have noticed me among the BBC news trucks — and you must surely be thinking that her murder was an underground job."

Barnes decided that he had a lot to learn about professional relationships, particularly with the media. It felt like she had come to him with an apple in one hand, and then, while his guard was down, feinted with the other hand and slugged him with a body shot.

"The favoured theory is domestic violence at present, by an as-yet unidentified partner," he said, opting for the party line.

She made a derisive snorting sound on the other end of the line.

"That's contradictory in itself. If you're a criminal for long enough you learn a lot about police procedure, and that the police don't have unlimited resources, that more crime is happening all the time. That requires more manpower, and the older stuff gets shifted down the pile."

"A police officer was murdered, Emily. It will never go away."

"It will be in the hearts of her family and friends forever, but it will only be in the public eye for as long as it's in the papers. The nationals swanned into town long enough to bag a few headlines and some sticks of rock, then buggered off again. Feed me the details, Barnes. I can make sure her memory stays alive. I've been onto my editor with the idea of running a proper investigative column."

"As opposed to folklore pieces about clifftop erosion?"

"Look, if you give me a green light here, I might not have to write any more local interest bollocks. If I can convince my editor that I've got a source on the murder team, he might give it a second thought."

"It's a moot point, Emily. I've been pulled off the enquiry."

"What? Why?" The disappointment in her voice was genuine, as if a careful plan had been upended at the final hurdle.

"Long story. And I still don't see how you're linking the armed robbery at the building society with Harriet's murder."

"I don't buy the domestic violence theory for a second. You have an improbable armed robber doing over a bank the day after the main suspect for Harriet Holden's murder is killed in a fire — and your bank robber was only inches away from the scene. Somebody wanted to make bloody sure both the police and the press knew about that armed robbery. Not only that, but they wanted Garrett to be caught. Why would that be? Does *he* know something about something? Was it a warning?"

Barnes thought of Garrett's drunken ramblings about "the Dutchman", which were little more than a raw piece of intelligence. The fact that a reporter had more or less guessed at it made him wince. And how the hell did she know Garrett had been at the scene of Van Leer's murder? She was either very insightful or Barnes was not the only source she was cultivating.

"Let me leave you with this," she was saying in his ear. "If the bank robbery *was* a set-up, it could have meant somebody on the Christchurch team was onto something. And frankly, it's not that I don't trust the cops, but you being pulled off seems a bit too much of a coincidence."

"You're in the wrong job, Poirot," Barnes said, and clapped the phone shut.

He sat for a moment, Emily's words reverberating in his brain. Could she be right? Could it be that they'd come too close to finding Holden's killer, and that this was this the very reason why the murder team was being scaled down and sent back to their normal duties?

Emily's pitch had been clumsy, but among her attempts to bargain he thought he had glimpsed somebody motivated by truth. She wasn't after a quick headline, otherwise he wouldn't have entertained another conversation with her.

He thumped the empty glass back on the table. Who was he trying to kid? The "hero cop" piece had been an attempt to seduce him, with the promise of more on the table. And he knew that he wanted it — like an addict desperate for a rush, he would snatch at success if it helped him forget about failure.

He sat for a long time, thinking about Holden, about Eve, already feeling a million miles away from the ambitious, idealistic officer he had been only a matter of weeks ago.

He wanted to make Eve proud, he knew that. But not at any cost. He wanted to solve all her problems, to *save* her, but he knew he couldn't, and the feeling of failure was unwavering as a consequence.

The one thing he knew was driving him was Holden. He still believed this was something he could fix, even if he had to do it alone. Emily was right. Holden had died, and while she would never be more than twenty-six, the immediate impact of her death would become more distant, one day at a time, until it became about other things entirely. Barnes couldn't shake the feeling that most of the people involved in the mechanics of the investigation and the furthest reaches of its impact were more interested in saving their own collective skin. Maybe the righteous overtones of Emily Varela's strategy *were* the only lifeline.

The bar filled up around him as the afternoon drinkers became the Saturday night crowd. The bar became noisier, the lights grew dimmer and the space became precious. Barnes watched them file in. He stayed in his seat and watched pockets of conversation, watched as the drink touched them and dissolved their inhibitions.

Saturday night. He looked at his watch. He and Eve had made no plans, and it weighted his heart to realise he did not know what she was doing tonight.

He sent her a text message. *What are you doing? Are you home?* He left the phone on the table. There was no reply, so he slipped it back into his pocket.

A shriek of female laughter rose up from a group clustered near the whitewashed fireplace. Barnes looked over and saw a well-dressed group of young professionals enjoying their evening. The men wore suits; the women wore evening dresses or smart outfits. There was laughing, touching, skin on skin; some innocent, some exploratory, some forbidden.

One of them caught Barnes's eye. He nodded slightly at her. She smiled back.

Natasha Warwick.

She excused herself from the group and sidestepped her way to the front of the crowd queuing at the bar. She leaned forward on the bar, folded her arms under her breasts, flashed a killer smile at the gap-year barman and was served within seconds.

Subtle.

She walked over to Barnes's table, holding a glass of white wine and a bottle of Corona.

"Hello, Officer." Her tone was playful, her smile wide. "Mind if I join you?"

Barnes said nothing, his mind still revolving around his conversation with Emily Varela, but gestured to the chair Hadian had left. He did not return the smile.

She wore a black cocktail dress with a plunging neckline and a slash in the thigh. Her make-up was a little excessive, but the silver choker and teardrop earrings were a nice touch.

"You look good," he said, without a trace of humour.

"Thank you. Office do. Not sure what the occasion is. There might not be one. A few drinks here, then we have some kind of fancy function room booked at the Grand."

"Do the CPS always cut loose here? I thought it was a police-only establishment," he said.

"Ah, the neophyte in you is still apparent, Officer. This pub is the favourite of every professional outfit in the town, particularly the legal profession. In fact, I'm surprised to see you here."

"Oh, yes?"

"Well, you have a home and a pretty wife to tend to. Do you have any children?"

Barnes looked away, the question like ice on his skin. "No."

"Well then, are you on duty?"

"No, not on duty."

"Then how come you're here by yourself? One might almost think you were waiting for someone." She raised one eyebrow, sliding the bottle of beer across the table to him.

"Meeting with the DCI. He left a while ago. I'm going home in a minute. And I'm afraid I don't drink."

"What a pity." She was smirking. "Lifestyle choice?"

"Something like that. So, for a single girl like you I suppose the weekend is non-stop debauchery. Can I ask why you don't have the home and the dutiful husband?"

His words were sharp, his tone fatalistic, and her smile slipped a little.

"You're a rather intense young man, aren't you?" she said, holding his gaze as she sipped her wine. "I'm divorced, thank Christ. Been single nearly two years. If I were a man I'd be having a midlife crisis about now. As it is I'm simply enjoying myself."

"Enjoying yourself with anyone regular?" he asked. The question sounded like a challenge.

"Why don't you just come right out and say what's on your mind?"

She leaned forward on her elbows. Barnes, unable to help himself, glanced at the freckled tops of her smooth breasts, then looked quickly away. She noticed.

"Officer, are you flirting with me?" She was smiling again. He could smell the wine on her breath.

She reached out and placed a hand on his. The train he was unwittingly riding was not yet a runaway, and this was one choice that seemed easy. He had enough on his plate without having to worry about this.

He pushed her hand away and stood up. The ambient noise in the bar suddenly sounded like the fire that had consumed Howard Van Leer.

"So serious, Officer." Her voice was playful, but she looked hurt.

"If I've given you the wrong idea, Natasha, then I'm sorry. I don't want this."

He walked round the table and out of the pub, pausing for a moment outside to watch her through the window. She sat for a moment, stirring the wine in her glass with a little finger, then got up and rejoined the laughter.

* * *

He drove home. The house was empty. He had no idea where Eve was. He thought of the sweating bottle of Corona Natasha had left on the table with his name on it, and suddenly remembered a six-pack of Heineken that had been on ice since Christmas, courtesy of one of Eve's cousins.

He dug them out from the bottom of the fridge, fed the dog and collapsed onto the sofa. Forbes stood in the doorway and tilted his head inquisitively.

"Who are you, my wife?" Barnes said to the dog, who sensed his tone and went to curl up in his basket.

Barnes opened a bottle and took his first drink in ten years.

It went down well, although for ten years' abstinence he'd been expecting a little more bang for his buck. He got started on the second almost immediately.

He took another drink. And another. And then another.

Vague urges — to be aggressive, to call Natasha, to call Eve, to go out drinking all night, to eat the contents of the fridge — came and went, none strong enough to act upon.

The only thing he desperately wanted to do was have a long, idle chat with Harriet Holden. But he knew he couldn't.

Instead, he rummaged around carelessly in his briefcase for Holden's demo CD. He cranked the volume up, and her voice, clear as a bell and pitch-perfect, filled the room as if she were sitting right there with him.

He sat rigidly through "Without You", waiting for the bottled-up tears to come rushing out, suddenly craving the loss of control, that orgasm of grief, but he was disappointed. In the drunken jumble of thoughts and feelings, he thought of her wasted body, wondering if she'd been able to conceive when she was alive, if she'd wanted children, reminding himself that now she would never do anything.

He'd expected the alcohol to lubricate his emotions and had prepared himself to finally give in to them, but — nothing. He wondered if they were too deeply buried. Maybe they were never really there. He didn't know. A note-perfect rendition of "Walking on Sunshine" did nothing for him either.

By the time the demo wound up with "Moon River" he'd polished off the pack and had fallen asleep. He lay on the sofa, MTV projecting mute, aversion-therapy images onto his face.

The beer-induced stupor was like a black fog, so he did not hear his phone when it vibrated gently on the table.

It had taken a while to filter through, but the text message was from Eve, replying to his earlier message:

No not at home, out clubbing. Rescue me, Chief! X

But Barnes was asleep.

CHAPTER FIFTEEN

Three things were making Barnes drive at a pace totally unsuitable for the conditions.

The first was the telephone message he had received from Sussex House earlier that day. The recordings of Van Leer's prison telephone calls had finally arrived. Despite pulling Barnes off the Op Christchurch enquiry, Hadian had presumably not yet got around to reallocating the action to retrieve them to someone else — it was still allocated to Barnes on HOLMES.

Having arranged to collect the tapes after hours, Barnes had raced to Sussex House, an ugly rectangle of concrete and glass on a Hollingbury industrial estate, hoping to get there before someone discovered he was working under the radar. Sussex House was the operational base of all the major specialist departments in the force, and despite his urgency Barnes had paused long enough in the lobby to drink in the directory on the lobby wall — the soon-to-be-launched Major Crime Branch . . . Force Crime and Drug Unit . . . Hi-Tech Crime Unit . . . Specialist Investigations Unit . . . Covert Policing Unit . . .

Real police work.

And now he was racing back to Eastbourne, the tapes in a polythene exhibit bag on the seat beside him. He was desperate to listen to them, but the Mondeo was equipped with only a CD player, and he needed to get back to the office to dig out a tape machine. This was the second thing making him drive like a maniac as the night descended on the deathly quiet A27.

The third thing was the headlights in his rear-view mirror, on main beam and gaining fast. As Barnes raced past Lewes he eased off the throttle slightly, flicked the mirror to reduce the glare and jabbed his rear fog lights on. A sudden release of adrenaline made his thighs ache and his heart beat hard in his chest. He was doing seventy-five, but the headlights were growing in his mirror at an alarming rate.

He applied the brakes early at the bottleneck on the approach to Beddingham. The car was now immediately behind him.

As he entered the roundabout Barnes heard the clutch of the car drop and the engine howl as the driver slid up the inside to get ahead of Barnes before the bottleneck.

Barnes wrenched his steering wheel to the left to narrowly avoid the collision. The car was a pale metallic convertible Mercedes. Barnes couldn't quite make out the colour under the sodium carriageway lights, but he knew that it was green. The same car that had driven at him the night of Van Leer's murder. He fumbled on the front passenger seat for his radio.

The car was level with him for a split second. Barnes managed a sideways glance at the driver, but saw only the peak of a baseball cap. He heard the loud *thump-thump-thump* of a powerful bass system, then the Mercedes roared away, its rear lights glowing. The carriageway lights ended once they were off the roundabout, and the road became shrouded in darkness, but Barnes had managed to note the registration number.

Suddenly angry, he dropped a gear and thundered after the Mercedes, yelling into his radio for backup. But the

Mondeo was no match, and the Mercedes quickly became just a pair of red dots in the distance.

Barnes wanted to ask the control room to run the vehicle through the system, hoping that a traffic patrol might be able to intercept it, but the air was busy, with every spare unit assigned to a job.

He pulled onto a lay-by and hit the interior light. He found his notebook and a pen, and scribbled down the registration number of the Mercedes.

"L2D GBH," he said aloud as he wrote. "Cute."

He checked the tapes were okay, and, after a brief interlude at the Beddingham level crossing, headed off again.

Outside Firle he opened the window to let in some air, and felt the night's moisture on his face like icy breaths.

As the road rounded onto the Firle straight he began to increase the pressure on the throttle again, but eased off again as something ahead caught his eye.

The Firle straight was a notorious stretch of the A27 that had claimed a number of lives. The road was poorly lit, and calming measures to prevent the temptation of unwarranted overtaking had yet to get off the drawing board.

The thing in front of him grew larger as he headed towards it, his headlights cutting a tunnel of light through the suffocating black. He wasn't sure what it was, but it looked like something in the middle of the carriageway. He slowed to around thirty and squinted forward, then a glint of metal cut through the darkness and he slammed on his brakes. The tyres made an unholy shriek as the car juddered to a halt.

The Mercedes was lying on its roof in the middle of the carriageway, flames of vapour dancing in the beam of the headlights. Beyond the car the Firle straight was empty, stretching into the darkness, flanked on both sides by nothing but the desolate black countryside.

Barnes checked his mirrors. Nothing behind him. He pulled his car onto the verge and grabbed his radio and torch, anxiety at what he might find overridden by a grim desire to know who was behind the wheel.

He ran over to the car. The engine was dead, and there was a strong smell of petrol. The headlights were still on, and the stereo was playing loudly — the *thump-thump-thump* of the powerful bass echoed in the still air. It was the only sound Barnes could hear.

The Mercedes was a soft-top, and had been smashed almost completely flat by the impact. Barnes got onto his belly and shone his torch through what was left of the driver's window.

To his surprise and frustration, the car looked empty. Barnes shone his torch across both seats. There were no back seats to speak of, and the car was resting flat on its windscreen so he couldn't tell for definite if the driver had been ejected. He checked the seatbelt. The driver hadn't been wearing it. Blood was streaked across the dashboard. It dripped off the controls like thick red paint.

He stood up and checked the front of the Mercedes. The remains of a fox were spattered across the grille and bumper, enmeshed in the metal like a gruesome novelty decoration. He walked back past his own car, following a trail of glass shards, and about a hundred yards down the road found the rest of the fox. He looked back at the wreck, a feeling of horror growing in him. The guy had been driving like a maniac when he chose to overtake Barnes. In the darkness, he must have only seen the fox at the last second, stamped on the anchors and rolled it. Barnes was no expert, but estimated that at that speed, with virtually no braking time, the car would have rolled at least six times. The driver must have been flung out of the car.

He fiddled with his personal radio until he got reception, and called in the crash as he walked back to the mangled Mercedes. He called it as a fatal, even though he hadn't found any bodies. Being a night duty, the nearest traffic car was doing motorway patrol on the M23 up near Gatwick, and would take the best part of thirty minutes to get to him. The eerie sound of the incessant bass thumping through the night had become too much, and he reached through the crumpled frame and used the end of his baton to poke the "off" switch on the dash.

A couple of local patrols came free. They closed the roads and set up diversions to avoid further crashes. While he waited, he asked the control room to check the vehicle. Sorry, they said, PNC is down. Problems at Hendon, they said. *Expect it back soon — ten minutes or so?* Barnes told the controller that was no problem.

The night traffic car arrived, and two serious-looking cops who looked like ex-squaddies began measuring, marking and preserving. They asked for a name for the investigation, and got Op Cheriton. Barnes thanked them for coming. They were tired — it was their second fatal of the night. They were glad to have a detective on the scene — there weren't enough of them to start searching for a body as well as controlling the scene, even if there was no chance of survival. They looked relieved when Barnes said he would start looking.

It didn't take him long. His torch caught something in a grass verge, about fifty yards east of the scene. He walked towards it. The torch picked it up again. A tiny glint, flashing in the torchlight.

He moved closer. The voices of the traffic police grew fainter, the reach of the dragon lamps grew less, until it was just Barnes, his torch, the darkness — and the tiny reflective thing hiding in the verge.

Blood was flicked across the road surface, like paint from the brush of an exuberant artist. It led to the verge, and Barnes stepped into the grass. The glint was now recognisable as a gold tooth in a row of grinning teeth that had been mashed through the face of the dead driver.

The body was in some long grass about ten feet from the roadside, heaped in a way that defied conventional anatomy — Barnes could not tell where the torso ended nor where the limbs began. A shard of skull half an inch thick had lifted clear of the head, hair and blood pasted to it like a coconut smashed open on a rock.

The injuries were extensive, the sight gruesome, but Barnes felt nothing other than the shivering cold that had by now seeped into his bones from the cool moisture of the night.

"*Quo vadis*, you silly sod?" he said, shining his torch down onto the dead face of Phil McDermott.

CHAPTER SIXTEEN

Barnes watched his wife for some time from the driver's seat of the car.

He was parked across the road from the entrance of the nursery. Eve was standing outside the nursery doors, saying goodbye to a large group of kids aged about three or four, as their parents arrived in rotation to collect their offspring.

She looked good. Watching her from this distance, he realised how happy it made him to know intimate details, like how she'd picked that day's outfit the night before and how she'd coaxed him to iron the top for her because his ironing skills far outstripped her own.

The kids clearly loved her. They hugged her legs and jumped up and down and tried to get in on the conversations she was having with their parents, little hints of possessiveness as they tried to remind mum or dad that this was *their* teacher.

She hugged them back and ruffled their hair and knelt down to the quieter ones. Barnes wondered if any of the parents knew how desperately his wife wanted a baby, and, if they did, whether they would feel any discomfort at the thought of the vicarious maternal gratification she gained from teaching their children.

One of the fathers — a well-built man, about ten years older than Eve, looking about six-three, six-four — touched Eve on the arm while they were speaking. She threw her head back as they laughed and chatted, and when they left she touched his hand after bending down to kiss the boy. A sick, hot feeling swelled in both his stomach and his loins as his mind momentarily ran away with itself, and then it was gone.

Eventually the last car drove away, and Barnes, feeling somehow helpless, walked over as she was locking up.

"The old woman that lived in the shoe," he said, smiling.

She smiled back. "If only."

He pulled her close, and whispered in her ear. "Come on. Let me take you home."

She cupped his face in her hands.

"Barnes, I've been doing some thinking. I've got an opportunity here to see to it that my problem doesn't interfere with your future. Barnes, I don't want you to look at me in ten years and feel like you should have found someone else when you had the chance."

"Eve, I know how you feel, but . . ."

"I don't think you do, Barnes. And I know it's stupid, but I can't help thinking about all those women you work with. All about your age, and they could just run upstairs with you, hop into bed and you could be a dad nine months later. Simple. We'll never be able to do that, Barnes."

"Listen . . ."

"And whenever I think those things, I can't help but think of poor Harriet, and the way you obsess about her. About finding the man that killed her."

"Harriet? What's she . . ."

"Did you love her, Barnes?"

"What?" He began to laugh, incredulous.

"What's so funny?"

"Eve, it isn't just you. It's me as well."

"What do you mean?"

"I went to the consultant. My sperm sample was empty. I'm shooting blanks, Eve."

Tears filled her eyes, her sadness genuine. She touched his face.

"Barnes, I'm so sorry."

"No, it's a good thing."

She frowned.

"How so?"

"It means we're in it together. How can I resent you when we've both got the same problem?" He laughed again, a hysterical edge to his voice.

"I . . . I don't understand." She was pale.

"It's very simple."

"No, I don't understand why you're happy about this. I mean, *both* of us infertile? What are the chances of that? I'm starting to wonder if someone's trying to tell us something. Maybe we're just not meant to have children."

"I don't believe that."

"Barnes, the couple over the road have just had their first. When it's quiet you can hear him crying. I can't stand it. How can something so easy for other people be so hard for us?"

"I . . . I didn't know."

"Barnes, look." She shut her eyes. "I'm going to stay at my mum's for a while. Just some time to think."

His heart plummeted. He was tempted to pretend he hadn't heard his wife.

"Eve . . . are you leaving me?"

"I love you, Barnes, but I don't want to be the one to ruin your life."

She kissed him on the mouth as the taxi pulled up, and went to retrieve the overnight bag from inside the nursery doors — the one she'd already packed, early that morning.

Intimate details. This was one he hadn't known about.

* * *

The thoroughness of any police investigation can be virtually predetermined in certain areas, but is less predictable in others. Scene management, forensic examination, setting the parameters of the house-to-house enquiries, examining CCTV footage and following up sequential lines of enquiry — these can be determined by mathematically precise strategies, and validated in the knowledge that each decision will be scrutinised by a defence lawyer.

The results of such enquiries, however, leave a lot open to chance. The net of witness appeals can be thrown over a huge catchment, but each news bulletin, media release, press conference or leaflet drop depends entirely on the right people bearing witness, and also the success of appealing to a potential witness's civic duty in coming forward.

Such are the vagaries of a police investigation.

The murder of a police officer was high-profile, but only for a limited time. As Emily Varela had speculated, and as Paul Hadian knew for sure, the public interest shelf life of any case was limited, and if witnesses were not secured in the vital first week, then there was a risk they would be gone forever, while the snapshot in their minds that could have proved so crucial began to decay.

People called in, but it was all useless. A blonde girl had been seen in the street. Was it Holden? No idea. Suspicious behaviour in and around the hotel. No surprises there — the place was rife with crime. A voice in the night heard shouting "I'll kill you" — an almost daily occurrence at the Atlantic Hotel. The detectives knew that the investigation was hampered by probable low-life witnesses who were either distinctly unmoved by the murder of a police officer or loath to testify against a cop-killer. Or perhaps both. Moreover, the vast number of transients in the area who came and went on a sporadic basis, leaving no paper trail, meant that there was no way of accounting for everyone who had been in the hotel between when Holden was killed and when she was found.

Barnes had been working day shifts since being assigned to the enquiry, but had since returned to his regular shift pattern, which included night duty rotations on a regular basis. He didn't mind working nights. Some of the older detectives hated nights, and spent them asleep in the office. Barnes, however, was not an older detective, and, exactly as he had done as a uniformed officer, used his night duties to go hunting.

His first night tour was the following Wednesday. He arrived in the office and took a handover from the late-turn DC, who gave him a quick briefing and hurried home.

Barnes checked his watch. It was still relatively early — he calculated that he had maybe an hour or two to catch up on some files before he ventured out. The stack of files on his desk had grown. He worked from the bottom up, and pulled out the assault file containing the CCTV tape from the previous Friday. The last time he'd tried to review this particular file he'd ended up rolling about on the floor with an armed robber. He glanced at the phone and toyed with the idea of taking it off the hook.

He made himself some tea and ventured into the CCTV control room next door. He sipped his drink and chatted with the operator while he surveyed the banks of screens covering the centres of every town in the east of the county.

After exchanging pleasantries, he found a quiet corner and sat down with the file. He pulled the videotape out of the file and played it on one of the unused monitors. With the film was an audio recording of the accompanying police radio traffic, consisting largely of the CCTV operator's commentary.

The film started. A group of six men were squaring up to each other outside one of the town centre's less salubrious establishments. On closer inspection it appeared to be a group of smartly dressed young men circling another man. The lone man wore a baseball cap and a black singlet. Barnes noted his wiry physique and squinted at the grainy footage.

He wasn't sure, because the cap was partially obscuring the man's face, but it looked like Robbie Fortune, the curious resident of the Atlantic Hotel.

As Barnes watched, one of the group threw a beer glass at Fortune and yelled something. Fortune covered his eyes

— the glass struck his forearm and bounced onto the ground a few feet away from him, where it smashed. Things were getting nasty.

Fortune drew a knife and beckoned the group towards him. The knife glinted in the glow of the street lights, and on the audio recording the CCTV operator barked that some patrols were needed, and quickly.

The group hesitated, Fortune's total lack of fear arresting their confidence. Then they appeared to decide among themselves that they could take this strange-looking man. They slowly advanced and surrounded him, drunken bravado animating their movements. Barnes folded his arms and watched the screen, his pulse quickening.

Fortune didn't wait to be entertained by any pre-battle rituals. He sprang forward like a cornered cat and, driving forward with his hips, landed two good punches on two of the group. His two victims were sent immediately to the ground, semi-conscious and dead weight. This gave a green light to the others, who jumped on Fortune and began raining blows onto him. These were clumsy, scattergun attempts — nothing like Fortune's professional-looking strikes — and although the overall effect looked savage, very few connected anywhere important.

Fortune swung the knife out in front of him, in wide arcing movements. He caught two of the group across the chest; stripes of blood appeared on their neatly pressed white shirts. They clawed at themselves and staggered around on the spot. Barnes let out an involuntary gasp. The audio recording lapsed into a moment's stunned silence, and then the CCTV operator started yelling for units to hurry up.

Fortune had injured four of the six and so far appeared relatively unscathed. He landed another two haymakers that sent the two stab victims to the ground. The remaining two circled him, but two determined lunges with the knife were enough to make them turn tail and run.

Fortune had defended himself, but it didn't end there. He concealed the knife, then, with vicious accuracy, took a brief run-up and swung a huge kick at the head of one of the two he had stabbed. Barnes winced when it connected.

The victor approached his now unconscious victim, and lifted his head from the pavement to check for signs of consciousness. There were none. Fortune dropped the man's limp head carelessly back onto the concrete. A pool of blood began to spread slowly across the pavement — under the distorted amber wash that tinted the image, it looked black.

The CCTV operator, aware of his own duties as an investigator and collector of evidence, had focused the camera on Fortune's face and zoomed in on the image.

Flashing blue lights appeared, just visible in the periphery of the screen, signalling the imminent arrival of the emergency services. Fortune looked around him, then up and directly at the camera that was glaring at him accusingly, and took to his heels.

Barnes stopped the tape and sat back, tapping his pen on the desk while he thought. He'd briefed Hadian about Robbie Fortune — that they couldn't find a record for him, that he may have been the one to make the bullshit phone call to report his neighbour Howard Van Leer missing. The DCI had told Barnes he would get the intel unit to do some work on Fortune.

Barnes had heard no more since then. Maybe Hadian forgot. Maybe he hadn't forgotten at all, but the outcome of the intel unit's research was none of Barnes's business — he was no longer on the enquiry, after all. Maybe they'd been watching Fortune for weeks, and were hours away from arresting him for Holden's murder.

No, that didn't make sense. If Fortune was under surveillance then the assault on the videotape would have been prevented, or at least interrupted. The first responders on the tape were there as a result of the CCTV operator finding the incident, nothing more than that.

Maybe Hadian was just humouring Barnes and had no intention of following up on his information. Maybe he didn't really want him in the CID at all, and just wanted suspects for Holden's murder close to him.

Barnes flung his pen across the room. He got up and started pacing with anger, which brought the headaches on. Then he slowed down and channelled his anger into action. The file had been passed to him as having an unidentified suspect. He alone had made the ID of Fortune from the CCTV footage, which meant Fortune was now a named suspect in this GBH investigation.

Which meant he was wanted. Which meant Barnes was going to go and get him.

He hesitated momentarily. Hadian had said he'd recruited Barnes into the CID because he made his own luck, but also that trouble had a way of finding him. Were the two notions so different?

He went back into the office and began to kit up — stab vest, baton, pepper spray, handcuffs, radio and car keys — and suddenly he missed his uniformed duties. Life seemed so much simpler then.

With that in mind — not to mention the fact that every time he was on his own he seemed to get in trouble for something, despite his best intentions — he went down to the custody block looking for some assistance. As luck would have it, a solo patrol cop had just been stood down from a cell watch — he was young and keen, and so Barnes co-opted him into helping out. The two of them walked to the garage to get the Mondeo, and they drove into town.

Eastbourne town centre was busy. Gangs of drunken youths roamed the streets, laughing and singing and shouting. They kicked over bins, swung from road signs and loitered in the road. It was low-level, but it was still early, and it wasn't good-natured. The evening would get worse. Uniformed patrols circled the town — on foot and cycle, by van and car.

Pockets of disorder were swept away quickly by the patrols. Drunk and disorderly, abusive behaviour, criminal damage — anyone with more than a few clever words to spit at the patrols was quickly cuffed and bundled into one of the vans to prevent further trouble. For a while it looked as though the police were winning.

Barnes headed for the Atlantic Hotel and parked outside. He could see the tiny window to Robbie Fortune's room. It was dark. No movement. Barnes's impromptu crew partner logged the arrest enquiry with the control room so they knew where they were and what they were doing, then the pair of them got out and walked to the front doors of the hotel.

They paused as they approached, and Barnes turned to look down at the steps of the hotel, where he could just see the basement window of the room in which Holden's body had been found. It was in darkness. Strands of police tape could still be seen inside.

He hadn't forgotten her. Hadian may have reassigned him, but he was still going to find her killer, one way or another. Even though he was, at that moment, working on another investigation entirely, a dull, nagging feeling in his stomach told him that Robbie Fortune somehow held some insights into her death.

The hotel doors were locked and the lobby through the glass was dark. Barnes backed away slightly and exchanged glances with his crew partner — the thought of breaking in having occurred to both of them simultaneously — and then Barnes saw a figure on the street briskly approaching the hotel. His system braced with a surge of adrenaline. He squinted. The figure came closer. It was Fortune. He was trotting, and looking around anxiously. He slowed down to a walk as he reached the hotel.

Barnes held his baton up behind him with one hand and his warrant card out in front of him with the other. His oppo moved around to outflank Fortune and cover Barnes.

"Police! Stand where you are, Robbie."

Robbie Fortune looked like he had no intention of obeying the command until he heard his name, whereupon he screwed his eyes up and edged closer.

"It's DC Barnes, Robbie. Empty your pockets."

Fortune did as he was told. Coins and a lighter clattered onto the wet pavement, and then he spread his hands in demonstrable compliance.

Barnes edged closer, baton held up behind his shoulder; wide, searching eyes roving all over Fortune's body for tell-tale signs of fight or flight — agitated foot movements, eyes seeking out target areas on Barnes's body, flared nostrils, rapid breathing.

Barnes locked an arm up under Fortune's armpit; his oppo did the same on the other side and reached around to the back of his belt for his handcuffs. Barnes was impressed — the officer's movements were swift, precise. Fortune's eyes widened when the cold steel snapped onto his wrist and he heard the unmistakable sound of the ratchet sliding home — the sound of his liberty evaporating, and doubtless one he'd heard many times before.

"The fuck is *this*?" He tensed his arms up and shook the cuffs indignantly. There was a note of outrage in his voice, as he evidently realised this was not just a stop-and-search, but by then it was too late.

"Robbie, you're under arrest for wounding with intent to cause grievous bodily harm." They led Fortune to the back of the Mondeo, but their prisoner tried to twist away. Barnes put one hand on the side of Fortune's face, and the other on his upper arm, and Fortune was jerked face-down onto the boot of the car. His skin looked grey in the street lighting, and there were little white scars all over the side of his neck.

"GBH? Me? Fuck that. This is bullshit," Fortune dribbled onto the metal, sounding like a cat hissing as he inhaled.

"Last week. Six idiots in Langney Road, outside the Curzon." Fortune's aftershave and sweat were sticky on Barnes's hand, and he could feel the rough stubble and the hollow of Fortune's mouth under the ball of his palm.

"Don't know what you're on about." Fortune's mouth was squashed between the boot lid and Barnes's hand, and his voice was like someone gargling.

"There's video footage, Robbie. It's all as clear as day. How about you make this easy for yourself and tell us what you did with the knife?"

"On video, my arse. I want a lawyer. I ain't telling you shit. Get me a fuckin' lawyer, you pig."

Fortune tensed his body and tried to push the two cops off him. Barnes relaxed long enough to allow Fortune to lift them both up with his back; then, when he was at an angle of about forty-five degrees to the car boot, they forced Fortune back down again. Except this time, Barnes aimed him behind the car. The three of them crashed down onto the road, and there was a thumping *whoof* as Fortune's wind was knocked out of him.

Barnes's oppo took the opportunity to truss Fortune's arms and legs with Velcro restraints — the phrase "hog-tied" was no longer allowed, but that was exactly what it was — and then Fortune was slung in the back seat of the car.

They drove to the station through the middle of town, Fortune wriggling and grumbling on the back seat while Barnes's oppo held him in place. The kid appeared to be thoroughly enjoying himself.

"Where's the knife, Robbie?" Barnes asked again.

"Fuck yourself."

Barnes gave it up as a bad idea, but his oppo called up on the radio to ask for a dog handler and a couple of units to trace Fortune's likely route for the knife. The control room sent a patrol car and a dog handler. Barnes nodded at him in the rear-view.

Closing time had been and gone, and now the revellers were all on the streets — animals released from their cages. The disorder was increasing, and the patrols were now struggling to cope, not least because closing time brought with it an increase in calls to domestic incidents, which pulled the resources away from the town centre.

As he drove, the car silent apart from Fortune's raspy breathing, Barnes tried to remember what a Wednesday night in the first flush of summer looked like before he'd joined the police, but the memory was elusive.

* * *

The tiny, stuffy interview room smelled like sweat and the bad breath of every prisoner that had ever been in there. The room was silent while Fortune and his solicitor, Joan Byatt, watched the screen intently.

Barnes concentrated on Fortune's expression, but even he could not tear his eyes away from the part where he'd kicked his prone victim in the head. Byatt did not react, having already seen it once. When Barnes had first showed it to her as part of his initial disclosure, she had been unable to suppress a grimace.

The video came to an end. Barnes shut it off.

"What do you want to tell me about that, Robbie?" he asked quietly.

"It's obvious, ain't it? I was defending meself. There were six of them, one of me. Wankers!" he barked at the now-black screen. He was still trembling with righteous outrage.

"Self-defence? Then why did you have the knife?"

Fortune threw his hands up in exasperation, as if every question Barnes asked was a stupid one that he should know the answer to.

"I always carry it. Protection. Good job too, or it'd be *me* in the hospital."

"You know that's an offence, don't you?"

"Officer, we're looking at a clear case of self-defence resulting in unfortunate injury. Charges of possessing a bladed article have not been discussed," Byatt interjected in a nasal tone that bordered on the supercilious.

Barnes had not met Joan Byatt before, and he had taken an instant dislike to her. She was from Wedderburn's, the same firm as Phil McDermott. She was a skinny, elfin creature, somewhere between thirty and forty, with crafty eyes and a naked contempt for police officers.

Barnes held Fortune's stare for two seconds before turning to look at Byatt. He looked to Fortune again.

"Robbie, your legal representative is suggesting that we should not be talking about the offence of possessing a bladed article because I only told her about the four separate counts of assault — two of them serious — before you consulted with her. However, if you are claiming self-defence, it's my duty to explore that claim."

Barnes kept his eyes on Fortune, who looked from Byatt to Barnes and back again — despite his obvious agitation, he looked confused. Barnes could sense Byatt bristling in the corner of the tiny room. He had learned this trick from his interview training — to studiously avoid any direct interaction with the suspect's legal representative, and to redirect any interjections straight back to the suspect. Barnes had not used it with confidence before, largely because his preferred style was to generate a positive atmosphere in the interview and extract information from an over-eager suspect. He was, however, more than happy to ignore Byatt, and it appeared to have an immediate effect.

Barnes continued. "Why did you have the knife, Robbie?"

"Officer, my client has answered that question."

"Did you know that it's an offence to carry a knife like that in public?"

"Officer, my client has answered that question as well. If we're going over the same old ground, I think we should wrap this up."

With toe-curling patience, Barnes drew breath and addressed Fortune.

"Robbie, this is your interview. Yours and mine. Your opportunity to put forward your side of the story, mine to test any account you give me with the facts I already know." He checked his notes. "And, in actual fact, you weren't given an opportunity to answer the first time I asked you if you knew that it is an offence to carry a knife in public." His eyes remained fixed on Fortune.

"I don't fuckin' know, do I? What I do know is that it's a fuckin' good job I *did* have it." Fortune's unblinking eyes did not leave Barnes.

"We've all watched the tape, Robbie. Let's say you were genuinely in fear for your immediate personal safety, and did what you had to do to defend yourself."

Byatt tutted. Barnes ignored it.

"Now you can disagree with this, but I think your claim of self-defence is probably valid — up until the point where you decided to punt that man's head halfway up the street." Barnes leaned forward. "What have you got to say to that?"

Fortune eyed his solicitor, an ugly scowl forming on his face. She put a finger to her lips.

"No comment," Fortune said, with a faintly triumphant tone.

"On the video, the man is lying on the ground, totally still, because you had already punched and stabbed him. To me, he looked pretty much out of the game already. So you tell me how kicking him in the head was self-defence?"

"No comment." Fortune folded his arms and exhaled.

"You knew he was down and out, but you thought you'd put the boot in anyway, didn't you? Teach him a lesson?"

"No comment."

"How did the fight start, Robbie?"

"No comment."

"They were obviously squaring up to you, ready for a rumble. Who started it?"

"No comment."

"Were they jibing you? Or was it the other way around?"

"No comment."

"You walked into town with a switchblade on you. You picked a group of drunk, stupid idiots and goaded them into fighting you."

"No comment."

"When you'd finished with them, you picked one for kicking practice. You went looking for trouble, didn't you?"

Fortune's self-control snapped, and he suddenly tensed. He leaned forward and slapped his palms onto the table, his black eyes blazing with anger.

"No fucking comment!" he yelled.

Barnes's challenges had been deliberately provocative, and he had half-expected a reaction from Fortune; despite this, he had to force himself not to flinch. Having seen what Fortune was capable of, remaining impassive was not easy.

Barnes shut the recorder off and got to his feet.

"I expect you to either charge or release my client without delay, Officer," Byatt huffed. She emphasised the word *release*, checking her watch at the same time.

"I can't do that until I've discussed the case with the custody officer. I need his authority to charge."

Fortune's eyes widened and his hands dropped off the table when he heard the word "charge". He'd obviously received conflicting advice, and he shot Byatt an outraged look. Byatt avoided his eyes, and Barnes thought he saw a flicker of anxiety on her face.

Barnes showed them out of the interview room into the solicitor's consulting room next door. Byatt sat down at a small table, but Fortune paced up and down, his movements animated, as though he were shot through with electricity. To facilitate legal privilege, the consulting room was also heavily soundproofed, but Fortune did not wait for the door to shut before he started yelling.

"Charge? You said self-defence! You said keep quiet and I'd be home by morning . . ."

Barnes allowed the door to close on them, and the sound was cut. He went into the custody office and collared the sergeant.

"Might want to keep an eye on the consulting room, sarge," he said.

The custody officer put down his Robert Ludlum paperback to look through the window in the door. He was a sandy-haired man with thick glasses and huge forearms who liked to bring in an acoustic guitar and play folk songs on night duty. He scowled when he saw Fortune pacing up and down, yelling.

"She's all right. He's not threatening her, just got a strong opinion." The custody officer went back to his Ludlum.

"You're not a fan of Joan Byatt either?" Barnes felt a sudden urge to shake his hand.

"Mangy old cow."

Barnes felt a trifle relieved, and relayed the circumstances of the case. The custody officer listened patiently.

"Well, there's more than enough to charge him," he said, when Barnes had finished speaking. "Have you seen his previous?"

Barnes frowned. "He told me before that he'd done some time, but I couldn't find any trace of him."

"We ran him through LiveScan. There's no trace of him on the name Robbie Fortune, but his file name comes down to Grigory Michalek — and that's a different story."

Barnes turned to the giant whiteboard on the wall, where a custody assistant was erasing the name FORTUNE and writing MICHALEK in bold marker pen.

The custody officer thrust a sheaf of papers into Barnes's hand. Barnes felt a flutter of excitement at the new information. Did Hadian know this already? Had the intel cell already dug it up? It was possible, but not definite. Getting someone into custody was the best way to verify their identity, and since Barnes and Nightingale had questioned him at the Atlantic Hotel, Fortune had more or less kept his nose clean.

"Nasty bastard. Likes to take chunks out of cops," the custody officer said as Barnes flicked through Fortune's previous convictions. "There won't be any issue in refusing him bail."

"Actually, I'd rather we didn't," Barnes said suddenly, his mind still racing.

The custody officer looked at him sharply.

"What? He's up for two GBH charges using a knife. He's got previous for serious violence, including on police officers. You got a reason to let him roam the streets?"

"He won't be roaming the streets exactly. But his name keeps coming up in the Christchurch murder investigation. There's nothing concrete coming in yet, but we don't want him in prison just yet. I want to let him run, and put surveillance on him." Barnes was thinking on his feet, and the words were tumbling out almost as fast as his brain could process the turn of information.

"DC Barnes, I think there's a real need to consider the safety of the public here. This man is violent and dangerous."

"Sarge, if there's a surveillance unit on him twenty-four-seven then we limit the risk. If he starts playing up, then they call it in and we have uniform on him straightaway before he can do any damage. I'm willing to take the risk."

"I'm not sure I am."

"If you're not happy, call DCI Hadian."

The custody officer made the call. Hadian — once he had recovered from being woken up in the middle of the night — was initially reluctant and took convincing, but in the end backed Barnes and said he would arrange a surveillance team. The custody officer argued, but eventually conceded the point of view.

The custody officer hung up the phone, and Fortune was taken from the solicitor's room to the charge desk.

"Do I get me clothes back?" he asked.

"No," answered Barnes. "They've been seized as evidence."

Fortune looked down at his white paper suit.

"I thought only murderers wore these."

"You stabbed two people and kicked one of them in the head. They're still in hospital. Who knows what could happen to them?"

"Officer, if you are implying that my client will be facing further charges, then I want further disclosure," Byatt said.

Barnes ignored her. Fortune began to bristle as the charges were read out, and Barnes's eyes flicked back and forth from the charge sheet to Fortune. The custody officer was doing the same.

When Barnes finished the caution, Fortune put his hands on his hips and looked at the ceiling.

"Two fuckin' GBH charges! Fuckin' unbelievable," he groaned.

The custody officer noted this as Fortune's reply to caution.

"How can it be GBH if it's fuckin' self-defence!" he demanded, of no one in particular.

Only Barnes offered to assist him. "Robbie, if it's self-defence then that's down to a court to decide, not us."

Fortune found some focus for his upset, and he stepped forward and jabbed a finger at Byatt.

"You! You said it was self-defence, easy! You said I'd be out!" His tone was choppy and aggressive, and she stepped back in alarm, her us-against-them bond seemingly broken.

"It *is* self-defence, Robbie," she said weakly. "It's just the police—"

The custody officer cut her off.

"Calm down, Mr Fortune," he warned, stepping out from behind the desk.

Tears formed in Fortune's eyes, and he turned around on the spot, unsure of where to look or what to do. He started to pace up and down, throwing his arms in the air.

"GBH. Fuckin' GBH! I done time for GBH already, oh fuck . . ."

The relief in Byatt's face was palpable when Fortune turned his attention to the custody officer.

"You fuckin' pigs! I ain't going back to prison. I fucking ain't!"

Fortune was screaming now, arms flailing as if directing traffic, fists clenching and unclenching. He set his feet like a boxer's and Barnes recognised the transition in body language from verbal to physical aggression.

Barnes put down his paperwork and stepped forward, but the custody officer reacted faster. He stepped towards Fortune and calmly hooked a massive arm around the man's neck, pulling his head down so his face was under the custody officer's armpit. Fortune started to struggle. The custody officer whispered something to him that Barnes did not catch, and then Fortune went limp and began to sob.

The custody officer released him. Fortune slid down the wall into a sitting position and buried his face in his hands. The tears began to flow; hoarse, raspy sobs that turned his face red.

"Fuck, *fuck*. I can't go back to prison. I *can't*," he wailed. There were flecks of spittle at the corners of his mouth.

"Right, let's wrap this up," the custody officer said sternly, his patience evaporating.

Byatt stirred. "Sergeant, can I please insist that—"

"I wasn't talking to you, Ms Byatt," the custody officer snapped. "If you want to make representations about my decision to grant bail, you'll get your turn in a moment."

Byatt was silenced.

"No opposition to bail, sarge," Barnes said, watching Fortune intently. "Just some conditions."

"The usual?"

"Yeah. Curfew, residence, no contact with witnesses."

"Fine." The custody officer began scribbling on a clipboard. Byatt looked surprised.

"What's your address, Mr Fortune?"

In light of the news that he was being granted bail, Fortune seemed to regain some semblance of control. He hauled himself up to the desk, rubbing a finger under his nose and sniffing loudly.

"I . . . I just moved. It's in the harbour. Sovereign Harbour. Santa Ana Court, Barbuda Quay. Number twenty-one. Not sure how you spell all that."

The colour drained from Barnes's face. His heart began to thump. *Howard Van Leer's bail address.* He opened his mouth to speak, to protest, to demand a further interview, but another voice told him to keep quiet and ride it out.

Robbie Fortune signed his bail sheet and Barnes showed him and Byatt out of the station. It was gone three in the morning, and all the lights were off in the deserted main foyer.

Barnes unlocked the heavy oak doors and Fortune trudged out of the station, flanked by Byatt. Grove Road was dark and silent, the air filled with the threat of rain. The solicitor whispered something to her client, and Fortune made a sarcastic reply before sloping off towards the railway station.

Barnes and Byatt stood side by side for a second on the steps of the police station, watching him go. Once he'd gone Barnes felt an irresistible urge to leave Byatt without further acknowledgements. She foiled this.

"Two charges for GBH, two for ABH pending. With his record he'll get at least five years, easily. Why didn't you oppose bail?" She was still looking away down Grove Road at the departing shadow of Robbie Fortune.

Barnes turned to face her for the first time that evening.

"You've got a point," he said. "The way I hear your firm treats its clients, he'd have been safer in prison."

As rejoinders go, it was below the belt, but worth it. He turned and walked back into the station before she could answer, slamming the heavy oak doors behind him.

CHAPTER SEVENTEEN

Barnes rang the doorbell of the tiny terraced house in Willingdon Trees and shifted from foot to foot as he waited. He was wary of Eve's mother, who did not suffer fools gladly. She had always been pleasant enough to Barnes, but now, having heard her criticise nearly everyone that ever came up in conversation, he suspected he would be getting the same treatment.

It had been three days since Eve had gone to her mother's house, but it felt like three months. Butterflies danced in his stomach, and he wondered how a five-year marriage could revert to first-date nerves just because the environment had changed a bit.

To his relief, Eve answered the door. His heart leapt. She looked fresh and clean — her face was free of make-up, her hair wet and combed behind her ears. She was wearing an old grey Nike hooded tracksuit top that was two sizes too big for her. It was spattered with paint, and he was surprised by the possessiveness he felt when he realised he'd never seen it before.

He produced the bunch of flowers from behind his back and offered them shyly.

"Hi, Barnes." She took the flowers and kissed him on the mouth, but she didn't smile. "They're beautiful."

"Been busy?" he said, pointing at the paint splotches on her top.

"Just a bit of painting. Thought I'd finish that poppy. I . . ."

He pulled her to him and buried his face in her hair. She returned the embrace with similar enthusiasm for a few seconds, and then extricated herself.

"Pleased to see me?" he said, trying to present a relaxed front that he didn't really feel.

"Of course I am. You should have phoned, though. I've only just got out of the shower."

"I thought I would surprise you."

"I am surprised. Sorry, please come in." She took his hand. He resisted.

"I thought we could go for a drive."

She hesitated. "Okay. That would be nice. Let me put these in a vase. Come in a minute."

He looked past her shoulder into the house. He didn't really want to make small talk with Eve's mother.

"That's all right. I'll wait in the car."

"Suit yourself. I won't be long."

He went back to the car and waited for her. She emerged five minutes later. As she approached the car, Forbes, who had been dozing in the back, got to his feet and began to leap up and down with excitement.

She hugged the dog and made a fuss of him for a few minutes, and then got in beside her husband. Before her door had closed he had leaned over and laced his hands through the hair on the back of her head, pulling her towards him again. She didn't resist but kissed him deeply, letting out a small gasp, and her hand had already clawed down his front to his loins before she composed herself and pushed him away again.

"I thought we could go to the seafront," he said after they'd got their breath back. "It's a gorgeous evening. Summer's almost here."

She smiled, and put her hand on his leg while he drove.

They double-parked near the pier, and Barnes rushed across the road to Dayville's, their favourite ice cream parlour, to buy two huge cones.

Eve held them while he drove further up the seafront. They found a spot near the bandstand, in front of the Cavendish Hotel. There was a brief hiatus while they performed a concentrated licking operation on the rapidly melting cones. Forbes yowled when he saw that they were feeding their faces, and Barnes lobbed him a couple of biscuits.

They watched people walking and skating and cycling along the upper promenade. The sun ignited the sky as it sank, catching the vibrant patchwork colours of Carpet Gardens, the row of vivid flower beds lined with immaculate arrangements that stretched like thick flags along the upper promenade. On the horizon, the white landing platform of the Sovereign Lighthouse was visible, looking like a plane that had landed nose-first in the drink and stuck there.

Barnes spoke first.

"Get any rum raisin on my upholstery and I'll smack you."

"Promises, promises."

"So, when are you coming home?"

"It's only been a few days."

"Well, how long do you need? How much thinking do you need to do?"

"I don't know."

"The house is huge without you. I miss you. Forbes misses you."

There was a splutter of agreement from the back.

"I miss you too."

"So come home." He twisted in his seat so he was facing her, and spread his hands as if the solution was obvious.

"You think this is easy for me?" she said, her voice shaking with a rawness he had never heard before. "I'm trying to do right by you. I don't want you to hate me. I don't want you to one day feel that I was the worst mistake you ever made. I'm doing this while there's still time for you. But that doesn't mean I like it. It doesn't mean I don't still love you."

Barnes clasped her hands in his.

"Eve — honey — I *want* to take the chance. You can't just hide from life in case something goes wrong. And I know you mean well, but it's for me to decide how I live my life, and I want to live it with you. For better, for worse, remember?"

Tears started to well in her eyes. He brushed them away with a gentle finger. The seafront lights began to flick themselves on, like a string of pearls — tiny white globes suspended between the lamp posts, bobbing gently in the breeze.

They were silent for several minutes, then Barnes pointed through the rear windscreen at the Cavendish Hotel on the other side of the road.

"Remember?" he asked. "If walls could talk, eh?"

She laughed through her tears.

"Our suite looks empty now. No guests. We could spend the night."

"Barnes . . ."

"I know, I know, you . . ."

He didn't finish his sentence. The crashing sound came from behind him, destroying the peaceful conversation in the car like an explosion.

He turned and looked at the window of the driver's door. It was destroyed, huge spider web cracks sprawling out from the centre. Confusion creased Barnes's face. *Was it a seagull?* He touched his wife's hand. Forbes, jolted from his daydreams, began to bark, rapid-fire, from the back of the car.

"Stay in the car."

He got out of the vehicle, and saw a large rock lying on the ground next to his door.

"*Bastard!*"

Robbie Fortune stood at the rear of the car wearing a black basketball singlet and jeans. He was wired on something. His legs were braced, his fists clenched, his body red and coiled for violence. Barnes had seen his capacity for violence before, and fear rooted him to the spot.

"You fucking pig bastard!"

Barnes fought to stay calm.

"Robbie, what . . ."

"You shut up. *You fucking shut up!* You think I'll let you send me back to prison? I ain't going!" Fortune snarled. His black eyes were veiled with chemical rage, and there was nothing there to reason with. There was a sound like a *click* — and Barnes saw the flash of the blade in Fortune's right hand.

To Barnes's horror, Eve got out of the car and stood by the door, wide-eyed and pale. She clutched her phone in a shaking hand. Fortune turned his attention to her.

"And I'll fucking slice you too, bitch!"

"Eve, get back in the car! Call 999," Barnes yelled.

Fortune advanced. Instinctive concern for his wife eroded Barnes's fear and galvanised him into action. He reached down to where the rock was lying at his feet and heaved it like a shot-putter over the car. It struck Fortune on the right shoulder and stunned him, but he was neither injured nor disarmed. There was momentary relief, however, as his attention was deflected away from Eve back to Barnes.

"Gonna show me your balls? Didn't think you had any, copper. I ain't going back to prison. You'll have to kill me first," Fortune growled.

He moved towards Barnes, the knife held out in front of him. Barnes took refuge behind the open driver's door. Then he remembered — there should be surveillance on Fortune.

"Come on, pig. Fight me. Let's see who's standing at the end."

"Don't hurt him. *Leave him alone!*" Eve cried from the other side of the car.

"Without your fucking army of mates, I bet I win," Fortune snarled.

Eve's exclamation had awakened a feeling deep in Barnes — a feeling of aggression, of anger, and pride. The fear dissipated. Why was his wife telling Fortune to leave him alone? He wanted Eve to be telling him to leave *Fortune* alone. Inside the car, Forbes was going nuts, barking and growling and running around in circles.

He waited behind the open driver's door as Fortune moved towards him from the rear end of the car, then, when the time was right, he kicked out, connecting with the door at full stretch.

The door swung shut, collecting Fortune as it went. Fortune yelped like a wounded dog, and Barnes sprang forward. Fortune swung the blade in an arc, in the same way as Barnes had seen him do to the kids on the CCTV. He missed Barnes by inches, and Barnes grabbed at the arm holding the knife. He took hold of the wrist and tried to force it downwards, tried to shake the blade loose. But he could feel the strength that Fortune had in his arms, and it was no use.

Fortune got up on his toes, his trainers squeaking on the tarmac, and butted forwards with his head — short, staccato movements that Barnes managed to avoid. He needed to get into a position to take Fortune to the ground, but it was too dangerous to let go of the knife.

He managed to position himself so he was almost behind Fortune, who was slavering and growling incoherently. There were no sounds other than the scuffling of feet on the concrete and Barnes's clipped breaths — as if he were afraid to breathe, as if each breath might be his last. Barnes couldn't see or hear Eve, and had no idea what she was doing. He was beginning to tire, the strength leaving his body.

But he couldn't give up, couldn't allow Fortune to get to his wife. In a final effort, Barnes raised his open hand above his head and chopped it down into the back of Fortune's shoulder socket, causing him to double over. At the same time he swung his right knee upwards, where it connected with Fortune's midriff. Barnes heard his opponent groan as the wind went out of him, and seized his moment. He struck Fortune twice in the side of the head with his knee; Fortune buckled, and Barnes was able to take him down, where he pinned him prone with his knees. Fortune continued to struggle, and Barnes heard him bark "*killya, killya*" in a kind of disjointed tattoo. He could feel sticky sweat from Fortune's armpit on his fingers.

Relief washed over Barnes as he heard sirens approaching from the town centre, then, to his dismay, he realised that the knife was sticking into his palm. He winced as he withdrew it.

Fortune must have felt the pressure on his back momentarily lifted, because he lurched upwards, causing Barnes, off balance, to topple over.

Barnes fell on his back as Fortune sprang to his feet. He inched towards Barnes, drinking in the fear on his face, then the sirens and blue lights were on top of him, and he took off across the road.

The police van stopped sharply, and the Local Support Team piled out, led by John Callaghan. Three of them took off after the rapidly departing Fortune.

"A surveillance unit called it in," Callaghan said. "Are you okay?"

"No, I'm fucking not," answered Barnes. "That prick stabbed me."

"There's an ambulance on its way," said Callaghan. "Don't worry, we'll catch up with him. My chaps don't run too fast, but surveillance will pick him up if they don't. Who is he?"

"His name's Grigory Michalek, but he uses the alias Robbie Fortune. Try the harbour. Santa Ana Court."

Callaghan jumped back into the van and it pulled away after the others. Clutching his hand, Barnes walked slowly over to where Eve had been standing. She had fainted during the fight, and was half-standing, half-slumped on the doorframe.

The ambulance arrived and took them both to hospital, where they were treated in separate bays. The A&E nurse was soft and sympathetic. She swabbed his hand and cleaned him up, then took a blood specimen and stitched the wound.

He asked for a telephone. The nurse brought it to him, and he made a call while his injury was cleaned.

DCI Hadian answered straightaway.

"Boss? It's Barnes. Listen, I think we have a good suspect for Harriet Holden's murder."

CHAPTER EIGHTEEN

There were no lights in the office other than the dim desk lamp and the reflection of the VDU on his face.

Along with a fictitious date of birth, the name Robbie Fortune was obviously a brand-new alias, likely to have been created the minute he walked out of prison, or possibly invented on the spot when Barnes and Nightingale came knocking on his door.

Barnes tried to ignore his throbbing hand long enough to think. Essentially, Fortune had been spoken to as part of routine house-to-house enquiries, which meant he was technically a witness — initially, at least. Thus, there was no reason to immediately disbelieve his credentials. The intelligence cell would have — *must* have — checked him out, but a speculative check wouldn't have thrown up a single match. Robbie Fortune had no record on the Police National Computer or any other system.

Grigory Michalek, however, was a different story. Once Fortune was arrested and taken into custody, his fingerprints had been taken and had immediately flagged up his ID as Grigory Michalek, with the alias Robbie Fortune now indelibly marked on Michalek's PNC record.

Michalek had arrived in the UK from a small town
south of Bratislava in 1991, a couple of years before Slovakia
and the Czech Republic divorced — long enough, apparently, for all traces of his accent to disappear completely. He
had arrived alone on a container ship and sought unskilled
work in London and the South East. Eastbourne appeared to
be just one stop in a job-hopping tour of England's seaside
towns.

For a man with his propensity for violence, the list of
previous convictions was remarkably short, but then Barnes
realised this was because Robbie Fortune had spent great
chunks of his life in prison. His first stint as a labourer in
Lewisham had been interrupted after nine weeks when he
was arrested for breaking a pool cue over a man's head in a
pub. His first conviction by an English court saw him with a
three-year prison term; his latest release had been nine weeks
ago from HMP Belmarsh after serving a seven-year term for
pushing a man through a plate-glass window on the fifth
floor of a hotel. This had occurred outside the Sussex force
area, which might explain how Fortune had arrived in town
undetected, despite the existence of an intel unit monitoring
prison releases. Inter-force communications were often rudi-
mentary at best, and it was easy for cross-border movements
to slip through the net.

Barnes checked his watch — nearly 3 a.m. The surveillance team should have been on Fortune round the clock.
Why hadn't he been caught yet?

Van Leer had been ready to talk. The fact that he had
been kidnapped from a prison van in transit and then bru-
tally murdered — but not before the police had been lured
to where he was found — suggested at least some marginally
organised villains. Van Leer's death meant that there was now
virtually nothing in the way of intelligence or evidence that
might lead the police to what he might have otherwise been
ready to tell them.

The last possible opportunity was that something would
be on the prison tapes. It was surely a matter of time, but

Hadian had not yet asked about them or come looking for them. Barnes had listened to them twice already — once to get a sense of the main headlines, twice to fully transcribe the contents into his notebook — and now, he was going for a third time, to start pinning down the extrapolations that were simmering in his brain.

Barnes made a bitter-tasting coffee and pulled the tapes from the polythene bag. There was a covering note — Van Leer had made four calls during his two short periods in prison. Two to his legal firm — which Barnes couldn't touch — and two more to the same mobile phone, a mobile phone that the intel cell said belonged to his older brother, Dominic Van Leer. This was a new name for the enquiry, a potential new lead.

He slipped some headphones on and hit play.

The tapes began with the sound of a phone ringing. In the background the sounds of male prisoners talking, jeering and playing pool could be heard.

The receiver was lifted.

"*Hello?*" The voice was gruff, deep. Barnes didn't recognise it.

"*Hello? Hey, it's me, big brother!*" Howard Van Leer — unmistakable.

"*How are ya, pal?*"

"*Yeah, cookin', mate. Well, not bad, considering.*"

"*You got caught, then?*"

A moment's silence.

"*It happens.*"

"*More often than not, in your case. You talk to Phil?*" On the first listen, Barnes had scribbled *Phil = Phil McDermott?* in the margins of the transcript. This time around he circled it. He checked the date. The conversation had taken place before Van Leer burgled McDermott's house.

"*Nah, been waiting for him to call me.*"

"*Lazy fuckin' shite. I sent him down to talk to ya.*"

"*Yeah, yeah. What do we pay him for?*"

"*What you mean 'we'? I'm the one pays the fuckin' twat.*"

"*Yeah, I know, I know.*" The tone was defensive. "*Just lookin' out for me big bro'. Maybe Phil needs reminding of what he owes us.*"

Barnes wrote this last comment down verbatim and put a question mark next to it.

"*All right, all right, don't talk too much. These phones are fuckin' tapped, ya know.*"

There was a moment's pause on the tape. Barnes frowned, staring at nothing. Van Leer Senior was apparently too careful to talk much on prison telephones. Barnes hoped — and not for the first time — that the conversations wouldn't be worthless.

"*Anyway . . .*" the older Van Leer continued, "*. . . you just leave that down to me.*"

"*Bro, can you send me some money and fags?*"

"*Yeah, no problem, pal. I'll bring them to you myself.*"

"*You're coming to visit?*"

"*Yeah. Is that a problem?*"

"*No, 'course it isn't.*"

"*You'll need to sort me out a visiting order.*"

"*Oh yeah, yeah. Hang on.*" There was the sound of rustling paper. "*Let me write this down on the form. Er, name . . . ? Oh, it's Van Leer, innit?*"

"*Same as yours, you fuckin' numbnuts.*"

"*Okay . . . VO for Mr Dominic Van Leer . . . visiting in May . . .*" Van Leer was writing.

"*Got that sorted then? I'll see you next week.*"

"*Okay.*" There was the faintest hint of trepidation in Howard Van Leer's voice.

Then there was a click as the receiver was replaced, and the tape stopped. Barnes shut his eyes and replayed the voice of Dominic Van Leer in his head. The voice that called him outside the conference centre? The same voice that tipped him off about the armed robbery? The voice that called the police from the Atlantic Hotel? Maybe. No way to be sure.

He ejected the tape and replaced it with the other one. This conversation was recorded two days after Howard

Van Leer was sent back to prison for breaking into Phil McDermott's house. Barnes pressed play. The phone rang.

"*Yeah?*" Dominic Van Leer.

"*Dom, it's me.*" Howard's voice was quiet, strained.

"*Yeah?*"

"*Bro, I'm going away for this. I ain't coming out for a long time.*"

"*You couldn't do it, could ya?*" Dominic Van Leer was unhappy. "*I put my fuckin' neck on the line to get you bail — surety, nice flat, everything — and you couldn't stick to your fuckin' conditions for more than a couple of days.*"

"*What was I meant to do? You . . . you put . . . my room . . .*"

"*Fifty grand you cost me.*" The interruption was abrupt. "*Fifty . . . fuckin' . . . grand. I said they'd put fuckin' surveillance on ya. And Phil's house? Phil's fuckin' house? What's the matter with ya? You cut up his fuckin' wife?*"

"*I thought . . . you said . . . he was slacking off. He needed reminding of what he owes us.*"

"*Nah, you said that. And if I was of a mind to tell Phil to pull his socks up, I would be the one to decide how to fuckin' do it. And I would also decide who to do it — and it wouldn't have been you, you useless little junkie. You went looking for a house to screw, and you picked Phil's 'cos it was an easy target. You're too fuckin' lazy — too fuckin' desperate — to even case a place properly. And cutting up his old lady just ain't on. That's another five years, minimum.*"

"*Dom, I . . .*"

"*So don't pretend you was trying to do me a favour by giving Phil a kick up the backside. You did it 'cos you're a thieving junkie scumbag, end of.*"

Howard was quiet on the other end of the phone. Barnes heard another prisoner in the queue behind him yell at him to hurry up.

"*Dom . . . what about the copper?*"

"*What?*"

"*Officer Barnes.*"

"*What about him?*"

"*He . . . he gets everywhere.*"

"*'Course he does. It's all going to plan, so far.*"

"I'm worried about him. He's sticking his nose in all over the place."

"'Course he is — he's a Cunt In Disguise. That's his job. Don't you worry about DC Barnes, we got him exactly where we want him. Robbie's keeping him busy."

"Did he take the bank job?"

"Brother, for fuck's sake. I already told ya about these phones."

"Oh yeah . . . sorry."

"I think, brother, you only need to be worrying about yourself."

"What ya mean?"

"I mean, without sugar-coating the pill, you're becoming a bit of a fuckin' liability. Did I mention I'm fifty grand in the red 'cos of you?"

"What? I . . ."

"Gavvers are talking to you a bit more often than I'm happy with. My worry is that, sooner or later, you'll start talking."

"I won't! 'Course I won't! I ain't a grass!"

"Maybe not, but you are a drug-taking scumbag, which means you only look out for number one."

"I'm your brother, Dom. I would never . . ."

"Yeah, you are. Watch your back, little brother."

The receiver was replaced by Dominic Van Leer first. Then the noise of the crowd in the prison recreation room was silenced as Howard Van Leer also hung up. Barnes checked the date. Four days later, Howard Van Leer's body had been dumped in a beach shelter.

He stopped the tape. The hiss stopped, and the empty office was filled with witching-hour silence. Barnes pulled the desk lamp over his notebook and read his notes. Dominic Van Leer was being careful — he knew that the prison telephone conversations were recorded. But they had let slip a few useful pieces of information.

Phil owes us.

Don't worry about DC Barnes. Robbie's keeping him busy.

It's all going to plan, so far.

Did he take the bank job?

Watch your back, little brother.

Barnes chewed his pen and thought about it. Howard Van Leer — dead. Dominic Van Leer — elder brother of the deceased. Phil McDermott — criminal defence solicitor with practices that seemed to go beyond the usual lawyer–client privileges — also dead. And now Robbie Fortune, using the same bail address as Van Leer. That had been unexpected — now he was definitely linked to the Van Leer brothers.

Howard Van Leer hadn't killed Holden — there was no better alibi than being in police custody at the material time. But he had clearly known something about her murder, and when he was finally ready to talk, somebody wanted to shut him up permanently.

Fortune? He was certainly capable, but why? Why would he want to kill Holden? He hated all police, but why her? Fortune would have killed Barnes on the seafront, of that he had no doubt, but that had been a little different. Was there something about Holden, some link to Fortune that they had yet to discover? It was possible. For all the investigation into Harriet Holden's lifestyle, habits and associates, they knew so little about her. Her boyfriend still hadn't been identified, although Barnes doubted very much whether Fortune could claim that particular privilege.

Don't you worry about DC Barnes, we've got him exactly where we want him.

Barnes thought of the Mercedes, the jogger, the urgency in his meetings with Emily Varela. He thought of the armed robbery — HERO COP. Stefan Garrett, the improbable armed robber. Barnes had seen Garrett's accomplice before as well, but had yet to place her.

Nightingale? Shortly to be sacked from her job in professional disgrace. With the exception of her drink-drive arrest at the hands of Callaghan, she hadn't been seen since that night on the OP — unless you counted Van Leer's kidnap as a positive ID. Where was *she* in all this? Bent cops and robbers make strange bedfellows.

Barnes shook his head and made coffee. It didn't help. No one can function fully at three thirty in the morning, he thought.

He returned to his computer and ran Dominic Van Leer through the PNC. His last conviction had been thirteen years ago, for minor possession of a Class A drug. 12 months' conditional discharge. A nothing sentence. But from the conversation he'd had with his brother, he hardly sounded like a nine-to-five straight guy. It was more likely that Barnes's first notion had been correct — that Dominic Van Leer was active but careful.

He ran the name through the local systems. He had a file on the intelligence system, but, again, the information was old. Dominic Van Leer's personal details were there, along with his physical description. His last known address, like most of the criminals in the town at one time or another, was the Atlantic Hotel. Barnes suspected that this was also out of date.

There was a flag next to Dominic Van Leer's name — IF SUBJECT ARRESTED CONTACT DCI DENNIKER AD918 FIB 24HR PAGER/CELL. Barnes noted the name and chewed it over. Denniker had an interest in Van Leer, but this was over four years ago — he had climbed two ranks since then. Dominic Van Leer had not come to notice for a good while.

He scrolled through the first half of the 108 pages in the file. There were no surprises. Van Leer appeared to be suspected of a great deal, but a lot of the intelligence was useless — unconfirmed, uncorroborated and nothing that could be acted on. One thing was clear, though — the information was chiefly centred around drug supply and associated violence.

INFORMATION RECEIVED THAT SUBJECT IS BRINGING LARGE AMOUNTS OF HEROIN INTO EASTBOURNE TOWN FROM LIVERPOOL. METHOD OF SHIPMENT NOT KNOWN.

SUBJECT BELIEVED TO BE DRIVING FORD TRANSIT VRM F392 PJK AND IS USING FOR SUPPLY OF CLASS A.

SUBJECT CARRIES BASEBALL BAT IN THE
BOOT OF HIS CAR TO INJURE BUYERS
WHO CANNOT PAY HIM.

SUBJECT CAUSED GBH TO RIVAL DEALER
USING FIREARM AS ASSAULT WEAPON —
USED BUTT TO STRIKE VICTIM IN FACE.

SUBJECT IS MEETING UNKNOWN
ASSOCIATE FROM ESSEX TO COMPLETE
DEAL FOR SUPPLY OF CLASS A BELIEVED
CRACK COCAINE.

It went on. But when Barnes cross-referenced the intelligence submissions against the database of recorded crimes, nothing came up besides that possession offence thirteen years ago. There had been rumour, speculation and conjecture, but Dominic Van Leer had not been caught for a crime for a long time.

Idly, Barnes put McDermott's name in the NAME field. No hits. Then, he sat up a little straighter, and typed PHIL MCDERMOTT into the free text field.

One hit. He sat up. Phil McDermott's name appeared in Dominic Van Leer's intelligence record. Barnes scrolled through till he found it. B-grade source intelligence from three years previously.

INFORMATION RECEIVED THAT SUBJECT
RECENTLY WENT ON HOLIDAY TO THE
BAHAMAS WITH ONE PHIL MCDERMOTT.
COMMENT — SUBJECT'S SOLICITOR IS
PHILIP MCDERMOTT OF WEDDERBURN
& CO.

Barnes switched to the collision recording system. He ran "Op Cheriton" through the search box to bring up the record of Phil McDermott's fatal crash. He read the OIC's notes. An off-licence carrier bag containing several bottles of liquor and traces of cocaine had been found in the passenger seat of McDermott's Mercedes. The OIC had made the observation that the deceased had strapped the bag into the seat, but hadn't bothered putting a seatbelt around himself.

Awake now, he entered Santa Ana Court into the system. Several hits — it was the bail address of Howard Van Leer and Robbie Fortune, and also the address given by a Melanie Denton when she reported being the victim of a mobile phone robbery last year. Barnes skim-read the MO — set upon by two black men in a BMW who attacked her with baseball bats and stole her handbag, cash, benefits book, mobile phone and a small amount of heroin. There was comment from the investigating officer — quite apart from the inexplicable complaint about the theft of a controlled substance — the injury, a small graze to the forehead, was inconsistent with her description of the attack. There were no witnesses and no one identified from photographs. Read between the lines: totally fantastic, and sounded like a junkie's stock attempt to get a crisis loan.

There were also a couple of general neighbourhood complaints — one from a neighbour, one anonymous piece of Crimestoppers information — reporting suspected drug-dealing and associated antisocial behaviour at the address. The neighbourhood teams had the reports on their radar, but they appeared to be sandwiched in the middle of a very tall in-tray.

He tried to take it in, and began to list confused questions in his notebook. These were basic intelligence database checks — surely they had been completed at an early stage of the investigation. He rubbed his eyes, and realised that at the time the checks were completed, the information may not have meant anything. That, or someone had made sure they weren't done.

Barnes bit his lip as it occurred to him that the investigation suddenly seemed to be unfolding in front of him, that he was *making* the investigation, there and then. He got up and walked over to a shelf of alphabetised files containing images that would, once upon a time, have been called mugshots. He pulled down D–G and thumbed through the yellowing Polaroids until he found one of a woman with blonde, drawn features with the caption *DENTON, Melanie*. Barnes made a positive identification — the girl with Garrett at the armed robbery. The girl that dropped Cathy Nightingale off at the OP.

He sat down and continued typing, scribbling notes as he did so. He recognised further intelligence as reports he himself had submitted, such as the information on Sovereign Holdings Ltd and the £100,000 security.

He switched to the internet. Santa Ana Court had been put on the market eighteen months ago as part of a new development. It had been bought by an investor who rented it out via a letting agency in the town — Sunshine Coast Apartments. It cost a fee to access the detailed history of the property, but Barnes was able to find out that the let was advertised in February of that year, and that it had been occupied and paid for more or less straight away.

He wrote this down and then sent an official-sounding fax on police headed paper to the agency requesting full details of the let. There was no legal weight behind it, but it looked the part. It had to be worth a go — as with most requests for information to help an investigation that didn't involve a warrant, the success depended entirely on how pro-police the recipients were.

He tried to process the information in front of him. It was no good. He was too tired, in spite of what he had learned. He needed to see the flat. He needed to get in and search it. He flagged the address on the intel system with his name, stretched in his chair, and an idea came to him.

The DC investigating the seafront assault of Barnes by Fortune was called Pryor — who was one of few that were not, thankfully, part of the pro-Nightingale/anti-Callaghan set. Barnes tried his mobile — as it happened, he was on duty, having been called out to a stranger rape an hour previously. He was standing in a dingy alleyway in Langney trying to avoid a sudden spring shower when Barnes called.

Fortune had yet to be arrested, and Barnes asked Pryor politely if he had any plans to get into Santa Ana Court. He told Barnes that he'd been round there twice with an arrest team — no answer on both occasions, and that his next move was to get a warrant.

Barnes offered to get the warrant for him — Pryor was initially resistant, saying it was really his job to do so, but acquiesced when Barnes told him that the big, sore wound in his palm was a very small piece of a much bigger pie. In fact, Pryor sounded almost grateful. Investigations into assaults on brother officers were deserving of a premium service, but most detectives could privately have done without the addition to their workload.

Barnes did a quick stocktake of what he had — two neighbourhood complaints, and the confirmed bail address of an outstanding suspect. It would have to do.

It was gone eight when he was finally shaken awake by Hadian. The office was starting to fill. The radio was on, the kettle was boiling — the office transformed from the hollow blackness of the night duty.

He tried to tell Hadian about what he had found out without betraying that he had been working on Christchurch on the quiet — Hadian refused to hear it. He sent Barnes home to sleep, and said that whatever it was, it could wait till later.

Barnes slept heavily on his sofa. He was woken by the afternoon sun streaming through the bay window, and he woke up sweating and disorientated after a nightmare in which a laughing Robbie Fortune got the better of him and carved him open with his knife.

When he was fully awake, his stomach surged with butterflies. He wanted this to be over. He wanted to quit the force and go and work in a shop. And he desperately wanted Eve back. The way he felt when waking up, he would have walked barefoot to China on a bed of hot coals if only she would come home. He checked his phone — no messages. Not from Eve, and no message to tell him Robbie Fortune was in custody. He lightly fingered the keys and thought about calling his wife, then decided against it.

He took Forbes with him for a quick sprint around the park in Huggetts Lane. The park was empty, the flat green expanse lit gold by the sun above the South Downs, rush-hour traffic rumbling past the trees. After a shower and two bowls of cereal, Barnes felt a little better. He drove back to work, arriving at the station a little after 4 p.m. All notions of regular shifts seemed to have evaporated — the feeling that he was inching closer to Holden's killer meant he only went home to sleep and change clothes. The rest of the time he was at work. Maybe that was another reason Eve had gone to her mother's. Maybe it was just as well.

He walked into the office and sifted through the post that had arrived for him during the day. There was a fax from the letting agency. He sat down to read it.

The first page didn't tell him anything he hadn't already secured from the internet. Page two revealed that the tenant was Sovereign Holdings, a company with a box number as its correspondence address. The rent had been paid six months in advance, and the company appeared to have transacted with the agency almost entirely remotely.

Almost.

The third page was a photocopy of a passport. The agency had added a footnote to say that this was the proof of ID provided by the company's representative when the lease agreement had first been signed.

The photocopy was of poor quality, but the text was legible, and the reproduction of the photograph was just recognisable. To Barnes's amusement, Phil McDermott appeared to be smiling in the photograph — a big, shit-eating grin, with his gold incisor just visible in the murky black copy.

Barnes rubbed his forehead and smiled, theorising that this much help could only mean some cop had once been kind to the sender's mother. Add a dead guarantor to the neighbourhood complaints and the fact of Fortune's bail address.

He bundled the information together and dashed over to a metal filing cabinet in the corner of the office. His heart drummed with excitement as he pulled a blank search warrant from a drawer marked MISUSE OF DRUGS ACT 1971.

He scribbled the details onto the warrant and ran downstairs to the cell block. DCI Hadian had gone home, but the duty inspector was reviewing prisoners in the cell block.

She looked harassed — a tired-looking woman in her forties, red-faced with stress, the kind of cop that has been dragged kicking and screaming back to the front line after hiding behind a desk for too long. Barnes didn't know her. The cells were full, and she looked in danger of blowing a gasket. Good.

Barnes approached her, waving his warrant. She told him it would have to wait; he mustered his best indignant *I'm a very busy detective* expression, told her it couldn't, and she obviously realised that there was only one way to get rid of him quickly. She signed the warrant, and Barnes raced back upstairs to use the phone.

The clerk of the court grumbled about the anonymous report, but, as all the pieces of information appeared to corroborate each other, agreed to squeeze him in before the magistrate disappeared for the day.

Barnes sprinted round to the court and swore out the warrant in front of the magistrate, throwing in some editorials about the dangers of drug dealers preying on vulnerable children. The clerk rolled his eyes, but the magistrate was female, middle-aged, well-dressed — and absorbed every word with wide eyes, hyperbole and all. The warrant was duly approved and signed. Barnes spewed thanks. He left the court and was about to sprint back to the station when he saw Natasha Warwick walking out of Court 2.

He saw her and toyed with the idea of ignoring her, but she was too close and had already made eye contact. Christ, this was the last thing he wanted. The urge to bury his head in the concrete was overwhelming.

"Hello, Barnes." She was clutching a stack of files.

"Hello. What can I do for you?" Polite, but cold and uncomfortable.

"Listen, I just wanted to say I'm sorry about the other night." She looked him dead in the eye.

"It's okay. Listen, I'm quite busy . . ."

"No, it isn't. Come in here." She beckoned Barnes into an interview room designed for defendants to consult with their advocates privately.

She shut the door.

"It wasn't right of me to make assumptions about your marriage or how faithful you are to your wife. I don't want to add to your problems." She put her files down on the table.

Barnes let out his breath.

"It's not easy being that candid," he said, thawing out a little.

"I'm not a little girl, Barnes. I know myself. I know my own faults. The alcohol didn't help, I'm afraid."

The apparent sensitivities of the situation suddenly seemed unnervingly juvenile, and Barnes cut her off. "Natasha, there's a big conspiracy surrounding Harriet Holden's death, and I think it goes higher than the street. It's about to blow wide open. I need someone in the CPS to be onside. I need an ally, not a lover."

She gripped his forearm.

"I've told you once before — exploit your hypotheses, whatever it takes. If you have the evidence, the senior investigators can't ignore it. I will support you. I will lay the charges against McDermott and whoever else—"

"McDermott's dead," Barnes said.

She inhaled sharply and her eyes widened. It took a moment for her to regain her composure.

"I will work with you on this."

She stepped forward and touched his face. Her eyes were shiny. He didn't move.

"At least tell me your first name," she said.

"It's Rutherford," he answered.

She held his gaze, her expression soft and unchanging, then dropped her hand and went to the door.

After a moment's pause, she opened her mouth to say something, then turned and hurried to her car.

Barnes watched her go.

Whatever it takes.

CHAPTER NINETEEN

Barnes ran to the station. Once there, he called John Callaghan, one of the few people he felt he could trust — or, indeed, who would give him the time of day — and asked him to put a team together to execute a search warrant the following day. Barnes told him it would probably be a quick job, that he didn't expect to find much, but he was desperate to get in there and rip the place up. Callaghan's curiosity was piqued, and he readily agreed without asking any uncomfortable questions. Not that Barnes had been expecting any — it was just a drugs warrant, and only he knew that it might bust open the doors of Operation Christchurch once more.

The next call was to Emily Varela. He didn't say much — time, date and address, then he hung up before she could ask any questions.

He exhaled deeply and slowed down his pace. He tucked the warrant into his inside jacket pocket and returned to the office.

* * *

It was a little after seven that evening when he started hammering on Paul Hadian's front door in the Old Town. Late spring was beginning to dissolve into early summer, and the sun was dipping behind the Downs a little later every night.

The DCI came to the door, still in his work suit, his tie loose and his dishevelled shirtsleeves rolled up to the elbows. He held a crystal tumbler of amber liquid in one hand.

"Barnes? Would you like to tell me why you are pacing up and down my front garden?" He sloshed the whisky around the heavy base of the tumbler.

"Sir, sorry for the intrusion at home. We need to talk. It's important."

Hadian bore an expression that, if worn by the parent of a troublesome teenager, might have read, *What's he done now?*

He pulled his front door closed and got in the Mondeo with Barnes. The evening was balmy with the promise of summer. They drove to Langney Point and looked out across the lock as the daylight began to fade.

The tide was out. Little egrets and kittiwakes sat perched in the mud. A lifeboat launch sat silently on a slim channel of water, poised for the next call, and out on the Channel the *Sospan Dau* was working its way up and down the shore, sucking up detritus from the seabed and spewing it back onto the beaches.

Hadian sighed.

"What a clusterfuck," he said for the third time since leaving his house. Barnes finally bit.

"What happened?"

Hadian stared at Barnes as if seeing him for the first time. "Well, you know about the disagreement we had about the press conference, because you were listening through the keyhole."

Barnes said nothing.

"Mr Denniker did eventually turn up to address the press. That bullshit he spouted in the office about resting easy in our beds — he recited that verbatim."

"Think he rehearsed it?"

"He rehearses everything. But I haven't got to the best bit yet. He tells the conference that Van Leer would have been charged with conspiracy to murder. Then, for reasons best known to himself, he says that we aren't looking for any other suspects. So then some skinny bird from the local rag sticks her hand up and says — how come you're not looking for other suspects when, by definition, a conspiracy charge means that there must be at least *one* other suspect?"

"What did he say to that?"

"What could he say? There was what you might call a pregnant pause. Poor Sally Holden looked like she wanted the ground to swallow her up. I had to wrap it up pretty quickly after that. Imagine — the nation's press assemble, and the commander is upstaged by some local hack barely out of nappies."

"Did you get her name?" Barnes asked, closing his eyes momentarily.

"Yeah."

"Don't tell me. Emily Varela?"

"That's her. The one responsible for your 'hero cop' piece." Hadian pursed his lips and looked out to sea. "So why are we here, Barnes? Are you about to tell me you've been working on Christchurch on your own?"

"Sir, I think if I hadn't, some stones might not have been turned over."

"Meaning?"

Barnes took a deep breath.

"Look, I'm genuinely sorry, I know you pulled me off, but all I want to do is find Harriet's killer."

"Don't we all, lad."

"But somehow I'm a *pawn* in all this. It's *me* that keeps getting the bloody anonymous phone calls. It's *me* that's been to A&E three times in as many weeks. It's *me* that's somehow managed to piss off half the workforce. I don't know why, but, like it or not, I need to try to use that to my advantage. To *her* advantage."

Hadian eyeballed him. Barnes decided to get to it.

"Phil McDermott's dead," Barnes said.

"Yeah, I know. Car crash. In more ways than one."

"The car he was driving. It was registered to Dominic Van Leer — at an address in Santa Ana Court, Barbuda Quay."

Hadian frowned. "Wasn't that Howard Van Leer's bail address?"

"It's Robbie Fortune's as well."

"What?" If most senior detectives were vexed by information bypassing them, then Hadian was no exception.

"The night we agreed to let him run and put surveillance on him. That was the address he gave."

"Did he now? The one in the harbour?" Hadian asked, clicking his tongue rapidly against his teeth, like a metronome. "Well, there's your link between Fortune and Van Leer. Fortune could be our co-conspirator. What do you think?"

"You know what I think. I don't think Van Leer had anything to do with Harriet's murder. I think his reaction was genuine, and—"

"And he had an alibi, I know. Well, you know I don't agree that Van Leer had nothing to do with it, but I'll meet you halfway. I don't like the victimology. There was a reason for Harriet being put in Van Leer's room, but I don't know what it is."

"Somebody — maybe Fortune, maybe not — called us from the Atlantic Hotel to report concern for Howard. Nightingale said at the time that was crap. Whoever called us *wanted* us to find her body to stitch up Van Leer. He was just a stooge to keep us looking the other way. He had an alibi for the murder — he was in prison — but from listening to the tapes of his phone calls, my guess is that the night he ran from the apartment is when he found out her body had been dumped in his room. He was scared."

"A warning? Was someone worried he was going to talk?"

"He *did* want to talk — just not when we first went to see him in prison. He was full of it. But he was also an unpredictable, junk-addicted burglar who kept getting caught. Maybe whoever put the body in his room knew that, and knew that he was a weak link, whether he talked or not."

"None of which explains Harriet. She was picked for a reason."

Barnes didn't immediately answer. Just the mention of her name caused her face to rise before him, stirring feelings he could neither name nor control.

"The boyfriend has to be the link, except we can't identify him," he finally said. "But then how do you explain the choice of dump site?" Barnes looked out at the darkening sea. His voice was quiet.

"That's what I mean about the victimology not being right," Hadian said. "I mean, there's no chance she was in a relationship with Fortune, is there? She didn't like a bit of rough?"

"No way." Barnes shook his head. "An association with someone like Fortune would have jeopardised her entire career. Her career was everything to her."

"Poor kid. We knew so little about her."

An ambulance raced past on Prince William Parade, blue lights and sirens screaming. Hadian put his fingers in his ears, and removed them when it had passed.

"Dominic Van Leer?" he said eventually.

"Howard's older brother. Howard called him from the prison. I've got the tapes."

Hadian raised an eyebrow.

"I know, I know, but listen. The tapes confirmed one or two things. First, McDermott was up to his neck in it."

"I bloody knew it."

"Second, the armed robbery at the bank was organised by Van Leer Senior. I'm convinced of it. There isn't enough on the tape to stick a conspiracy charge on him yet, but it's a good start."

"Go on."

Barnes's tone grew more urgent. The pieces, so desperate for someone to put them together, seemed to fall into place as he spoke.

"Well, before Garrett did the robbery, he mentioned new people in town. They sounded like extortionists, or maybe Eastern-bloc dealers. No names, but Fortune is a Slovakian import, and Garrett mentioned 'the Dutchman'."

Out on the mudflats, a huddle of seagulls suddenly took off, screeching as they went.

"You're thinking big brother?"

"Yes. Garrett was terrified, especially after we found Howard's body. I'm thinking there's an organised crime group operating at the centre of this thing."

"Propaganda is half the battle with OCGs." Hadian drummed his fingers on the dashboard. "Spread the word among the scum, give it a year or so, everyone's terrified — next thing you know, fucker's got a book out."

"Sir, there's something else."

"I'm listening."

"When Garrett did the armed robbery, he left with a woman. She disappeared when I arrested him. Wasted no time."

"Garrett didn't say anything about her, but then he's pretending to be loopy. He's convincing." Hadian's tone was faintly sour. "I sent a pair to the court cells to quiz him about the possible murder weapon — this 'bust of Beethoven.' Barely got him to string a sentence together. Did you check the photo albums?"

Barnes nodded.

"I couldn't place her at first, but she's the girl that dropped Cathy Nightingale off at the OP the night Van Leer attacked McDermott's wife. Cathy said she was job, but she clearly isn't."

"Not a skinny girl, about twenty? Blonde?"

"That's her. Her name's Melanie Denton."

"I think she's Cathy's bit on the side," Hadian said. "I saw them together a couple of times. She didn't want to talk about it, especially when I said she looked like a druggie."

"Well . . ." Barnes began with a grimace. Ethical dilemmas aside, he could sort of understand the objection.

"Did you check her record?" Hadian said, interrupting.

"No. I can do it now."

He switched on the Mondeo's mobile data terminal and entered Melanie Denton's details. Her record appeared after a few seconds.

"Yes, she's known," Barnes muttered. "Theft, assault, drugs — the usual."

"Of course she is," Hadian said. "Fuck, this isn't good. If Cathy's girlfriend is CRO, who knows what kind of pillow talk there's been."

Despite the detectives' cynicism, Melanie Denton had only recently troubled the clerks of the Criminal Records Office. As Barnes scrolled through her nominal record, he realised she'd only come to notice in the last few years. She'd had a relatively normal upbringing — reasonable education, a fistful of GCSEs, working parents, and had been brought up in a part of town that wasn't all bad. But she stumbled into smack at about sixteen years old, and it all went south from there.

"What about Cathy?" Barnes asked.

Hadian rubbed his face.

"Bloody Nightingale. I swear she'll put me in the ground. She's still on suspension, so she could be anywhere, but her first hearing for the drink-drive thing is in a couple of days. We can nab her at court, buy her a coffee and ask her some uncomfortable questions."

"Okay."

"But first we'll visit Fortune," the DCI said. "You and I. Call it a bail check. But we need to do some more research on this apartment first. Get the deeds, find out who owns it, that kind of thing. See if we can find out some more about this company."

"Already done it. I got hold of the letting agency. The flat's rented by Sovereign Holdings. No address, only a box number. Rent paid well in advance, by cash. They would have transacted with complete anonymity, if the agency hadn't insisted on proof of ID, so they used their frontman's passport."

"Go on."

"McDermott." Barnes just about managed to conceal his sense of triumph.

Hadian shook his head in disbelief. "Scumbag."

Barnes straightened in his seat. It was time to close the deal, and he hoped his segue from discussion to action came off with the skill of a seasoned senior detective.

"Sir, Fortune isn't in custody yet. I want to get inside Santa Ana Court. First thing tomorrow. Early. I've got a warrant."

"Barnes, you don't need a warrant for an arrest enquiry . . ."

"I know. Pryor's tried a few times without luck. This is a search warrant for drugs. John Callaghan's bringing a busload."

"A drugs warrant? How'd you get that?"

Barnes shrugged. "Everything we already knew plus a couple of neighbourhood complaints was good enough for the JP. It's here in my briefcase." Barnes indicated towards the back seat with his thumb.

Another pause. Hadian's suspicious look dissolved into a smirk — for good or ill, Barnes had impressed his boss.

"Well, who am I to argue? I'll see you at the office. Five thirty. First one in buys coffee. I can't drink shite coffee at that time of the morning."

* * *

Barnes took the drive home at a gentle pace, his head swimming with the next day's possibilities. He wasn't quite sure what he might find, but his stomach was surging with adrenaline at the irresistible thought that the answers Holden desperately needed were behind the doors of Santa Ana Court, either in the form of Robbie Fortune or whoever was protecting him.

The sky was clear and dark except at the edges, where it glowed pink, the edges of the clouds gouged red like strands of candyfloss.

He touched the brakes as he approached the house — and saw Eve's car parked outside. The boot lid was up. Barnes's heart leapt. *She's coming home.*

He parked behind her car, peeked in the boot and trotted up the steps to the garden path. The front door was also open. He entered the house, whistling, and saw her overnight bag sitting in the hallway. The almost-finished poppy canvas was back in the living room.

"I'm home, dear! Can I help you with your bags?"

No answer. The house was deathly silent. No TV, no running water, no excited Forbes. No signs of life at all. He checked all the rooms on the ground floor — empty. He went to the bottom of the stairs and called up.

"Darling?"

Still nothing. He jogged up the stairs, the unease spreading like overflowing liquid from his stomach to his brain, knowing something was desperately wrong, but clinging to some small hope that his imagination was getting the better of him.

He peered through the railings of the banister as he ascended — and saw two feet lying on the bedroom floor, the rest of her body concealed by the partially closed door.

"No," he whispered, horror strangling his mind.

He slipped on the stairs, grabbed the banister and scrambled up in a daze. The door crashed against the wall as he burst into the bedroom.

His wife lay on the floor on her back, her face a battered mess of bruises and cuts. Her left eye was purple and swollen shut. Blood had been pouring from her nose, but had now started to clot around her face. There was a small pool of blood that had soaked into the carpet, but he couldn't tell if she had any freshly bleeding wounds. Forbes was lying quietly beside Eve, wedged against her body as if trying to keep her warm.

"*No no no!*" he screamed, sinking to his knees beside his beloved wife. Forbes got to his feet, alarmed, and padded into the hallway where he sat down. The room began to spin.

Barnes could feel himself losing it. His vision blurred, and he fought to keep hold of himself.

"Honey, can you hear me? Eve, say something. It's Barnes." His voice was so shrill that he did not recognise it.

There was no sound. He frantically checked her breathing and pulse, then gingerly felt for broken bones. He was too afraid to move her. He could smell the rich tangy stench of his wife's blood, which cast him instantly back to Howard Van Leer's room.

He fumbled with the keys on his mobile phone. His hands seemed heavy and clumsy. He punched 999, and realised in that moment that out of all the times other people had dialled the same number and he had responded, he had never fully understood what it was like to feel as desperate as they did in those moments.

He fought to keep calm. While he waited for the call to be connected he pulled her to him. Only then did he notice the upended bedside table, the lamp on the bed, the smashed dressing table mirror and the array of cosmetics littering the carpet. In the centre of the chaos were daubs of red across the bedroom wall.

BAD COPS WILL BURN

The call was connected.

"This is DC Barnes, warrant number Charlie-Bravo two-two-three. I am off-duty at my home address. My wife has been seriously assaulted. I need an ambulance and a patrol car here straightaway."

He lost it when the call taker began to ask him stock questions, like if anybody was still in the house, how old his wife was and if she was breathing, if she was conscious.

"Listen, I am a police officer! Someone's tried to kill her — get an ambulance, now! I don't know . . . I don't know if she's conscious . . . I can't tell."

He looked up at the slogan on the wall again, just as he noticed the first sharp trickles of smoke drifting into his lungs.

"Fire . . ." he whispered into the phone. *"The house is on fire!"*

He dropped the phone, and carefully levered his arms under Eve's limp arms and legs. He hoisted her up, as carefully as possible, hearing the first growl of flame erupt somewhere downstairs.

He stumbled down the stairs, slipping at the bottom, nearly dropping Eve. Forbes raced ahead, sensing danger, and began to bark at the front door. Barnes reached the foot of the stairs and chanced a look back at the galley kitchen, where the fire was already ablaze and spreading fast. He breathed blinding smoke, and coughed insanely, latching onto the dwindling rational sense that told him the way out — between the staircase and the front door — was still clear, although not for long.

He couldn't open the door. It was a simple Yale catch, but with his hands full, he could only lift Eve up and then drop his elbow to try and flick the catch.

After seven attempts it had not worked, and his arms felt like lead. The catch in front of him was disappearing from view as the hallway filled with choking black smoke. He looked down at Eve's face, and then back at the kitchen, the fire creeping closer along the hall carpet, curling the edges of the poppy canvas, daylight obliterated by a curtain of black and yellow.

As smoke engulfed them, he felt resistance suddenly snap, and the urge to just give in and sink to the floor overcame him. At least they would die together. The dog stopped barking and lay down.

It was only a tiny whimper from Eve that prompted him to drop her legs briefly to free up one arm, just long enough to open the door.

He rushed out, coughing up his panic, Forbes close behind him. He dropped Eve onto the lawn as carefully as he could, while the fire ripped through the house they had worked so hard to prepare for a lifetime together, for a family.

She lay unconscious among the bluebells. He rested his head on her chest and felt shallow breaths, and a dull rhythmic throb from her heart. He didn't know what else to do. He cried that he loved her, over and over. His tears fell onto her bloody face, and, not knowing what else to do, he held her.

* * *

He rode in the ambulance with her, the world outside carrying on as normal; trees and lights and concrete flicking by, only visible through the tiny window in the wall of the ambulance. The lights and sirens caused cars to stop and heads to turn, then as it passed the ambulance was immediately forgotten.

The driver was testing the ambulance to its limits. Barnes had not seen him, but he recognised the bespectacled paramedic riding in the back, who was managing to both tend to Eve and write on a clipboard without falling over. He was professional and efficient, despite being the size of a Ford Transit, but there was none of the usual banter that had passed between him and Barnes when their paths had crossed before.

"I . . . I checked her vitals," Barnes managed. "And I don't think anything's broken."

The paramedic nodded without looking up. Barnes figured it wouldn't be unreasonable in the circumstances for the paramedic not to place too much trust in Barnes's first aid skills at that moment. Lord knew he didn't particularly trust them himself.

An older patrol officer whom Barnes didn't know rode with him in the ambulance, while the fire crews battled with the blaze at his house. The officer was pleasant and sympathetic, but obviously didn't know Barnes was a cop. Barnes had been first on the scene of many serious incidents, and he'd always done the drill on arrival — tend to the victim, secure the scene, commence the log, support relatives, canvass for witnesses, avoid cross-contamination of scenes, get CID, get SOCO, get ambulance, start the search . . . he'd always tried to be professional, methodical and self-assured, to give the victims and their families the confidence that he knew what he was doing.

But he'd never been able to properly empathise — until now. Now that he was on the other side, thoughts of procedure had gone out of his head. His wife was the victim, and he didn't care about what the police were doing. He just held her hand to his face and whispered to her. All he cared about was her being okay.

The ambulance arrived at the hospital and the two paramedics clattered the trolley into the treatment bay like a couple of bobsledders. The familiar faces of the A&E nurses looked at Barnes with awkward sympathy as they cut away clothing and fitted drips and monitors and oxygen. The smell of blood faded away, usurped by disinfectant. He watched the medical team engage their skills for a short time, but when Eve looked less like his wife and more like part of the hospital furniture, he felt the strength leaving his legs and the sound of the world fading in his ears.

It's like she doesn't belong to me anymore.

Sally Holden's voice in his head.

Self-control threatened to abandon him completely, but he managed to compose himself enough to wrench his body from the treatment bay while they worked, fear in his chest like a disease.

Hadian and Denniker were already sitting in the waiting area. They jumped to their feet when Barnes emerged.

"Barnes, Jesus. I'm so sorry." Hadian put his hand on Barnes's shoulder. Denniker muttered similar platitudes about taking as much time as he needed and doing what needed to be done.

Barnes did not hear them, but allowed himself to be led to a seat. He'd known Fortune was violent and dangerous, but each time he'd encountered him his job had served as a buffer. This time, it had been personal. The sanctity of their home had been invaded, and Barnes felt raw and vulnerable, like his entire belief system had been tossed in the air and smashed like a vase. It was his *job* that had done this to his wife.

Hadian got him some water, and the pressure in his chest eased a little.

"Who . . ." Hadian began.

"Robbie Fortune," Barnes said quietly, his eyes fixed on the floor. He was suddenly exhausted. "Fortune's done this, and he's *got* to be good for Harriet Holden's murder."

"The patrol teams are out now looking for him. They'll pick him up," Hadian said.

"It's been two days. He hasn't been arrested yet. I don't understand how he managed to break into my house and inflict grievous bodily harm on my wife if there was a round-the-clock surveillance team on him."

Hadian and Denniker glanced at each other. The edge to Barnes's voice was like a razor.

"Barnes . . . the surveillance team was redeployed earlier this week." Hadian's voice was quiet.

Barnes breathed through his mouth. The anger was growing, gripping his chest with a vengeance.

"Sir . . . I don't understand. I don't understand." He was clenching and unclenching his fists.

"It's complicated, DC Barnes," Denniker began.

Barnes stood, and turned to face him. Denniker's clumsy attempts at sympathy were falling well short, and his every word was lighting touchpaper inside Barnes.

"What's so complicated, *sir*?" He spat the mode of address like a profanity.

Denniker's eyes narrowed.

"The surveillance team is a Force resource, with limited staff. Each division puts in a bid for what they need and why their need is greater than everybody else's, and the team is deployed accordingly. They'd been on our patch for a while, on Howard Van Leer. It was decided that it was time they moved onto something else."

"What exactly did they move onto? Something worth-while, I hope," Barnes said, unable to help the sarcasm.

"I can't comment on that."

"Meaning?"

"Meaning I don't *know* what they were deployed to."

"I would *like* to know what was so fucking important." Barnes was angry now, the room spinning.

There was a silence. An ambulance raced into the resus bay, blue lights flashing.

"Barnes, go to your wife. Be with her," Hadian instructed. "I'll get a couple of the uniformed guys to guard her."

"Don't bother. I'm not going anywhere. We're still on for tomorrow? Five thirty, yes?" Barnes's jaw was set with grim defiance.

Hadian looked shocked.

"Barnes, you can't be serious. You are to take a leave of absence and support your wife. The LST can handle it. We'll bring Fortune in, and he won't come out again."

Barnes looked at the ceiling while Hadian spoke, then fixed his gaze on him.

"Sir, we have to do it tomorrow, and I have to be there." He looked at Denniker. "I think we may find more than we bargained for."

"Barnes, quite understandably, you're not thinking straight. Sit down, and I'll get coffee." Hadian disappeared off to find a vending machine.

Barnes inched a little closer to Denniker.

"What was so important, sir?"

"I'm not sure I like the tone of your questioning, Officer."

"With the utmost respect due to you, sir," Barnes continued, in a tone that suggested anything but, "and in recognition of the fact that you are a senior commanding officer, why did you pull the surveillance off Robbie Fortune?"

"As I just said—"

"That's fucking bullshit. He was charged with three counts of GBH, he attacked my wife and me on the seafront, and now he's broken into my house and tried to kill her. What the hell was so important? They could have called it in. They could have prevented this happening."

"As I recall, DC Barnes, it was *you* that insisted on granting bail to Mr Fortune the last time he was in custody. Both the custody officer and DCI Hadian were reluctant, but were convinced by your intervention. I think you need to audit your decision-making before you start pointing the finger."

Barnes blinked rapidly, his vision suddenly blurred. *Was this his fault?* He had been trying to catch a criminal. That had been his motivation, nothing else.

"Then why the hell wasn't I told that the surveillance was being pulled off?"

"Unfortunate timing, Officer. It must have got lost in the paper loop. There's probably an email to you right now. Have you checked your phone messages?"

Barnes wanted to punch him, and very nearly did.

"Mr Denniker, don't let's forget the conversation you and I had at your house."

Denniker smiled. "Refresh my memory."

"You ordered me to plant evidence on an innocent man."

"I recall no such conversation, Officer. Are you suggesting you may have pursued some kind of impropriety in your exuberance to nail a murder suspect?"

"You and I conspired to stitch up Howard Van Leer. That's what happened."

"A fruitful imagination, Officer."

Barnes stopped, not believing what he was hearing.

"Your wife," he said with a dry throat. "Your wife remembers me coming to the house."

"Yes, I invited you there to give you your excellent exam result. And if my wife, having had another stroke, could tell you what day of the week it is, then I generally regard that day as being a good one for her."

"No one will believe it. I could go straight to Professional Standards and tell them everything . . ."

Denniker's eyes gleamed, the rage apparent in his quiet voice.

"Well, I wish you the very best of luck. I, of course, will deny everything, and will vehemently claim that you are trying to upstage me to deflect blame from yourself and expedite your own ambition. I am a *senior commander*, and you are an obnoxious, self-righteous little shit. I think I know who will get better odds.

"And if you threaten me again, Constable, I will be relentless in my efforts to have you instantly dismissed, facing criminal charges, and prevented from ever holding any job that pays more than four figures a year." Denniker's breath was sour.

Barnes fought to keep from being intimidated. He moved closer to Denniker.

"What does Dominic Van Leer have on you?"

Denniker didn't move, but Barnes thought he saw something change, almost imperceptibly, in the commander's face.

CHAPTER TWENTY

There was no life in the town centre besides scavenging gulls and a handful of homeless people curled in sleeping bags in the doorway to the Arndale Centre and the railway station. This was not a particularly common sight — the rough sleepers habitually occupied the beach shelters — but Van Leer's murder had pushed them all north.

Barnes and Hadian drove through the town, with Callaghan following in a police van. Barnes looked out of his window and saw a carpet of early-morning mist blanketing the Levels on either side. The telegraph poles that stretched away into the distance rose out of the fog, as if suspended in the sky. A train appeared in the distance, ripping the vapour apart like discarded breaths as it headed out of town. It raced underneath them as they traversed the flyover.

Conversation was scant. Hadian had asked after Eve, and Barnes told him she'd had a good night. She was concussed, had a splinter fracture of the left forearm and was suffering the effects of smoke inhalation, but the prognosis was good.

The doctors expected her to make a full recovery. They didn't believe a weapon had been used, just that Fortune

— for that was who it surely was — had used his fists. Once her face had been cleaned up the damage didn't look as bad.

But Barnes felt no relief. The thought of his wife, alone in their house and defenceless against her cruel attacker, was almost too much to bear. That he had not been there to protect her made him nauseous, made him flinch like someone was aiming punches at his face. He had vomited twice during the night, all the time thoughts clamouring in his head about the Van Leers, Fortune, Nightingale, McDermott and now Denniker. And Harriet. Always Harriet, and how her poor naked corpse had lain alone in silence before anyone had even *started* down the road to justice for her.

Hadian shifted in his seat.

"Who's on the LST?" he asked, indicating behind him with his thumb.

"Callaghan."

Hadian groaned.

"He's a good copper. I know he breached some sort of unwritten code, but his hand was forced. I trust him." Barnes glanced at Hadian as he said this.

Hadian changed the subject.

"If Fortune is here, I want you to stand down and let the LST take him," he said.

"Please don't give me any orders. Not this morning," Barnes answered, pulling into Sovereign Harbour South. A huge orange sun rose slowly in the east.

"Please, Barnes, just promise me that. I'm sticking my neck out even letting you come along this morning."

"If it makes you feel any better, sir, just tell yourself that you didn't have a choice. Even if the Home Secretary ordered me to keep away this morning, I would be here."

Hadian sighed.

They pulled into Barbuda Quay quickly and quietly, and stopped outside the block.

Emily Varela was waiting outside with a photographer. Barnes made the introductions, and Hadian shot him an enquiring look while shaking Emily Varela's hand. Barnes made a hand signal — *later*.

The two detectives, seven uniformed officers and two members of the press assembled in the lobby. The lift was not large enough to take all of them, and two trips were necessary. Barnes shepherded the group so Hadian and Callaghan did not ride together. The lift was new, and it raced smoothly upwards. Barnes produced the warrant from inside his pocket and smoothed it out. Nobody in the lift spoke.

The doors slid open, and the men filed out into the hallway. The wait for the second group seemed to take forever, but after the minor hiatus they assembled outside the apartment. The hallway was silent, apart from the faint sound of a television from elsewhere in the building.

Two of the uniforms crouched and slid past the door of the apartment. Two more took a position on the other side, whispering and shuffling. The entry man moved to the door with the method-of-entry instrument — a huge metal battering ram affectionately referred to as "the bosher". He was followed by the remaining officer, who was equipped with a DVD video camera and had *"Evidence Gathering Team"* emblazoned across the rear of his body armour, and Callaghan, who held an enormous steel crowbar. The photographer was right behind them, and the detectives brought up the rear.

There was silence. The air was heavy with tension. The video camera was raised to the door. Callaghan looked momentarily over his shoulder at Barnes and then tapped the shoulder of the entry man for the go. The bosher was swung in an arc at the latch. It took only the one hit — the door flew open and the LST piled in, yelling. The camera went *click-click-click-click-click-click*.

Barnes examined the door and frame as they entered. Hadian whistled.

"One hit. Remind me never to buy a place in the harbour."

The apartment was clearly new. Halogen spotlights pockmarked the ceiling. There were white walls and carpet, black leather furniture, a glass coffee table and four straight-backed black metal chairs.

But the entire place already had the feel of drug abuse. The table was littered with old reefers, tinfoil and burned teaspoons. Syringes were spread over the floor. The carpet had cigarette burns spread across it; unwashed dishes and cups lay on the floor. There was a footprint on the glass balcony door. The smell of dirty clothing and body odour was unmistakable. The central heating was fully cranked up.

Hadian grimaced. "This place is a death trap." He picked his way through the rubbish and slid open the balcony door to let some air into the stuffy apartment, and stepped onto the balcony.

"What a dump," muttered Emily Varela.

Callaghan approached Barnes.

"It's empty. No one here," he said.

"Shit," Barnes pursed his lips. "Shit, shit, *shit*. Should have kept obs on it. Where the hell is he?"

Hadian re-entered the room as the search team got to work.

"Not much of a view," he observed. Barnes looked — beyond the surrounding wings of Santa Ana Court, the only things visible were cranes, JCBs and the churned-up mud of a huge construction site.

Barnes walked around the apartment, and found the telephone in the short entrance hallway by the now-destroyed front door. It was off the hook, and had fallen down onto the floor from its position on the telephone table. He produced a digital camera and took some shots. He put the camera away, pressed his knuckle to the bridge of his nose and shut his eyes.

Who had been here? Howard Van Leer had run from here in a panic before burgling Phil McDermott's house and assaulting his wife. Then Robbie Fortune had used it as a bail address. Had there been anyone here in between? Had Fortune ever even been here?

Barnes's eye was distracted by a cardboard box near the telephone table. He moved over to it and crouched down.

It was full of brown jiffy bags, A5 size. He pulled on two pairs of latex gloves, one pair over the other, and picked an envelope out of the box. Written on the front in black marker pen were the words "TO BE HANDED IN AT POLICE STATION," in some admirable — but likely doomed — attempt to create a ready defence for anyone found in possession of one of these envelopes. Barnes carefully prised open the envelope and pulled out a cellophane pack containing a block of white powder.

In spite of himself, Barnes chuckled.

"We've got something, sir," he called, and threw the pack to Hadian, who examined it. "Cute, eh?"

Barnes photographed the box *in situ*. When he had finished Hadian pointed the LST towards the box, and Barnes stepped out into the hallway. There was another apartment across the hallway. He banged on the door several times, but there was no answer.

Barnes wondered what sort of behaviour the occupants had been forced to tolerate. Threats, intimidation, visitors at all hours. Equally, however, the block was a new build and many flats were still vacant — perfect criteria for Van Leer in selecting his den. Or maybe it was a holiday let — a little hideout for rich Londoners sneaking to the coast on August weekends, maybe pocketing a little bit of recreational gear themselves.

He walked to a heavy fire door and pushed it open, revealing a brightly lit stairwell. He pictured Howard Van Leer tearing down these stairs, too afraid to wait for the lift. He replayed that night in his head — that was the last time Howard Van Leer ever got to taste freedom.

He returned to the apartment. The LST were animated — it looked like a big haul. The EGT officer moved swiftly in between them all to film the seizure.

"If this is pure, there's a fair amount here," Callaghan said.

Hadian was pleased. Barnes just shrugged. Callaghan carried the box carefully into the lounge, and cleared the coffee table of crap with one kick of a large boot. The EGT officer followed him diligently. In pairs the team began to carefully remove, weigh and itemise the contents of the box.

Barnes was about to speak when a voice came from behind him.

"You boys don't like knocking, eh?"

Barnes spun round on his heels. A small, ratty-looking man with a complexion like gunmetal stood in the doorway of the apartment, examining the damage. He wore a red Hawaiian shirt that hung off his slight shoulders and tufts of hair stuck out from under a dirty baseball cap. He had not an ounce of fat anywhere on him, and his skin was tight on his bones.

"I'd think very carefully before you say any more." Barnes was over to the man in an instant. "Who are you?"

The EGT officer tapped Callaghan on the shoulder, and the team paused their sifting through the box of jiffy bags. The EGT officer moved alongside Barnes and filmed the man standing in the doorway, who stared into the lens with cunning, grey eyes. He didn't speak.

"I said — who are you?"

The man smiled. "I'm not saying a word. I'm taking your advice. I would like to have some *proper* legal advice, though. I want a lawyer."

Hadian moved forward and flanked Barnes.

"Why? Got something to hide?"

The man spread his hands.

"Do I look like I'm delivering pizza?"

Barnes stepped forward. "You're Dominic Van Leer, are you not?"

The man shrugged. "Who?"

"Listen to me carefully," Barnes said. "Turn around and put your hands behind your back." He heard Hadian inhale sharply, mirroring the butterflies in his own stomach. "I think this apartment is yours. You're under arrest for possession of Class A drugs with intent to supply."

The photographer began to snap. The man called Dominic Van Leer did as he was told, but only after he'd lashed out long enough to knock the photographer's camera to the floor.

"Get that fucking thing out of my face," he snarled. Barnes and two LST officers grabbed him.

"Whoops," Hadian said. "That would be assault and criminal damage as well."

The cuffs went on. Hadian instructed the two LST officers to ferry the older Van Leer to the cells and get him his lawyer, and they duly went — searching Van Leer and finding his driving licence in his wallet prior to departing. The rest of the team resumed the search.

The photographer began to gather the pieces of his damaged camera with a dejected look on his face. Barnes went to shake hands with Emily Varela.

"Thanks for coming. Sorry about your camera."

"Same time next week?" she grinned, clearly enjoying the excitement.

Barnes looked around him, and guided her by the arm into the kitchen. She gave him a curious look, and he quietly told her about how Eve had been assaulted. He told her to meet him at the hospital later and he would explain. She nodded, and left with the photographer.

Barnes and Hadian stepped out onto the balcony. A warm breeze blew in off the Channel.

"A heads-up on the press being here would have been nice," Hadian said.

"You look fine, sir."

"That isn't what I meant."

"It's a reciprocal agreement. I trust her."

"I hope so, for your sake. Does she know about Eve?"

"Yes." Hadian rolled his eyes. "She won't print anything unless I say she can, but not if her source comes from somewhere else. If it gets leaked to the press at all, I'd rather be the one doing it."

"How high up does Van Leer go?"

"He's not just street. He's not big-time either, but he's on the way. He's not been convicted in thirteen years. He's patient and clever, and it sounds like he had a reasonably prominent defence lawyer laundering his dirty work for him."

"And now he's in a cell. He won't be there long, you know."

"Doesn't matter. He's back in the system, that's the main thing. We'll release him on bail — tight conditions — and keep an eye on him. I checked the intelligence files — most of the current stuff is vague and unreliable. The good stuff is all old. The chief super had a flag against him when he was a DCI."

Hadian looked up, frowning. "Denniker?"

"Yeah. Make of that what you will."

Barnes walked back inside and went over to Callaghan.

"You done?" Barnes asked.

"Yeah. There's a couple of kilos here. If it's Class A then it's not the bust of the century, but a nice little haul."

"I wonder if the jiffy-bag defence will hold any weight."

Callaghan made to leave, then stopped and turned back to Barnes. Hadian moved away and pretended to examine the kitchen.

"Barnes, I've a small favour to ask." He took a small white square of paper out of his breast pocket and gave it to Barnes. Barnes examined the image on the passport photograph.

"It belongs to Cathy Nightingale. It fell out of her pocket when the traffic guys took her away. I've been meaning to give it back to her. Could I ask you to do it? I wouldn't trust anyone else with it."

"Of course," Barnes said.

"If you're getting a hard time because of what I did, then I'm truly sorry. I really had no choice."

"The hell with them."

"Thanks, Barnes."

Callaghan led the LST out, followed by the detectives. He made a clumsy job of securing the apartment by fitting a huge padlock. They returned to the vehicles.

Hadian's phone rang as they were getting back in the car. This conversation was even shorter.

"That was the custody officer," Hadian said as they got in the car together. "Brother Dominic has asked to speak to Mr Denniker in private."

* * *

Barnes drove home. The kitchen was blackened and stank like a barbecue, but, according to the fire service, the house was just about habitable.

He walked Forbes, the events of the day having cushioned the thoughts of Eve that had tortured him all night. As soon as he was alone, however, they returned with a vengeance.

After a few hours' sleep, interrupted by the scratch of the cloying remnants of smoke on the back of his throat, he returned to the hospital, where Eve was conscious, but groggy from painkillers. All traces of her warm, sweet smell had gone, replaced by the antiseptic on her wounds and the powerful tang of hospital disinfectant that stifled the air. He helped her sip some water, then stroked damp strands of hair from her forehead and promised her everything would be okay.

She managed a smile and was able to whisper, *"Hello, Chief. When do I make my statement?"*

He kissed her forehead and told her not to worry about it, that there was no rush. He squeezed her hand and whispered, *"Who did this? The man on the seafront?"* She nodded, and he bit his lip as tears filled his eyes. Tears for her pain, for her bravery. Tears, he knew, for his own guilt at not being there to protect her.

He talked to her about the children they would have, about walks on the Downs, about the dog, about a little cinema in New York that played *Breakfast at Tiffany's* every Sunday. He promised to take her. He promised to make up for not being there. He made a lot of promises.

Eventually the sun began to cast long shadows across Eve's room, and Barnes held her hand until the light

334

disappeared completely and the hospital room was shrouded in gloom. A white street light flicked on outside, changing all the shadows.

She slept. Barnes sat back in his chair, pulled his tie loose and tried to make himself comfortable. His eyes had begun to close when his phone vibrated with a message.

It was from Emily Varela: *I am at hospital. Are you here? Meet me outside A&E?*

Barnes left the room, stopping to talk to the two patrol cops outside. He hadn't wanted them there, but Hadian had insisted, and they had turned out to be decent guys — sensitive but fearless. They were a little older than Barnes, and didn't have the common-room idiocy about them like some of his younger peers — exactly, Barnes realised, as he wanted himself to be perceived.

He thanked them, walked down to A&E and looked around the waiting room for Emily. He stepped outside, where a man in a dressing gown smoked while holding onto a mobile stand that held both his intravenous drip and his chest drain. The cause-and-effect immediacy of the image made Barnes wonder whether the guy would have been better off just digging his own grave and being done with it.

She was standing outside the ambulance loading bay in a heavy-looking parka, two pigtails sticking out from under a Billabong beanie hat. She was clutching her notebook and a small bag decorated with flowers.

Barnes walked towards her, past a row of three ambulances backed up to the doors of the resus unit. Two paramedics were cleaning out the back of one of them.

Barnes and Emily stood underneath the blue neon strips that illuminated the canopy above them.

"Jesus, you look awful," Emily said. Barnes looked at his reflection in the mirror glass of the resus bay windows and saw she was right. He was pale, with dark rings around his eyes, like a Halloween mask of the Grim Reaper. For a second he didn't recognise himself.

"How is she?" Emily said, pointing at the hospital.

"Could be a lot worse, thank you for asking. She's conscious, and she'll make a full recovery. She's looked better, though, and she's got a busted arm."

"Who?" she asked, lighting a cigarette. She offered him one. In the circumstances he was momentarily tempted, but declined with a weak smile.

"Robbie Fortune."

"The guy who knifed those young lads?"

"The very same. Please, Emily, keep Eve's assault out of the papers. I don't want it to be public knowledge."

His tone was raw, his voice shaky. She looked him in the eye and exhaled smoke slowly.

"Consider it done. Hey, we saved the camera. Got some good pictures of the raid. I'm working on a headline: *style over controlled substance*. What do you think?"

"Cute."

"What happened to the suspect?"

"Bailed for twelve weeks. We've got to get the drugs analysed, then prove they were his. A fingerprint would be nice, but that's wishful thinking. I might be able to tie him to the apartment, though."

"Who is he?"

"Dominic Van Leer."

She frowned. "Van Leer?"

"Howard's brother. We think he's a bit further up the food chain than his little brother."

A radio crackled from behind them. The paramedics hurriedly finished their cleaning and tore out of the bay with blue lights flashing. Barnes squinted at them until the lights were out of sight, then turned back to Emily. She was still frowning.

"Mind if I think out loud?" she asked, treading her cigarette butt underfoot.

"Not at all, but not too loud."

"Harriet Holden's body was found in Howard Van Leer's room, correct?"

"Correct."

"Howard Van Leer is suspect number one, even though he has an iron-clad alibi. So the police stick a conspiracy charge on him — or were about to — then you find forensic evidence to suggest he had been inside Harriet's flat at some point in the past. How am I doing?"

Barnes just nodded. So far she had not made any notes.

"Then Howard burgles his solicitor's house and stabs his wife, and the solicitor — perhaps reasonably — decides to beat him up in a rage."

"I didn't think you believed me when I told you that."

"I didn't, at first. But I know you a little better now. I don't think you're capable of that kind of creativity."

He laughed. It was unexpected, and felt good. "Thanks."

"Van Leer is then kidnapped on the way back to prison, probably by his own people — right about the same time that he decided he wanted to postpone his destiny by talking to you lot. Then his body turns up on the beach, and the only witness besides you suddenly commits armed robbery and signs the rest of his life away. Not to mention being as mad as a box of frogs." Her eyes were drilling into him as she spoke.

"That's about the size of it."

"I'm not making the connection," Emily said with a frown. "You're putting big brother forward for Harriet's murder?" Her voice was suddenly loud in the still night air.

"No, I'm thinking Robbie Fortune."

"But there isn't enough. And what motive has he got?"

Barnes bristled for a moment at her insensitivity, and felt his hands start to tremble. He dug them in his pockets. "He's quite clearly a cop-hater, for one. But I think it might have been a contract."

"But who put it out?"

"Emily, this is speculation. There's no evidence. It's got to stay out of the papers, at least for now."

"You don't have to put that disclaimer in every four sentences, you know. You were saying Fortune killed Harriet on a contract?"

Barnes paused and looked over his shoulder. Had he heard something? He listened hard for a moment, but there were no sounds other than the rumble of the traffic on Kings Drive.

He turned back to Emily.

"I was saying *maybe*," he said in a whisper. "He had no motive that I can think of, other than his hatred of the police. But I think that Fortune is in Dominic Van Leer's pocket."

"Shit, really?" Now the notebook was out.

"And also Phil McDermott." Barnes's voice was getting quieter and quieter.

"Who?"

"The Van Leers' solicitor. The one whose wife was attacked by Howard."

"Oh Christ, that's good." Her face lit up as she scribbled. "You think he's bent?"

"He was. As a . . . shush a minute."

"What's the matter?" She looked at him, frustration in her face at the information flow being interrupted.

"Sssh!" he hissed, and peered over her shoulders to the expanse of rough, unmade ground beyond the helipad that served as an overspill car park during the day. It was unlit and in the still air it was like a thick black curtain behind her, the only light coming from the red lights blinking slowly on top of the incinerator chimney. There could have been a small army of cop-hating psychopaths down there, and he wouldn't have been able to see a thing. Under the blue strip lights of the ambulance bay, however, Barnes and Emily were sitting ducks.

"I think there's someone there," he whispered. His mouth was dry.

"We're being watched? Oh, this gets better," she said.

What was wrong with this woman? She was actually excited. He grabbed her arm and yanked her between the two ambulances.

"Emily, I don't mind telling you that I am scared of this Fortune character. He broke into my house and nearly killed my wife. He's capable of anything, and I don't think you should be quite so glib about your safety." His voice echoed in the small fluorescent canyon created by the walls of the two ambulances, and he could hear his heartbeat fluttering loudly in his ears, as if there was an insect in there trying frantically to get out.

She raised one eyebrow, amused by the admonishment. He shook his head. It was like trying to get through to a child.

"Okay then, Mr Policeman, we'll talk later."

"Go to your car. Take a circuitous route, and don't go home until you're sure you're not being followed. If you are, keep away from home and call the cops. And a taxi. Here." He pressed some money into her hand.

The smile vanished.

"Do you actually think I'm in danger?" she asked, her eyes widening.

"I think we all are. Now go."

"Okay," she said, a slight tremor to her voice. "But I can pay for my own taxi."

She slipped the note into his breast pocket and walked briskly to her car, looking left and right over her shoulder as she went. Her car was the only one left in the main car park, and he crouched down, waiting for a dark figure to leap from nowhere and grab her, or for a car to go roaring after her from the blackness.

But she drove away without incident. He watched her go, pulled out his torch and shone it into the darkness.

A light breeze had risen and was sweeping over the Cross Levels — he could just hear the bushes moving in the air outside the Day Surgery Unit. He walked over to the bushes and pulled his baton from his belt.

Fear was licking at him now. He had overpowered Fortune once, but he put it down to luck and didn't relish an opportunity for him to get even. The rage that came to the surface when he pictured his wife's battered face would be more of a hindrance than a help if it came to a fight.

He swept his baton two or three times at the bushes, slicing the ends of the plants.

"Police!" he called in a shaky voice. "Come out." He walked towards the helipad, feeling blades of grass brushing his ankles as the wind blew harder. He felt totally exposed.

The ground in front of the Day Surgery Unit spread out in a wide expanse of grass with the A&E helipad at the centre. Behind it, the ground sloped away to a road far below him which led under the main building into a concrete canopy that serviced the mortuary.

He shone his torch from his vantage point near the helipad, sweeping it back and forth across the grass. Nothing.

Without warning he heard an engine start, and a car pulled out from the mortuary onto the service road. It had no lights. It accelerated away, high revs in first gear, before shifting up. It barely slowed at the gate, and nearly collected the reflective barrier arm as it rose.

Barnes ran across the grass towards the car. It was on the hospital road proper now, and heading towards Kings Drive. He sprinted towards it, but the driver accelerated away and got onto the main road before it flicked its lights on.

The wind was stronger on the flat land surrounding the helipad. Barnes swore loudly, his voice swallowed quickly by the wind. He hadn't even seen the make or model, let alone the registration number or the driver, and under the street lights it could have been one of any number of colours.

The realisation that Eve could be in trouble suddenly hit him, and he turned on his heel and sprinted back into the hospital. He bolted through the quiet A&E department and ran up the stairs two at a time to Eve's ward. He tried in vain to tell himself it was nothing, but the images of someone coming back to finish Eve off while he was outside were much more commanding. Any other time he would have written it off as paranoia or groundless worry, but Eve's injuries — like the fear that sat in his stomach like cold water — were very real.

He burst into the ward. A lone nurse stood by a station, reading some notes. She looked up in surprise when Barnes ran in. He ran to Eve's room. The two cops were still stationed outside, their expressions mirroring the alarm on Barnes's face.

She was fast asleep, lying on her back, her breathing whistling uncomfortably through her injured nose and mouth. Her dark hair on the pillow seemed to be the only part of her Barnes recognised. He bent over and put his hands on his knees, relief flooding through him like a feeling he did not deserve, the metronomic *blip-blip-blip* of her heart monitor slowly steadying the world around him.

He kissed her hand and tried to sleep.

* * *

It was still dark when his phone vibrated again. He woke with difficulty from a fitful sleep punctured by bad dreams — it took him several seconds to adjust. Eve was still asleep. She had turned onto her side, and her breathing sounded more comfortable.

He went outside to the main ward. The two cops had been relieved by night shift guys. Younger, but polite, helpful and obviously alert. He smiled hello and took the call.

"Barnes?"

"Who's this?"

"It's Cathy Nightingale."

Barnes didn't answer, sidelined momentarily by the adrenaline that felt like someone had blasted cold air through his sinuses.

"Barnes? Are you there?" Her voice was thick, as if her cheeks were rammed with boiled sweets.

"Yeah. What do you want?"

"Listen, you and I need to meet."

"What for?"

"Get in your car. I'll see you at Birling Gap."

"Now?"

"It has to be now."

* * *

341

The wind had picked up when Barnes got to his car. It was a little after midnight. The humidity was thick in the air, and Barnes felt the storm coming.

The road swept upwards to the highest point of the South Downs, then snaked downwards again towards Birling Gap. The wind was strong on the cliffs, and Barnes felt the car rock. The lights of trawlers out on the Channel bobbed up and down in the rough waters, the sky and sea like one thick purple curtain, the horizon indistinguishable in the murk. Barnes eyed Belle Tout away in the distance, and thought of Denniker.

He pulled into the rough gravel car park at Birling Gap, the tiny fissure on the coastline engulfed on either side by the dark outlines of the Seven Sisters. On the east side of the car park stood a row of six disused terraced cottages, built by the Admiralty in the nineteenth century to house coastguards. There had originally been eight, but with the gradual erosion of the cliffs, the two southernmost cottages had been demolished to prevent them falling into the sea.

Near the edge of the cliff a car flashed its headlights. Barnes drove slowly over to the car and parked next to it. He got out and walked over, apprehension churning his gut.

The driver's window slid down. The faint strains of Annie Lennox — "Walking on Broken Glass" — could be heard from the radio, and a cloud of exhaled booze wafted into Barnes's face.

"Get in," Nightingale said. Her eyes shone in the gloom, emeralds in a darkened cave.

Barnes hesitated momentarily. As he wondered whether these were the same eyes behind the balaclava the day Van Leer was kidnapped, he realised he had every reason to be afraid of Cathy Nightingale.

But his need for answers outweighed his fear, and in a deft movement he reached through the open window, grabbed her slender right wrist and snapped on a handcuff. Before she could protest, he attached the other cuff to the steering wheel.

Barnes walked around the car and slid into the passenger seat. Under the beam of the car headlights he could see the southern face of the six coastguard cottages. Faded wallpaper and light patches were visible on the interior of the end cottage where paintings and furniture had once been — a door on the second floor opened out into nothing but the storm and the cliffs below. It made Barnes want to run for shelter.

"Fair to say you don't trust me, then?" Nightingale said, tugging ineffectually at the handcuffs.

Her voice still sounded thick. At first Barnes thought it was the booze, but then, in the darkness, he realised there was something wrong with the shape of her face.

Barnes switched on the interior light. The right side of Nightingale's face, from the jaw to the temple, was puffy and swollen. Her right eye was smeared with a purple bruise, and there was a lump on her forehead like a boiled egg.

"Jesus," Barnes said. "What happened to you?"

Besides the injuries, she had lost weight, and in the weak glow of the light the shadows in her face were long and drawn. A sickly-sweet smell of perfume, sweat and whisky came off her in waves.

"Upset the applecart," she said, and then spluttered a cracked, humourless laugh that sent a chill down Barnes's spine.

Nightingale reached inside her jacket with her free hand and pulled out a packet of Silk Cut. She fumbled with it for a moment, and then looked at Barnes, her eyes pleading and pathetic.

"What do you want, Cathy?" Barnes's jaw flexed as he lit a cigarette for her, his senses heightened for any surprises.

"We need to talk." She sucked on the cigarette.

"Hadian and I were looking for you. We had quite a lot of questions," Barnes said.

Nightingale said nothing, but picked up a pint bottle of Jim Beam from the footwell. She held it between her knees, unscrewed the cap and, with closed eyes, tipped her head back and took a long pull with her free hand.

She wedged the bottle back between her knees, not bothering with the lid, and wiped her mouth with the back of her hand. Barnes noticed that it was trembling.

"What have you done, Cathy?" His tone was accusatory. "I want to know. Are you part of Van Leer's crew?"

Nightingale turned to face him. The handcuff chain pulled tight and clinked against a bracelet on her wrist. It was a sudden movement, like a dog straining on its leash, and Barnes flinched.

"You have to understand," she said, her tone urgent. "A career detective isn't qualified for much else. My job was making friends with scumbags, but once you lose your rank, it's only the scumbags that will have you. Do you get that? I've been . . . running some errands." The cigarette bobbed in her mouth as she spoke. "I had to pay the *rent*," she said in a whisper.

"Errands? Like driving Range Rovers?"

Nightingale took a deep breath.

"Make no mistake, Howard Van Leer got what he deserved."

She was silent for a moment, and the corners of her mouth turned down.

"That's why you and Hadian wanted to question me, right? Something about loose lips sinking ships?" She cackled briefly at her own wit, and then looked off into the distance ahead of her.

"Cathy, if you're going to speak in code, then I'm out of here." Barnes went to open the door. She stopped him with a strong hand on his upper arm. He could feel her fingers, hard against his jacket.

"Wait. Please wait. You need to hear this."

He turned back to look at her. Her eyes were wide, the tendons standing out on her neck.

"What do you *want*?" he said.

"I'm on borrowed time here, Barnes. You have to listen." She removed her hand from his arm and switched off the radio. Annie Lennox was silenced. Nightingale exhaled deeply and her voice dropped to a whisper, as if someone might be listening. "Dominic Van Leer wants you."

"Tell me something I don't know. He's unleashed his puppy — Fortune."

"No, he doesn't want you dead. He wants you to *succeed*. He's been throwing you *bones*." The cigarette had burned to the hilt in her shaking fingers, and she dropped it on the floor.

Barnes just stared at her dumbly.

"Don't you see, Barnes? Van Leer has been putting you onto some jobs. Decent jobs, with press coverage. Jobs you can build your career on."

"Why . . . why would he do that?"

She smiled thinly in the electric yellow light.

"You're so green. It's really quite sweet. Give and take, Barnes. He staged that armed robbery for you. You understand? He *staged* it. You must have realised he would want something in return."

"What can I give him? I'm only a constable."

"But not for long, am I right? It's what Denniker would call strategic perspective. I call it selling your soul."

A gust of wind rocked the car. Lightning flared in the distance over the Channel, and gouged itself on the heavy, purple sky as the storm inched closer.

"Denniker? Somehow I'm not surprised. What does he have to do with it, exactly?" Barnes was opening and closing his fingers on his lap.

"Denniker has *everything* to do with it. How do you think he got to where he is? Big, high-profile arrests, that's how — all staged by Van Leer, all in exchange for immunity when Denniker got to the top."

"Christ, how *old* is this fucking guy?" Barnes said, starting to feel numb.

"Older than he looks. Old enough to keep his eye out for fresh meat. The heir to the commander's throne. And that, my friend, is you."

She took another pull of the whisky, and her body shuddered.

"But why . . . *why* did he have to hurt my wife?"

Nightingale gazed at Barnes. There was sadness in her eyes.

"So you couldn't say no," she said quietly.

"Jesus." Barnes put his head in his hands and raked his fingers over his scalp, anger and frustration swimming in his head with nowhere to go. "The bastard. That *bastard*. I don't . . . I *can't* believe this."

He tried to process it all, dumb with shock. Had he achieved *any* of his successes on his own merit, or had he just put his wife in danger? He shook his head. He wanted to give it all back, just rewind the clock and start again. Was that too much to ask?

Nightingale touched his arm, as if she could tell what he was thinking. He looked up at her. Her eyes were like those of a child trying to show sympathy to an adult without fully understanding what troubled them.

"How do you know all this, Cathy?" Barnes said, eventually. "Have you been feeding information back to Melanie Denton? To Van Leer?"

He angrily pushed her hand away, and she covered her eyes again. Her chest began to hitch as she fought the tears. "I did what I had to do, okay? To survive."

Barnes's shock was already starting to dissipate, as if, now it had been spelled out, the explanation was obvious. When it came to catching criminals, sustained success could only be achieved by cheating.

The picture became clearer. "Dominic Van Leer is a drug dealer," Barnes said. "He's got the apartment in the harbour. He must import the gear over the water. The company, Sovereign Holdings, he must launder the cash through there. Phil McDermott — the recently departed Phil McDermott — was his frontman."

"What . . . what happened to him?"

"Car crash. It wasn't pretty."

Nightingale shook her head as the car rocked again, a smile of wonder on her lips.

"What, in this life, is *pretty*?" she said, as rain began to lick at the windows.

"Van Leer must have had Denniker over a barrel," he said. "If Denniker tried to back out of their deal, Van Leer could just threaten him with exposure." Barnes had to admit it was clever. He suddenly thought of Emily Varela, and her theory that the armed robbery was to deflect attention from Op Christchurch. "And any time he feels things are getting too hot, he can just create a diversion."

"Best smokescreen for organised crime," Nightingale agreed. "Any time Van Leer's got a shipment coming in, he just has to create havoc. Keeps us busy, and the little prick loves it."

"What about Harriet? Where does she fit into this?" Barnes asked. He was afraid of the answer, but he wanted to bleed Nightingale dry.

"I'm not sure. Poor girl. She . . ."

Her voice tailed off, and her eyes filled with tears again. She drummed the steering wheel with her fingers while she tried to keep a lid on it. Barnes felt a small stab of pity penetrate the curtain of anger that surrounded him. He had not seen her like this before.

"So, you just have a theory about Van Leer blackmailing Denniker," he said. "Where is the proof? How do we—"

"Shut up and listen," Nightingale interrupted. "Has Denniker asked you to do anything that could compromise you?"

Barnes shut his eyes and pressed a clenched fist to his forehead, suddenly feeling like an animal trapped in a gunsight.

"He asked me — *told* me — to plant evidence on Howard Van Leer. To fit him up for Harriet's murder."

"Oh, shit." Nightingale ran her hand through her marcel wave, and then, in the gloom, a wry smile appeared on her lips. "Then I guess we're not so different, after all."

"Fuck yourself. I'm nothing like you."

She suddenly leaned across and gripped his knee, her strong fingers like a crab's legs. "You've got to take him down,

Barnes. You're young, impressionable. Tell Professional Standards he ordered you to do it, that he threatened you. You might survive it."

"It's an act of dishonesty. I'll never work again."

"You've got to do it. Even if you are implicated, it's a small price for taking that bastard down."

Barnes twisted in his seat.

"Don't preach to me. Why the hell are you putting all this on my shoulders? Why haven't *you* gone to Professional Standards?" he said.

"They wouldn't believe a word. They'd see me as a disgraced ex-cop with a chip on her shoulder and a grudge in her pocket . . ."

"You *are* a disgrace!" Barnes shouted. It made Nightingale jump, and the bottle of Jim Beam fell from her knees into the footwell. Whisky leaked over the rubber floor mat. "Why are you laying all this shit at *my* door, Cathy? If you're trying to clear your conscience, you can forget it." Barnes leaned over towards her and unlocked the handcuffs.

"Why am I *telling* you?" Nightingale said in disbelief as he freed her. "This is all I've got to *give*."

Barnes got out of the car and slammed the door. Then he remembered something, and walked around to the driver's window. The wind on the cliff edge was ferocious now, and he had to steady himself on the car as he walked.

"Cathy, I've got something for you." He produced the passport photograph Callaghan had given him and handed it to Nightingale. She fingered it for a good few seconds before looking down at her ex-husband's face. She stared for a moment, then flipped it over to read the back.

Barnes exhaled.

"Cathy . . . tell me honestly. Tell me you weren't the one that leaked her address. Tell me you didn't give them Harriet."

Nightingale didn't answer, didn't look at him, but instead gazed over at the crumbling coastguard cottages.

"Less than twenty years before the sea gets the next one. Only take a bit of shingle to keep them standing, but the miserable bastards won't allow it." She sighed, and shook her head. "It's all just falling away into the sea."

Barnes backed away and walked to his own car. He started the engine, the rain drumming on the roof, and drove slowly over the unmade ground onto the winding road that led back towards Beachy Head and Eastbourne. Before the undulating South Downs enveloped him in the darkness, he looked in his rear-view mirror to see if Nightingale was following him. All he could see was a heavy curtain of black.

* * *

The lightning flashes were increasing in both intensity and frequency. Her last confession spent, Cathy Nightingale reached over to the back seat. With the photograph still in her fingers, she put the shotgun in her mouth, her teeth chattering against the barrel.

In the darkness, the flash of the muzzle was indistinguishable from the lightning, and the explosion drowned in the rising wind.

CHAPTER TWENTY-ONE

The hospital was quiet when Barnes returned. The storm was virtually on top of them, and the wind whipped a cold spattering of rain across his face as he left his car. He walked slowly through the hospital, his footsteps echoing in the dimly lit, empty corridors, and felt utterly alone.

Barnes entered the ward. It was in darkness, besides the pale glow of a lamp at the nurses' station and some night lights dotted around the bed bays.

He stopped dead.

The two chairs were still outside Eve's room, but the two uniformed officers were not.

His heart pounding in his chest, he ran for the door and burst in.

The bed was empty.

No . . .

Fighting panic, he ran to the nurses' station and yelled at an alarmed Filipino nurse.

"Where is she?"

Desperately hoping there was a simple explanation, he looked at the list of patients on the wall in case she'd been moved in his absence, but her name was still there.

He punched in a telephone call to the control room. No one had been stood down. As far as the control room was aware, the two night duty cops would be replaced by the early shift. The controller couldn't answer when Barnes asked where the hell they were.

She'd been taken. He knew it. He ran down to the night security office and banged on the door, waking the security guy. He made him go through and check all the CCTV in the building for the last hour. He told him what he thought had happened, and told him he would be back in fifteen minutes.

He ran back to the ward, terror creating a strange out-of-body feeling, like he was watching himself in a nightmare. The two young uniformed guys were back outside Eve's room. Neither of them looked older than twenty-two. Barnes stared, wide-eyed. They knew she had gone. They were scared, and their fear made them look even younger than they were.

"What . . . happened?" Barnes asked through clenched teeth.

"We were here. All night. Then there . . . there was screaming from one of the other wards. Out in the corridor," one of them said, a waver in his voice. "Two voices, one male, one female. She was screaming, 'Help me, help me.' We went to check it out."

"*Both* of you?" Barnes shut his eyes.

"Yeah. We couldn't find anything. None of the night staff reported any disturbances, although they'd heard the noise. We just got back, and saw . . ." He pointed at Eve's empty room.

Diversion. Just like Nightingale had said.

Blue lights now — cars racing towards the hospital. Footsteps in the corridor as officers piled in. Somebody flicked a bank of switches, and the main overhead lights came on in the ward. Hadian was there, flanked by uniforms, having instructed the control room to contact him immediately should anything happen to Barnes's wife. He directed a couple of uniformed guys to secure the room, and sent the two in disgrace to canvass the nursing staff for witnesses. He went straight to Barnes, concern illuminating his face.

"Fortune? Or Van Leer?" he asked, signalling a young constable to fetch coffee.

"Both together, most likely." Barnes leaned on the nurses' station and tried to make some sort of sense from the chaos in his mind.

"There's more on the way. We'll get the CCTV."

"I've already been down there. They've kidnapped my *wife*, Paul."

"I know. Has she got a mobile phone? We may be able to triangulate."

"Of course she hasn't," Barnes said, throwing his hands in the air. "She was semi-conscious with morphine and all she had was the bloody hospital gown on her back."

"Have they made contact?"

"It isn't a fucking ransom demand. Fortune just wants to kill her."

"We don't know that. There may be another reason." Hadian gripped Barnes's shoulders. "Listen to me. We're going to find her, okay? And she'll be fine."

Barnes didn't answer. He replayed his conversation with Nightingale in his head — he could only hope that there was another reason for kidnapping Eve.

As he thought this, his phone rang in his hand. He moved away from the uniformed commotion and flipped it open.

"Yes?"

"It's difficult getting you to play ball, DC Barnes," the voice rasped.

"Van Leer?"

"Sssh, no names. Before I go on, look out of the window of the south stairwell. You'll see a car. Black 911. Come down to it. Alone."

"If you hurt her, I swear—"

The line went dead. The screen of the phone cracked under the pressure of Barnes's furious grip.

Barnes sensed Hadian behind him. He turned.

"Who was that?" Hadian asked, his eyes narrow.

"No one," Barnes said.

"Was it Fortune? We need to be putting traces—"

"Sir, due respect and all that, but this is my wife, and I'll do it my way. Don't forget somebody like Denniker is sitting in an office somewhere deciding on the strategy for this kidnap. You'll forgive me if I don't trust them to do a very fucking good job."

Barnes ran to the south stairwell, his footsteps echoing in the darkness. Droplets of rain were beginning to swarm down the window, the white arc lights of the car park projecting them onto his face. He looked down and saw a car parked a little way from the hospital, near to the nurses' residence. Smoke curled up from the driver's window.

He took the stairs at a sprint and ran out across the wet road. It was raining hard now, fat drops lashing the concrete. It fell in his eyes, his mouth, his ears — the only sound he could hear.

Barnes stood for a moment in the rain, then walked over to the Porsche. He took slow steps, breathing through his mouth, feeling like everything that had gone before was just a lie, or a dream.

He stood by the window and looked in as it slid down. Dominic Van Leer sat in the driver's seat in an oversized blue Hawaiian shirt. He had no cap on today, and his hair was untidy on his receding hairline. In the seat his slight frame made him look like a child was driving the car, and his stubbled, unkempt appearance made him look like nothing much at all.

Some small part of Barnes wanted to defer to Van Leer, to succumb to his manipulation, to throw himself to his knees and pledge devotion to his cause and all the schemes he could dream up, if he would only let Eve go.

Another part wanted to understand him, to sit down and go over all the things Barnes had supposedly done to upset him, to apologise for whatever had led to this moment.

But these were small voices. Anger fuelled him now, a tight skin of self-control encasing him for when he needed strength.

"Unlike you to come in person," Barnes said. His voice was taut, to conceal the tremor.

"Well, as I was bailed so soon, I thought I would come and thank you personally for arresting me on a wing and a prayer."

"All the stories I've heard about you — I thought you would have sent one of your troops," Barnes said, shaking his head. "Sounds like you command a small army, Van Leer."

"Stories, DC Barnes, are just that. I guess Mrs Nightingale has been blowing my trumpet again. But on some occasions you just have to make an appearance." Van Leer started rolling another cigarette.

"You double-crossed Howard. It makes sense. He had an alibi for her murder. When we visited him in prison, he was full of himself — probably because he had you behind him, and he knew what you were going to do to Harriet."

Van Leer stared at him. His eyes were black, like a shark on a hunt.

"What he didn't know was that you were going to stitch him up by dumping her body in his room. He found out the night he ran from the apartment, didn't he? He thought he was going to have to go into hiding, so he burgled the most convenient place — McDermott's house — to get supplies together, not banking on being arrested the moment he walked out.

"Neither were you, for that matter. I think you told Howard that if he didn't kill himself, someone else would, and in a much less pleasant way. Unfortunately, he didn't have the bottle, and got to find out what you meant. You burned him alive? Your own *brother*?"

"You'll never know, will you?" Van Leer placed the cigarette in his mouth, lighting it with a Harley Davidson Zippo. The lighter flared briefly — in the glow his skin looked grey.

"Did you kill Harriet Holden?"

"Who?" Van Leer's eyes were totally empty.

"Did you send Phil McDermott to follow me?"

Van Leer grinned. His teeth looked grimy in the gloom.

"Phil was a useless cokehead, Officer Barnes. So is Joan. Surprised you never noticed. They got wicked habits. I've no doubt that when he rolled my beautiful Merc he was off his head. When people got habits, you can own them. It ain't just defence lawyers, either. Certain Crown prosecutors are pretty pliable too, although it seems — and I respect you for this — it seems you were a bit too Catholic to fall for Miss Warwick's charms."

Barnes's eyes widened and disgust welled up in him. *No, Natasha, not you too.* He desperately didn't want to believe she was in league with Van Leer, but now he'd said the words, it suddenly seemed obvious. He may never have been tempted, but that didn't mean he hadn't been flattered. Now, of course, he felt ridiculous — how could his stupid fat ego have thought her interest was anything *but* a honeytrap? Frustration coursed through him — was there *anyone* he could trust?

Van Leer was smiling, and Barnes knew his expression had betrayed him. He forced himself to stay focused.

"Did you supply them all with their dope?" he said.

"Nice try. There's laws against self-incrimination, you know. I might not decide to speak to you again, DC Barnes. Anything else you want to say?"

Barnes raised his eyebrows and looked up for a moment, as if he were really considering it.

"I didn't finish my sentence before," he said. "If you've hurt her, I'll rip your fucking throat out."

Van Leer grinned again and flicked the roll-up at Barnes. It bounced off his leg and hissed in a puddle.

"Why don't you get in?"

"Fuck you."

"She's fine. Robbie won't touch her. He's sorry for what he did."

"He will be."

Van Leer frowned. "Now come on, DC Barnes. Playground aggression will get us nowhere. This is all strictly business. But before we go on, I would like to know if you've done anything really fucking stupid like bringing the cavalry down on me, or making any unwise telephone calls based on what Mrs Nightingale — useless waste of space — may have told you."

"It's just me here."

"Are you sure? There's one or two marked police cars out the front there."

"It's the shifts changing over."

"Ah yes, some young and eager recruits, no doubt. It was all a bit easy. Hmm . . . they've got no one to guard now, of course."

Barnes leaned on the doorframe and clenched his fists.

"DC Barnes, I don't want to hurt you, I want to do business. You must have guessed that by now. You took the robbery, you nabbed Robbie for assault, and at some point you'll crack the murder of Constable Harriet Holden. You're a rising star in the ranks and the press. I just want to make it a bit more official, and then you can do something for me in return."

"Like you did with Denniker?"

Van Leer's narrow shoulders appeared to slump a little.

"You see, Mrs Nightingale shouldn't have gone shooting her mouth off like that, if you pardon the pun."

"What do you mean?"

"You should be flattered — you were the one she chose to have her final conversation with on this earth."

"You killed her?"

"Alas, the wash-up of a cop known as Catherine Nightingale took her own life about half an hour ago, shortly after you took her last confession at Birling Gap. May she rest in peace."

Van Leer crossed himself with mock-solemnity, and then spluttered a laugh.

"She's . . . dead?" Barnes said, the nerve with which he had steeled himself slipping a little.

"I don't think the boys in blue know yet. God knows how they'd run a cop suicide *and* a kidnapping in the middle of a night shift with the numbers they've got. Do you see what I'm driving at?"

"Why don't you enlighten me?"

"I don't know the detail of Mrs Nightingale's closing submission to you, but she had nothing to gain by lying. My point, DC Barnes, is that if she advised you to blow it open and start upsetting people like myself and Mr Denniker then it makes tonight's course of action sadly necessary."

Barnes blinked water out of his eyes. It dripped down his neck and into his shirt.

"For fuck's sake, Officer, it isn't hard to grasp. As a wise man once said — we just want to be left in peace. You get your wife back, I go about my business without worrying that you're going to come crashing through my door again. We're all happy. You just remember that we'll do it again if, in the future, you get a sudden attack of the morals."

Barnes said nothing.

"What did you think of the sign-writing? Bit crude, I know, but it added a bit of a fun, a bit of spice. Robbie doesn't spell so good, so I kept them simple. And little brother was too thick to be anything other than a corkboard. Just a face for the paperwork, so to speak. Honestly, you'd be amazed how easy it is to buy information — like pigs' addresses . . ."

Barnes's arm shot out and clamped around Van Leer's throat. He squeezed — Van Leer's eyes bulged and he clawed at the detective's hand. Rain dripped from Barnes's hair down his face — tendons stood out on his neck as he grimaced with the effort.

"Where *is she*?"

The chrome barrel of a pistol appeared slowly and deliberately from below the doorframe. It glinted in the arc lights of the car park; Barnes found himself mesmerised by the accusing black hole, and slowly released his grip.

Van Leer coughed and sucked in air in big gulps, not taking the gun or his eyes away from Barnes.

"Come on then," Barnes said in a voice he did not recognise, with a bravado he no longer felt. "Do it."

Van Leer didn't answer, but slammed the Porsche into reverse and backed away at speed, the tyres spinning wildly in the wet. Barnes started to chase after it, but Van Leer stamped on the brakes and Barnes realised he was now in the car's path. His eyes widened as Van Leer dropped into first gear. The car lurched forwards, engine yowling, the headlights blinding Barnes as they fired towards him.

For a moment there was only scorching yellow light and rain, and at the last second Barnes hurled himself towards the pavement, smacking his knee on the kerb as he rolled, the Porsche narrowly missing him as Van Leer floored it away out of the hospital grounds and back into town.

Barnes pulled himself up and tried to hobble after the car, but there was a sharp bolt of pain in his knee, and in any event the car was already gone. He dropped to one knee in the road, the rain pouring down his face.

* * *

Barnes returned to the hospital, taking slow, exhausted steps. The ward was alive with police activity, but the activity slowed as he walked in. Cops and hospital staff turned to look at this strange, hobbling, soaking-wet creature that was virtually holding onto the wall for support. Then a kind nurse broke ranks from the sea of gaping faces — she got him a chair and brought him towels and a scalding hot coffee.

Hadian walked slowly over.

"Van Leer's got her." Barnes's voice was toneless.

"What does he want?" Hadian asked.

"To be left alone."

"That's it?"

"That's it. This is a warning. He wants carte blanche to run his business. If we don't let him, he'll kill her." Barnes gulped the coffee, burning the roof of his mouth. He barely felt it.

"He must have a deal about to go down or something. So what are the terms of the release?"

"We didn't get that far. I tried to strangle him, and he drove off." Barnes's voice was flat, his whole body numb.

Hadian put his hands on his hips and looked at the ceiling.

"I must need my head examining, letting you go off and deal with him like that."

"They'll call back. At this moment in time I still don't trust anybody to do it right and keep her alive."

"You think assaulting him in the middle of a negotiation is doing it right?"

Barnes waved his hand. He was past caring about the rules.

"Look, you're right. You're in charge. Run it how you want. I'm going to lie down."

"You going home?" Hadian seemed relieved.

"No."

Barnes walked past his wife's hospital room. It was a crime scene now. SOCOs were examining it and taking photographs; blue tape was stretched across the doorway; officers carefully questioned confused patients and tired staff.

He went to the waiting room and sat down for a moment, staring wide-eyed at the ceiling. The room was dark, lit only by the glow from a nearby vending machine. His eyes closed.

* * *

He jerked awake half an hour later. His mind was an excited jumble, and torturous fantasies about Eve's location and condition threatened to cripple him. He had to banish them, had to focus on the logical progression of facts and get on with things — just like any other investigation.

He got up and hobbled out of the waiting room. The ward was silent. The operation had moved out of the hospital and into a new room at the Major Incident Suite. Barnes drove there slowly, the last scraps of sleep making everything feel more unreal than it already did. The storm was raging now — squalls of wind swept across the Levels and the rain pummelled his car.

Hadian had been home for a change of clothes. He was sitting at a desk with a couple of detectives running through the process of negotiation. He looked up as Barnes approached, and stood.

"Barnes, there's really no need for you to be here. Go home and sleep. I'll call you if something happens." The sympathy was still there, but his patience was stretching, and it was clear he wanted Barnes out of the way so he could get on with things.

Barnes didn't say anything, but turned and shuffled out of the room, like a zombie. The room Hadian was using to run the investigation into his wife's kidnapping was adjacent to the one used for Harriet Holden's murder.

He hoped to God that they didn't give it an operational name and stick pictures of Eve all over the walls. He surmised, correctly, that if things got to that stage then they would revoke his security clearance and keep him from entering the building.

The Christchurch incident room was empty, all resources now pulled away to the live kidnap operation. He flicked on the lights and padded across the floor to the whiteboard. He stared at the smiling eyes of Holden's poster-size photograph.

"Sorry, Harriet. We haven't forgotten you."

He stared for a moment, and wondered if he, like Sally Holden, would soon begin the process of grieving for his loved one. Somehow the thought that his wife was still alive somewhere, scared and in pain, was worse than if she were dead.

He perched on the edge of a desk and stared, his eyes wide and dry. He couldn't tear himself away from those smiling eyes. He wondered if her boyfriend was grieving somewhere, if he would always remain a suspect as long as he was anonymous, or whether his theory about Fortune had been correct.

He stared and stared. *You poor thing. We will find him. One day.*

He stood up and touched the surface of the picture. He looked at the floor, lost in thought, dimly aware of his own breathing. He tried to remember what her voice sounded like. He tried to imagine that, had she lived, she would have found happiness. He tried to take comfort in the fact that she was now at peace. He said a silent prayer for her, and in that moment let her go.

He took his fingers from the poster and slowly backed away.

He turned to go, walking across the silent, open-plan room.

And stopped.

And snapped his head back around. His eyes widened as he stared again at the picture.

The *picture.*

And ran out of the room.

* * *

He tore into the adjacent room and sprinted over to where Hadian was sitting. The other detectives had gone.

"Sir, give me your swipe card," Barnes said, planting both palms on the desk.

"Barnes, what—"

"I said — *give me the fucking swipe card.*"

"Barnes, you really need—"

Barnes leaned across the desk and yanked the card from where it hung on a lanyard around the DCI's neck. It came away in his hand and he ran out of the room, feeling Hadian's stunned gaze on his back.

Barnes took the stairs two at a time until he got to the third floor, then he ran along the corridors until he got to the room he wanted. He used Hadian's access card to let himself in. The sign on the door read *Op Christchurch — Exhibits.*

He started pulling boxes from shelves — rifling through them, flinging them to the floor, muttering "come on, come on" until he found what he was looking for. He held it above his head triumphantly and ran back to Hadian.

"Look at this," Barnes said, flinging the item onto the desk.

"Yeah, I've seen it before," Hadian said, rubbing his neck.

It was inside a polythene exhibit bag. It had only been opened once — carefully cut along one side by the analyst at the FSS, then replaced and sealed with a signed and dated label.

It was a photograph.

It showed Harriet Holden at the foot of the Arc de Triomphe on a sunny day in Paris, wearing mirror-lens aviator sunglasses, a plain white T-shirt and jeans. Her head was cocked to one side, and she was aiming a lopsided grin at the camera.

"This is the exhibit that we got Howard Van Leer's DNA from, isn't it?" Hadian asked.

"Yes."

"And? He's dead. It's useless."

"You think? Look at it again."

Hadian held the photograph in front of his nose and peered at it.

"What am I supposed to be looking at?"

"Dammit, look *closely*."

"I am. Is it a magic picture or something? Is the killer going to mysteriously appear in front of me?" The frustration was showing on Hadian's face.

"More or less," Barnes said. "Look at her face."

"I *am*, Jesus. Barnes, will you tell me what I'm supposed to see? Please end my misery and tell me what the fuck you're driving at."

"Look at her sunglasses."

"Okay."

"Who can you see? Reflected in her sunglasses?"

"Well, I assume . . . yeah, there you go. The person taking the photograph."

“Exactly.”

Hadian looked closer. Recognition made his face go slack.

“Oh, good Christ.”

CHAPTER TWENTY-TWO

The rain had stopped, but the wind was vicious atop Beachy Head. It had been the warmest day of the year so far, but at that time of night, on the undulating expanse of clifftop three hundred feet above sea level, the wind chilled them to their bones.

Barnes had insisted that they confront him alone — no uniform, and no PSD yet. Hadian agreed. They took the unlit driveway up to Belle Tout and parked outside the iron gates. They walked slowly to the door.

Barnes rang the bell. Hadian shoved his hands in his pockets and looked around him.

"How are you planning to play this?" the senior detective asked.

"No idea." Barnes backed away from the door and stared upwards at the lighthouse. A gull soared by, close to his head. Barnes jumped. Its beating wings sounded like someone panting.

"This place gives me the willies," Hadian said. "A whole slice of the cliff came down a couple months ago."

"Devil's Chimney."

"Come again?"

"That's what it was called."

"Well, we'll be lucky to get out of here in one piece. Why was it called Devil's Chimney?"

"I'm not sure. I think because it was a bastard to climb."

The door opened. Clive Denniker stood there, with his hands on hips.

"Barnes. Paul. It's gone 2 a.m. What can I do for you?" He was dressed casually, and did not look like he'd been asleep.

"Sir, we . . ." Hadian began.

"This is official, I'm afraid, sir," Barnes interrupted. "May we come in?"

Denniker looked faintly amused.

"I'm quite sure I don't know what you mean, Barnes, but come in anyway."

They entered Belle Tout and followed the commander to a room that he and his wife Ellen used as a lounge. All the lights in the house appeared to be on. On the way they passed another room that had the door open. Barnes looked in as he passed, and saw Ellen Denniker sitting on a divan, in the same evening wear he had seen her in on his last visit. She was staring into space, a vacant smile on her lips.

Denniker saw where Barnes was looking, and pulled the door shut.

"My wife is not well. She had another stroke," he said by way of explanation, then took them into the lounge. He offered them each a seat; Hadian took one, Barnes declined.

"Sir, this is a little awkward . . ." Hadian began.

"You were Harriet Holden's boyfriend," Barnes said.

Denniker was silent, arrogance on his face.

"However misguided your assertions, DC Barnes, I would still like to know what gives you the right . . ."

"I'll tell you what gives me the *right*," Barnes said, his voice rising. "You are corrupt to the core. You have all kinds of cosy agreements with Dominic Van Leer — in fact, you owe your career to him. He threw you some high-profile cases in return for a blind eye to his drug dealing."

"Fascinating, Officer. Do please continue." The commander feigned apathy, but Barnes could see a tiny line of sweat on his brow.

"Once he had done that, you were in his pocket, but he wasn't in yours. You realised too late that you had the rough part of the deal — he could back out, you couldn't. Not that there was any reason for you to back out — the fear of being caught must have dissipated years ago.

"So I wondered why you would want to get out of it at all. Like I said, it wasn't fear. I only realised recently that it was probably your supreme arrogance. I think you decided that once you made ACC, you would be too powerful for Van Leer to control. I think you told him that you no longer needed his services, and that you couldn't guarantee his protection anymore."

The corners of Denniker's mouth had turned downwards. He blinked in the light.

"And I think Dominic Van Leer probably smiled, went home and ordered Robbie Fortune to butcher Harriet Holden. As a warning to you."

"Officer, where—"

"And you couldn't stomach being outgunned by Dominic Van Leer, so you tried to damage something close to him and play him at his own game — you fabricated evidence to convict his younger brother. That's why you were so desperate to charge him. Two problems with that — first, Van Leer is so cold-hearted he wasn't fazed by the thought of his own brother doing time for a crime he didn't commit. In fact, he virtually told him that if he didn't commit suicide someone else would take his life. Van Leer and Fortune killed Harriet, then they dumped her body in Howard's room and made an anonymous call pretending to be concerned about Fortune's neighbour. Big brother knew that Howard was a weak link and would roll over at some point. Who knows, maybe Howard had let him down before. Either way, they couldn't take the risk so they second-guessed him — the dump site was a warning to him, but the murder was a warning to you.

"And second — you fucked it up. The reason I know all this is because they're now trying to do it to me. You're yesterday's news, commander. They've set their sights on me now. But I didn't want to play your game, so now they've taken my wife, and plan to do to her what they did to Harriet if I don't sign up."

Denniker lowered himself into a wing chair and crossed his legs. He looked at Hadian, rolled his eyes and smiled, as if sharing some unspoken knowledge, like a parent enduring a tantrum from a small child. Hadian did not meet his gaze.

"It's a pity, Barnes. You had the opportunity to take over from me. We could have been a team. Dominic won't live forever — you could have watched him roll into the grave, the debt settled. And I could have guaranteed your rise to the highest ranks. You would have done better than me."

Denniker shook his head. Hadian was agape.

"I'm not interested."

Denniker smiled, showing yellow teeth. "Unfortunately, DC Barnes, you already made your play. Planting evidence on an innocent man who was later burned alive is unlikely to expedite your career."

Barnes felt Hadian's stare, and for a moment felt a sense of shame at having let down his boss.

"Dominic Van Leer has assaulted and now kidnapped my wife. Do you really think I could care less what happens to my career after this? Besides, I will claim that I was bullied by a superior officer who took advantage of my junior status and length of service. But I will admit it, and I will take you down with me."

Denniker steepled his fingers in front of him and blew laughter through his nostrils, nodding as he did so.

"You are intelligent, but bereft of guile, Barnes. You could have gained such political advantage. What a pity."

Barnes inched towards him.

"I will see to it that you and Van Leer sit together in the dock."

"For all your sermonising, you lack real insight. How effective do you think you will be by adhering to the rules? Rules are made by men, like you and me. Just men. Not gods, not geniuses, just men. Men who take their positions through birth or inheritance. What makes these men different to you or me?"

"I don't know. But the rules work for most people. What makes you so special that you're not above breaking them?"

"You idealistic little prick." Denniker sat forward and gripped the arms of the wing chair. "The practices that cripple us are made by faceless politicians — anonymous bureaucrats who have never had to fight a gang of drunk men armed with knives on a street corner at midnight. I told you once before — we need to play by our own rules if we are to be any sort of effective measure. We need to make our own justice."

"I just want to know where my wife is."

"You think I know?"

Hadian stood and moved closer to Denniker. The two men flanked him, and Denniker's eyes flicked from one to the other, the uneasy look growing by the minute.

Hadian's voice was low.

"She was your girlfriend? You stood there and acted as if she was just another murder victim. You pretended that you didn't know her. You never let on once. How could you stand there, completely neutral, and give false eulogies like that? Did you even care for her?"

"Where is your evidence, Detective Chief Inspector?"

"Do you deny it?" Hadian's voice was rising, the Welsh burr becoming more pronounced.

Denniker was silent.

"You evil bastard," Hadian said, almost shouting. "She was killed because of your greed. She had virtually no one, and she ended up with a prick like you. A prick that denied her existence."

Denniker stared at Barnes. "I will *bury* you."

"I've called PSD," Barnes said. "They're on their way. I've told them you're unhinged. I've told them you're a flight risk."

Denniker appeared to shrink into his chair. Like a cornered animal, Barnes recognised the fight-or-flight instinct beginning to take hold. He had seen such a countenance many times before on the street, but never on the face of a senior commanding officer.

Then Denniker was on his feet. He launched forward with both hands and connected with the centre of Barnes's chest — hard enough to knock him off balance and send him toppling over an ottoman onto the floor.

Hadian was there before Denniker could go any further — he stepped forward and swung a massive right hook that connected with the commander's left temple. Denniker slumped back into the seat, semi-conscious.

"I've got a lot of questions for you," Hadian said to Barnes, helping him to his feet.

"Later. Let's get him out of here."

They went to Denniker and took an arm each.

"Did you really call PSD?" Hadian asked as they hoisted the commander up.

"Of course not. That's coming later."

Hadian fumbled for some handcuffs.

"Hold on," Barnes said. "I'd better speak to his wife."

They dumped the now-groaning Denniker back in the chair. Hadian stayed with him, while Barnes went to the other room, trying to think of something to say to Ellen Denniker about what had happened.

Barnes knocked on the door and slowly opened it. Denniker's wife was still sitting on the divan. Barnes stood in the doorway and knocked again, but she did not appear to have heard him. She was still staring out of the window. The furious Channel, vast and black, could not be seen in the dark, but it could be heard.

"Mrs Denniker, are you all right?"

Barnes stepped over the threshold and walked up to her. He picked up an empty prescription bottle by her feet. The date on the dispensing label was only four days ago.

He touched her lightly on the upper arm. She looked up at him and smiled.

"Mrs Denniker, did you take all these?"

"Oh yes. Clive looks after me when I'm feeling poorly."

"I need to tell you something," Barnes said, pulling out his phone to call an ambulance.

"Of course, dear."

"It's about your husband."

"Such a wonderful man. I hope he hasn't been boring you with his stories about the project."

"The project?"

"Yes, dear. We have to move our house away from the cliff edge before the end of the year, otherwise it will just fall away into the sea."

"Yes, I did know about that. He didn't mention it today, though. He was a little distracted . . ."

"Yes, sometimes he can be. The project has become quite an obsession for him, though. He wants to document everything. He's talking about writing a history of the town as well, along with his memoirs."

"They will be quite a read, I'm sure." The call was connected. Barnes gave the ambulance call taker enough information to get them rolling, and then cancelled the call. "Look, Mrs Denniker . . ."

"Won't they, though?" She smiled faintly. "I only hope that the newspaper hasn't beaten him to it."

"I . . . the newspaper?" Barnes frowned, like a bright light had been shone in his eyes.

"Yes. They're running a serial on coastal erosion in Eastbourne. I hope they don't lose interest. I saw *you* in the newspaper, dear. A hero, they said. Your wife must be very proud. It reminds me of when Clive was a young detective, wanting to get noticed. He was a hero too. And he so *badly* wanted children. We both did."

Her eyes filled with tears. Barnes shut his eyes, wondering if this was an insight into his own future — his career steamrolling ahead, leaving a trail of destruction in its wake, his wife approaching old age like a lonely shadow, all sense of her own identity decimated by her husband's ambition.

"She's a nice girl, I must say," Ellen Denniker continued, wiping her eyes with dutiful stoicism.

"Who?"

"The journalist. Emily."

"You've met her?"

"Why yes, she's been to the house several times. She's
had tea with Clive and me, interviewed us, taken photographs
of the lighthouse. She asked all about him. Very interested in
his career . . . Was there something you wanted to tell me,
dear?"

Barnes opened his mouth to speak, but was distracted by
a shout and a loud crash from the other room.

He ran to where Hadian was now sitting on his backside, touching a bloody nose.

"Where did he go?" Barnes yelled.

Hadian pointed to an open door that led from the lounge
out the back of the lighthouse. It was swinging in the wind.

"That way. Bastard got the drop on me. He was faking
it."

"Are you okay?" Barnes said as he helped the DCI to
his feet.

"Seen plenty worse at the bottom of a ruck. Come on."

They ran outside onto the clifftop, and were immediately grabbed by the claws of the wind.

"Where is he?" Hadian shouted.

They scanned the clifftop, but it was useless. They could
barely see. The wind seared their eyes, and Barnes felt tears
whip across his face.

"Come on," Hadian yelled. "There's dragon lamps in
the car."

They ran back to the car and rooted around in the boot,
then edged across the clifftop, taking nervous, shaky steps as
they swung the lamps back and forth, seeking out anything
alien to this wilderness.

Then Barnes gripped Hadian's forearm and pointed
across the cliff.

"Look!"

Hadian looked to where Barnes was pointing. Two forms were just about visible in the gloom. Denniker was half-carrying, half-dragging his wife out across the black clifftop. The wind caught her pale evening gown, causing it to billow out behind her as she tried to keep up with her husband.

"Oh my God," Hadian said. Barnes was already running.

The wind caught Barnes's jacket as he ran, sending him on a sideways drift away from the direction he was running in. Long, black grass masked dips and ruts in the landscape, forcing Barnes to little more than a trot. He was dimly aware of Hadian following.

Barnes's eyes had adjusted to the darkness, but in the storm, the edge of the cliff was not visible; the sky, the sea, the cliff — they all seemed to be part of a single blanket of smoky darkness. Ellen Denniker's ghostly evening gown was the only thing that gave Barnes any indication of how close he was to the edge.

"Sir!" he yelled, but his voice was lost on the wind, and Denniker showed no indication of having heard him.

Denniker stopped moving. Barnes stopped also, now only a matter of yards from the commander and his wife.

"Sir!" he yelled again. Denniker finally looked up, his usually neat hair tossed into a wild tangle by the wind.

Barnes squinted, trying to read Denniker's expression. He couldn't make it out.

"Don't do this," he yelled. "Come back inside. We can work something out."

Barnes wasn't sure, but Denniker seemed to smile. He saw the commander's mouth moving, but all he heard was the wind shrieking in his ears. He edged forwards. Denniker held a hand up.

"What? What is it? I can't hear what you're saying," Barnes shouted.

Then there seemed to be distance between Clive and Ellen Denniker — the commander holding both his arms outstretched towards his wife.

Barnes squinted again, wondering for a moment why Denniker seemed to be holding his wife at arm's length. Then realisation hit him — he had already pushed her.

She seemed to teeter there for a moment, looking over at her husband, her head slightly lopsided in that winsome way Barnes had seen before — a manner symptomatic of the condition that was eating away at her mind.

Then she was gone.

"*No!*" Barnes screamed, and rushed forwards.

He stopped within a few feet of Denniker, and held out a hand imploringly.

This time Denniker really did smile — a pained, scowling grimace. Then he took a step with one foot, and then the other, giving himself up to oblivion. Just before he fell, Barnes saw the commander looking over at his beloved house.

The wind continued to envelop Barnes, and he felt as if he had no control over his legs or his balance. He dropped to his belly and edged forwards on his elbows to the cliff edge.

The jagged white chalk rocks glowed through the murk five hundred feet below, but there was nothing else to see. The world began to spin, and Barnes shoved himself back from the edge before fear and panic pulled him over too.

Hadian was there when he stood, and the DCI took hold of Barnes's arm until they were clear of the cliff edge.

* * *

When they got to the car Hadian called FCC and asked for a coastguard search-and-rescue team. Barnes made another call, punching Emily Varela's number into his phone, muttering angry expletives as he did so.

She took a while to answer, and Barnes blinked, seeing Ellen Denniker's evening gown dancing before his eyes, as if on a repeat reel. His mind tossed up an image of her twisted body impaled on the rocks, and he flinched.

When the journalist finally answered, she spoke in a hoarse whisper.

"Hello?"

"When were you planning on telling me?"

"Barnes?"

"Yeah. You've been playing us off against each other, haven't you?"

She didn't answer.

"Come on, Emily. I know you've been to Denniker's house, and you never told me, not once. Did he tell you about me? Did he tell you what grand plans he had for the town?"

She still didn't answer.

"Dammit, Emily. Are you still there?"

"Okay, okay. I went to Denniker's a couple of times." She was rasping.

"Yeah, for tea and cake. I heard. But I don't understand it — if you were so cosy with him, how come you publicly humiliated him at that press conference?"

"We are not *cosy*. And I think the word 'humiliation' might be a trifle strong."

"Oh, really? A small-time hack pointing out the deficiencies in the future ACC's knowledge of basic policing? *I* would have been humiliated."

"Thanks a lot." The hurt in her voice was obvious.

"What did you interview him about?"

"Barnes, this really is not the time . . ."

"Don't fuck me around, Emily," he barked. "What did you *interview* him about?" The sea was black through the windscreen of the car, but he was staring at nothing, concentrating fiercely on her words.

"Talking about the coastal erosion pieces, mainly. The collapse of Devil's Chimney. But we got onto you and your career, and your ambition. And him, and how he got to the top, and the plans he had for you. Listen, Barnes—"

"He isn't at the top anymore," Barnes said, interrupting her. "He's just thrown himself and his wife off Beachy Head."

There was a stunned silence on the other end of the phone.

"Oh my God. Are you serious?" she said eventually.

"He was corrupt to the bone, Emily. I can promise you an exclusive when the story breaks, but first I need to know what you've said about me to anybody else, and what you know that you've withheld from me. It's important."

"Barnes, listen—"

"Dammit, Emily, they have my wife! If you don't . . ."

His voice tailed off as the penny finally dropped.

"Emily," he said carefully, "why are you whispering?"

"I can't really talk . . ."

"You haven't done anything stupid, have you?"

"Well . . ."

"Emily, did you approach Dominic Van Leer as part of this little investigation you've got going? Tell me you didn't."

More silence.

"Oh, tell me you didn't. Emily, where the hell are you?"

"Actually, I'm on the beach. About two hundred yards from the Martello Tower at Sovereign Harbour North."

"What on earth are you doing there at this time of the morning? I thought that tower was derelict."

"Barnes . . . you might want to get some troops down here."

CHAPTER TWENTY-THREE

Of the seventy-four original Martello Towers, the elliptical defences spread along the south coast of England built to repel Napoleon, only twenty-five remain. Some have been purchased, restored and converted into private residences. Some, like tower seventy-three — known as the Wish Tower, standing on Eastbourne's Grand Parade — are seafront tourist attractions bolstered by tea rooms, a puppet museum and a memorial to Eastbourne's war dead, known as Peace Garden. Some were demolished to allow for the orchestrated expansion of retail, entertainment and industry in and around Sovereign Harbour. And some stand derelict and unused, waiting for the relentless pounding of the Channel to eventually claim them.

Napoleon never attacked, and the Martello Towers never served their intended purpose, but in the eighteenth and nineteenth centuries the coastguards used the towers as outposts to catch and fight smugglers.

Tower sixty-four stands on a low-level strip of shore, east of Langney Point, against a backdrop of construction sites and the concrete carcasses of future Sovereign Harbour residences mummified in industrial plastic sheaths, awaiting their unveiling. The tower outlived its neighbouring counterparts, and now stands desolate, awaiting restoration or destruction.

At half past three on a stormy May morning, this strip of beach was remembering the kind of nineteenth-century clamour when coastguards and smugglers clashed on the beach.

The storm was slowly easing. Emily Varela felt it as she sat in the driver's seat of her car, her breath steaming up the windows. She resisted the urge to start the engine and get some warmth through the car. She had brought a pair of high-powered binoculars with her, but in the semi-darkness they were useless. She swore and threw them on the passenger seat.

She was parked inland, in the middle of a construction site, her car partially hidden by a huge concrete girder. The wind rattled cables against an array of flagpoles bearing contractor logos, and, looking out at the marina, she could see hundreds of boats — a forest of masts fingering the sky as they bobbed in the water.

Barnes had been the first person to describe her endeavours as an "investigation". Despite his reproachful tone, as if he had been speaking to a child who did not know any better, his use of the word had only encouraged her. But now she realised, alone and cold on a black expanse of shore, the unforgiving Channel crashing against the earth, that she was out of her depth.

Approaching Dominic Van Leer had been unwise. She knew that, but she had neither assessed the idea properly for risks nor had the necessary people behind her in the event of it all going wrong; rather, out of fear of being laughed at or talked out of it, she had decided to go it alone.

Van Leer's general reaction had been one of amusement. He complimented her for having some original ideas. He asked her what she hoped to achieve by approaching him directly, and what it was, exactly, that she suspected him of. He asked her if she really believed he would consent to being publicly named in the press.

Her play was weak. She suggested putting pressure on the police, by highlighting inadequacies in their practices and insufficient resources to effectively combat the drugs trade along the coast. She even suggested a blanket gag on reporting his criminal activities, and a greater focus on other crime reporting, to divert the attention from his business. He threw his head back and laughed. He told her she didn't have that kind of influence. He told her she wasn't dirty.

Then he'd put a large knife on the table where they had been sitting. Her eyes flitted around the murky pub in which they'd met, for probable exits and possible assistance. But this was Van Leer's turf — the doors were closed and guarded, and most of the clientele were indebted to him for one reason or another, and therefore obliged to turn a blind eye at the very least.

He grinned and told her she was stupid, and in over her head. He told her not to do anything foolish like print his name. He told her not to make up stories about him. He told her if she did, he would cut off her fingers and post them to her editor. Then he laughed and told her no news is good news.

A shaft of light cut into the gloom as a door was opened. She took her cue and scurried out into the sunlight — ashamed of her own fear, chastising herself for having big plans but rushing to see them through. But anger also crept in — anger at having been treated that way, the anger of a middle-class upbringing that did not really understand the desperation and violence that lurked within the radius of Devil's Chimney.

She looked at herself in the rear-view mirror. If impetuous behaviour was going to be her particular Achilles' heel, then so be it. And so, with no better plan in mind, she decided to follow Dominic Van Leer.

* * *

Eve was still groggy from the painkillers, and it dulled the edge of the fear she knew she ought to be feeling. Her wrists hurt. Her hands had been bound behind her using a pair of Cathy Nightingale's now-redundant handcuffs. They had been locked tightly, and the metal ate into her wrists. Her broken arm had been agony, but so far the morphine was just about keeping the pain at bay.

She did not know where she was. She was sitting awkwardly against what felt like a brick wall. She was cold — the flimsy hospital gown offered little protection — but someone had put a rough blanket around her shoulders. Her left eye was still swollen shut from the bruising, but it looked like she was in a large, circular room. Her right eye adjusted to the dark after a while and she could make out shapes — there was a ladder leading up to a platform a few feet away from her, and the wind was whistling through arched doorways on the opposite wall that led out into the night. The room was not residential — in fact, it looked like a disused warehouse of some kind. But she could hear the sea — the rolling, rising waves crashing rhythmically onto the shore. It sounded very close.

Then voices. Strained, hushed voices. Two male voices. One with a coarse, gravelly edge to it; the other deeper, calmer.

Then a third voice. Female. She spoke in muffled tones — one of the men told her to shut up, and she obeyed.

The storm had broken quite suddenly, and the two male figures appeared in one of the archways, silhouetted black against the clear, navy-blue sky. Eve leaned her head against the wall, a feeling of helpless dread licking at her. She tried to focus on the few stars she could see. She tried to think. What had happened to the two policemen outside her room? They must have been called away to something, or maybe somebody senior decided that she was no longer at risk and keeping the guard on was not a good use of resources.

But when Barnes left the hospital room, he had promised he would be back soon. Hadn't he? If he had come straight back, he would have raised the alarm straightaway. So surely everybody would be looking for her. But she didn't know where she was. She didn't know why they had taken her — did they mean to kill her, or was there going to be some kind of ransom demand? Who would they make the demand of? It could only be Barnes, and it didn't make sense that they would demand money from him — they had none.

Maybe it was Barnes they wanted to kill, and she was just bait. She didn't know. Nothing made sense. She shivered, and tried to shrug the blanket further around her, but instead it fell off one shoulder. She cursed in a high-pitched half-sob. She fought the tears, praying the morphine would last a bit longer, forcing herself to think clearly and to fight panic.

Then she heard the boat.

* * *

The balloon went up. Barnes relayed Emily's location and what little she had seen of the activity, and theorised a drug shipment over water. Hadian agreed and made calls to Force Command and Control, apprising the Force gold commander, who listened carefully and began to formulate her strategy. Divisional patrol officers were put on standby, as were dog handlers, PSU serials, armed response vehicles, hostage negotiators, intelligence analysts, the coastguard, the helicopter and a dedicated rescue team to pull Eve and Emily Varela out of danger.

This was it. This was crunch time. They were one hour — maybe less — and a single police operation away from learning Eve's fate. It might already be too late. But then again, it might not. He couldn't stand it.

Barnes touched Hadian's arm in between calls.

"If they don't think they've made their deal, they'll kill her."

"I know."

Barnes sat in the darkness in Denniker's office. An amber street light from outside the office cast the only light across the room, its beam sliced by the blinds on the window, leaving lines of light scored onto the walls.

He scrolled through the incident log on the computer terminal and read the text. The strategy was vague and even ambiguous in parts. He tried to tell himself that it was the best that could be done with the information they had. The possibility of disrupting a drop of Class A drugs but knowing that to do so would, in all probability, result in the death of a policeman's wife, had created an impossible stalemate. Barnes had been involved with incidents like this in the past — many times the opportunity to act was put off in favour of talking about it a little longer.

He read to the end of the log, then flicked back and forth between the pages. There was a lull in the activity. He timed four minutes with no update on the log, and sensed a stalemate. Everybody was on standby. Everybody was waiting on everybody else — for a command, a direction, new information. Four minutes during which Eve was sitting somewhere out there, in pain and terrified beyond comprehension.

The thought that on a different night, it would have been Denniker taking his turn on the rota as Force Gold made Barnes understand the fallibility of everyone involved. They were, after all, only human. Mistakes could be made.

He made up his mind. If Eve did not survive tonight, he was not going to live with himself knowing he'd sat in an office and done nothing. After another ninety seconds he grabbed a radio and the keys to a car. He walked to Hadian's office. The DCI was doing the same as, Barnes imagined, everyone else involved in the operation at that moment — sitting, staring at the computer, waiting for an update.

"I'm going out there," Barnes said. "I can't sit here any longer waiting for nothing to happen." He stuck his jaw out, expecting dissent.

"Good idea," Hadian said. "I'll come with you."

* * *

Hadian drove. Barnes called Emily again. He put the call on loudspeaker.

"Emily, it's Barnes. What can you see?"

"Not a lot. The storm's blown over and the moon's out, which helps, but I think I'm too far away. I've got binoculars, but it's too dark to see much."

"Listen, Emily, do they know that you're there?"

"I don't think so."

"Don't think. Be sure. You followed them to the beach from the town, yes? It was — what — about three a.m. at that time? There wouldn't have been much else on the roads. They would have been suspicious of any vehicle behind them."

"My lights were off. I was miles behind them too. I thought I'd lost them once or twice. When I saw them turn off towards the beach I slowed right down to let them get there, then kept on going. Straight past. I carried on east a little further, then turned onto one of the building sites just inland from the beach."

Hadian frowned, impressed, as he heard this. "She's in the wrong job."

"How far away are you?" Barnes glanced at his boss while he continued speaking to Emily.

"Not sure. Fifty, sixty yards. They're west of my position."

"Can you be sure it's them?"

"It must be. They're standing on the beach, near the derelict Martello Tower at the north harbour. Three of them, looking out to sea. One might be female. I haven't seen any more."

"Female? Could it be Eve?" Barnes's voice was frantic, desperate to latch onto the faintest glimmer of hope.

"Barnes . . . I don't know what she looks like. This woman is thin, looks like she has long hair. She's moving about the beach with the other two. If it is your wife, she doesn't look like she's been kidnapped."

"It can't be Eve. She's injured . . ." The end of his sentence tailed off as his chest hitched and the glimmer of hope vanished. Hadian looked over at him. Barnes fought to keep calm. "Sounds more like Melanie Denton."

"Who?"

"Never mind. What sort of cover have you got?"

"I'm in my car. The lights and engine are off. The windows are steamed up and wet on the outside. There's another four or five cars dotted around the site. I'm in the middle of the building site, and I've got good cover from a concrete building shell."

"Okay, sit tight. We're on the way."

Barnes clapped the phone shut and turned to Hadian. "I don't like it. They could have spotted her and not let on."

"If Van Leer is about to receive a drop and thought he was under surveillance, he wouldn't hang about. He'd get out of there."

"Maybe. And then he'd kill Eve and make sure I know about it. I don't like it, boss. We don't have enough information. Emily may be keeping good obs but it's too dark and the terrain is too unfriendly. If we take the beach they'd have time to kill Eve before we even got close."

"We need him to think he's successfully collected his shipment before moving in. Maybe after they leave the beach and get back on the road."

"Yeah, but then we risk losing them altogether. We've got to assume that Eve is with them, or at least nearby. They wouldn't risk letting her out of their sight. She's their collateral."

Barnes tried to think. Van Leer had hinted that there was some kind of criminal activity imminent. To ensure he was allowed to undertake it with impunity, he had kidnapped Eve and threatened to kill her if he was disrupted. He hadn't said what was being planned, or when, where or how it was going to go down. But Emily Varela had, out of blind courage and wounded pride, kept a tail on Van Leer and had led Barnes straight to Eve — and now the police had the advantage. The question now was, how to get Eve out alive before they had a chance to kill her?

He knew one thing — they didn't have long.

* * *

Eve didn't know much about boats, but in the darkness her senses had become heightened, and she concentrated on the sound. It had an audible motor, but it didn't sound very big. The sound was distant at first, then got louder and overpowered the noise of the waves as it approached the shore.

Low voices now, the words indiscernible. All male. Accents? Maybe Eastern European? She couldn't tell. Then the sound of physical activity in place of conversation — items being moved. Grunts — heavy items? Things being moved from the boat to the shore, or the other way around?

Her legs were numb with cold, and she tried to wiggle some kind of circulation back into them. She tried to shuffle to the right, to get a better view out of the archway facing the shore. A jolt of pain shot up her arm, and she just managed to clamp the cry down in her throat. She didn't want to remind them she was still here and give them ideas.

A wedge of moon was illuminating the beach now, but the shore sloped away from the room she was in and obstructed her view. She tried to move a little more. If only she could work out where she was, she might be able to think of a way out.

She thought of Barnes and how frantic he must be. She pictured his face, and there was a hot feeling in the back of her throat. The tears came — real, free-flowing tears as she began to believe the possibility that she might not see him again.

The moonlight was eclipsed as a figure stood in the archway, and the room became dark. The figure advanced towards her. She shrank back against the wall, sending another lightning rod of pain down her arm, and turned her head away. Was this it? The figure knelt beside her and touched her face. It spoke in a rough, gravelly voice.

"Don't cry, beautiful."

* * *

The moon was bright now. Emily's eyes had adjusted to the dark and she could make out the people moving on the beach. She thought she could recognise one as Dominic Van Leer — not a positive facial identification, but the build, gait and height made it a very strong possibility. She had only seen Robbie Fortune from the CCTV stills of the town centre stabbing given to her by Barnes, but the second one could very well be him. He was wearing a baseball cap. The third was definitely female. Looked blonde. Skinny.

They were looking around now. They kept looking up at the sky, then at their watches. They didn't like the moonlight — it was like a relentless searchlight, and they scurried around, heads bowed. The one she believed to be Fortune pulled his cap down lower on his head and began shining short flashes from a powerful flashlight out to sea.

She shivered, and thought of Barnes's wife. They must both be beside themselves.

The *Sospan Dau* was visible beyond the activity on the beach, her huge yellow stanchions bright in the moonlight, as she gargled and sprayed roaring black muck back onto the shore in a relentless torrent.

Emily knew she'd been rash and not terribly sensible — and she'd been called worse — but she had enough sense to realise that Van Leer was probably waiting to receive a shipment of drugs. Fortune must have been signalling to the carrier.

She looked at her watch. Getting towards four. Daybreak couldn't be far away. Which meant the drop must be due any time now.

She heard a sound and dared to open her window a fraction. The sound of the waves seemed to penetrate everything, but she could hear it in the distance. It started like a low humming noise, then it became a buzzing noise, then it became the sound of an outboard motor echoing through the darkness.

It became visible a few minutes later, and the dark form of a motorboat approached the shore. Three figures jumped from the boat and began to unload packages about the size of shoeboxes. They were smaller than she expected, and she didn't think it would take very long to unload it all from a boat that size.

She looked at her watch. It was happening in front of her. So what were the police waiting for?

Then it occurred to her that they might be waiting for her.

* * *

Barnes drummed his fingers on the dashboard. They had stopped at a makeshift rendezvous point about a mile out from where Emily had described her position.

He could feel Hadian watching him, and for a moment he felt sorry for dragging him into this. The DCI was a good man who just wanted some decent staff around him, but his latest recruit had managed to haul him into a shitstorm inside of six months.

Hadian spoke.

"I know what you're thinking. If Van Leer knew or even suspected there was a sting in the offing, he would get out before he got his hands dirty. What could he hope to gain by going ahead with the drop and risking fifteen to twenty years in prison?"

"He isn't that stupid," Barnes said.

"Exactly. We've got an advantage here. He doesn't know about Emily. He thinks we have no idea about what's actually going down tonight."

"But what guarantees have we got that he will even release Eve once he's completed his deal? Look at what happened to Harriet," Barnes said.

"That won't happen to Eve."

"How can you say that? All the time we sit here doing nothing we're not giving ourselves very good odds. She might already be dead."

Barnes breathed heavily.

The radio crackled on the car set, and the voice of the controller came over the airwaves.

"Unit please, for an immediate response to the Last Stop public house. Reports of two large gangs fighting at the location. Knives have been seen by the informant, and there is uncorroborated mention of a firearm. Several calls received. Units, please respond."

Barnes stared at the radio set in disbelief, like it had just signed Eve's death warrant.

"Shit," Hadian said, reaching for his own radio. "What timing. That's going to pull all our troops out of here. Sounds nasty. FCC will have to take the reins on this as well. Shit. What are the chances?"

What, indeed. Barnes sat staring straight ahead, trying to recall the conversation he'd had with Nightingale.

Hadian was on his phone to Force Gold, trying to negotiate a minimum number of officers from other districts to attend the fight report. He virtually pleaded with her to keep all units on standby around the harbour, to resource the fight by some other means.

Barnes looked out of the window. The lights of Langney Point twinkled in the distance, and from somewhere below the horizon the morning sun began to emerge from beyond the Cooden coastline.

He thought of Nightingale.

Van Leer will create havoc.

Diversion is the best smokescreen.

Barnes touched Hadian lightly on the arm.

"Let them go," he said.

"Hang on a second, ma'am," Hadian said into the phone, then turned to Barnes. "What did you say?"

"All the units on standby. Send them to the fight. Blue lights, sirens, the works. Tell them to take the coast road. Ambulances too. The more obvious, the better."

"Then we'll have virtually no one here."

"I know. But I bet you there is no fight."

"What?"

"Just trust me."

* * *

"I'm sorry for what I did. I'm sorry I knocked you about."

Fortune pulled the blanket back around Eve's shoulders, although it did nothing to assuage the now-violent shivering that had taken hold of her.

"Can you take these cuffs off?" she whispered. "They're hurting my arm."

"Sorry, princess. I can't do that. We've got some business to take care of, then Dom wants to let you on your way. Believe it or not, he's afraid of your pig husband."

"You broke my arm, you kidnapped me from hospital and handcuffed me before the plaster had even set. How do you expect me to accept your apology?"

Fortune made a hawking sound in his throat and spat on the ground.

"I said Dom wants to let you go, but I'm not so sure about it. Thanks to Officer Barnes, I'm looking at another five years in prison, easy. Now, let's say you think about handing him over to me, then you might have a way out of this."

"You're not talking sense. You need help."

"Don't patronise me." His voice was like a razor blade. "Either you give him up or the inside of this tower will be the last thing you ever see."

She recoiled as he moved closer. She inhaled cold air, and a wave of fear coursed through her.

"It doesn't have to be like this." His voice softer now. "You could make it easy on yourself."

He touched her face with rough fingers, then traced a line along her jawline, down her throat, and then pushed two fingers into her sternum in the shape of a pistol. Slowly, his hand moved and cupped her left breast through the flimsy material of the hospital gown. Powerless, she screwed her eyes shut and tried to move away from him.

"Hey . . . *Robbie*," a voice from outside hissed. "Get out here."

Fortune stood and turned his back on Eve. She heard him start to leave, and opened her eyes. He was walking away from her. The relief was compounded by the sight of blue strobe lights reflecting on the walls around her. Sirens in the distance, mingling with each other. It sounded like several police cars. At last.

New courage surged through her.

"Hey."

He turned in the archway, silhouetted in the moonlight.

"You deserve everything you get."

He carried on walking.

* * *

Emily Varela dialled Barnes's number with shivering fingers. For a moment she thought he wasn't going to answer.

"Barnes?"

"Emily? What's going on?"

"You tell me. I've just seen a load of police cars leaving the area. Where are they all going?"

"Fight at the Last Stop pub."

"Oh shit. You mean you're not sending anyone in? The boat is here. They're making the drop now. I can positively identify Dominic Van Leer on the beach. And Robbie Fortune. I don't know the female."

"Are you sure?"

"Am I sure? The moon is like a spotlight. They're running around under it like ants under a magnifying glass. Fortune keeps going back and forth into the Martello Tower."

"He does?"

"Yeah, I think your wife might be in there."

Barnes's breath caught in his chest.

"Okay, sit tight," he said. "I'm going to make a call."

"What—"

He terminated the connection. Emily Varela took the phone away from her ear and looked at it.

The phone slipped from her grasp. It clattered onto the doorframe, and hit the steering wheel on the way down, landing between her feet. As she bent down to retrieve it, her head

389

nudged the button on the steering wheel. A short, sharp blast of car horn undid the silence.

"Shit. Oh . . . *shit!*"

Her head snapped upwards to look at where the activity was taking place. The three figures on the beach were now still, and three pairs of eyes were looking in her direction.

One of them began to advance. She remained in the driver's seat, frozen by fear. Dominic Van Leer walked towards the car, then broke into a run, his expression under the moonlight changing to a snarl.

Emily turned the key. Nothing happened. The engine turned over, but refused to catch.

"Come on, you fucking car!" she hissed.

She tried again. The chugging sound of the engine turning over became lazy and slow as the battery died, like the dying pulse of a failed resuscitation. Van Leer slipped on the shingle, and could only run at an awkward half-pace over the uneven ground.

She shrieked, and fumbled to unclip her seatbelt. She wrenched the door handle, forgetting that she had locked the door. Panic began to lick at her brain as Dominic Van Leer approached.

The ground levelled out, and he picked up speed. He was almost upon the car when she flung the door open. She timed it badly, and Van Leer had time to extend his leg in a sharp kick.

He connected with the door, which slammed shut, striking Emily's head and knocking her back into the car. She lay across the front seat, and Van Leer walked around to open the passenger door. He grabbed a handful of hair and yanked her onto the cold ground.

She wailed with pain, and tried to speak. She managed "Please . . ." and then Van Leer struck her across the temple with the butt of his gun, knocking her senseless.

* * *

Hadian called FCC. Barnes watched him as he spoke.

"The fight is a diversion. The civilian keeping obser-vations has just identified Dominic Van Leer and Robbie Fortune. They are receiving items as we speak from a boat that's just run ashore — suspected Class A. Van Leer orches-trated the fight to give himself cover — if we're all tucked up dealing with a big fight at the other end of town then he's got all day to make his drop."

Barnes strained to listen while the gold commander spoke.

"The civilian followed four people in a car to the location — only three got out at first. Person number four matches the description of the hostage. No, she didn't lose sight of them at any time. And their activity at the scene indicates the hostage might also be very near." He eyed Barnes while Gold spoke again. "Subject can't have missed the units going to the fight — it was like the funfair. Send them all back, on a silent approach. The pub fight was a hoax call. Yes . . . yes . . . okay."

He flipped the phone shut.

"What did she say?" Barnes asked.

"We're going in."

* * *

They were talking frantically on the beach. There was only one calm voice — Eve didn't recognise it. Hope thudded through her — then the sirens grew fainter and the reflection of the blue strobe lights off the walls became less intense, and she realised the police cars were going in the opposite direction.

In the darkness, she hung her head in despair. The one they had called Robbie came back to the archway. The blade of a long knife glinted in his hand.

"Did you think they were coming for you, princess? Unfortunately they suddenly got very busy. Funny how these things happen in twos, innit? And at opposite ends of the town too."

He advanced again until his form was again filling her view, the moonlight obscured. It seemed that he had someone with him, standing very close.

"Brought you a friend to play with," he said, and flung a woman's still body onto the ground beside Eve, who jolted and tried to move away. He lifted the woman's chin. "Hello? Can you hear me, you interfering bitch? Reckon you were keeping the pigs updated, yeah? Well, I don't like fuckin' grasses." He hauled her upwards by the hair; the woman's tiny frame meant this didn't require much effort. She began to moan incomprehensibly.

"For Christ's sake, leave her alone!" Eve cried.

Fortune said nothing, but drew his arm back and punched forward with the blade. It slid between the woman's ribs, the punctured flesh yielding too easily, a gurgling hiss escaping her lips.

"No! You bastard . . . *you bastard!*" Eve screamed, staring in horror as Fortune withdrew the knife. She became aware of something warm and wet under her legs, and realised that it was blood spreading across the ground.

Fortune moved to her, and wiped the blade clean on the thigh of her thin cotton nightgown. She gritted her teeth and braced her body for what was about to happen, saying a silent prayer for herself and her husband.

Then she was aware of a third presence in the room. Heavy breathing. Oh God, what was going to happen to her? She felt the fight go out of her as all her hope vanished, like vapour sucked into an air vent, and she prayed it would be over quickly. This third presence edged towards her, light feet tapping on sandy ground.

Then it barked.

* * *

Dark forms stormed the beach. Barnes and Hadian followed behind firearms officers and dog handlers in plain clothes. Searchlights from out at sea flooded the shore like a net, shining out from a coastguard cutter patrol that flanked the boat making the drop and from the powerful Nightsun of Hotel-900, the police helicopter.

A cacophony of sounds shattered the morning silence — loudhailers boomed from out at sea, the armed officers roared commands, and the dogs barked furiously as they raced after their unwisely departing prey, whose panicked shouts filled the air.

Barnes racked his baton and crept to a side doorway of the sixty-fourth Martello Tower. He peered in, and his blood raced hot through his veins. He saw his wife, cuffed and dirty, slumped against the cold wall. He saw the still body of Emily Varela lying next to her. He saw the back of Robbie Fortune, facing down a large German shepherd straining at its leash, barking furiously. He saw the handler, giving commands to both Fortune and the growling dog. Fortune was still, with his hands out to the side, but was still holding the knife.

Barnes moved in behind Fortune. The dog handler was warning him for the final time to drop his weapon, lie down and put his hands behind his back, or the dog would be released.

Two armed officers appeared either side of the dog handler in protective helmets and face masks. Two red dots appeared on Fortune's chest.

In a single swift movement, Fortune lunged forward, snatched Eve to him and held the knife to her throat.

"Armed police! Drop the knife!" yelled one of the armed cops.

"*No!*" Barnes yelled, unable to stop himself. Fortune's face contorted as he spun on his heel to face down Barnes, bringing the blade over his head as he charged towards the detective, gripping Eve's throat with his other hand. Her face was half dead with pain, fear and cold.

In a parody of a gentlemen's duel, Barnes skittered forwards on his feet to meet the lunge, swinging his baton up in an arc to arrest the blade as it plunged downwards.

The parry was off-target; the baton missed the knife, and Barnes felt the blade tear into the flesh of his arm. There was a moment's numbness, then a warm feeling as blood began to gush from the wound. The red dots were circling around Fortune like mad insects as the two armed cops tried to get a clean shot.

Fortune carelessly released his grip on Eve, who slumped, dead weight, to the cold ground of the tower. Fortune turned his entire attention to Barnes as he moved in for a second strike with the blade; Barnes, distracted by both the wound on his arm and his wife collapsing onto the ground, did not react quickly enough to the second lunge, and caught another sideways blow across the sternum. Barnes was dimly aware of his flesh being sliced cleanly open, and the curious sensation of the blade dragging across the bone.

Barnes felt his knees buckle and more warmth gush down his chest. He slumped against the cold wall of the tower, only barely registering that the dog was being released.

Fortune inched towards Barnes to finish him off, then turned back to Eve, his blade poised for more carnage. She moaned softly.

Barnes saw the rest in flash frames. He pushed himself off the wall with all the strength he had left.

The handler flicking his dog loose. Barnes bringing his baton in from the side. Fortune bringing his arm down towards Eve, brandishing steel. The German shepherd leaping into the air and clamping its jaws around Fortune's wrist. The baton meeting the side of Fortune's head.

Two shots were fired from the doorway. Fortune's skull crumpled at the temple under the force of Barnes's baton, and he crashed into the cold stone wall face first. He dropped to the ground and lay still.

The dog handler handcuffed Fortune and yelled for a paramedic. His yelling brought more cops into the tower. Barnes dropped the baton and staggered to his wife. He collapsed to his knees and pulled her to him. One of the cops — in fact, one of the two that had been guarding Eve's room

when she was kidnapped, although Barnes did not notice this
— removed Eve's handcuffs and covered them both with a
blanket. Barnes stroked his wife's face and hair.

She murmured something, and the sound of her voice
could not have been sweeter. She opened her eyes, the knotted clouds lifted from her expression, and the pink edges of
the sun tipped over the horizon.

EPILOGUE

Eve was treated at hospital for hypothermia and concussion. The ordeal had prolonged the recovery of her broken arm, but the prognosis was still one of full recovery. Barnes refused to leave her, and so they wheeled a trolley round next to Eve so he could be patched up alongside her.

Robbie Fortune was treated under guard for fairly serious head injuries sustained from the impact of Barnes's baton, as well as a bullet wound to his shoulder — the other round having missed its target.

A couple of days later, Barnes went with the coastguard search and rescue team to where Clive and Ellen Denniker had joined the hundreds of other souls who have thrown themselves from the top of Beachy Head onto the rocks below.

The bodies had been spotted by helicopter, and Barnes went by lifeboat to the foot of the cliff. He carefully picked his way over to their bodies. The fall had distanced them by several metres, but as they lay lifeless, twisted on the rocks, they seemed to reach out to each other. The crumbled remains of Devil's Chimney lay further up the beach, and the Channel roared and churned around their bodies.

PSD obtained a search warrant for Belle Tout. Barnes wanted to be part of the search team, but was told to keep away.

Instead, he went to Sally Holden and voiced his hypothesis that her daughter had been a victim of greed and had been caught in the crossfire of egomaniacal battles between Dominic Van Leer and Clive Denniker. He apologised sincerely for the lack of evidence that would enable their prosecution. Sally Holden told him that without knowing where her daughter died, she would never be able to truly lay her to rest. She told Barnes that no parent should have to bury their child.

He also visited Emily Varela in hospital with a huge bunch of flowers that he took to her bedside. He thanked her for having courage, self-reliance and a thick skin. He thanked her for saving the life of his beloved wife. He apologised for calling her a hack. He asked why she had said she could positively identify Fortune and Van Leer on the beach when it was obvious that she couldn't. Through the pain she forced a smile, and shrugged.

The Belle Tout recovery project was thrown into turmoil — the Dennikers were childless, and no heir had been nominated in either of their wills to fund and oversee completion of the project.

There was pressure on the local authorities to continue funding the move as a matter of national and historic importance, but the corruption and suicide had left a sour taste in the mouths of many, and with the myriad unanswered questions and rumour surrounding the Dennikers' deaths, the project was abandoned.

Belle Tout was left vacant to face down the changing seasons, and await the day when the crumbling coastline would eventually be eaten away far enough to claim the lighthouse — when the entire structure would come crashing down five hundred feet to be swallowed by the raging Channel.

* * *

Dominic Van Leer was taken down by a dog handler and two armed officers. He was compliant on arrest, but refused to answer any questions during his interview. He was charged with drug trafficking offences, kidnap and conspiracy to pervert the course of justice. Paul Hadian also added an additional charge of conspiring to kidnap and murder Howard Van Leer, but there was insufficient evidence to prove it, and it was later dropped. He pleaded guilty to all charges on the advice of his solicitor, and believed his convictions would prove only a temporary setback in his business affairs.

The details of Van Leer's anticipated "setback" finally reached court. Barnes sat behind the prosecutor and listened to the summing-up by the particularly unforgiving circuit judge at Lewes Crown Court. Barnes surmised that maybe Van Leer's supporters, cronies, henchmen and associates had a better notion of what would be handed down that day and decided it best to stay away, for when Van Leer received his sentence of twenty-one years in prison, he was alone in the dock, and the gallery was empty.

Nobody wept.

* * *

To Barnes's relief, the house insurance paid out quickly. He and Eve moved away from the bad memories and bought a small cottage in Litlington, nestled at the foot of the Seven Sisters and the Cuckmere Valley.

Eve was at her mother's when the removal men dropped off the last of the boxes. Barnes roamed around the empty house, trying to picture their belongings in place, trying to call it home. Forbes trotted around the house, inspecting the new surroundings.

At Eve's request, her easel had been unpacked first and was now propped against the fireplace. The pencil outline of a flower was visible on a new canvas.

Barnes had already located their portable television, and the lunchtime news played while he tried to unpack.

He recognised his boss's voice from the set and stopped to watch it.

At a press conference, Hadian had gone public with his confidence about a successful prosecution had Denniker lived to see trial, and that was sufficient, in the minds of some, to prove beyond all doubt that the suspicions surrounding his intractable corruption were true.

Barnes clicked off the set. The room was quiet again.

He rubbed his eyes. The deaths of Clive Denniker and Cathy Nightingale meant that the conspiracy shrouding the murder of Constable Harriet Holden remained an ambiguous entity, a mist of questions condemned to drift unanswered through history, and the "neatly packaged morsels of evidence" that Clive Denniker once spoke of remained elusive as a consequence.

They never found the original scene of Harriet Holden's murder.

The phone rang, interrupting his thoughts. It was Hadian.

"I know why you did what you did. You're stupid, and you were dishonest, but I don't blame you."

Barnes was silent.

"Will there be a tribunal?" Hadian asked.

"I don't know. They've served papers. It's possible."

"Good luck."

"Thanks, but if they sack me I'll thank them for it."

"Robbie Fortune won't stand trial."

"I know."

"He suffered long-term brain damage as a result of the injury to his head. He's in a secure unit. *Committed to full-time psychiatric and rehabilitative care in a secure unit at an undisclosed location.*"

"Are you reading that?"

"Yeah. Can you tell? Something else I'm reading — Ellen Denniker's post-mortem toxicology report showed potentially lethal levels of various prescription drugs."

"I don't need to know that. They're both dead."

"If Denniker kept his wife docile with carefully administered amounts of controlled drugs, then the truth died with them. We'll never know."

"I saw your press conference on the television. There's plenty we'll never know," Barnes said. "Like whether sliding your house fifty feet further inland is a good way to dispose of a crime scene — a piece here, a piece there."

"As you say, a lot of unanswered questions. Enjoy your holiday, Barnes."

Barnes sighed and hung up. He pulled an envelope from the top of a box. Inside were two airline tickets to Madrid, and a local fertility clinic that had found a couple of likely donors within days, without the need for a second mortgage. The place was tiny, and had taken some serious research to locate. He hadn't told Eve yet. He couldn't wait for the look on her face.

He smiled and tucked the envelope into his pocket. He pulled open a box marked "Barnes's Clothes", and found his running shoes and shorts. He looked around the stacks of boxes, and began to get changed.

He was tying his shoelaces, one foot propped up on a box, when he heard her voice from behind him.

"Are you off somewhere, Chief?"

He turned to see Eve standing in the doorway of what would become their lounge. She was wearing running shorts and swinging a pair of trainers from side to side in her left hand.

"I thought I might come with you. Not too fast, now."

They drove back into town, so Barnes could show her his favourite route along the promenade. He carefully tucked the envelope into the glove box. He would show her over dinner.

They ran together. They took it slow.

The sun began to drop in the sky as they approached the Levels and headed to the seafront. A string of lights above the promenade flicked on as the sky went from blue to pink to orange, turning navy blue at the edges of the horizon. Fishing trawlers cruised out in the Channel, pursued by clouds of gulls, and the *Sospan Dau*, its task finished, inched slowly west, taking a wide berth around Beachy Head for fear of what detritus its powerful pumps might encounter.

Eve wanted to rest. She stopped and leaned against a wooden groyne, the pebbles clacking underfoot. Barnes crouched next to her while she rested and placed a hand on her tummy, gently caressing the possibilities of their future. She told him his hand was warm.

Barnes watched the lights above the promenade stretching away to a point in front of them, grateful that someone had thought to light their way.

THE END